What others are saying about

The Penitent:

"Wow! I just finished reading *The Penitent* by C. David Belt. What can I say about this book? How about amazing! The book is told from Moira's point of view, and it was thrilling to read. This book takes you in so many emotional directions: spiritual, happy, sad, sighing at the romantic parts, scared, and the reader will be thrilled from the first page. The characters are more fleshed out in this, the second volume. You'll find yourself falling in love with them all over again. The author knows how to insert gospel truths into a vampire novel in a way that you never thought would be possible. It's not preachy, but touching and informative. The author inserts many Book of Mormon stories and uses them in a way to teach vampires and the reader gospel truths. The plot continues from the first volume picking up with the same characters, and adding new exciting ones as well. I found myself riveted to this novel. The author wrote so much excitement into this volume that it will become addictive. This volume is brilliant, thoughtful, inspiring, and Moira is as always, loveable!"
—Book Junkie Reviews

"I eagerly anticipated the 2nd installment and was not disappointed. The continuing theme of repentance, forgiveness and redemption flowed throughout the book. I was very interested to read from Moira's perspective as one who HAD killed for revenge and blood as opposed to Carl's innocent and "unwilling" perspective in the first book. The individual character development was exceptional as well as the growing and evolving relationships. I was particularily intrigued with the interactions between Winnie and Moira. Over all, it was a great read! And now I will eagerly anticipate the concluding 'chapter.'"
—Loretta Julander, Hooper, UT

"This is a real page-turner that will interest anyone in vampires, and even LDS history."

—Rick Steadman, Salt Lake City, UT

"The sequel ups the ante on the action and the intrigue of the story, and leads the read through an exciting adventure with well-drawn characters you can't help but care about."

—Michael Young, author of *The Last Archangel* and *The Canticle Kingdom*

"While you should really read the first book first, there is enough recap in the second book that you could read it alone. He tells just enough so the new reader knows what's going on.

"This book contains more of the Latter-day Saint beliefs and contains references to stories from The Book of Mormon. A key story is described in enough detail that all the readers will be acquainted with the highlights and understand its significance to the penitent vampires. And Belt also mentions some other stories that illustrate the same point, but does not give any details. I don't think it will be confusing for the reader.

"I especially liked the author's comments at the end of the book. You should check it out."

—Deborah Carl

"It was a great read! There's enough recap at the beginning to understand what's going on without having to read the first book, but I'd suggest reading *The Unwilling* first anyway, because it gives a much fuller understanding of the main character's psychological journey. The moral struggles the characters face are fascinating and once you start reading the book it's hard to put down."

—Olya Polazhynets, Khust, Ukraine

The Penitent

The Children of Lilith
Volume II

The Penitent

C. David Belt

ISBN: 978-1-4276-9581-9 hardcover

ISBN: 978-1-4276-9579-6 paperback

ISBN: 978-1-4524-9110-3 e-book

Cover design: Ben Savage

PARABLES

PO Box 58
Woodsboro, MD 21798
http://www.parablespub.com
parables@parablespub.com

*For Cindy, who is
my Moira, my love,
and my inspiration.*

Through many dangers toils and snares
I've already come.
'Tis Grace that brought me safe thus far
And Grace will lead me home.
John Newton

But in a larger sense we cannot dedicate, we cannot consecrate, we cannot hallow this ground. The brave men, living and dead, who struggled here, have consecrated it far above our poor power to add or detract.

Abraham Lincoln

I am prepared to meet my Maker. Whether my Maker is prepared for the great ordeal of meeting me is another matter.

Sir Winston S. Churchill

Chapter 1

THERE'S SOMETHING seriously wrong with me.

I cannae Sleep.

Or, to be more precise, I dinnae *want* to Sleep. And since I can catch a full day's rest only once each week, abstaining could have . . . consequences. It makes me irritable. It affects my judgment. It increases the ever-present likelihood that I might . . . slip up.

And if I slip up, people die.

Ach! I'm so hungry!

'Tis another thing that's worrying me. I should nae be hungry! Nae even a wee bit! I Fed just after sunrise! We both did. Carl, my husband, and I consumed two quarts *each* just before we went to bed. 'Twas a bit of a luxury, those two quarts. *One* should've been sufficient, enough for a week in a pinch. But here I am, lying in bed beside my Sleeping husband, and all I can think of is how *hungry* I am, how *tired* I am, and how much I *dread* going to Sleep!

'Tis nae use.

I rise from bed. Carl does nae notice. To all appearances he could be dead. I slip into my dressing gown and make my way to the living room. I take several turns about the room as I try desperately to think of something else, *anything* other than my hunger, my weariness, and my fear.

A scratching sound! Aye, lassie, focus on that. Someone's at my flower bed again, digging it up. And I'm nigh certain I know who 'tis. That's twice this year. I should peek out and catch . . . but, nae, 'tis the side facing the Sun.

My stomach growls.

Perhaps just a wee pint more.

I walk into the kitchen. Though nobody's watching me, I try to keep my pace casual, walking, strolling as if I'm nae in a hurry, as if I'm nae desperate to get there. *Why do I bother? There's nary a soul to see me. Who am I trying to deceive? Myself?*

I open the refrigerator, and the cold air transports the sweet fragrance to my nostrils. To be sure, 'tis tainted by the odor of the preservative, but that cannae mask the nectar of . . .

There! Outside! Something far sweeter than the contents of my icebox!

Evil.

Though I cannae *smell* it just yet, I can feel the general direction.

Quickly I close the refrigerator and head to the window. A cautious glance, while I carefully stay in the shadows, reveals nothing about the source of the evil, but it does show an overcast sky.

I shudder with relief, and my mouth begins to water. In a trice, I rush to the door and throw open the chest beside it. This is my emergency kit. I retrieve all the things I need: the bottle of heavy-duty spray-on sunscreen, the sweatpants, sweatshirt, gloves, boots, sunglasses, cloak, and hood. In just a few seconds, I've applied every bit of protection. Only at this point, when I'm prepared, do I pause for a wee tick to be sure there's still a *reason* to venture outside.

Aye, the evil's still there. Sweet corruption.

I open the front door quietly so as not to alert anyone to my presence. *Aye, but I want to throw it open!*

And the scent of pure evil washes over me. The honeyed fragrance engulfs my senses. Drool spills from my eager lips.

So close!

The familiar rage builds like a smithy furnace stoked by a bellows within me. *Here! In my very neighborhood, practically on my front lawn!*

Through the red haze of my wrath, I barely notice that my flower beds are indeed torn up, the destroyer having fled. I dinnae care for that. The one I Hunt now has done far worse than petty vandalism. Nae, the evil I smell can be caused only by murder and violence.

The scent turns my head to the southwest. I cannae see the source, but the direction is certain. I follow the airborne spoor across the street and to the right toward . . . *Aye! That open garage!* 'Tis the Murphys' home. I can see two cars, neither one of them running. Now I can hear voices—hushed but emphatic voices.

". . . my money, *cabrón?*"

I dinnae recognize the voice.

"Tomorrow! I'll have it tomorrow!"

That voice I recognize. 'Tis Aaron Murphy. I dinnae know the the family well since they are nae in my ward, but Aaron's the oldest boy in the family. He's plays football or baseball or some other sport at the high school. I do hope he's nae the source of the evil.

I approach the garage with all stealth, fighting hard to contain the mounting rage and the ravenous hunger.

"You said that yesterday, man. And the day before that. You been hiding from me!"

"I swear, Manny! Tomorrow!"

"You don't get it, *muchacho.* I give you *product.* You sell it to your little friends at school. You give me my *money.* I give you more product. You sell it.

You give me money. You get to go on making everyone think you just a good little Mormon boy. That's how it works."

"Please, Manny!"

"Not this time, *cabrón*! I gotta teach you a lesson. Today, I'm just gonna break your fingers."

I round a corner of the garage and take in the whole scene. In the confined space between a compact car on the left and the Murphy family's minivan on the right, Aaron, the all-American boy, is pinned against the larger vehicle, held there by a big Hispanic man complete with bandana, gold chains, tattoos, multiple piercings, and a nasty-looking switchblade. Manny, the thug, has one hand at Aaron's throat. The other hand holds the knife an inch away from the lad's eye.

"Next time I *cut* off one of your fingers, *muchacho*. Just try catching a football like . . ."

A snarl rips from my throat.

Manny releases the boy and spins to face me. He looks startled, but nae frightened. Aaron's head snaps in my direction, but he remains rooted to the spot. *He* looks horrified.

The thug's face twists in an evil leer. "Beat it, *chica*. This is none of your business."

I laugh low and menacingly. "Ach, nae, rat. *Ye* are my business."

I step into the shade of the garage, safely out of the muted sunlight. I throw back my hood and pull off my sunglasses, setting them on the trunk of the sedan. I fix Aaron's eyes with my own and say with Persuasion, "Lad, go stand over there and wait for me while I deal with this." Aaron's expression goes slack, and he turns obediently and walks to the far wall of the garage.

I return my gaze to the gangster, who's staring at Aaron in amazement. "Now, rat," I say, "face me. Look into my eyes and see the hellfire that awaits ye."

Manny looks at me, his face a mask of fury. "Listen, *puta* . . ."

I open my mouth wide, revealing my dripping fangs.

His brown eyes go wide, and the color drains from his face. *"Madre de . . . !"*

I advance toward him, savoring his terror as I will the honeyed sweetness of his evil blood. I want to tear this vermin to shreds . . . *after* I consume his life.

Still brandishing the knife in one hand, he fumbles at his breast with the other and lifts a rather large and ornate gold cross on its chain. He holds it toward me as a talisman.

I cower back, shielding my face from the crucifix.

Through my fingers, I can see Manny's face split in a leer of triumph. "That's right, *zorra*. Now you know who's . . ."

I straighten up, no longer feigning fear. I shake my head slowly from side to side, laughing softly. "Ooh, did I give ye a wee moment of hope, ratty? That bonnie bit of jewelry cannae protect ye from me."

Any color remaining in Manny's face is gone. He's as white as a maggot. His knees tremble, and a new odor wafts in my direction as he wets himself. The knife falls from his hand. He still holds the cross forward, but that hand shakes violently.

In an instant I close the few feet between us and plunge my fangs into his neck. Sweet, evil blood, pulsing with life, shoots into my waiting mouth. At first the villain struggles, trying to push me away, but as the Seed in my saliva enters his bloodstream, his struggles cease. He begins to moan with pleasure as the Seed-induced euphoria grips him. His hands find my shoulders and then my neck, and like a lover, he holds me close.

Kill! Kill! Kill! Take it all! Tear him limb from limb! Send him to God unrepentant with the blood of innocents on his hands!

What am I doing? Stop! Stop! Stop! I'll kill him! Ne'er again! I cannae take another mortal life! Nae now! Ne'er again!

So sweet! I'm so hungry!

How can ye be hungry, lassie! Ye've Fed and Fed well! Stop!

KILL!

I tear my lips from his neck. I stare at it, at the sweet evil blood flowing weakly, oozing from the already partially closed wounds. *Take it all! He deserves death!*

With a snarl, I lick the wound to allow the Seed to Heal it. Then I release the waste of flesh.

He staggers a bit and then leans against the minivan, panting and pale. He lifts a hand toward me in a pleading gesture, a look of longing on his face. He tilts his head to the side, exposing his neck for me. "*Mas. Por favor. Mas.*"

I look him in the eye. With Persuasion I say, "Ye will leave this place, and neither ye nor your associates will e'er bedevil this lad or his family again. Ye will go immediately to the police and confess all your crimes. *All* your crimes. Ye will provide the police with the information and cooperation they need to put ye and your associates away and see that ye all pay for your crimes. Ye will spend the rest of your miserable life yearning for my touch and fearing my return. Ye will dream of me every night. And ye will ne'er e'er speak of me to anyone. D'ye understand?"

He nods. "*Si.*"

"Now go. Find a policeman."

He staggers past me and outside, casting me one final look of longing.

I turn my attention back to Aaron. He's still standing at the rear of the garage, gazing at me. His expression is blank.

I fix his eyes with my own. "Aaron, laddie. D'ye know who I am."

He nods. "Yes. You're Sister Morgan." His voice is flat, devoid of emotion.

"Aye, well, ye will forget what ye have seen me do this morning. D'ye understand, laddie?"

"Yes."

"The bad man left when he saw me and that's all. D'ye understand?"

"Yes."

"That's grand." I release him from my Persuasion.

He blinks stupidly. Then he looks at me as if seeing me for the first time. "Sister Morgan?"

"Aye, laddie."

"Uh, did you . . . see that guy?"

"Aye, laddie, I did."

"I think . . . Um, I think he was gonna mug me. Good thing you came when you did. Scared him off!"

I laugh mirthlessly. "Nae, laddie. Ye know as well as I that was nae what happened here."

"I . . . I don't know what you're talking about." His hands are trembling.

"Ye've been destroying lives, Aaron. Ye've been selling drugs to other lads and lasses."

"What? No way!"

"Ye've done a horrible, wicked, selfish thing. Ye must confess, accept the consequences, and try to repay the evil ye've wrought."

"You're high!" His bonnie face—and I'm sure many a good young Mormon lass has mooned over it—twists suddenly in anger and fear. "Get out of here, you crazy b . . ."

"Aaron?" Sister Murphy . . . *Carol's her name* . . . opens the door from the house. She's wearing an apron, probably been fixing breakfast for her family. The nauseating aromas of mortal food waft from the kitchen behind her. "Aaron, honey? What's going on?" She spies me. "Sister"—her eyes dance about as she searches her memory for my name—"MacDonald?"

I nod. "'Tis Morgan now."

"Oh, OK." She looks confused. "What're you doing here?" She shakes her head. "I'm sorry. I know that sounds rude, but what are you doing in my garage?"

"She was *hitting* on me, mom!"

I laugh. *How pathetic!*

Carol Murphy looks at her son in shock. Then her gaze turns back to me, her eyes narrowing in suspicion.

Ah, well. 'Twould nae be the first time I've been accused of bewitching the young and nae-so-young men in the area.

I sigh. "Don't be daft, Carol. Check in the lad's . . ." I test the air. "Check in the lad's backpack."

She looks at me. Then she glances at the backpack inside the sedan. Suspicion is replaced by doubt. "Aaron, honey, let me see your backpack."

His eyes go wide. "Mom! Cut it out! You're not going to listen to her, are you? She was coming on to me!"

"There was a man in here," I say, "in your garage. A man with a knife." I point at the discarded weapon lying on the floor between the two vehicles. "That knife. He was threatening your son with it. I scared him off."

"Don't listen to her, Mom! She's lying!"

"That man was supplying your son with cocaine," I continue, "which Aaron has been selling to other children at school. Take a look in his backpack."

"SHUT UP!" Aaron screams.

"Give me your backpack," his mother commands.

"No, Mom! Please!" He's crying now. "Don't!"

She pushes past him, opens the door of the sedan, and retrieves the backpack from the car. After closing the car door, she lays the bag on the hood and begins to rummage through it.

All the while, Aaron pleads with her. "Don't, Mom! Please! It's not mine! She put it there!"

In a few moments she has removed a plastic bag containing many wee bags of the damning white powder. Tears stream from her eyes. She turns to face her son and clutches the bag in her fist, holding it between them.

"Inside," she says softly.

"It's not mine!" the lad blubbers. "You gotta believe me!"

"Now," she whispers.

Aaron utters a foul oath and runs into the house, slamming the door behind him.

Carol turns to me. She cannae meet my eyes. Her lip trembles. "Thank you, Sister Mac . . . M-Morgan. I'll take it from here."

"Moira. Call me Moira. I'm so sorry, Carol."

She turns to go.

"Carol?" I call after her.

She stops, but does nae turn toward me. "Yes?"

"Ye should know that the man who left here . . . he'll be in police custody soon. I . . . I'll see to that. They'll find out soon enough about Aaron and what he's done. 'Twould be better for him if ye were to contact the police before they come looking for him. And 'twould be very bad indeed for you if they were to learn that ye had disposed of the evidence. Nae that ye'd do such a thing, mind."

I can hear her swallow hard. She nods.

"If there's anything I can do . . ." *Ach! That sounds so trite!*

"You've done enough." She keeps her back to me.

Ah, so that's how it is. More's the pity. I've made another enemy.

"No," she says, "that's not fair. You ... saved my boy's life." Now she turns, fresh tears streaming from her eyes. Then she sobs.

Gently, I put my arms around her. After a moment, she hesitantly returns the hug.

"Your son needs ye ... now more than ever," I whisper. "Repentance is a miracle. I can testify to that. Ye'll have to help him find his way back."

She nods mutely.

I hold her for a bit longer. Then she pulls away and says, "I've got to call Jerry. And ... the police."

She turns and walks slowly into the house. As she closes the door, she hits a big button beside it, and the garage door starts to close.

Poor lass. That poor lad. That poor family. They've a long road ahead of them.

I throw my hood over my head and duck into the muted sunlight. *Muted, aye, but still so bright!* The garage closes behind me. I glance up at the clouds and ...

Pain! My eyes!

I snap them shut.

I forgot my sunglasses! They're still in the garage!

The pain's replaced by the maddening itch of the Seed's Healing.

How could I be so glaikit, so stupid! Such a ninny! Now, I'm blind!

I'll be able to see again soon, but for the moment I'm lingering in the daylight, and I cannae see to find my way home!

Ach! I want to claw my eyes out! The itch is so bad!

My skin begins to feel hot. Surely I've nae been out in the light so long! 'Tis my imagination! It has to be!

Fire! Death by fire! I cannae conceive of a worse way to die! It needs only one patch of exposed skin. From there it'll spread, consuming my clothes, exposing more skin ...

I open my eyes. My vision is cloudy, but I can see. And 'tis clearing.

There! Home! Shelter!

I force myself to run *slowly* across the street and toward home. 'Twould be very bad if my friends and neighbors saw how fast I *can* move.

Ach! I feel hot!

The door is there before me. Aye, my poor flowers're destroyed. *Nae time for that now, lassie. Get inside!*

I reach the door, throw it open, and reach the safety of the darkness inside. Slamming the door behind me, I throw off the cloak.

'Twas my imagination after all. There's no smoke, no smoldering flesh.

I breathe a sigh of relief.

I start to pace around the living room. *Why, lassie? Why did ye risk so much? Ye cannae possibly be hungry! Ye've had four quarts in the past few hours! The human stomach can hold only about six! Ye risked exposure to the Sun. Ye risked exposure to your friends and neighbors! Ye very nearly took a mortal life! 'Twould render all the centuries of repentance for naught! Aye, ye took a monster off the streets and stopped another monster-in-the-making, but ye cannae be so hungry!*

I stop dead still and look in horror at the bag of blood in my hand. I'm standing in my kitchen in front of my open refrigerator, and I'm holding a bag of blood. I was about to Feed *again*.

And I don't remember getting here.

I hastily return the blood to the fridge, close the door, sealing off the smell of the nectar inside, and fall to my knees.

Father in Heaven, there's something seriously wrong with me. Help me please!

Chapter 2

THE BLOOD IN THE refrigerator is untouched, but I'm exhausted. I need Sleep. Perhaps this unnatural hunger is aggravated by lack of rest. I cannae take risks like today's.

I change back into my nightgown and stow my emergency gear away in the chest by the door. I have to replace the sunglasses with one of the many spares I have, but all is back in place.

I walk slowly to the bedroom, carefully keeping my eyes away from the kitchen. I snuggle in close to my dear Carl, though he takes nae notice. How could he? Naught but the scent of blood or the setting of the Sun can wake a Sleeping vampire.

I lie here, holding him, but I cannae bring myself to close my eyes.

My mother was a dreamer.

Her dreams had meaning. Nae every dream, of course, but there were some dreams, and she could always recognize them, that were meant to tell her or her family something. Rarely was it anything to be happy about. She did nae speak of this talent to anyone outside the walls of our home, fearing others might call her a witch. And my father would nae listen.

She dreamt one night of a murder of corbies, what'd be called a flock of crows today. "They were large birds, were the corbies," she told me the next morning as I was milking the goat. "But they were nae black. They were red as heartsblood. They descended on a wee flock of sheep: a ram, a ewe, and a wee ewe lamb. 'Twas like a boiling pool of blood. They ripped the ewe and the ram till there was nought but tattered bits of bone. The lamb they left torn and broken, barely alive. Then they flew away. The lamb then arose on its broken limbs, restored to full vigor, but its wool turned black, and its eyes shone with an evil light."

Of course, she knew this dream was an omen of evil. She tried to tell my father. He would nae listen. He should have listened. We should have fled.

The next day, word reached us that Bonnie Prince Charley had led the highlanders to disaster and ruin. Half were slaughtered. The rest captured. Charley had fled. And Donald, my Donald, my betrothed, was captured and hanged.

A week later, the English raided our village. They razed our farm. My father and mother were murdered. Me, the English beat and violated. They left me for dead.

But I arose from the ashes. I sought out the Ancient One, the Daughter of Lilith, who haunted the kirkyard. She instructed me, administered the Oath and the Ritual, all at my urging. Three days later, I arose as a vampire.

And I had my revenge.

Aye, and I paid a terrible price.

For more than two and a half centuries I've nae dreamt. Nae even once. The Children of Lilith dinnae dream when we Sleep.

A few months ago, I began to dream again. 'Tis the same dream, over and over.

And I, like my mother, know the dream is a portent of . . .

The sharp point of the iron spike is pressing down into my palm. The white-robed, hooded figure of a man leans over me and holds the spike in place with one hand. The golden image of the Sun is emblazoned on his robe. The pressure of the hard iron alone causes me pain, but the man's other hand holds up a wooden mallet, poised as if to strike.

He brings it down, and I feel the spike driven into the flesh of my hand. I scream in agony, but only in my mind. Nae sound escapes my lips. I dinnae move. In point of fact, I struggle to hold my body still as a second blow of the mallet drives the iron farther into my flesh and into the wood behind it.

I want to scream, but I cannae make a sound.

Through the red haze of pain, I become aware of the ritual chanting of many voices coming from all around me. I cannae concentrate on the words. There's only the pain in my hand and the new spike being pressed into my wrist. The mallet rises again. Once more I feel pain as the new spike drives through my flesh.

The mallet strikes again and I feel more flesh ripping, more bones breaking as my wrist is nailed to the wood behind it.

Still, I'm mute in my agony.

The process is repeated on my other hand and wrist. Then finally my feet are nailed to the wood. The chanting increases in volume as other white-robed figures around me close in. Many hands grasp the wood of the cross and lift it and me upright. The agony in my hands, wrists, and feet doubles and redoubles as the spikes began to bear the weight of my body. Each movement as I'm hoisted upright sends new bolts of pain thundering through my wounded flesh.

Along with the pain I can feel the horrible itch of the Seed as it tries to repair the damage, but cannae expel the invading iron. I cannae think of anything except the pain and the itch.

And the unfulfilled need to scream.

Suddenly I begin to drop and pitch forward as the cross is lowered into a hole in the ground. I feel the flesh rip again.

I can hear the chanting fade away as the figures move back, behind, and away from me. I dinnae care. I just want to be delivered from the pain. I try desperately to pull my hands free, but something stops me. I try to fly up and away, but I cannae. All I can do is silently endure my agony. My breathing becomes increasingly labored as the unnatural position of my body pulls at my internal organs.

A white-robed figure walks out in front of me. From the Sun emblem on his chest, I can tell he's the man with the mallet, only now he bears a spear. The head of the spear looks ancient. It looks like 'tis made of iron.

The Sun-emblazoned figure, holding the spear aloft, advances toward me. The chanting crescendos till it thunders in my ears. He thrusts the spear up and into my side. I cannae breathe. The physician in me thinks clinically that the spear must have pierced my diaphragm. The Seed repairs it quickly, of course, and my labored breathing resumes.

Why can I nae fly away? Why can I nae escape? Why can I nae scream? I cannae get my body to obey me.

Then a new sight fills me with horror. The sky is lightening. I did nae ken that I was outside until this moment. The sky above the mountains to the east is brightening. Soon the Sun will begin to top the mountains, and I will be exposed to his deadly rays.

The chanting gets louder even as the robed figures move out of my range of vision. They have to hide from the Sun. I can see the rays touching the tops of the trees that line the clearing where I'm crucified.

As the light touches the top of my head, my hair bursts into flame. The light falls rapidly, and my face is illuminated, and I'm ablaze. Incredibly, my burning lips move, and I say, "Father, into thy hands I commend my spirit." And then I'm engulfed in flame.

And I awake screaming.

Beside me, Carl Sleeps on like the dead. So I lie there, trembling, sobbing, clinging to him as the dream lingers vividly in my memory.

I've been having this same dream frequently for nearly a month now. It does nae happen every time I Sleep, but when it comes, I wake up screaming. There are little variations in the dream, but the basic elements are the same: the crucifixion, the white-robed figures, the leader with the Sun emblem on his chest, the inability to scream, the ancient spear, the inability to escape or help myself, the last words of Christ as I burn. I dinnae ken what it means and this frightens me. It frightens me that I'm having dreams at all.

I've nae told Carl, my husband, about it. There's nary a thing he can do. Except *be* here.

My husband. How I do love that phrase! Even though he's Sleeping, his very presence is such a comfort. For so long, all I could do was mourn Donald, my former betrothed, executed by the English more than two and a half centuries ago. I did nae believe that marriage and happiness were possible for me, damned as I was, a creature forever barred from Heaven.

Or so I believed.

Then Carl came into my life. My dear, brave Carl, the first and only Unwilling vampire in all the long history of the Children of Lilith. Carl is a good and decent man who did nae choose this . . . *life*, as I and every other vampire did. His very existence turned all that I ever believed about my condition on its head.

Now at last, I'm a bride, sealed in the temple of God for Time and all Eternity to the man I love. The way to Heaven is open to me again, if I can remain true, if I can control this unnatural hunger.

Like the Anti-Nephi-Lehies of old, I've covenanted to murder no more. I've nae taken a mortal life in centuries. If I fail . . . I fear for my very soul.

And with God's help . . . I know I can keep that covenant.

I've found redemption.

I've found love.

I have a purpose in my life and every reason to be happy.

Every reason except for one: I cannae bear a child. No female vampire can. The Seed, the biological component of vampirism, would reject and expel any fetus, as it would reject and expel any foreign object.

But for a very short time, less than a single day, there was Ben. Ben, my poor, wee bairn! How I miss ye, laddie!

My phone rings.

At such a time as this? Nobody who knows us would call at this hour of the day, nae at home! Who could it be?

The phone rings again.

Well, I'd rather talk on the phone than Sleep right now!

I snatch the phone from the dresser and flip it open. "Aye?"

"Sister Morgan, it's Bishop Adams."

Ach, nae! Someone saw me! Stupid! Daft and stupid!

"Aye, bishop," I say, trying to keep my voice calm. "What can I do for ye?"

"Moira, I'm sorry to call during your . . . sleep time."

"Think nothing of it, bishop. I was awake."

"Oh, good! I just felt . . . *prompted* to call. Are you all right?"

Maybe he does nae know! Maybe nobody saw me.

"I'm grand, bishop. Just grand. Having a wee bit of trouble Sleeping, which is very odd for . . . people like me."

"Yeah, I thought you told me that"—his voice drops to a whisper—"that *you* and *Carl* are very hard to wake once you go to sleep . . . in the day, that is."

Bishop Adams is one of the few mortals who knows my true nature. Even his wife, Laura, does nae know.

I chuckle. "Aye, nigh impossible to wake before the Sun sets, unless we smell blood."

"Yeah." He laughs nervously. "Uh, how . . . did it go?"

"How did what go?"

"The sealing. You said you and Carl were going to have your son sealed to you while you were in Florida. How did it go?"

"Oh, aye. 'Twas a very sweet and poignant moment for both Carl and me. The Orlando Temple is beautiful. Have ye ever been there?"

"No, I haven't. I've never been to Florida."

"Ye should go sometime."

"Laura wants me to take her to Disney World. You're a trendsetter in this ward, you know that?" He chuckles. "That *is* why you went to Florida, right?"

"Aye, for our first wedding anniversary."

"I'm so glad it worked out . . . with your boy, I mean."

"Well, we have ye to thank for that, don't we?"

"I'm glad I could help a little."

"'A little?' Bishop, ye processed and pushed through our petition to have him sealed to us! I'm sure that was nae mean feat!"

"Well, there was the matter of no birth certificate and his actual age. How old was he?"

"Ben was at least a hundred and fifty."

"But he looked only eight or nine?"

"Aye, the leader of the Cult of vampires here in Salt Lake could nae Convert him till he was at the age of accountability and could consent. Though how a slave boy could refuse his master anything is beyond me!"

"So, Ben was really a *slave* to that Michael Beumont character you told me about? The one Carl . . . uh, *killed* last year?"

"Aye, Michael was a slave owner in the old South. He was a *monster* long before he became a vampire."

"And he . . . *abused* that boy? Ben? I mean, Michael abused Ben . . . sexually?"

"Aye."

"That poor kid. He never had a chance, did he?"

"Nae."

"At least not until you came along—you and Carl—and freed him."

Tears spill from my eyes. "Aye, he endured a century and a half of horrific abuse. It twisted him, but I have to tell ye, bishop: once Carl freed him from Michael's control, he seemed like any other little boy."

"How . . . ? You never told me how he died."

"He was murdered by another vampire. She beheaded Ben right before my eyes." *Rebecca slew him. I was nae fast enough to stop her. I cradled his severed head in my arms and I watched the life fade from his eyes. I could do nought but weep and watch as he voicelessly mouthed, "I love you, Mama. I love you, Papa."*

"Oh, my word! I'm so sorry," the bishop says. "I . . . I shouldn't have asked."

"Nae, it's all right. I . . . He's with God now. He cannae suffer any more."

"You're right."

"And, bishop, if I'm true, if I keep my temple covenants, I'll see him again and he'll"—my voice breaks—"He'll call me Mama."

◢ ◢ ◢

If I can remain true. If I dinnae give in to this unnatural hunger.

I'm lying down next to Carl again. I snuggle closer. I wish Carl could snore. His breathing and heartbeat are so slow that a mortal would think he was dead.

I should nae fear to Sleep again. The dream ne'er repeats itself on the same day. It should be safe to close my eyes . . . just for a wee bit . . .

Ben's head rolls across the dais. I run screaming after it. I scoop it into my arms. For one wild moment I look about for his body so I can reattach his head. But I know 'twill nae do any good. Ye can reattach a limb, but nae a head, *I told Carl once.* 'Tis too complex even for the Seed to repair.

I sit down on the floor and cradle Ben's head in my arms. I rock it back and forth. I stare into his beautiful black face and brown eyes. He's trying to speak to me, but he nae longer has lungs or vocal cords. So he merely moves his lips. Then suddenly, impossibly, I hear his voice. With tears streaming from his eyes, he says, "I trusted you, Mama. Why did you let Rebecca kill me? You must have wanted *me dead. Why didn't you love me, Mama? Wasn't I good enough for you?"*

I'm screaming, "Nae! Nae! Nae! Ben, my poor wee bairn! I loved ye! I'm sorry I was nae fast enough to stop her!"

Tears gone, his disembodied head leers at me, and says, "Do you want me to suckle at your breast now?"

I awake screaming again.

Chapter 3

HAND IN HAND, we fly out over the Great Salt Lake, enjoying the rush of cold air on our faces and in our hair. I love the feel of my clothes whipping about me. Carl has been teaching me the aerobatic maneuvers he learned years ago in the Air Force. We do loops, barrel rolls, Immelmanns, and cloverleafs. I think the cloverleaf is Carl's favorite. I must confess that I like the simplicity of a loop. When I reach the top of the loop, looking up at the stars, gravity begins to overcome centrifugal force, and the blood is pulled from my eyes. Colors begin to fade to gray, and the lights of the stars seem to shine brighter. Then the blood returns, and the colors sharpen again.

Tonight we're going to concentrate on "formation flying." I dinnae see the point of flying close to each other, but nae touching. I'd rather be holding my dearie's hand.

"Formation flying allows you to cover each other better," he explained before we left the ground. "The leader is looking forward. The wingman is looking at and past Lead, watching a whole different patch of sky. The wingman crosses over to the other side of Lead from time to time in order to view the other *patch of sky."*

"What about the sky behind us?" I asked.

"The sky behind us and above us," he said, "is harder to watch with just two of us. That's why you make occasional turns to look behind and above."

"I see," I replied, but I did nae see at all. It seemed to me that ye could do all of that while still holding hands . . . but I did nae say that to Carl. It seemed so important to him to teach me this. So I indulge him.

Carl lets go of my hand. I move a couple of feet to the left and down and I assume the "Number Two" role. Carl is the lead. I'm the wingman.

Carl begins a slow turn to the left. This is harder than it looks. I need to make constant adjustments to stay in the same relative position.

I start to slip out too far to the left. I correct back quickly to the right and in toward Carl and . . . Ach! I've slid right past and under him. Now I'm on his right and too low.

I gradually move to the left and then up. *That's it, lassie.* I slide slowly under and behind Carl. As I approach the "Number Two" position, I start to move a little bit to the right again to slow my movement to the left. *That's*

15

better. This time I'm able to control my location relative to "Lead."

Carl rolls out of his turn and then starts another. I stay with him this time by making minute corrections. When he rolls out of this turn, he looks back at me and, seeing that I'm still with him, grins his lopsided smile that I love so much. Then he turns his attention back to the sky in front, below, and above us. This reminds me that I'm supposed to watch the sky to our right while maintaining my position.

And that's when I see the winged figure rapidly closing on us.

I move forward and take Carl's hand. We decelerate, and I point out the approaching vampire. We knew this day would come. Once we destroyed the Cult of vampires here, we knew Lilith would send someone to investigate.

Neither one of us is armed, but we're nae defenseless. I'm a master at armed and unarmed combat. I've been training Carl, and he's doing well, learning rapidly. Still, if the approaching vampire is armed, flight (and by that I mean running away) might be our best option.

"Laddie," I say, "we must be prepared to flee."

"Roger," Carl replies quickly. In spite of the situation, I suppress a wee smile. When he's in the air, he reverts to pilotspeak. By "roger" he means, "I acknowledge or I understand or I agree" or perhaps all three together. It seems to me that pilotspeak is designed to be terse *and* precise and often ends up being simply *terse.*

"The safe house?" I suggest.

He nods. "Roger that." This must be the *I-agree* version. "Let's hold here until we see what his intentions are."

We clasp hands as we watch the white-winged figure (apparently male) dramatically slow his approach. He's now floating slowly toward us in an upright posture, holding a sword.

I squeeze Carl's hand. "See the way he's holding the sword, the hilt toward us?"

"Roger," he replies, nae taking his eyes off the newcomer.

"'Tis a sign he comes in peace," I say. "He's offering his life to us, were he to make an aggressive move."

"Am I supposed to take the sword from him?"

"Normally, I would say nae. Ye would just acknowledge the gesture, and he would sheath the weapon. Given that we're unarmed, 'twould seem prudent to receive the weapon. But *I* will take it, mind ye. Your training is coming along nicely, but I'm better."

He grins, but he does nae look in my direction. "Roger that."

"Besides, laddie, ye have ne'er handled a bastard like that, and I have."

"Bastard?" This time he glances in my direction momentarily.

He thinks I'm upset and using foul language, though he has ne'er heard me use such. "'Tis a type of sword," I say. "The term refers to a broadsword that allows ye to place both hands on the grip or, in your case, on the grip and pommel, since your hands are larger than mine. Such a blade is nae typically wielded with both hands, as a true *great sword* would be, but ye can use both hands in a pinch. 'Tis also called a 'hand-and-a-half' sword."

He cocks an eyebrow, but says nary a word.

"Laddie," I say with a smirk, still watching the slowly approaching vampire, "'bastard' has nae always been the epithet it is today."

"Roger."

"Now, when he offers us the sword, *I* will take it. That'll lead him to assume that *I'm* the Master." He winces at the term for the leader of a vampire Cult. *I know what ye mean, laddie. It gives me the willies too.* "However, *ye* do the talking. That'll keep him off balance."

He nods. "Roger. Wilco." *I understand and I will comply,* I translate in my head from pilotspeak to the King's English.

Ah, my military man! How I love him!

Now, lassie, focus on ye're about. "Still, be prepared to flee if I tug on your hand." I keep my whisper so low that only Carl can hear me. *I hope that only Carl can hear me.*

The newcomer halts a few yards away from us at the same altitude we're holding. He's still pointing the hilt of his sword toward us. He looks wary and . . . something else. *Hopeful?* He's clean-shaven, and his blonde hair is closely cropped. He has blue eyes that shine from a handsome, if somewhat severe, face. He's dressed casually: blue jeans and a dark blue, long-sleeved shirt, unbuttoned at the collar, but buttoned at the wrists.

I extend my hand to take the proffered weapon. He moves forward and places it in my hand and then lets go. Once I have the weapon, he moves back a yard or so.

He looks straight at me. He has decided that *I'm* the Master. "I'm Rolf." I can hear a hint of the German accent that the name implies.

Carl says, "I'm Carl. This is Moira."

Rolf starts visibly when Carl speaks (rather than me).

"What're you doing here, Rolf?" Carl says.

Rolf looks from Carl to me and then back to Carl. He seems to collect himself after the shock and says, "What *are* you?" He pauses for a moment. When Carl does nae answer, he continues, "You're not mortal. You're not vampires. You're not *evil*. What are you? Are you . . . angels? The ones I heard about?"

"Angels?" Carl asks. He seems confused. I must confess that I'm a wee bit puzzled, myself.

"The angels who defended the Mormon temple in Ogden," Rolf responds. "I've heard . . . stories."

Ah, that's it. Carl said the incident would come back to haunt us.

"No . . . and yes," Carl responds cryptically.

Rolf looks confused.

"*No*, we're not angels," Carl clarifies. "And *yes*, we're the ones who defended the Ogden Temple."

"Then . . . what are you?" Rolf looks as baffled as ever.

"We're vampires like you," Carl says.

"Impossible," Rolf replies. "You have no wings."

I realize with a jolt that I've forgotten this simple fact: vampires have wings. The wings are a mental projection, but Carl discovered last year that we can fly *without* projecting them. At first, it took an effort of will to fly without them. Now it's second nature to us.

Ben was the only other vampire to succeed in "turning the wings off."

But now is nae the time to be thinking of Ben.

Carl glances at me. I nod in understanding. I know what he intends.

Our wings spread out behind us and beat insubstantially at the air. There is the sound of beating wings, but there is nae the movement of air.

Rolf looks stunned.

"Does this make you more comfortable?" Carl asks with a wee smile.

I squeeze his hand, and our wings blink out of existence. *I dinnae like them anymore. Now the wings make me feel . . . unclean.*

Rolf looks at us in wonder. "*Himmel!* How . . . how did you do that?"

"A discussion for another time," Carl says calmly. "What're you doing here, Rolf?"

Rolf opens his mouth as if to speak and then stops himself. He does this a few times before he finally says, "I've come seeking those who dissolved the Salt Lake City Cult."

I was on my guard before, but upon hearing this, I shift Rolf's sword to a more aggressive position. It's all I can do nae to force Carl behind me.

Rolf notes my fighting posture with his eyes, but he continues, "Rumors have spread among the Cults and the Renegades . . . Renegades such as myself . . . that the Salt Lake Cult was destroyed, its Master and all the Teachers killed. There was a new Master for a very short time. Some say it was only for a few minutes. And then the Cult was suddenly *dissolved*. It simply ceased to be. That hasn't happened since the Flood of Noah."

When we say nothing, he continues, "Rumor *also* has it . . . that it was the work of . . . *Penitents.*" He looks at us with an expression I cannae quite read.

I squeeze Carl's hand before he can say anything. *I* want to handle this one. "And if 'twere the work of Penitents," I say cautiously, "what then?"

Rolf looks from Carl to me and says, "Then, I've come to *join* you."

Chapter 4

THE RED-FACED MAN *twisted and choked and wriggled like a worm on a hook. He kicked at me and both clawed and beat at my hand and arm without effect as I held him up against the wall of his wee home. The winter wind howled through the open doorway, the door itself lying in pieces where, moments earlier, I'd smashed it in. Snow billowed about the room, and all the candles were extinguished. The only light came from the fireplace. Behind me, the sergeant's wife, with a bairn in her arms, screamed in horror. A wee lad of nae more than six years clung to her leg and shrieked as well.*

"Ye are Albert Cooper, Sergeant of the King's Own Royal Regiment (Lancaster)?" I demanded, my fangs extended.

His only response was to beat at my wrist and to splutter and spit.

I loosened my grip on his throat slightly, and I heard the intake of a tortured breath.

"Answer me!" I hissed.

"Yes," he choked out. "Please, spare me wife and children! Kill me, but let them go! Have mercy!"

"Mercy?" I shrieked, drowning out the wind for a moment. "I will show ye as much mercy as ye showed Donald MacDonald. Ye commanded the squad that hanged him for a traitor."

"I did me duty . . . served me king and country," he managed to choke out.

"James be your king! Bonnie Prince Charley be your prince! Nae that German pretender!" I spat. "Ye killed my Donald and for that ye will die!"

The wee lad grasped me around the knees and said, "Don't kill me daddy!"

I ignored him.

"Please spare me wife and children!" Cooper cried, his voice hoarse.

I began to lower him, to bring his pulsing throat toward my waiting lips. His blood smelled sweet, but 'twas nae the sweetness of true evil. Nae like the men who raped me, killed my family, and left me for dead. Nae as sweet as that, but sweet all the same. I had nae Fed in the weeks I'd spent tracking him down. I was very hungry. Drool filled my mouth and spilled from the corners of it. He was the last of them. The final man I had to kill. I'd slaughtered all the rest. Nae Feeding, except for them. Killed them all.

For my Donald.

For my father.

For my mother.

For my stolen virtue.

For me.

For vengeance.

Cooper looked at my fangs waiting to sink into his flesh, at my mouth waiting to drain his life, and into my eyes, and he saw the fire of hell burning there. He began to scream high and loud.

And then I felt a sharp pain in my leg. I looked down. The wee lad had bitten me. He was biting me still.

Rage and hate consumed me, nearly blinding me. I dropped Cooper to the floor. I wheeled about and lifted his son into the air with both hands. The lad shrieked. 'Twas a horrid sound of pure terror. It stoked my rage. I wanted to tear, to rend, to dash his brains out on the wall. He hurt me! Me! He touched me! I would nae be hurt again! Nae again! Nae by any English dog or pup such as this!

"Please! Please spare me son!" the lad's father pleaded. "Spare the boy! Don't kill me boy! He's done nothing! Kill me!"

I looked at the screaming child. A tremor shook my body as my rage melted away and horror chilled my very blood.

What had I become? Vengeance was one thing, but this . . . this would be murder! *What kind of demon would murder a child for nae more than defending his father? The lad was innocent, and I was about to . . . to . . .*

And what of the father? He was nae evil. I knew it. I could feel it. He had nae but served his king. My Donald had served his prince. Were they so different?

My Donald was dead. He would nae return to me. I grieved his loss. I'd done terrible things in his name. I had given up . . . I had lost . . . sold . . . my immortal soul.

I quickly but gently placed the child onto the floor, and I fled into the night, into the howling wind and the blowing snow.

Hell is a place of fire, they say. Nae. Hell is filled with a bitter cold. Hell is a void. Hell is the emptiness of the damned soul.

I was going to murder a child!

What had I become?

"What was your turning point, Rolf?" I ask. We're standing on the side of a mountain east of Salt Lake City. 'Tis nae far from the spot where Ben is buried. I'm still holding the sword pointed at Rolf. I cannae sense evil in a vampire the way I can in a mortal. I'm nae going to take his claim that he is a Penitent on its face.

"Would you mind if I were to sit?" he asks. "I haven't Fed in over a week, and flying is exhausting for me."

I nod at him, pointing with the sword to a likely rock.

"Go ahead," Carl says, "but you'll understand if we're . . . cautious with you."

"Of course," Rolf says as he sits down quickly. His heart rate is elevated, and his breathing is somewhat labored. With the Moon shining on his face, I can see that he does look ashen and wan, malnourished. He *looks* as though he hasn't Fed recently.

"My turning point, you say?" he responds after a moment. "You mean, what made me want to repent?"

"Aye."

He nods. "Ironically," he says with a bitter chuckle, "it was Adolf Hitler. Adolf Hitler and a nameless Jew."

"What d'ye mean?" I ask.

"I was young when Adolf Hitler came to power in Germany. He was *mesmerizing*, and I was entranced. His words made so much sense to my young mind. I believed with all my heart in his teachings about the Master Race, Aryan superiority, and the inferiority of the "lesser" races. I eagerly joined the Hitler Youth and later the Waffen Schutztaffel (the 'Fighting SS,' you would say), which at the time was open only to pure Aryans. Later, because I could speak perfect English with a nearly flawless British accent (my mother was educated in England, you see), I was recruited into the Sicherheitsdienst (the 'SD' or 'Security Service') as a spy and assassin."

"What department?" Carl asks suddenly.

His interruption startles me. Apparently, it startles Rolf as well.

"What?" he asks, confused.

"What department in the SD?" Carl asks again.

"Department B, although I did missions for Department D as well," Rolf replies, perplexed.

"The West and America. What about C?" Carl presses.

I glance at Carl. He meets my eye, then winks and nods quickly. *Ah, that's it! He's testing Rolf. He's probing to check the validity of his story. I had nae idea that Carl was such a WW II enthusiast.*

"No," Rolf replies, "I didn't speak Russian or Japanese, and I couldn't pass for Japanese anyway. I didn't do work for E, either, before you ask, because I didn't speak Polish, Czech, or any other Eastern European languages."

Rolf understands the purpose behind Carl's question now too.

"OK," Carl says, "go on."

I guess he passed the test.

"One of the members of my unit was an especially skilled assassin with an extraordinary number of kills. He was accorded special status. His name was Günther Paul Müller. I admired him and wished to emulate him. He took me on as a protégé and eventually taught me the secret of his success: he was a vampire. A very *old* vampire. More than a thousand years old."

"A thousand years?" I say in shock. "I've never heard of one so old . . . save Lilith herself."

"Yes, quite ancient for one of us. He Converted me. And I *reveled* in my new power. I was *unstoppable*. I was the Aryan Übermensch."

Superman, I translate in my mind.

"Vampirism appealed to me," Rolf continued, "because I was of the Master Race and I could Feed off the lesser races. They existed only to serve me, to sustain me, and to sate me. I could do what I wanted with them: use them, consume them, and discard them as the vermin I believed them to be."

I stare at him in horror.

He nods at me. "I know. It was what I believed at the time." He sighs. "But with vampirism came also the *knowledge* that the Nazis were *evil*. I was constantly surrounded by people whose blood cried out to me. At first, I embraced the evil. Oh, I gave in to the urge to kill some of my fellows from time to time, but I wanted to advance the cause of the Führer. I *believed* in it. The strong *should* prey on the weak, I convinced myself. If some or even *most* of the leaders were evil, that was because they indulged certain appetites and *not* because the Aryan cause *itself* was evil."

He looks at me again. "You asked. So I'm telling you. You must understand the devil I was."

"Go on," Carl prompts.

"You see, over time, though, it began to gnaw at me, gnaw like a rat slowly eating my guts from the inside out. With each assassination, each good man or woman that I killed, I began to doubt the *rightness* of the cause. On one occasion, I met Reich Minister Heinrich Himmler who commanded the SS. I was shocked to sense that Himmler was truly evil, but I dismissed my concerns because, well, Himmler's appetites were well known. Perhaps he was secretly disloyal to the Führer, I thought. It had to be that."

He pauses for breath. "When, at long last, I stood in the presence of the Führer himself, I was shaken to my very center to find that he, Adolf Hitler, my beloved Führer, to whom I had pledged my life and my absolute loyalty, was evil and corrupt to the core. Now my guts felt like there was a whole *colony* of rats chewing on them. Hitler had been a *god* to me. Only . . . then I knew that he was *not* a god; he was a *demon*."

A tear falls from his hollow eyes. "I'd followed him . . . served him faithfully for years. I'd embraced vampirism the better to serve him. I had *fantasies* of Converting him so he could be immortal and reign over the Thousand-Year Reich for the entire thousand years and beyond. That was all shattered when I realized he was a monster."

He looks me right in the eye.

"A monster like me," he says.

Shaking his head, he continues, "I was so shaken by my encounter with the Führer that I felt driven to see the fruits born of our 'glorious cause.' I visited Auschwitz." He waves a weak dismissal. "I won't describe the horrors there. They've been described and documented enough. I will tell you, however, what *I* found there."

"And what was that?" I ask.

"Evil. I found great evil. I'd been taught that the *Jew* was evil. I'd believed the Jew needed to be exterminated. But what I found was that *we*—my people, the *Aryans*, the 'Master Race'—*we* were the evil and corrupt ones. Among the emaciated Jews I found some corruption, some pettiness, but this can be found in all races. No, what astounded me was . . . I found *nobility*.

"From the cover of trees, I observed a work detail in which a skeletal Jewish man saw another skeletal comrade fall as he was hauling wood. I don't even know if the fallen man was the Jew's *friend* or not. He may have just been a fellow inmate in misery. The Jew looked around quickly to see if he was unobserved. He crawled over to his comrade and tried to rouse him. He knew if the guards saw them, it might mean death for both of them.

"The Jew shook his comrade. He spoke to him in German with a Polish accent. He urged and then pled with him to get up and get back to work. The fallen man said he was too weak. They'd had virtually nothing to eat for several days. He couldn't move.

"And then I watched something that astonished me, something that *changed* me. It was my 'turning point,' as you would say. The Jew bit into his *own wrist* with one of his few remaining teeth. He opened a vein and put the oozing wound to his comrade's lips. He fed the man with the only source of nourishment he had to offer.

"He gave him his own blood. I had taken blood by force to make myself immortal. The Jew gave his life's blood to save another. And even I am aware that drinking blood is against Jewish law. It must have been the last extremity. Maybe the Jew didn't even know the other man. He never called him by name. I have no idea. I don't think it mattered. The fallen man was a fellow human being, and he was in need. Nothing else mattered.

"I don't know what happened after that. I don't know if the Jew's sacrifice saved the other man or not. I don't know if they both died. I don't know, because I fled.

"I flew away and left that awful place of death and misery. I fled the sight of the only true nobility I'd ever witnessed. I shed my uniform as I flew. I couldn't bear to have the vile symbol of the Nazis against my skin—against my evil, unclean, many-times-damned skin. Naked, I flew high over Europe. Eventually, I flew across the Mediterranean to Africa. I found a cave in a mountain in central Africa, and there I stayed for weeks. I wept and I starved. I contemplated how I would end my foul existence.

"Many times I thought about exposing myself to the Sun. I never did, not because I was too cowardly to do it, but because eventually I decided that it was far too quick a way for me to die. I deserved to die slowly and painfully, wasting away like that Jew at Auschwitz.

"And waste away I did. It was agony beyond anything I'd ever known. Eventually I lapsed into a coma. I don't know how long I remained like that. It might have been months."

Rolf pauses. He seems to be having trouble catching his breath. I listen to his pulse. 'Tis rapid. The doctor in me is very concerned. On the other hand, I'm still cautious. I *want* to believe him, but . . . I don't know if I can.

"Forgive me," he says. "I don't mean to go on like this. I'm . . . very hungry."

"Then what?" Carl asks.

"What?" Rolf says wearily.

"What brought you back?" Carl presses.

"Laddie," I say, "I'm nae sure . . ."

"Go on," Carl says to Rolf. His voice an uncustomary edge I dinnae like.

"You were once a soldier . . . no, an officer, Carl?" Rolf asks.

Carl stiffens. Then he says cautiously, "Yes."

Rolf looks at me. He smiles wanly. "Your husband knows that *now* is the time to press the attack: when the enemy . . . or *potential* enemy . . . is weak." He looks at Carl. "Yes?"

Enemy? Well, I've nae lowered the sword yet, have I?

Carl nods. "Go on."

"Very well." Rolf sighs.

"After I lay in the coma for some time, I was awakened by the smell of prey. And not just prey: it was the sweet smell of pure evil blood.

"There were six men: six large black men chasing a lone black girl, the moonlight shining on their dark skins. The girl couldn't have been more than ten years old. She had fled into my cave, and the men followed her, trapping her there.

"How their blood sang to me! I rose from the rocky floor and stood before the men. I was a terrible sight as I stepped forward into the moonlight: pale and naked and as skeletal as that Jew at Auschwitz. I must have appeared to be a demon from the abyss. The men cried out and fell to the ground, but they were unable to flee; their legs would not obey them. The girl fled deeper into the cave behind me.

"Instantly, I fell upon the closest man before he could catch his breath to scream a second time. I drained him. The others finally found the use of their legs and turned to run. I spread my wings and flew after them into the night. I hunted them in the jungle.

"I slaughtered them all.

"Then I returned to the cave.

"By that time, I was Healed, my body restored, but I was bone tired. The girl was waiting for me. She bowed herself to the earth and stayed there. I took a girdle, a kind of skirt, from my first victim and wrapped it around my loins.

"I came to her and offered my hand to raise her up from the floor. She refused at first, but eventually got to her feet. Then she said a few words in a language I didn't understand. When I didn't reply, she said many other things I didn't understand before finally backing out of the cave and then turning and running away down the mountain.

"I was very tired, so I lay down and went back to Sleep. When I awoke at sunset, I found that the body of my first victim was gone, dragged away while I Slept. There was also an offering of food (gourds, a goat's leg, and sweet potatoes) left at the mouth of the cave.

"Over the coming weeks and months I slowly became the protector of the girl's village. A neighboring tribe had been slowly killing them off, driving them farther up the mountain. All the men were dead. The women and children were alone.

"Over time I realized they thought I was a god of some kind. I got them to stop bringing food offerings after I kept returning the food each night. So they started making offerings of clothing, jewelry, and flowers.

"They wouldn't approach me or speak to me. Even the girl never spoke to me again. I couldn't learn much of their language, although I could hear them speaking, when they were unaware.

"I tried to observe them at night. Though I could not understand their language, I tried to pick out their names. I think I picked out a few, but I couldn't learn even the name of the girl I saved. So I made up names for each of them in my head. I called her 'Nachtblume.'"

What a bonnie name!

"I protected them for nearly a year," he continues. "Every week or so, raiders attempted to come upon the village by night, and every time, I drove them off. After each raid, I would go to the enemy tribe and take blood from the more corrupt men, not killing them, but leaving them weak for several days.

"One night, I arose from my Sleep and I left my cave to watch over the village. As I approached from the air, I knew that something was wrong. The village was too quiet. And I could smell blood and ashes everywhere.

"They were all dead, slaughtered as I Slept, the village burned to the ground. I sat in the middle of the ring of burned huts, and I wept.

"I buried them all. I wrote the names I'd given them on stone markers I set up. I carved the names into the stone with my finger."

I cannae help but glance in the direction of Ben's grave.

Rolf wipes away a tear. "When I finished burying them, I flew to the village of the enemy tribe with the intent of killing all the men. Then I thought about the women and children who would be left behind. If I killed their men, they'd be alone to fall prey to someone else.

"In the end, I left them as they were. Vengeance would not bring back the dead.

"And so I fled my mountain.

"After that, I roamed the world. I lived off the blood I took from the truly evil, but I never killed again. I've encountered many of our kind, mostly Renegades, over the years, but I've avoided becoming entangled with Cults. I don't wish to be forced to kill again, as I would be if a Master commanded me to do it."

I know exactly what ye mean, laddie. I shudder at the memory of lying motionless on Michael's bed, unable to move, bound by his command alone, waiting to be raped.

Until Carl rescued me and helped me to break the Master's command.

"A few months ago, I heard the rumors of what happened here: I heard the Cult had been dissolved. I heard the new Master had killed the old Master and all of the Teachers and then had summarily dissolved the Cult. Lilith was said to be beside herself with fury. I heard she sent agents here to find those responsible. Her agents failed to turn up anything, except for the story of the angels who defended the Mormon temple in Ogden. Because the angels didn't have wings, everyone assumed that they couldn't be vampires. They might have been *actual* angels for all anyone knew.

"Word has spread among the Penitents that . . ."

"What?" Carl and I cry together.

"There are other Penitents?" I say incredulously.

"Yes, of course," Rolf replies.

"Where?" Carl asks.

"How many?" I say.

Rolf looks from Carl to me and then says, "Dozens that I've met."

"*Dozens?*" I say.

"I'm sure there are many more that I haven't met. Maybe a hundred scattered around the world.

"A hundred?" Carl says.

"Yes," Rolf replies, "and most of them are coming here to Salt Lake City."

Chapter 5

WHY WOULD THE PENITENTS be coming *here*?" I'm still trying to get used to the idea that there are *many* Penitents. For all my life, I believed I was the only one still alive. "And how could there possibly be so many?" *According to the stories I've heard, Penitents lose hope before very long and take their own lives.*

Rolf looks at me curiously. "As for why they're coming *here*," he says, "they're coming *here* because someone *here* broke Lilith's power. Someone dissolved a Cult. That someone was a Master, even if only for a few minutes. No Master can defy Lilith and dissolve a Cult. There's no greater command, save one."

"And what would that be?" Carl asked.

"No Master or Teacher must ever create an Unwilling vampire," Rolf responds.

Both Carl and I gasp. *I was nae taught that! The Ancient One who Converted me did nae mention that.* Carl and I glance at each other, and our eyes lock for a moment. *Apparently there is much Carl and I were never taught by the vampires who Converted us.*

Our reaction is nae lost on Rolf. "*Has* someone Converted an Unwilling vampire?" he asks incredulously.

"Um," Carl says a bit sheepishly, "that would be me."

"*You* Converted an Unwilling vampire?" Rolf says.

"No," Carl responds, "I'm the Unwilling vampire."

"The Curse!" Rolf exclaims.

I nod. "Aye."

Rolf's referring to the ancient prophecy made by Adam. Vampires call it the "Curse."

"And it shall come to pass in the last days," Rolf recites, "when Unwilling and Penitent shall join in the house of the Lord in the top of the mountains, the mother of night shall fall, and death shall come upon her children."

"Yep," Carl says grimly, "that's the one."

"You are the 'Unwilling,'" Rolf says.

"And I'm the 'Penitent,'" I say.

"What makes *you* the 'Penitent'?" Rolf asks. "That could be anyone."

I shake my head.

"Unless," Rolf says hesitantly, "the two of you were joined 'in the house of the Lord in the top of the mountains.'"

"Moira and I were married in the temple last year," Carl says.

"But the part about 'the top of the mountains?'" Rolf says.

"Utah is a Ute Indian word meaning, 'the top of the mountains,'" I say.

"*Himmel!*" Rolf exclaims in a breathless whisper.

"Amen," Carl agrees solemnly.

We stand in silence for a while until a thought occurs to me.

"This area cannae sustain a hundred or more vampires, even if they dinnae kill anyone," I point out.

"What do you mean?" Rolf asks.

"Moira and I have Fed only from living mortals a handful of times in the past year," Carl says. "We Hunt only violent criminals and then we take only a quart or so. And we actually went Hunting one time."

He does nae know about my foray this morning. Although I did nae seek it out.

"The other times, evil . . . *presented* itself to us. Even so, law enforcement or the media takes notice. They see a pattern."

"You mean, like when you defended the Mormon temple?" Rolf says.

"Aye, we just happened to be there," I say. "Right time, right place."

"And even that ended up being spread about," Carl adds. "Also, I had a police detective after me last year."

"And that ended . . . badly," I say.

Rolf looks at me curiously.

"He sought out the Cult, and he and his whole family died as a consequence," I explain.

"So, if you don't Hunt, how are you Feeding?" Rolf asks.

I start to open my mouth to answer, but Carl quickly squeezes my hand and says, "We'd rather not say just yet."

I shoot Carl an annoyed glance. *Why is he being so protective of that particular piece of information?*

"Ah, yes," Rolf says with a weary nod, "I understand. You don't know if you can trust me. I *could* be one of Lilith's agents, sent to find out and *deal* with whoever dissolved the Cult."

"The thought had crossed my mind," Carl replies flatly.

That's my husband: thinking like a military man! If we tell Rolf our primary source of food is expired or contaminated donated blood, that clue could lead him to the fact that I work in a hospital. Which, in turn, could lead him to find out where we live, and then we could be in real danger. So Carl was prudent to withhold that bit of information. At least until we know whether or nae we can trust Rolf.

"Well, then we have a problem," I point out. "Rolf, ye obviously need to Feed and right soon. We cannae trust ye with our . . . secret. At least nae yet."

"And I don't want to lose contact with you," Rolf says. "I came here to learn how to break Lilith's power as you two have. And now I find myself in the presence of the prophesied Unwilling and Penitent, the harbingers of doom. If there's a path to redemption, it lies with the two of you, even if it means death for all of us. At least it would rid the world of the plague of Lilith and her Children. It would rid the world of *us*."

"So, what do we do?" I ask.

"Perhaps, I could show you how a Renegade Penitent Feeds to set your minds at ease about me," Rolf suggests. "I won't kill. None of us will."

Carl looks dubious.

"The last thing a Penitent wants to do is kill," Rolf tries to reassure us, "and the last thing a Renegade wants to do is attract attention. I want to avoid any of Lilith's Masters. I don't want to be a slave."

"We *all* want to kill," Carl says. "It's part of our condition."

"What I mean is," Rolf says quickly, "a Penitent wants to avoid killing prey at all costs. It's the proof of our Penance. That . . . and trying to serve the mortals around us."

"Why have ye nae Fed recently?" I ask.

"Travel, partly," Rolf says. "I started in Poland."

He must notice my raised eyebrow, because he follows that statement with, "I visit Auschwitz every decade or so.

"As for the rest . . . I've been watching the Mormon temple in Ogden. I didn't know what I was looking for . . . the 'angels' maybe. It happened about the same time as the dissolution of the Cult. I thought the two incidents might be related. I was afraid to leave the temple site for fear I might miss . . . what I was searching for. I just haven't had time to Hunt for evil, and I didn't encounter any at that place.

"Tonight, I thought I'd examine the site where the Cult was located. As I flew here, I saw the two of you pass across the Moon. You had no wings, so I thought you must be the angels of God. And that's when I . . . approached you."

He falls silent except for his labored breathing.

Carl looks at me and then says to Rolf, "Excuse us for a minute. Don't go anywhere."

Rolf nods and says, "I'll wait right here."

Carl gives a slight tug on my hand, and the two of us fly up and away from the mountain. We keep our eyes on Rolf, though.

"What do you think?" he asks in a whisper when we're a safe distance away.

"I dinnae know, laddie," I reply. "I *want* to trust him."

"My gut tells me he's on the level," he replies, "but, if Lilith *has* sent agents to investigate, Rolf is *exactly* what they would be like. He told us he used to be a spy and assassin. Maybe he still is.”

"I can tell ye this much, laddie: his state of advanced starvation is *real*. My guess is he has a day or two at the most before he'll be comatose. And, as ye well know, controlling the urge to Feed is very difficult. Most vampires dinnae even *try* to control it. I find it very hard to believe that any but a true Penitent would deny himself food for so long.”

"I say that we should let him show us 'how a Renegade Penitent Feeds,'" Carl says after a moment.

"Aye, laddie, I agree, but I *do* wish we were both armed," I say with a little flourish of Rolf's sword.

"Yeah," he says with a smirk, "that's a mistake we'd better not make again. We should have weapons with us when we fly and probably all the time at night. One of us could fly home and get a sword, but that would give away its direction. Besides, I don't think we should split up until we *know* this guy's the real deal.”

"Aye, laddie," I reply. "I think 'twould be best if we were to take Rolf up to Ogden for Hunting. He obviously has a refuge there where he's been passing the day safe from the Sun. That will allow us to retreat back toward Salt Lake City and make sure he does nae follow us.”

"Lead the way, pretty lady," Carl says as we start to fly toward Rolf.

"What are you *doing?*" The alarm in Carl's voice is obvious as he restrains Rolf. Carl's holding Rolf tightly by the arm as we hover above the streets of downtown Ogden. Rolf's wings beat furiously but insubstantially as they pass through both Carl and me like the mental phantoms they are.

"He's evil!" Rolf cries, as he tries to pull away from Carl, but nae so violently that Carl is unable to restrain him.

As for the *evil*, I feel the nigh irresistible attraction of the blood, drawing me as a black hole draws the light. The source of the sweet, sweet corruption is a lone young Hispanic man hurrying along the street below us.

With all I consumed this morning? I should nae feel so hungry!

Father, help me!

My fangs are extended, and drool is spilling from my lips. The urge to kill the man, to drain his life, to then rend the carcass into small pieces to leave for the rats is as potent as it has ever been in all my long life. As a vampire, I'm driven to kill the truly wicked and send them to the justice of God. But centuries of practice have helped me control my homicidal urges. Practice and regret for the seventy-two men I slaughtered in the name of vengeance . . . and the innocent child I would have murdered had I nae come to my senses.

Carl is, of course, reacting just as I am. And he has nae had centuries to learn to master his urges as I have. In spite of his compulsions, he still restrains Rolf.

I'm finding it hard to think of anything except the blood.

"Let me go!" Rolf cries. His German accent is more pronounced in his obvious distress. "He deserves to die!"

"So do ye, Rolf," I say, trying to focus. "Ye have probably done more evil than that . . . *animal* down there."

"But I'm only going to take a liter! Maybe two! I *know* you can feel the corruption! You can *smell* it!"

"You can't just *take* his blood," Carl says.

Rolf rips free from Carl's hold and spins in the air to face him. Rolf's expression is contorted in rage. "What do you mean I 'can't just take his blood'?" he snarls. "He's *evil*!"

"Ye have nae *proof*," I say as calmly as I can (which is nae as calm as I would like). "Ye must have proof. Ye must be defending yourself or others. Otherwise, ye are simply committing assault and *stealing* what does nae belong to ye."

"You're joking!" he snaps.

"Nope," Carl says. His control has improved dramatically over the past year since his unwilling Conversion.

"But he's evil! What proof do you need other than your own senses?" Rolf's anger is starting to give way to panic. His need to Feed is excruciatingly obvious.

Is mine as obvious? This should nae be happening!

"It's nae your blood," I say, lusting after the blood myself. "Ye cannae simply take it."

Rolf looks from me to Carl and back again, his jaw working as he tries to come up with a response. Then he wheels about and stares at the man below. Rolf's chest is heaving.

But he stays put. He hovers next to us, following the prey with only his eyes.

I understand his need. I, myself, have Fed well. *I dinnae need nourishment!* Rolf's need must be agonizing. The look on his face alternates between longing, pain, and rage.

"So be it," he says through clenched teeth. "Vater, gib mir Kraft!" he mutters under his breath.

Was that a prayer?

Suddenly, the prey slows to a more casual pace. He pats his stomach just above his belt. I sniff the air, trying to smell *anything* other than the corrupt sweetness of his blood.

There it is! The scent of gun oil, spent gunpowder, and steel. *He has a gun tucked into his pants, and he just checked it.*

"'Twill nae be long now, laddie," I say. "Be patient."

The prey reaches into his jacket and pulls out something that fits into the palm of his hand. He's putting it to the top of his head. 'Tis a nylon stocking. He's masking his face. He's about to do violence. I can feel it. And his target is the convenience store at the corner. "That's enough, laddie," I say to Rolf.

No sooner have the words passed my drooling lips than Rolf is speeding toward the prey.

He swoops down upon the man and lifts him into the air. The gun falls to the pavement with a thunk. The man does nae have a chance to even utter a scream before Rolf has plunged his fangs into the prey's neck. With the vampire's Seed-laden saliva in his bloodstream, the prey's scream fades almost sooner than it starts, and a look of ecstasy relaxes his contorted face.

I listen to the heartbeat of the prey. The heart slows. *Pumping that delicious blood through his pulsing arteries and veins.*

I'm ready to intervene if it becomes erratic or weak.

So close and so tempting.

Stop that, Moira MacDonald Morgan! Ye have better control than that, lassie!

I hold Rolf's sword at the ready. I could have his head off his shoulders without giving the prey so much as a scratch, if need be.

Then the prey would be all mine.

Lassie, ye are nae doing so well tonight. Why is that? Is it the stress of the dreams that ye are nae supposed to be having?

Rolf tears himself away from the man's neck. He stares at the blood for a moment and then licks the wound so that the Seed in his saliva can heal the man's neck, leaving nae trace. The prey is still alive, and I can tell from here that his blood pressure is low, but acceptable.

He'll live.

Rolf was true to his word and did nae take too much. The prey could stand to give up another quart, surely.

Stop it, lassie! What's wrong with ye?

Still holding his prey aloft, Rolf begins the distasteful but necessary process of Persuasion. Rolf did nae kill the man, and that's *good*, but this part is very important as well. What he does here may be just as *telling* as the fact that he did nae kill.

Rolf fixes his prey with an intense gaze. In a commanding voice he says, "You will forget that you ever saw me. You will forget what I did to you this night. You will forget, but you will fear me. You will not be able to name this fear, but you will dread my return all the same. You will go home and you will never hurt another person again. If you ever harm or threaten to harm another soul, I will come back for you. Do you understand?"

The Seed-induced euphoria and longing on the face of the prey is obvious. He's moaning and trying to pull Rolf's head back to his neck.

Equally clear is the fact that the Persuasion has worked (meaning that the man is *susceptible* to Persuasion).

And just as apparent is the fact that he does nae understand a word that was said to him.

"Do ye speak Spanish?" I ask Rolf.

"No, I don't," he replies with a grimace. "Do either of you?"

"Not a word," says Carl.

"I know a wee bit," I say. *I hope I dinnae muck this up! What I know is a bit of older Castilian Spanish from my travels long ago. 'Tis different from the Mexican version.* "Say this to him: ¡No daño a nadie!"

Rolf repeats it.

"Ask him if he understands," I say. "Say: ¿Entiende?"

Rolf repeats the question. The man nods.

"Now say: ¡Sea beuno!" *I'm nae sure that conveys the meaning that I want. If he were nae being Persuaded, he might laugh at that one.*

With each command, Rolf repeats it followed by the query, ¿Entiende?

"¡Olvidese de nosotros!

"¡Usted nunca nos vio!

"¡Confiese a la policia!

"There," I say. "That's close enough to what you said. Now put him down before someone sees us."

Before I give in to temptation.

Rolf returns the shaken man to the ground and then rejoins us in the air. The prey staggers off in the opposite direction from whence he came, taking his sweet corruption with him. *Is that the direction of the police department? I dinnae know, and I'm nae sure that he knows, himself. He'll find it eventually, I'm sure. So long as he leaves and takes his sweet blood with him!*

Carl drops to the ground and retrieves the gun. He bends it in half in his hands, wipes the fingerprints off with his shirttail and then tosses the weapon into the dumpster behind the convenience store. *The clerk inside will ne'er know how close she came to dying tonight.* Then Carl rejoins us in the air.

We start to climb to a higher altitude . . . mercifully increasing the distance between us and the pull of that evil man's blood.

"Except for the last part," Rolf says, startling me in my struggle for control.

"Aye?" I say. "What's that?"

"The thing you told me to say . . . the last part . . . the part about the police. I assume that meant he was to confess to the police," Rolf explains.

"Let mortal justice attend to him," I say, collecting myself.

"We don't kill," Carl says, "but he still needs to be brought to justice. He still needs to be . . . removed as a threat to others."

"I see," Rolf says. His voice is much stronger now that he has Fed. "But, doesn't that just call attention to your presence . . . sending him to the police?"

"Sure," Carl says. "There *is* that chance, but as long as we've . . . interacted with him, we might as well do as much good as we can. This way, we prevent violence tonight and have the potential to prevent violence in the future."

"But ye are correct," I say. "We've had problems because of it in the past."

"With so many Penitents gathering to this area, the danger of discovery will only increase," Rolf replies.

"We still have to do the right thing as best we can," Carl says, "even if it puts us at risk."

Carl levels off at an altitude where 'tis safe for us to fly. We should be hard to spot from the ground, and we're nae so high that we cannae breathe easily. However, we dinnae seem to be heading anywhere in particular. Carl makes slow random turns. *He's scanning the sky, looking for other vampires.*

"I assume you have a place to spend the day, Rolf," Carl says.

"Of course," Rolf replies.

"Let's go there so we can talk for a bit," Carl says.

Rolf nods.

"Take the lead," Carl says, gesturing in front of himself. Rolf moves ahead and turns toward downtown Ogden. We follow close behind. I keep Rolf's sword at the ready.

Something has been nagging at me since we met the newcomer. "Ye say, Rolf, that there may be more than a hundred Penitents coming to Salt Lake City?"

"Yes," he replies.

"Where are they? Speaking of the fear of discovery, why have we nae heard or seen any sign of them before? Ye would think there'd be a rash of . . . strange incidents. Their presence would nae go unnoticed, at least at some level. Surely ye are nae the first?"

"No," he says looking thoughtful. "I only heard of the movement a few weeks ago. Others have been gathering here for a while, or so I hear."

"Movement?" says Carl. "You mean . . . like a migration of vampires?"

"No, I mean a *movement*," Rolf replies, "as in a group of people working together for a common goal. Almost like an organization, but without a real leader . . . *so far.* That's why I came to find you."

Chapter 6

DOES THIS MOVEMENT have a name?" Carl asks as we sit in Rolf's modest hotel room. Carl and I sit together on the bed, and Rolf is in the single chair at the room's small writing desk.

The sword lies on my lap. Carl holds my left hand, while my right hand rests on the hilt of my weapon.

"I've heard two names," Rolf says, "but I think they refer to the same thing. Some call it 'the Congregation.' Others call it 'the Vampire Stake.' That last one sounds like a stupid joke to me."

Carl snorts beside me. "It probably *is* a joke, but it also makes sense, I suppose."

"How so?" Rolf says, puzzled.

"Ye dinnae know much about Utah or the Mormons, do ye?" I say with a wee smile.

Rolf nods and, pauses, then shakes his head. He says, "Utah was settled by the Mormons. They used to have many wives. Their leader was Brigham Smith. That's it. That's all I know."

"Joseph Smith and then Brigham Young," Carl corrects.

"OK," Rolf says with a perfunctory nod. "What of it?"

"A Mormon congregation is called a 'ward,'" Carl replies. "A larger gathering or collection of wards is called a 'stake.'"

"'Steak,' as in a slab of cow muscle, or 'stake,' as in what the hero drives into the heart of a vampire in a Hollywood movie?" Rolf asks.

"The latter," Carl replies, "but, more precisely, a tent stake, as in the stakes at the edges of the tent that connect to the center pole and keep the pole and the tent up."

"I see," says Rolf.

"It probably *is* a play on words, though," I say.

Carl nods. "And it *is* kinda funny," he chuckles.

"But, how could there be so many?" I ask.

"I don't understand the question," Rolf says. "What do you mean?"

"I've met so few Penitents," I say. "The few I've met lost hope and committed suicide. They don't last long. That's one reason why . . . I find it so hard to trust ye, Rolf," I continue. "At sixty years or more of penitence, ye have outlived all others I've ever heard of . . . except for myself."

"How long do most . . . last?" Carl asks.

"A year . . . maybe two. Most . . . far less," I say. "Carl and I met one just a year ago who lasted but a few hours."

"I . . . understand," says Rolf. "Those that do . . . survive . . . at least for a while . . . are the ones who find a purpose . . . a reason for living, for continuing to exist."

"What purpose did you find?" Carl asks.

"I became a protector of the innocent, particularly of the Jew, the Gypsy, and others that my race and I tried to exterminate. I've saved many lives. I've prevented much evil. But it isn't enough. It'll never replace the innocent lives I took."

Rolf hangs his head and says nothing for a few moments. When he raises his face to us again, his eyes are wet with tears. "My Offering was a Jewish woman," he says, speaking of his first victim. "She was terrified. I . . . *consumed* her. And I laughed and exulted as I did it . . . as her *screams* of horror and her *pleas* for mercy and her *cries* for God to save her . . . turned to moans of . . . Seed-induced euphoria . . . as I robbed her of her life."

His voice catches. "I knew her." His voice lowers to barely a whisper. "Her name was Gretl. She was . . . my nanny when I was a boy. She used to . . . *comfort* me when I was afraid of the dark."

His mouth works in mute agony. His shoulders quake. From his thundering pulse and his tortured breathing, he appears to be suffering the torments of the damned. I cannae believe he's faking.

He looks up at me and, in a choked voice, he says, "If I live a thousand years and save a million lives, I could never . . ." His voice trails off.

"I know," I say quietly.

"None of us can," Carl says.

"Then . . . ," Rolf whispers, "there *is* no hope."

"*We* cannae atone," I say gently, "but the Savior can, lad."

"There can't be enough forgiveness for me," he says, "not even with Him."

"The Book of Mormon tells of a wicked, murderous king named Lamoni," Carl says. "Lamoni executed his servants for the slightest mistake. He executed servant after servant because they were unable to defend his flocks from armed gangs. Then he sent new ones out. The new servants had no hope to succeed where their predecessors had failed. When they likewise failed, he executed them. He also led men in an unjust war against his peaceful neighbors. He had the blood of many innocents on his soul.

"One day, a man came to him from the neighboring country and asked to live with Lamoni and his people. His name was Ammon. Lamoni made Ammon one of his servants and sent him to guard the flocks, probably thinking he'd fail. Ammon successfully defended the flocks through the power of

God. When Lamoni learned of Ammon's deeds, he was afraid that Ammon was God come to punish him for his many murders. Instead, Ammon taught him about Jesus Christ and the infinite Atonement.

"When Lamoni learned about the Atonement and about the Savior, he gave up all his sins. He and his people buried their weapons and pledged never to kill again. Many of them laid down their own lives rather than break that pledge."

"And they *were* forgiven," I say. "They were *redeemed*."

Rolf says nothing, but his breathing eases a wee bit.

"But, my crimes were . . . ," he begins, but he does nae finish.

"Aye, your crimes were terrible," I say, "but so were Lamoni's. Put your trust in God and serve Him. Leave it in His hands."

Rolf is silent for a bit, and then he nods. "I've never heard of this Lamoni or whatever. What you're saying is all very new to me, but I believe you. Or at least I *want* to believe you. You've done what no one else has ever done. You've broken Lilith's power . . . or at least defied it."

Rolf looks up at us. "As for your other question, I've met a few Penitents in my travels. And, like you said, I heard tales of others who had committed suicide when they lost hope." He swallows. "But, there has been a huge surge in our numbers over the last few months."

"Why?" Carl asks.

"Because of the two of *you*," Rolf says, an eager, hopeful light in his eyes. "*You* broke Lilith's power. Nobody knows *how*, but apparently you did it. Actually, nobody knows *who*. Except for *me*, that is."

He continues, "Be that as it may, as news spread of the dissolution of the Cult in Salt Lake City, it gave hope to those who *wanted* to repent. Many have abandoned the old ways, embraced the legends of the Penitents, and gone Renegade. They've fled their Masters, being careful to avoid *other* Masters, and are slowly making their way here . . . looking for you."

"How," I ask, "are they hoping to find . . . whatever it is they're looking for?"

"And how is word spreading?" Carl asks. "From what you're saying, it sounds like Penitents are solitary . . . Renegades, as you put it."

"As for how they're hoping to find you," Rolf says, "*my* plan was simple: come to Utah and fly each night and hope to see a vampire or . . . an angel."

"Ye very nearly starved to death doing it," I point out.

"True, but that is what most of us are planning," he says.

"How do you know what others are planning? How are you communicating?" Carl asks again.

"Well, there's a blog." Rolf rattles off the name of an innocuous-sounding website. "This *is* the twenty-first century."

"A blog?" Carl says, rolling his eyes. "Who'd have thought?"

I shake my head, indicating 'twould nae have occurred to me.

"It's a bulletin board, really . . . like a support group for Penitents," Rolf continues. "Nobody gives personal information, not even names. We're terrified that Lilith will send Enforcers to hunt us down or put us under a Master's control. So, we just exchange thoughts, hopes . . . and vague plans . . . nothing more specific than gathering to Salt Lake City. Anything more specific could betray us to her."

Carl and I exchange a glance full of meaning. "She's going to be coming for us," he says.

"Aye," is all I can say.

We both know what that means.

"I hoped we'd have more time," my husband says.

"Maybe you do," Rolf says.

We turn our attention back to him. "What do ye mean?" I ask.

"Lilith has already sent agents to investigate," he explains. "As far as I know, they've returned empty-handed. Nobody knows you two are the prophesied 'the Unwilling and the Penitent.' *I* certainly had no idea. I'm just here looking for hope. Have I found it?"

"I think so," I say. "But ye must understand this, lad: there's another prophecy, this one from just over half a century ago. It was given by the President of the Church at the time . . . the Mormon Church. It mentions me by name and Carl by description. It says that we (my husband and I) are going to have to face Lilith someday. When we do, *if we've proven worthy*, we will kill her, but we will lose our lives in the process. When we kill Lilith, *all* of us, all vampires will die." *It also says that Carl and I will see our 'Redeemer's face in the resurrection of the just.'* "Ye see, lad, we must be willing to lay down our lives for our redemption." *Just like Lamoni.*

He nods. "I understand," he says. "But if such is the price, why don't we just starve ourselves to death or go out into the sunlight?"

I cannae suppress a shudder at the thought of death by sunlight.

"Because," Carl says, "that would simply be giving in to despair. Besides, suicide is never the answer. It's a terrible sin, unless it's a selfless act of sacrifice to protect others. It's not up to us to choose how or when we die. That's in God's hands."

"It's also nae our place to judge those who've given in to despair," I add. "God will judge whether they were in their right minds when they did it. But He *has* forbidden the taking of one's own life. So suicide cannae be the way."

"There are those on the bulletin board who say it's the *only* way," Rolf says. "Some say, if you're going to come to Salt Lake City, come fasting."

"Is that what ye were doing?" I ask.

"Not exactly," he says, his eyes having the unfocused look of someone lost in his thoughts. "Although, it *did* make some sense to me. No, I was mostly just too intent on finding . . . *you* . . . to worry about Feeding."

His eyes focus on us now. "So, please, tell me how you did it. How did you break free of Lilith's power?"

Carl looks at me, and I see there's still doubt in his eyes. I *want* to believe Rolf, but if we're wrong . . .

"Are ye nae curious about the wings?" I say, still looking into Carl's blue eyes. I see understanding in them. He knows where I'm going with this. He gives a slight nod. We both turn our gaze back to Rolf.

"Y-yes," he stammers. "Of course I am." He pauses and then says, "But surely my question is more important."

"Aye, it is," I say.

"But the two questions are related, I think," says my husband, effectively finishing my statement. "Why *do* vampires have wings?" he asks Rolf.

"So we can fly, obviously," Rolf says with a confused expression. "I don't see . . ."

"Our wings are immaterial," Carl interrupts. "They produce sound, but no *lift*."

"Everyone knows that," Rolf says. "They're manifestations of the demon inside us, the Essence that binds all vampires to Lilith."

"In other words, laddie," I say, "they're a manifestation of *evil*."

"They're projections of the mind," Carl says. "The Seed enhances our abilities. Our minds project the *image* and the *sound* of wings, but the wings aren't really there. We have wings because we *think* we do, because our Teachers *taught* us we do."

With obvious skepticism written all over his face, Rolf looks at each of us.

"Try it," Carl says. "Just try flying *without* them. You have to concentrate at first on *not* projecting them, but it's really easy once you get past it."

"What?" Rolf says, confounded. "Fly right here in the hotel room?"

"Just hover above the floor," Carl says. "Nothing fancy."

Rolf hesitates and then stands up slowly. He lifts off the floor a few inches, his wings instantly appearing. He shakes his head.

"Just concentrate," I encourage.

He closes his eyes and appears to calm himself. His breathing and heartbeat slow. His wings beat insubstantially at the air as he hovers.

"Ye can do it," I say. *I hope he can.*

He takes a calming breath, and then . . . his wings vanish! They flicker once . . . twice . . . and then they're gone.

His eyes remain closed, and he hovers, wingless, as a smile spreads across his face.

"This is *amazing!*" he says in a quiet voice.

I hear Carl breathe a huge sigh of relief. I realize I must have done the same.

"That'll do," I say.

Rolf opens his eyes and settles slowly back to the floor. As soon as his feet take his weight again, he stands there trembling. His heart is racing now.

"What does it mean?" he says in a voice filled with excitement.

"It *means* we're not alone," Carl says quietly. He stands up and offers Rolf his hand. "Welcome to the family."

Rolf takes his hand and shakes it warmly. "That's it? You believe me now?"

"Aye." Rising to my feet, I place the sword on the small hotel writing desk next to Rolf's chair. I give him a warm hug. Then I kiss his cheek. "We *do.*"

When I let him go and back up a step to stand next to my husband, Rolf says, "Why?" He holds up a hand. "I mean, don't get me wrong. I'm *glad* you believe . . . ever so glad . . . but I don't understand."

Carl motions to him to sit. Rolf takes his chair again, a wee bit unsteadily. Carl and I sit next to each other on the bed.

"It's the wings . . . or rather your ability to control them. We think it has to do with self-control," I say. "Vampires are all about giving *in* to their urges. Penitents are all about *denying* their urges. Last year, Carl discovered we dinnae need our wings to fly. He taught this to me. It took me a wee bit of effort, but I succeeded in 'turning them off,' if ye will. Now it takes nae effort at all."

"I tried to teach this to two other vampires," Carl says. "They were members of the Cult. One of them, a truly evil woman named Rebecca, couldn't even get them to flicker. The other"—*his* voice catches and tears come to *my* eyes "—was a child vampire who'd never killed and wanted nothing more than to be a normal child. He mastered it immediately. One embraced evil and failed, and one abhorred evil and succeeded."

Rebecca was unable to make the wings go away, but my poor Ben, to him it was effortless.

"Ye are the only other vampire to have done it, to have flown without wings," I say. "We believe ye must be sincere."

Carl nods in agreement.

"In some ways the Nazis were *very* disciplined," Rolf says with a smirk.

"Aye, but nae in controlling their baser instincts."

"Yes, as I know only too well," he says sadly.

Chapter 7

W HAT'S THAT SMELL?" the young OB nurse says, wrinkling her nose. "Ew! It smells like burning . . . *something*!"

I thrust my smoldering left hand into the pocket of my white coat. The pain is subsiding, but the itch of Healing is nigh unbearable now. In moments, it'll be back to normal, showing nae evidence of momentarily catching fire a second or two ago, but the smell and the whiff of smoke will linger for a bit.

How stupid of me to have closed the blinds in the patient's room myself, instead of making Sally, the nurse, do it. I thought I could keep out of the direct sunlight, but my hand was exposed for the briefest time. And, of course, I had just sanitized my hands, removing the sunscreen.

How I *do* hate sunny days! Ach, *hate* is nae the right word, but I *do* find them very *annoying*. Especially when I have to work.

Most of my co-workers *welcome* the sunshine, of course. On a day like today, I have to take special care to avoid direct sunlight as much as possible. And it's nae always possible to do so.

"It's fading now," Sally says, sniffing the air suspiciously. I'm lucky she did nae pull the fire alarm.

And if I'd set off the sprinklers, we'd have a bonnie mess.

I dinnae know Sally well. She has probably nae heard of my "sun allergy." I'm up on the OB ward today only because Dr. Harkness asked me to check on one of his patients.

Ah, that's better. The itch of Healing is gone now, so I pull my hand out of my pocket again.

"How are ye doing, Mrs. Lidle?" I ask the patient who's obviously upset. "Dr. Harkness asked me to check up on ye. I'm Dr. Morgan."

I glance at the fetal heart monitor. It is nae longer showing the baby's heartbeat.

"Is my baby OK?" the thirty-something mother says staring at the zero on the readout and the flat line on the paper.

"Ach, the baby's heart is strong," I say in a soothing tone. "The bairn just moved a wee bit." I can discern the baby's heartbeat easily with my vampiric hearing.

"Sally," I say to the nurse, "would ye be a dearie and adjust the monitor?"

"Certainly, Dr. Morgan," Sally says as she moves in to comply.

"Do ye know already if 'tis a boy or a girl?" I ask as I glance over the patient's chart. So many parents dinnae want to be surprised anymore. 'Tis a shame. 'Tis one of the joys and mysteries of life.

One I will ne'er experience myself. Nae in this life.

"It's a girl," she says in a strained, but satisfied tone. "Our first. We have three boys."

"I'd wager she'll be as bonnie as her mother," I say with a wink, "and her brothers will treat her like a princess."

Sally moves away from the bed, and the monitor resumes its scribing, replacing the flat line with the baby's strong heartbeat.

"Well, then," I say brightly, "it looks like ye'll be holding your bonnie wee lassie today. Ye've had a few false alarms with this one, I see, but ye will be staying with us this time. We'll nae send ye home until after the bairn comes." I give her a smile. She smiles back weakly. Poor dear's exhausted.

"We'll give Dr. Harkness a call and tell him to come in soon," I say.

"He's not here?" she says in a near panic.

"Dinnae worry, milady," I say with a small curtsy. "I'll be here until he arrives."

$$\blacklozenge \ \blacklozenge \ \blacklozenge$$

As it turns out, Dr. Harkness does nae arrive in time, and I get to deliver the bairn myself. How I *love* delivering babies! I cannae have children of my own, and so I became a midwife and later a physician so I could help wee ones into this world.

At least there were nae any serious complications with *this* one.

Mary MacGregor screamed again as the pain hit her, but 'twas weaker. She would nae last much longer. Her heart was beating unsteadily. Constance MacGregor, her mother-in-law, had waited too long to send for me. She would have preferred another midwife, any *other midwife. She stood behind Mary and supported her back as Mary sat on the birthing stool, gripping its arms weakly. Constance was wailing along with her daughter-in-law. The small stone house was lit by naught but a pair of candles and the ever-present peat fire. The smell of peat smoke would have smothered all other smells . . . were it nae for the fact that Mary had begun to bleed. That scent made it hard for me to think of anything else. I had nae Fed for several days, as there had been nae deaths recently (so that I could drain the dead bodies) and nae opportunity lately to Hunt murderers for some of their blood.*

"Can ye nae help her, Moira MacDonald?" Constance sobbed.

"I would've been able to do more if ye'd sent for me long afore this," I said, feeling the bairn above and below. "The bairn has nae turned as it should."

"A breech!" the older woman cried in rising panic.

"Nae," I say. "Twould it were so. The bairn will nae present at all this way."

Mary screamed again. She looked at me in terror. She kenned nicely what this meant. She would die and her bairn would die with her.

Nae this night. Nae if I've anything to say about it.

I took her by the hand. "Mary, I need ye to trust me. I ken what must be done. I must cut the bairn out of your belly. I may be able to save the pair of ye, but I must act now."

Mary looked from my face to her mother-in-law's.

"What say ye?" I pressed urgently.

"Cut it out of her?" cried Constance in horror.

I nod. "Aye."

"Ye are a witch!" she cried and cast about looking for a weapon.

There was nae time for this nonsense.

I turned my head and fixed the crazed woman with my unholy stare. "Constance, stand there and dinnae say a word. I will tell ye what to do." I could feel the Persuasion sap her will.

"Aye," she said in a dead voice.

Mary looked at me in terror. "Ye are a witch! The stories are true!"

"Mary, I'm nae witch, but if I'm to save ye, I must act now," I said calmly. "Please trust me." I did nae want to Persuade her as well. I hated doing that. It was wrong.

Mary screamed again and nearly fell from the stool. Constance was nae longer supporting her as she ought. I righted Mary and said earnestly, but with nae Persuasion, "Let me help ye, in the name o' God and all the Holy Angels."

She sat still a moment, staring at me . . . at my mouth . . . and then she nodded and said breathlessly, "If ye were a witch, your tongue would have burst into flame."

"As ye will," I said. I looked up at the older woman who stared blankly ahead at some flickering shadow on the stone wall. "Constance, help me carry her to the bed."

We lifted the ailing mother from the stool, knocking it over, in the process. We laid her on the bed, and I retrieved the sharpest knife from my bag.

I quickly lifted Mary's nightdress and went to work. Mary screamed as I made a slit down the lower part of her belly below the navel. I was immediately assailed by the scent of her sweet blood. How I wished I had Fed! The need to lap at the sweet red blood made my fangs extend. I clamped my mouth shut before Mary could see them. She was too busy howling in pain to look at me. I made another slit inside the first and another until I had pierced into the womb.

It was a struggle for mastery over myself and my demonic nature, but I soon had the bairn and the rest of the bloody mess out of her belly. I held the blood-covered wee lad upside-down and thumped upon his feet to get him to crying. And he cried lustily. I cut the cord and tied it. Then I handed the wailing laddie to his grandmother and told her to hold him. I would attend to washing him and drying him with saltpeter after I saved his dying mother.

There was nae other way to do this. Mary was too weak. I would have to make use of the Seed. I held the cut edges of her womb together and held my mouth over the wound. I opened my mouth wide and exposed my fangs. I let the scent of the blood nearly overwhelm me so as to generate as much spittle as I could. I let the Seed-laden drool stream down onto the wound. I trembled with the effort of holding back. I wanted so badly to Feed!

The Seed in my spittle knit up the womb, and then I did the same for the wound in

Mary's belly. The flow of the blood stopped. The spilled blood remained, though. I dared nae taste it, though. I would nae be able to hold back then. With a great effort of will, I forced my fangs to retract again.

I looked up at Mary. She stared at me with an unreadable expression. "Ye are nae a witch," she said breathlessly. "Ye are a demon from Hell." The color was coming back to her cheeks. The Seed was even now helping her body to generate more blood. Soon the Seed and its healing power would dissipate.

Her heartbeat was getting stronger. She would be weak for a while, but she should live to raise her son.

I took the bairn from his grandmother. She gave him up with nary a bit of protest. She just stared blankly.

I pulled a cloth from my bag and a jar of saltpeter. I inspected the bairn. He was ruddy, and all his wee bits were where they should be. I poured water into a basin and washed him swiftly so he would nae catch his death. Then I dried him with the cloth and sprinkled the saltpeter over the body, while I shielded his mouth, nose, and eyes. He fussed and he wailed, but he was a healthy lad. I repeated the washing and the application of saltpeter. I wrapped him in a bit of tartan I found near the bed. Then I handed him to his mother.

I helped her to sit up in the bed, and she took the bairn to her breast. She looked down at the wee bairn in her arms, and he quieted. Then she looked at me.

I awaited her verdict.

"I feel grand," she said dreamily.

That'd be the Seed in her blood. "Ye may be a demon," she said, "but ye are also an angel. How can that be?"

I smiled at her. "I'm what I am. Ye have your son, and ye will live to bear more sons and daughters to your husband. Will ye keep my secret?"

She smiled back. "What secret? That Moira MacDonald is an angel sent from God? Who would believe me? Will ye release my husband's mother?"

"Oh," I said with a wee laugh, "aye, that I will."

I turned to the older woman and called her name. She turned to look at me. I said with authority, "Constance, ye have a fine grandson. Forget your fears. I'm nae witch. I'm a midwife. Ye will remember this as a time of joy and nae of fear. D'ye ken?"

"Aye," she said.

And so I released her.

She blinked and looked about, confused. Immediately her gaze fixed on the bairn and his mother. Her eyes went wide. She clapped her hands and swiftly advanced on the bonnie wee laddie, cooing.

I instructed her to clean up the bedclothes and remove the blood. I was nae up to doing that this night. I did take the afterbirth and buried it at the foot of a tree. How I wanted to consume the blood from it! But I would nae deny the family the good luck.

Then I flew away into the night, my wings spread and beating, to find some hapless murderer or highwayman from whom to take a pint or two so I could slake my maddening thirst.

After I wash up following the delivery of Mrs. Lidle's first daughter, I pull out my plastic bottle of sunscreen and apply some more to my hands and arms.

I go through a *pint* of sunscreen on a day like today. I mix it myself. I mix it with rosewater. It is nae for myself; it's for my co-workers. I lost all appreciation for the scent of flowers two and a half centuries ago. At first, flowers reminded me of Donald and the long walks we had in the gloaming when we talked and dreamed of marriage, children, and our future together. This was, of course, in the days before Bonny Prince Charlie came and led him away to the Battle of Culloden and to his death. So flowers reminded me of what I had lost . . . what I'd given up so I could have my costly revenge.

As a vampire, my sense of smell is very acute. A shark can taste blood in the water a mile away. I'm surrounded by blood all day long. I'm surrounded by mortals and their delicious blood. That scent overwhelms all others. I've learned to deal with it . . . most of the time. I have to keep myself well Fed, though, in order to ignore it.

By special arrangement, I "dispose" of the blood that has expired or is found to be contaminated or just *looks* funny. I perform this duty for both the lab and the hospital blood bank. Normally, 'twould nae be the responsibility of a doctor, but I volunteered. The hospital administrator readily agreed, of course. Mortals *want* to trust my kind. They cannae help themselves usually. Only those possessed of very strong will, such as those who are immune to Persuasion, will easily refuse my requests or suggestions.

'Tis a terrible burden to know that, even if I'm nae using Persuasion and deliberately robbing someone of his or her free will (even if only for the moment), I can influence people to do whatever I want. This makes it hard to know if people like me for *me* or just because they cannae resist my unnatural charms. I have to be careful what I ask people to do. I never get involved in political discussions, because almost everyone would agree with me. Similarly, I have to be very careful in talking about the Church. People will trust me and believe what I say because of *me* and nae because of the truth. And 'tis important to believe for the right reasons. I, myself, took a very long time to join the Church.

Aye, we have to watch what we say to mortals. This is, of course, all very frustrating for Carl. He is passionate about politics and, of course, religion. Now, he has to limit himself. 'Tis amusing to watch him when he positively trembles with the barely suppressed urge to put in his tuppence, especially when listening to an ignorant ninny rail on with some nonsense or other about the Church or the war or whatever. He wants so badly to thump a wee bit of sense into some people!

My missionary husband! How I love him, and I thank God for him!

Rolf spoke of how a Penitent has to find a purpose, a reason for living. Helping others was mine, but now *Carl* is my reason. 'Twas *Carl* who brought me hope after my baptism failed to cure me of my vampirism. I had so hoped that it would!

My phone beeps. Carl has sent me a text. *"Running low on groceries. I love you."*

My abnormal hunger seems to be abated for the day, but, of course, I've consumed more blood than normal. And 'tis a good thing too: as a trauma surgeon, I encounter many patients whose evil blood cries out to me to consume it. My hunger seems to come on strong at night, but 'tis only once a week or so that the day is bad.

I dinnae like keeping things from Carl, but I dinnae want him to worry. And he *would* worry if he knew. He has nae seemed to take particular notice that we're consuming more when we Feed. But he does nae complain about getting "extra rations" as he puts it.

I decide to stop at the blood bank to do a quick inventory. Our supply at home is running low of course and I want to stock up.

There are eight units of red blood cells that have reached their expiration and two units that are labeled as "DO NOT USE." One is contaminated with Hepatitis B and one with flu. That gives us ten pints, once I mix it with plasma. I'll have to take care of that before I go home.

We're meeting with Rolf tonight to get an update. He has been pouring over the postings on the website, hoping to solve the mystery of why we've seen nae evidence of the Penitents that are supposedly gathering here. That vexes me. It makes nae sense. There should be reports of strange attacks on the criminal element. We've seen nae evidence of that, other than what can be accounted for by Rolf's activities.

I head to the break room to get my thermos. In the fridge, I have a thermos of blood mixed with just enough tomato juice to disguise it, but nae so much as to make me sick.

I retrieve my thermos and drink directly from it while sitting at a table. The taste of the tomato juice is disgusting as is all mortal food, but it's necessary for me to get nutrition at work so I can concentrate on my job.

Sally, the OB nurse, enters the room. She sees me and, after retrieving her lunch from the refrigerator, she asks if she can sit with me. I motion her to sit and quickly seal the lid on my thermos.

"Dr. Morgan, I know it's a bit presumptuous of me, but could I ask you a few questions?"

"Certainly, but call me Moira," I say.

"OK, Moh-rah," she says.

"Mwoh-rah," I correct.

"Moira," she says.

"Aye, 'tis an old name, nae so much in fashion now." I smile at her. "Ask your questions."

"You've been with the hospital for a while, haven't you, uh, Moira?"

I suppress a smile. "Aye."

"How well do you know Dr. Harkness?"

"Well, we've worked together on a number of occasions. I know him well enough. Why d'ye ask?"

"I don't think he likes me at all. I mean, he's so curt with me. I mean, I don't need to be friends with the doctors, but he just seems so . . . I don't know. I just don't get it. He seems to get on well enough with the other nurses."

"Why are ye asking me about this, Sally?"

"Because you seem to get along with *everybody*. *Everybody* loves Dr. Morgan. I mean, I know you're pretty and all . . . and you're very nice . . . but I don't see what I'm doing wrong with Dr. Harkness. It's getting so I *dread* being on shift when he has patients on the ward. I could go to talk to the Head Nurse, but I don't want to make trouble for him . . . or myself."

Ah, I ken what she's on about. I pat her hand. 'Tis with an effort that I dinnae pull my hand away as I feel the blood pulsing in her veins.

"First of all, Sally," I say, "one of the things that I dinnae like about Dr. Harkness is that he does seem to play favorites. I get along with him well enough, but I dinnae want to *hang out* as ye young people might say. I dinnae think there is anything ye can do to *make* him like ye or even be civil to ye. If it becomes unbearable, ye might try talking to him and tell him that ye want to be able to work with him, but ye dinnae know what ye did to evoke such treatment. The important thing is to talk to him."

She frowns. "That's easy for *you* to say. Everyone *loves* you."

"And *second*," I continue, "Nae *everyone* likes me. It's impossible to get *everyone* to like you. There are people who go out of their way to try to make my life miserable. I do my best to be nice to them, but, failing *that*, I must ignore them. 'God judge between me and thee,' as the scripture says."

My current nemesis is one Winifred Morrison. She lives in our ward. She despises me. Nae, "despises" does nae go far enough. She loathes me to the breadth and depth of her soul. She is miserable and seeks to make all around her miserable. But especially me. She is a bitter woman who let herself go to seed long ago. Her husband left her, nae for another woman: he simply left her. I felt sorry for the poor man and could nae find blame for him in my heart. She was always picking at him like a dog worrying a bone. She criticized him constantly, discussing things that should nae be discussed in public simply to belittle him or to show her "moral superiority." She claims nae woman can compete with me and that this is why her husband left. To be sure, 'twas nothing to do with her own shrewish behavior or the two hundred pounds she put on in the first five years of their marriage.

If there's one person in the ward who constantly points out the fact that I dinnae seem to age, 'twould be Winnie. I wonder what she would think if she had any notion of my actual age. She wants other women to know that she thinks I'm shameless and out to "get their men." Mercifully (for me), no-body seems to pay her any mind. Nothing infuriates Winnie more than that.

On the night that Carl and I were married, Winnie tried to disrupt our wedding reception. "I'll bet she's spent a fortune on that face. Do you have any idea how old she really is?" she said with a predatory grin.

Carl handled her magnificently, though. I could tell from his heart rate and the tension in his grip as he held my hand that he was laboring to keep his anger in check, which is nae mean feat for a new vampire. Winnie kept emphasizing my age to Carl. He was polite, but shut her down decisively by pointing out that he was technically old enough (in the biological sense) to be my father (despite the fact that I'm many times his chronological age). This sent Winnie stomping off in fury.

I'm reasonably certain that Winnie's the one who digs up my flower bed each year, but I would nae confront her about it. That'd give her more satisfaction. She makes her own hell. I dinnae need to add to it.

My pager vibrates and I look down at it and see that I'm being summoned to the OR.

"I have to go, Sally. Keep your chin up," I say as I give Sally's hand a friendly squeeze. "And ye will let me know how it goes?"

"I will," she says with a smile.

I quickly open and drain my thermos. If I'm going to operate, I will need to be prepared.

After scrubbing up, I enter the OR, and a nurse shows me the patient's chart. I skip to the pertinent details: female in her midfifties, morbidly obese, suffered severe fall, fractured both lower legs, broke four ribs, internal bleeding.

Time to go to work!

I look over at the patient. She has been intubated and is breathing pure oxygen in preparation for emergency general anesthesia. She can't speak with the breathing tube down her throat. I look at her face just as the anesthesiologist prepares to give her a propofol injection to put her under quickly. Her wide eyes lock with mine and her expression of fear and pain turns to one of abject horror.

She tries to scream around the breathing tube, but nothing comes out.

God surely moves in mysterious ways, does He nae?

Before she loses consciousness, I smile to reassure her, and, though she cannae see my smile, she can see my eyes. She knows me. That's why she is so frightened, of course.

I make sure that my voice is as soothing as possible when I say, "Hello, Winnie."

Chapter 8

WELCOME BACK, Winnie."

Her eyes fix on me, but she is still intubated and cannae speak.

"Ye are in Intensive Care. We very nearly lost ye. We should be able to move ye to a regular room in the morning."

Tears begin to pool at the corners of her eyes.

"I'm going to remove your breathing tube," I say. "Ye're going to be a wee bit hoarse for a while, but that's normal, so dinnae try to speak. Your voice'll come back soon enough."

As I remove her tube, I say, "We've set both legs, stopped the bleeding in your chest cavity, patched up your punctured lung, and bound up your ribs. Your anesthesia was complicated . . . and that's where we nearly lost ye . . . by the sleeping pills that ye did nae manage to vomit up. It appears that ye slipped in the vomit and that was probably when ye sustained your physical injuries.

"There," I say as I check her breathing, "that should feel a wee bit better."

The tears spill down the sides of her face into her gray hair. She looks fixedly up at the ceiling.

I sit next to her and take her hand in mine. "I dinnae know what drove ye to attempt to take your own life, but I . . . I can sympathize. I once tried to end my life . . . long ago. I felt I had nothing left to live for. I had done . . . terrible things. I could nae live with . . . what I had become . . . what I had *let* myself become. I tried to starve myself to death. It was a long, slow, and painful process. Perhaps . . . if I had chosen a *speedier* means of death, I would have succeeded. But I did nae . . . succeed."

Winnie appears to be ignoring me as she continues to stare at the ceiling.

"Anyway," I continue, "as I lay there, alone, in the dark, in agony, wasting away, I had lots of time to think, in spite of my pain. I considered that, though I could nae change the past, I could nae do any good for anyone, including myself . . . if I died. I could nae . . . *fix* anything. I prayed to God. I did nae know if He would listen to one such as I, but I prayed all the same. I prayed with my whole being. I told Him that I would spend the rest of my days serving others. I've tried to keep that pledge. It's why I became a doctor.

"It's taken me a very, very long time, but I found . . . peace . . . and happiness."

I sit quietly for a minute watching her face, but she does nae look at me.

"I would be your friend, Winnie, if ye would only let me. I bear ye nae ill will."

She looks at me now. Finally. Her lips move, but she cannae make her throat obey her. She tugs at my hand to pull me closer. I dinnae *need* to get closer to hear her slightest whisper, but I lean toward her face.

She closes her mouth and her jaw moves as if she's trying to swallow.

Then she spits at me.

The spittle does nae actually reach me. It simply lands on her face.

In all my life, I've ne'er seen anything so profoundly heartbreaking.

She begins to sob . . . huge, wracking sobs that shake her whole body. But the sound! She can give almost nae voice to her anguish. It is just the sound of air rushing through a wide tube.

I release her hand and retrieve a tissue to wipe her face.

At first she tries to block my hands, but she is too weak to stop me. I gently dab the spittle from her face. I feel only sorrow and pity for this sad woman.

"I'm sorry, Winnie," I say. "I'm sorry that my existence causes ye so much pain. I meant what I said, though. I *do* want to be your friend."

She turns her head away from me.

"Is there someone that we should contact? I've already alerted Bishop Adams."

She turns her face back to me, her expression a mixture of horror and anger.

"Dinnae worry, dearie. I will nae tell him anything about the pills. Ye slipped and fell. That's all I'm allowed to say, anyway."

She mouths, "I hate you," so distinctly that I cannae mistake her meaning.

"I know," I say simply.

She turns her face away again, but the awful, hollow sobbing resumes.

It's been a long, long day. I've stayed later than I normally do, waiting till Winnie was brought around. I've retrieved and mixed the blood, made the entries in the destruction log, and stored the blood in my oversized, insulated briefcase with sufficient ice packed for transport home. Now I really need to leave. Carl and I are going to Ogden to meet with Rolf, and it has been dark for a couple of hours already.

I'm heading to the locker room to change, my briefcase in hand, when something *tugs* at me. There is nae other way to describe it. I feel a sharp *pull* toward . . . where? The ER? Why? I need to leave! It is nae like the pull of evil blood. It is something else . . . It picks at the corners of my memory like a corbie worrying a bit of flesh from a corpse.

The English had left me for dead. I crawled into the remains of our barn and survived on rainwater and charred bits of goat flesh. The unfortunate creature had nae been able to escape the flames. So he fed me in my slow recuperation.

After several days I regained enough strength to venture out. I had nae desire to see what awaited me in the fire-ravaged ruins of our home, but I intended to bury . . . whatever was left of my parents.

The roof was gone, as were the windows, the door, and anything else that was nae made of stone. Even the walls, which were made of stone, had collapsed in places. Everything was blackened with smoke, and the stench of burning, mingled with rain and rot, still hung in the air, though the smoke was long gone.

When I found them, I saw that a portion of the wall had caved in on them. My father had tried to shield my mother with his body, but they were both dead all the same. It did nae matter if 'twas the crushing weight of the stones or the heat of the fire or the choking smoke: they were dead, and they were nae coming back to me.

I saw a single corbie perched atop my father, tugging a strip of charred meat from between his ribs. Once the bird got it free, he raised his head and swallowed it down his gullet. Then he dipped his head for another bit of my father.

I wanted to scream at him . . . to cast a stone . . . anything to drive him away, but I had nae the strength. He was a creature of death, and death had taken them from me. Death had taken my Donald. Death had come in the guise of the English, and they had taken my virtue. I felt so powerless to do anything.

The corbie cocked his head and stared at me with one eye. Then he uttered a squawk and returned to his meal.

I sat on the sooty dirt floor and watched him for some time. When he had eaten his fill, he flapped away . . . leaving me alone with the picked-over remains of my family.

I felt as though I should weep. I should've wanted to weep, but I could feel nae sorrow. All I felt was an emptiness . . . an emptiness that would be filled only with hate and rage.

I sat there, brooding in my dark thoughts as the rage and the hatred slowly built, until at last I stood and covered my parents, where they lay, with a mound of blackened stones.

The shadows of night fell, and as the cairn of my parents dimmed from my sight, I made a decision.

So be it. I would become a creature of death, a creature of night.

I would have my revenge.

Nae bothering to wash the soot from my hands, face, and hair, and wearing only the ruin of my bloody, ragged dress, I set off for the kirkyard. I knew just where to find the one I sought.

Like others in my village, I had heard the tales of the woman who haunted the kirkyard and preyed on men and only on men, leaving them pale and bloodless, but alive. All of them, the men, had a reputation for being rough with their mothers or their sisters or their wives or lasses in general. And afterward . . . afterward, they would nae so much as raise their voices to a woman.

I'd seen her once, myself. 'Twas on a night of a waxing moon, waxing almost to the full.

I'd been to visit the grave of my only brother, wee Robert, taken in his infancy. I'd placed flowers on his grave that afternoon, and I'd lingered overlong. The gloaming was past, and I should have been home long afore.

I was walking hastily homeward, when Alistair MacDonald came upon me. I was taken completely unawares. He must've been watching me in the kirkyard. He came up behind me and laid his hand on my hair. I pulled quickly away and told him to leave me be. He made lewd suggestions to me, and then he grabbed me about my waist.

I started to scream, but before the sound could leave my throat, Alistair was lifted into the air.

Above me, I saw what I thought to be an angel. She had wings of shining white feathers and was robed all in white. Her face was plain, but her eyes shone with the fire of righteous anger in the moonlight.

And she was holding Alistair aloft. He thrashed and made to scream, but then the angel (for so I thought her to be) bent Alistair's head aside, exposing his neck. I saw her mouth open, and I saw long sharp teeth like those of a wolf extend from her upper jaw. Alistair saw them as well, as he looked at her in horror. 'Twas then that he really did start to scream. He screamed like a wee lassie.

This was nae angel. She was a demon from Hell, clad nae in a white robe, but draped in the cerements of the grave. And her eyes shone, nae with the anger of Heaven, but with the fires of the Infernal Pit. She glanced at me and said, "Go!" Then she fastened her lips on Alistair's throat. His screams turned to moans.

I wheeled about and fled.

I called for help, but nae help came. I pounded on the door of the first house I came to, but they turned me away. I tried another and another. Nary a soul believed my tale . . . or perhaps they did believe, but would nae venture out to assail the demon.

In the morning, Alistair came to my home, white as a shade, and, in full view of my father, fell to his knees and begged my pardon.

I knew where to go to get the power *to seek my vengeance and punish those wicked men.*

I feel like I should *recognize* the tugging coming from the ER. It feels familiar somehow. Like being called . . . home.

It pulls me into the ER and into a specific room. There is a trauma team working on a patient.

An orderly steps back from the bed. His name is . . . Mark. Aye, that's it. The *tug* is most certainly coming from the patient.

"Mark," I say, "What's the story here?"

He looks at me and recognizes me. "Oh, hi, Dr. MacDonald . . . uh, I mean, Dr. Morgan. Sorry."

"It's all right, laddie. I was Dr. MacDonald for *ages*." *Ages and ages.*

"Anyway, we have a female, an apparent suicide attempt."

Another suicide?

"They say she tried to jump from a rooftop," he continues, "but she must have really had a running start. She landed nearly twenty yards from the building. Lucky for her, the grass and the soft ground saved her life. She doesn't have a scratch on her. No signs of internal bleeding. But it's funny, you know? The paramedics said that witnesses described her as having broken bones and being all messed up. But *nada*. Nothing there."

"Why all the fuss, then?" I ask.

"Well, take one look at her. Have you ever seen anyone so emaciated? She looks like those pictures from Auschwitz, you know?"

I move to get a good look at her. His description is a wee bit of an exaggeration, but she *does* look severely malnourished.

There it is again, that pecking at the edges of my memory.

A nurse gets an IV with a saline drip into her arm, and the others move back.

I listen to her heartbeat. It's weak, but steady. She's nae going to die immediately.

Something does nae *smell* right about her. *Why can't I place it? What am I missing?*

I get a good look at her face for the first time. Brown hair. Her features are drawn, almost skeletal. Even if she had more flesh in her face, I doubt she would ever have been considered pretty. She does nae look familiar.

Or does she?

In my mind, the corbie at last works the bit of memory free. A chill runs down my spine as I *do* recognize her face.

I *know* this woman! I *know* her!

In my shock, I nearly drop my briefcase full of iced blood to the floor.

I watch as the trauma team continues to work. Eventually, activity slows until there is only a single nurse standing, monitoring the patient's vital signs. Soon, she turns to leave as well.

I tap the nurse on the shoulder. She turns to me and I say, nae with Persuasion, but with that wee *edge* that my kind has when asking favors of mortals, "Give me a few minutes alone with the patient, will ye, Angie?"

"Sure, Dr. Morgan."

"Five minutes, please? And watch the door?"

"No problem," she says. Then she leaves, shutting the door after her.

I set down my briefcase on a stool and open it. I retrieve the bag marked "DO NOT USE: Hepatitus B." I shake it gently to mix it. Then I close the briefcase and carry the bag of blood to the patient's bedside. I tear open a corner of the bag with my teeth and then carefully pour a small stream of blood into the patient's mouth.

I'm careful nae to spill any when she closes her mouth to swallow. Then she opens her mouth again, and I pour a bit more. She swallows again.

Soon her hand comes up, and she blindly takes the bag from me. She pulls it to her mouth and greedily sucks the contents until the bag is drained.

Already, I see color coming back to her face and she looks less skeletal. But her eyes remain closed. Her Feeding is an unconscious reflex.

I retrieve the bag from my briefcase marked, "DO NOT USE: Influenza." I open a corner of the bag and place it to her lips. Her hand comes up, and she sucks at the second bag. I move to the other side of the bed and shut off and remove her IV. That would nae have helped her.

By the time she drains the second bag, she just looks slightly malnourished, as opposed to skeletal. I take the bag from her and place both emptied bags into my briefcase.

By the time I turn back, her eyes are fluttering open. She looks at me, and recognition widens her eyes.

"Moira?" she says in her ambiguous European accent. If you had to pin it down, most would call it "Cockney with German overtones," but "Middle English" would be more accurate.

"Aye, Sarah Smythe. 'Tis Moira. I wish I could say 'twas good to see ye."

She sits up. She works her mouth, tasting the blood *consciously* for the first time. Her eyes widen in unmistakable horror.

"What?" she cries softly. "You *Fed* me?"

"Aye." *What is she going on about?* "It's cold, but still nourishing enough for the likes of us."

"No! Why did you do that?" She looks genuinely distressed.

"Ye were comatose. It sounds like ye fell out of the sky. Ye were nearly starved to death. Why would ye starve yourself?"

She looks at me in exasperation. "Now I'll have to start all over! Why would you do this to me?"

"Do what?" I say.

"Feed me! I was almost there!"

"Almost where?" *This makes nae sense!*

She pounds her fist against the bed in frustration. "I was almost Sanctified!"

"What are ye talking about?"

"I've come to join the Congregation! I was almost Sanctified!"

Just then, my cell phone rings. I clamp my mouth shut in frustration. Then I say through tight lips. "Just hold that thought a wee tick."

I pull out my phone. It's Carl. I open it.

"Moira?" says my husband. He sounds a bit worried. "Where are you?"

"I'm still at the hospital, laddie. I'm going to be a wee bit longer. I'm sorry."

He is silent for a moment and then he says, "Everything OK?"

"Aye . . . I mean nae. Something has come up."

"Do you need any help? I can tell you're upset. Your brogue is a bit heavy."

That's one thing that is annoying about our relationship: my husband can read my moods like a familiar book. Bless him. And I *know* my accent gets a wee bit thick when I'm upset.

"Nae. I just need to take care of something here. Seems a very old acquaintance of mine has arrived here in Utah and she's a Penitent as well. She's here to join the Congregation."

"Really? And you know her?"

"Aye, I do. I should. She's my old Teacher . . . the Ancient One who Converted me."

Chapter 9

THE FIRST ORDER of business is to get ye out of here," I say. "We can discuss the ramifications of me saving your life when we're away from prying eyes and questions I cannae answer."

Sarah glowers at me.

"My shift is long over. We can leave now. I'll go and handle the ER desk. I'll be right back."

"Stop!" she says a bit too imperiously for my taste. "Just show me to a window."

"That's nae such a good idea. I've been seen with ye and there will be too many questions as it is. I cannae just . . ." My voice trails off as Sarah's shocked expression registers on me.

"What?" I say perplexed. "What is it now?"

"I . . ." she begins haltingly, "I'm your Teacher. The closest thing you had to a Master. How . . . How can you disobey me?"

Ah! That's it! "We really dinnae have time for this now," I say, slightly annoyed. "I'm nae subject to *any* Master. I'm free of Lilith's power."

The only way to describe her expression is one of . . . awe. "Then it's *true*," she says softly.

"Aye, 'tis true! Now . . . can we go?" I say, motioning her to get off the bed and follow me.

She swings her legs off the bed and stands. 'Tis well that they did nae have to cut her clothes off. She is still dressed in a simple brown skirt and tan blouse. 'Tis all a bit stained with a mixture of grass, earth, and blood, but at least I dinnae have to find anything for her to wear. Her shoes are gone, but that is nae matter. I just need to get her out of the hospital.

"Wait here and be ready to go," I say.

I ask Angie to watch the door for a tick longer and to admit nobody but me. The ER desk is nae problem either. Sarah had nae ID on her. She was nae admitted, and the only real record of her is the ambulance ride. Even there, she is referred to as "Jane Doe." I tell them to bill my personal account for everything and say that the patient desires to leave. There is nary a thing the hospital can do to force her to stay if she wants to leave and does nae pose a threat to herself or to others.

I go quickly to the locker room and change into my street clothes at vampiric speed. I toss my hospital sneakers into my briefcase. They *might* be Sarah's size. Then I return to the ER.

Angie is still standing guard at the door. I smile and thank her and tell her that the patient will be leaving. She accepts this, of course, without explanation.

Upon entering the room, I toss the sneakers to Sarah. "Here! See if these fit."

Apparently she has had time to collect herself. Without comment, she puts the shoes on her feet. They are a trifle big, but they're wearable.

"Give me a moment's lead, and then follow me out," I say quickly. "I've taken care of all the paperwork. As my husband would say, 'The plane doesn't fly until the weight of the paperwork equals the weight of the payload.' *My imitation of his western accent is quite good, if I do say so myself!* 'He used to be a bomber pilot."

"Your husband?" she says, her eyes narrowing. "You mean your Master?"

"Ach! Nae! I've nae Master! Nae Master but Jesus. Now, shall we go?"

"Then, you're the Master?"

"Nae Master! It's a new world ye have entered."

"Apparently," she says in wonder.

"I'll tell ye more in the car! Can we go now?"

"Yes," she says and nods at me.

As I emerge from the room, I see a commotion at the ER desk. John Tolman, one of the ER docs, is practically yelling at Angie.

"What do you *mean* she's leaving? That was one of the *most advanced* cases of malnutrition I've ever seen!" he says in obvious frustration and anger.

"Dr. Morgan said . . . ," Angie begins, but he cuts her off.

"I don't care *what* Dr. Morgan says," he snaps, "*I* say . . ."

"If ye would only have another *look* at the patient, John," I say, "ye would see that she is able to make her own decisions." I gesture back at Sarah, who has just emerged from her room. She looks almost normal now. She will need to Feed again soon, but for now, she can *pass* for normal.

His mouth snaps shut in anger, and he gives me a glare before looking past me at Sarah. Then his eyes go wide in shock. "What? How?" he splutters. "I *saw* her!" His gaze snaps back to me. "Moira, I swear you're a witch! What did you do?"

I snort. "I've nae been called a witch in *ages*, laddie. I simply gave her some fluids and something to drink. Now are ye going to burn me at the stake, or are ye going to let my patient go?"

"She's *my* patient and . . . ," he says with rising anger.

"Excuse me, doctor," Sarah says from behind me. Her tone is full of ice and venom. John shifts his attention to her, and she says with unmistakable Persuasion, "I'm *no* man's *patient* or anything else. I belong to *no man*! Do you understand me?"

His face slackens. "I understand."

"I'm going to leave now and you're going to forget all about me."

"Nae to forget," I hiss, "there are too many witnesses. Will ye Persuade them all?"

"Fine then," she snaps under her breath. Then to John she says, "You will *not* forget me. You will simply no longer worry about me. You will trust Dr. MacDonald."

"Dr. *Morgan*," I hiss again.

"Dr. *Morgan*," she corrects. "You will trust Dr. *Morgan*. Correct?"

"Yes," he replies.

"Fine," she says and releases him from her control.

He blinks twice and says, "Well, if Dr. Morgan says you're OK, I guess you can go. I mean, it's not like I can force you to stay. Besides, I *trust* Dr. Morgan."

"Thank you," she says, her voice dripping with sarcasm, and curtsies. *She curtsied!*

Angie stares at me with an expression of mixed surprise and amusement. "She your distant cousin or something? I mean, I *know* she's not your *sister*. She doesn't look anything like you (or sound like you, for that matter). What is that accent, by the way? German or British? But she *does* have your knack for getting people to *listen* to you." Then she adds with a whisper, "Only, she's not as *nice!*"

"Actually, she used to be my Teacher," I say. "Thanks, Angie." I hurry out the door with my briefcase filled with the remaining units of precious blood.

Sarah follows after me, but she gives John a withering look.

And if looks could kill . . .

◆ ◆ ◆

"Would ye mind telling me what that was all about?" I say as I pull out of the parking garage. Sarah, in the passenger seat of my car, looks furious.

"No man *owns* me. No man *claims* me," she says through tight lips, folding her arms. I know nothing about her background. I never asked and she never ventured, but I *do* remember that she had a reputation for preying only on men. Obviously, there is a profound resentment toward men . . . but that can wait. There are more important things at the moment than her misanthropic motivations.

"I meant," I say, "why were ye trying to starve yourself? There are quicker ways to die."

"I don't want to die," she says, "at least not yet. Not until I'm . . . ready."

"I dinnae understand your meaning."

"It's complicated." She looks pointedly out the window. "Where are you taking me?"

"We're headed . . ." *I was about to drive her to our home! I cannae risk that. Nae yet.* "We're headed to a neutral location. I hope ye will understand if I'm a wee bit cautious when it comes to trusting another vampire."

She nods quickly. "Of course."

"Excuse me a moment," I say and I pull out my cell phone. Then I put it away again. I might as well use the hands-free phone, since Sarah will be able to hear the full conversation anyway. I press the phone button on the mirror. I give the voice command to call Carl.

He answers before the first ring finishes. "Is everything OK?" It makes me smile to hear the concern in his voice.

"I'm right as rain, laddie," I assure him, but quickly add, "I'm nae alone."

"Your . . . Teacher?"

"Aye."

"OK, so . . . what's the plan?"

"Let's meet in Memory Grove Park," I suggest.

"The one with the little waterwheel to the east of the Church head-quarters building?"

"Aye."

"OK. That sounds good. Do you have your hanger?"

"Aye." He's referring, of course, to the eighteenth-century sword I've stowed in my bag.

"Is your . . . guest . . . armed?"

"Nae, she's at my *mercy*," I say, trying to make light of the situation. I glance over at Sarah. She does nae look amused.

"I'll see you there. I love you," he says.

"I love ye too," I say and terminate the call.

"You have it *all*, don't you," Sarah says.

"What are ye on about now?"

"You have *everything*." She starts counting off on her fingers. "You have physical beauty. You live successfully among mortals. You have a ready sup-ply of blood, so you don't have to kill or even Hunt. You have a man who loves you, a man you love in return. And, you're *free*." She puts her hands down. "You have *everything*."

Everything except a bairn of my own. Nae children in this life. Except for Ben. And he was ours for so short a time. But she is correct. I'm blessed, more blessed than I could possibly deserve. I have a temple marriage to a man I love more than life itself and who loves me every bit as much.

But wait just a wee moment. "Sarah, from what I recall, ye had nae use for men. Ye Hunted *only* men. Why would ye resent me my *marriage*?"

Sarah gives a bitter laugh. "That's right. I really thought I'd found a kindred spirit when you came to me, begging me to help you get your precious revenge."

She pauses a moment and then continues, "Did you know that in all my nine hundred and ninety-nine years, I've never Converted another vampire? You were the only one."

I glance over at her and shake my head.

"And you never came back." She says this in a flat tone, devoid of emotion.

Or does the lack of emotion cover a deep well of pain?

"I . . . reached a crisis," I respond, "and realized what I'd lost . . . what I'd given up. Ye were the embodiment of what I'd become. And ye were the *last* person I wanted to see."

"You became Penitent, then?"

"Aye, a few months after my Conversion."

"So soon? And you're still alive? I would have thought that . . . well . . . if the remorse came upon you in so short a time . . . that you'd try to kill yourself. You wouldn't have become as . . . *attached* to life as we older ones do when *we* reach such a 'crisis.'"

"I did try, Sarah. I starved myself. But, I had a change of heart. I decided to . . . *serve* humanity. To do *good*."

"As a doctor?"

"Nae, women could nae be physicians back then. Ye know that. I could nae bear children of my own, so I became a midwife. I became a physician much later."

"And you have a husband?" she asks.

"Aye, I'm married. I ne'er . . . other than the English . . . when they . . . violated me . . . I've remained pure . . . in that regard."

"And he's a mortal, your husband? Or is he one of us?"

"He's one of us . . . and yet . . . he is nae."

"What do you mean, 'he is nae'?"

"I mean, he's different. He has ne'er killed mortals for their blood, nae even his own Offering. He did nae *choose* this existence. It was forced upon him."

"Forced?" she says incredulously. She gasps and then her jaw drops as the full import of my statement hits her. "The Unwilling!"

"Aye." *Why did I tell her that?* "I should nae have told ye that. I dinnae know if I can trust ye." *I have to refocus the conversation here!* "Why were ye starving yourself?"

She bowed her head. "Because that's what we were instructed to do. He said, 'Come fasting. Purge yourself of mortal blood. Achieve Sanctification. Only then are you ready to meet God. Wait in the night sky above Salt Lake City. When you're Sanctified, someone will come for you.'"

"'*He* said?' *Who* said?" I demand. We're nearly to the park.

"The Keeper," she replies. "That's what *we* call him on his blog. He doesn't *refer* to *himself* that way (nobody uses names), but he's the *owner* of the site. He's been telling us how to achieve redemption."

And with that, we arrive at our destination. In what might be considered a modern day miracle in downtown Salt Lake, I find a parking spot nearby, in front of an apartment building on the hill just east of the park.

Well, Moira MacDonald Morgan, ye have nae done so well. Ye have nae learned what ye should have, and ye have revealed what ye should have nae.

I leave my briefcase with our food supply in the car, but I retrieve my sword from my bag. Sarah emerges from the car, but eyes me and my sword warily.

Seeing her look, I say, "It may nae be safe to go unarmed now. With so many gathering here . . ."

"Here? You mean *now?*"

"Nae, I meant to Utah. Nae, the only one coming to meet us is Carl, my husband."

"But you've met other Penitents?" She sounds eager.

"Only one," I answer, "but without more information about your Congregation, we dinnae ken who we can trust."

"You're not . . . not part of the Congregation?"

"Ach, nae! We had word of it only a few nights past."

"I thought that . . . surely . . . the Congregation must be behind the Breaking."

"'The Breaking'?"

"The Breaking of Lilith's power here. The dissolution of the Cult."

"Nae, that was just Carl and me. And Ben. Just my little family."

"Who is Ben?"

"Ben was"—my voice breaks—"*is* my son. He's dead now."

This brings a look of shock from her, but I push on before she can ask.

"We adopted him, so to speak. He was a child. He was part of the Cult here, but he joined Carl and me, and we *loved* him as our own. But he was murdered when the Cult was dissolved."

I motion to her to follow me toward the park, and we walk side by side, I with my hand on my sword.

"So, you were never part of the Cult?" she asks.

"Nae, although *Carl* was for a short time, or at least he pretended to be. 'Tis a long story, but suffice it to say that Carl was trying to entrap his sister's killer. She, the killer, that is, was one of the Teachers. After Carl was Converted against his will, he fled the Cult. He did nae ken what he'd become. I found him, and I helped him to adjust.

"We learned that the Master here was about to Convert all four of his Chosen at once. That would have meant at least eight more murders, and the

Cult could nae sustain so many. So Carl felt he had to act. We raided the Cult, and Carl slew the Master and one of the two remaining Teachers, each in single combat. By *killing* the Master, Carl *became* the Master, and he declared the Cult dissolved. The remaining Teacher attacked and killed Ben, and Carl slew her."

She grabs my arm and stops me. "How did Carl do that? Dissolve the Cult, I mean? Lilith has forbidden it! He shouldn't have been able to disobey Lilith's command. He swore the Oaths, didn't he?"

"Aye, he said the words, but he did nae *believe* any of it to be *real*. He did nae believe that vampires actually *exist*. He thought that the Cult was just a cult of personality. To him, the Oaths were just words spoken in what he thought was a fake ceremony made up out of whole cloth to bolster a fictitious religion. He *is* the Unwilling."

"But he should have been bound by the Master's command!"

"He ne'er *was* bound." I resume walking, and she follows.

"But *you!*" she says, a bit too loudly. "You took the Oaths willingly. You *bound* yourself to Lilith and her Masters. You should have been *compelled* to obey me!"

We enter the park, and I lead the way toward the waterwheel.

"Oh, ye're right," I say, "I *was* bound. The Master forced me to put a sword through my beloved Carl's heart. He, the Master, bound me with his command, and there was nary a thing I could do."

I shudder at the memory.

"But then," I continue, "there was Carl. He reminded me of one thing. Though I'm a vampire, I've given my life to God. I've been endowed and sealed in His holy temple. *Me!* After all that I've done, His Son redeemed me, and I serve *Him*. And God is more powerful than Lilith or even Lucifer himself. And once I understood *that* . . . I was free."

"But you still drink blood," she said.

We arrive at the waterwheel, and I turn to face her.

"Aye, that I do. 'Tis the only nourishment I can take. The Seed and the Essence make it so. But I dinnae kill, and if I must Hunt, I take only from the truly evil. So drinking blood does nae make me evil."

"But the Keeper said we have to abstain from blood."

"That's suicide for our kind," I reply. "But ye *can* survive without killing."

"And I've done so since long before I met you . . . for most of my long existence," Sarah says. "At least I haven't killed the *innocent* . . . and not even the *guilty* for a very, very long time. But it didn't make me . . . clean."

"It *is* crucial that ye dinnae kill, but ye cannae redeem *yourself*. Only God can do that."

She snorts. "I tried being a nun, you know. I mean, I still had to Hunt to survive, but I did everything else that was required of a sister. I gave myself to God for more than a century. Perhaps I'd be there still (and never have met you) if it weren't for Henry Tudor. He seized our nunnery for his bloody illegitimate Church of England. *Curse* that foul man!"

She trembles momentarily in her fury at the long-dead king. Then she sighs and says, "God didn't save our order. God didn't save me."

"Then why are ye here?" I ask. "Why were ye willing to starve yourself?"

She looks at me, and I see that her eyes are brimming with tears. "Because I'm *afraid*. I'm *always* afraid. I *became* a vampire because I was afraid. I was a third generation whore, beaten nigh to death by a man who wasn't satisfied with my wares. I didn't want to be afraid anymore. So I joined a Cult and became a vampire."

She shakes her head, and her expression is bitter. "But I just exchanged one form of bondage for another. I was a slave to my Master. He was worse than any other man I'd ever known, and I was his *property*, less than a *dog* to him. He forced me to do things even a *whore* wouldn't do."

"How did ye escape?"

"When I found an opening, a way to resist him without breaking his express command, I killed him in his Sleep, and then I fled. I've been alone, mostly, ever since. I tried to protect other women, but it never ends. There's always some man who'll treat them like so much dung under his shoe. And they keep returning for more. I'm damned and I make no *difference* in the world."

She waves her hands in obvious frustration. "I'm afraid to *live* and I'm afraid to *die*. I'm afraid of what awaits me *after* I die. I'm afraid to go on living. I can't abide the horrible, numbing *sameness* of it all. I can't stop the abuses by men, and I can't stop the pathetic grovelings of women. There's no point in going on as I am. I have nothing to live for. But, if I die . . ."

She jabs a finger at me. "But *you* . . ." she continues, "you have everything. You're happily *married*, of all things."

"If you hate men so much," I say, "why do ye envy me my marriage?"

"Just because I've never *known* love doesn't mean I don't *desire* it. I've never known the love of another human soul. Not my mother (who hated and resented me), nor the men who paid for the use of my body, nor the Master who enticed me with lying words . . . words which I was only too desperate to believe."

What a miserable existence!

"But," she continues, "I wouldn't know what to do with love if I *did* have it." The gall in her voice is palpable. "Anyway, you seem to be genuinely happy, and, yes, I'm jealous. Does that answer your question?"

"How would ye know if I'm happy? I am, but how would ye *know*?"

"It's so plain in everything about you. I've never met one of our kind who was *happy* . . . before now."

"Well," I say, "ye're about to meet another."

I can hear Carl approaching, from the rush of the air as he slices through it.

Sarah looks about with a bewildered look. She must have heard the rush of air. *She's expecting the sound of beating wings, I wager.* Carl changes from a prone flying posture (what he calls "superhero mode") to a vertical posture, and lands in front of us. He steps between Sarah and me, his basket-hilted sword drawn. 'Tis a clearly aggressive stance.

Sarah looks so shocked at the sight of Carl flying and landing without wings that she doesn't immediately step back from his drawn sword. He raises the sword slightly. She glances at it and takes a couple of steps back.

"You OK?" he says, never taking his eyes off her.

"I'm fine, laddie," I say, and I lay a hand on his sword arm. "I dinnae think she's any threat." It's nae so much that I feel I need to defuse the situation, I just need to reassure him. "I like that. Ye finally encounter another female vampire, and ye have nae kiss for your wife!"

He looks away from Sarah and turns to kiss me. It's nae a long kiss, but 'tis nae a mere peck either. "Sorry, my love."

I step up beside him, and we both turn toward my former Teacher.

"Carl," I say, "this is Sarah Smythe. She came here to join the Congregation."

He flashes me a look full of meaning.

"Sarah," I say, finishing the introduction, "this is my husband, Carl Morgan."

Carl glances at the sword in my hand and sheathes his blade. It's hard for him to relinquish the role of "protector of the maiden fair," but we both know that I'm by far his better with a blade. He extends his hand.

Sarah looks at his hand. Her expression is . . . odd. I expect to see caution, distrust, or even hatred. Instead she looks . . . resigned. She takes his hand and shakes it.

"So *you're* the prophesied Unwilling?" she says.

Carl looks at me in alarm. I shrug.

"I'm nae so good at . . . questioning, I suppose. I think I revealed more than I discovered," I say.

"Yeah," Carl says, returning his gaze to Sarah, "I suppose I am."

"And of course you had to be *male*," she says in disgust, but I *think* 'tis *mock* disgust. "I have to put my trust in a *man* again? God must be trying to teach me a lesson, and I don't think I'm going to like it. I'm being served a burnt pudding, and I don't care for the sauce."

"What?" Carl replies.

"Never mind. I've lived one year short of a millennium, and I've not met *one* man I could trust," she says, "and now I have to trust *you*."

"I'm . . . *sorry*, I guess?" He chuckles and looks nervous. "I don't know what to say to that."

"You can't help it. You were born this way." She releases Carl's hand and looks at me. "And I suppose that makes *you* the Penitent mentioned in the

Curse as well?"

I shrug my shoulders and nod. "Aye, so 'twould seem."

"And you were 'joined in the house of God'?"

Carl nods. "A year ago."

"Just *peachy*," she says through pursed lips. Then she sighs and nods. "What am I supposed to do, then?"

Carl shakes his head in confusion. "Do?"

She looks exasperated. "You're the ones who're at the center of the Curse. Aren't you supposed to *lead* us?"

"*Lead* you?" Carl says, clearly as lost as I am.

"Against Lilith!" she cries. "If you're not part of the Congregation . . . and you say Sanctification is a sham, you must be preparing to move against Lilith. You broke Lilith's power. Killing her is the only way to be truly free. You have to lead us. Surely you don't propose to go up against Lilith alone . . . just the *two* of you!"

"I have no idea," said Carl. "All I know is that we're supposed to kill her and that we will die when she falls."

"And when she dies . . ." Sarah says, "and we all die . . . Our only hope to avoid hellfire is to be on the right *side*: *your* side, apparently."

"OK. I get it. I *get* what you're saying," he replies with a dismissive wave of his hand, "but we've got more immediate problems."

"Such as?" she says. "What's more important than *salvation*?"

"Well, *nothing's* more important than that, but I don't know what we're dealing with. I know *nothing* about Lilith or how we can possibly go up against her. I need more information. I need to plan. *I don't even know where she is!*"

"Kansas City," I say.

He nods and then shakes his head. "That's a big place. I need to know where she is, how she's defended. And like *you* said," he points to Sarah, "we probably can't do it by ourselves." He pauses. "And, besides, we don't even know if we can *trust* you."

Turning to me again, he says, "Did you test her?"

I grimace. "Ach, nae!"

"Test me?" Sarah says. "What?"

"I'm sorry, laddie," I say. "I've been so distracted today."

"It's OK," he says and flashes his lopsided grin. "It's not every day you meet up with the woman who turned you into a vampire."

"What test?" Sarah insists.

"When Carl flew in, did ye notice . . . ," I start to say.

"You had no wings!" she cries, her eyes widening suddenly.

"That's right." Carl nods.

"How is that possible?" she says, eyeing Carl in a new light. "Is it because you're the Unwilling?"

"It's because we dinnae need wings to fly," I say. *Here we go again!*

"Try it," Carl says. "Simply imagine yourself flying without wings."

She shakes her head. "That's impossible."

I glance around and listen briefly for the presence of mortals. There is nae one.

I rise a few feet into the air without wings.

"That's impossible." Sarah's voice is a whisper.

"Try it," Carl urges again.

She looks at him and then at me as I settle back to the ground. Then she exhales loudly and closes her eyes. Her face becomes composed. She rises into the air, but her wings are clearly visible.

"Try harder," Carl demands.

"You know," she says through gritted teeth. "I don't *like* the idea of taking orders from a man, so *bugger off*! You're not helping."

She calms her breathing.

Carl opens his mouth, but I place a reassuring hand on his arm again. He nods in agreement, but his eyes never leave Sarah's beating wings.

"Ye can do it," I say, trying to encourage her.

She nods slowly and continues to hover.

Then her wings flicker and vanish completely.

A grin spreads across her face as she opens her eyes. I dinnae think I've ever seen her smile before. It makes her face seem almost . . . attractive.

"That'll do," Carl says.

I nod in agreement. "Aye."

Sarah drops to the ground. "That's amazing!" she says. "How is this possible? It's so . . . *liberating*!"

"Aye, 'tis," I agree.

"But what does it mean?" she says in wonder.

"It means, that I think we can trust you," Carl says.

"Why?"

"Because, it proves ye can exercise self-mastery . . . and because ye are willing to shed the symbols of vampirism. So far, we've found that only *true* Penitents are capable of flying without wings. At least, there appears to be that correlation."

"Didn't I prove my sincerity when I tried to Sanctify myself?"

"'Sanctify' yourself?" Carl asks.

"Starving herself to prepare to meet God," I explain.

"What are you talking about?" he says.

"This is apparently what the writer of the blog is instructing Penitents to do," I say. "Sarah collapsed from starvation. She was flying at the time and fell to earth. She was found by mortals and was brought into the ER in an emaciated condition. I revived her with a couple of our bags of blood. Rolf also said he was told to 'come fasting.' Remember?"

"That's right!" he says, slapping his forehead. "While I was waiting for you, I called Rolf. He thinks he's identified the blog owner."

"I thought he said they did nae use names or ID's on the blog," I say.

Carl smiles. It's a big Cheshire Cat grin. "Rolf, as it turns out, has some hacking skills. Apparently, users of the site refer to the site owner as 'the Keeper.'"

Sarah nods.

"Good. That's good," he says, his excitement building. "Anyway, Rolf thinks he knows the Keeper's name and his *physical* address. He lives right here in Salt Lake. When I talked to Rolf just before I got here, he said that the Keeper is online *right now.*"

"So we should go talk to him," I say.

"ASAP," Carl agrees.

"A sap?" Sarah raises a questioning eyebrow.

I lean toward her conspiratorially. "It's one of Carl's *military* acronyms. You get used to them." I wink at Carl. "It translates to 'As Soon As Possible,' but it really means '*now.*'"

"Ah, I see," she says. To Carl, she says, "Mind if I tag along? I want to meet this Keeper and give him . . . of course it would be a *man's* doing . . . a piece of my mind for the *agony* I've endured for the past few weeks."

"No offense, lady," Carl replies, "but for now, I don't plan on letting you out of my sight. Not till I know what's going on with this 'Congregation.'"

She smirks at him. "'Lay on, MacDuff, And damn'd be him that first cries, *Hold, enough!*'"

Chapter 10

I SWEAR WE NEED to take up sign language!" Carl growls as he closes his cell phone, ending his call to Rolf. "It's getting so we can't have a private conversation anymore!" He points his face meaningfully in Sarah's direction.

We're flying toward an address in the Rose Parks district. According to Rolf, that is where the Keeper, one Isaiah Bartlett, lives. Nae Rolf nor Sarah has heard of him. And, it goes without saying, nae Carl nor I have either. Up until we met Rolf, we had nae idea that any other vampires were in Utah.

We're nae flying in "formation," as Carl would call it. I assume that is because the "bogey" (meaning Sarah) is right here with us. Carl is in the center with me on his right and Sarah on his left. He keeps glancing back at her. Every once in a while, I see her wings flicker into view and then vanish. I suppose she still has to concentrate on flying without them.

"What is it?" I say to him, knowing full well that Sarah will hear every word.

"Look," he says in irritation, "I know I'm *young* and all, and I'm probably not as well versed in the classics as I should be . . . and I'm pretty sure that was Shakespeare, but I'll be darned if I know what she meant!"

Sarah snorts. "It's from *MacBeth*," she says, but there is nae even a *hint* of derision in her voice. "It's the last thing MacBeth says when he realizes he's probably going to die at MacDuff's hand. The witches told MacBeth that 'no man of woman born' could kill him. So when he faces MacDuff in combat, he's sure he's safe from harm until MacDuff tells him that he was born by caesarian section. 'MacDuff was from his mother's womb untimely ripped.' So basically, it's Shakespeare for 'Go for it.'"

She pauses and then she adds, "By the by, MacDuff kills him."

"O . . . K," Carl says, but I'm pretty sure he still does nae know exactly what she means.

"I think, my dearie," I say, "she means she's nae happy about the situation, but . . ."

"No," she says, "I'm not. I haven't followed a man *for any reason* for nearly a thousand years, but you two are my only option if I want to have the slightest chance of escaping Hell. So I'll make the best of it. If *you* don't trust *me*, well, it's hard for *me* to trust *you*. So, I understand. I'll put up with your mistrust. *You* do what you feel you have to."

"O . . . K," Carl says again. He smiles sheepishly for a moment and then adds, "It's not that I don't *want* to trust you. It's just that it's hard to trust anyone right now, *especially* the woman who . . ."

"Hey," she interrupts, "without *me* you wouldn't have your precious *wife*."

"God works in mysterious ways, laddie," I say with a smile.

"There, you see?" she says with a smile, mocking my own. "*God* sent me!"

"You're ganging up on me, aren't you?" He grins and shakes his head.

"Only a wee bit." I wink at him.

"Women!" he says, but he's grinning his lopsided grin.

"Men!" Sarah says, and she does nae seem amused.

"OK," Carl says, pointing at a modest house in a run-down neighborhood. "I think that's our target."

We begin our descent.

The smell of evil begins to assail me. It's getting harder and harder to ignore it. This area is riddled with violent crime. It would be so easy to find prey here . . .

I need to focus! What's the matter with me? I Fed just this afternoon from my thermos!

But it was nae the sweet savor of evil blood . . .

Stop it, lassie!

The smell of evil is nae coming from the house we're approaching. Nae, the sweet scent is coming from several directions around the neighborhood, but nae from inside the house itself. That alone tells us nothing. Vampire blood does nae *call* to us as the blood of evil mortals does. The only test we have to determine the Penitent status of a vampire is the "wings test." I pray it does nae ever fail us. *That's assuming it has nae already.*

We're standing at the door of the small house. The plan is simply to knock at the door, but we'll each keep a hand on the hilts of our sheathed swords.

"I'll do the knocking," I say. "I look a wee bit less *threatening* than you do."

Carl nods and moves behind me.

I can clearly hear the breathing and heartbeat of one person inside. I can also hear the sound of tapping on a keyboard. 'Twould appear that this is the right place.

I knock.

The typing stops abruptly. The heartbeat and breathing quicken. I hear the distinct sound of a sword being unsheathed. There are footsteps approaching.

Why would he come with drawn sword? He must be expecting trouble. From whom?

This is a bad neighborhood, 'tis true, but a sword is nae the right defense against mortals. It must be vampires that he fears.

He stops at the door, and I can hear him sniffing the air. Then I hear the hiss of a sudden intake of breath.

"Who are ye and what do ye want?" he demands. His voice has an accent that reminds me of Colonial New England, liberally sprinkled with the salt of the sea. I would nae be surprised to see a privateer with a peg leg and an eye patch and a parrot when the door opens.

If the door opens.

"We're Penitents, and we seek the Keeper," I reply.

I hear his breath catch at that name.

"There be no one here that goes by that moniker," he says.

"How about Isaiah Bartlett?" Carl ventures.

The man on the other side of the door curses under his breath, swearing oaths I've nae heard in centuries. *Definitely a sailor of some sort.*

"We just want to talk to ye," I say.

Sarah shoots me a murderous look. I glare at her, and she nods with an air of angry resignation.

"We wish to learn of the Congregation," I say.

Another stream of oaths. "Be ye Sanctified?" he asks finally.

"If by that ye mean to ask if we've starved ourselves nigh to death, then, nae," I reply.

"Be gone, the lot of ye!" he says. "Sanctify yourselves and be in the night sky. The Apostle will come for ye. But ye must be *prepared*!"

"Listen to me, you vile man!" Sarah says. "I came fasting! I was nearly 'Sanctified,' as you put it. I *fell* from the sky because nobody came for me and I was too exhausted to go on. I endured *weeks* of hell, and do you know what? I've met someone who has *real* answers! Someone who *actually* has the power to end our misery! Now open this *sodding* door, or I'll knock it down! There are three of us. You can't escape us all. We want to talk to you, and we *mean* to talk to you *now*!"

Even as she ends her tirade, the door opens.

There is nae peg leg nor eye patch nor birdie, but there is a squat man, barely five foot tall, thickly built of strong muscle. He is balding and bearded, though his upper lip is shaved. His beard shows streaks of gray amid lush black. He has a cutlass in his stout hand, and he carries it in the manner of someone who knows how to wield it.

"What be your meaning, '*real* answers'? The power to end our misery?" he asks. His tone is less surly than it was.

I smile at him and I say, "Might we come in, Mr. Bartlett?"

"Have I a choice?" he asks.

"Of course, you do," Carl says. "But this conversation is not for mortal ears."

He nods and steps aside, motioning us to enter. He glances outside, around the sky and around the neighborhood, and then he closes and locks the door.

"Pray forgive my lack of manners," he says, "but I fear Lilith's agents. If ye can find me, others can as well."

He ushers us into a small living room that has a single sofa, a small table and chair, and a television on a sideboard. On the table is a laptop computer. He motions for the three of us to sit on the sofa. He lays his cutlass on the table next to the computer and waits for us to sit. Carl places Sarah on his left and me on his right, and then he sits between us. Bartlett pulls his chair a wee bit away from the table, then straddles the chair and rests his arms on the back of it.

"Ye know my name," he says. "Tell me yours, if it please ye."

"I'm Carl Morgan," my husband begins the introductions, "and this is my wife Moira. This is Sarah Smythe."

"And ye are Penitents?" Bartlett asks.

"That's right," Carl replies.

"But ye look well Fed," Bartlett says, puzzled, "except for ye." He points at Sarah with her still hollow cheeks and sunken eyes. "*Ye* came fasting as instructed, didn't ye?"

"Yes," she says through tight lips. "*You* don't look like you've skipped any meals lately."

"The Apostle says I need to keep up my strength," Bartlett explains. "I have a mission to carry out to save those of us who seek redemption. I must not kill, and I must take only the blood of the truly evil. But ye must *know* that, being Penitents yourselves." He has a twitch in his right eye, a tick that seems to come and go.

"Who is this 'Apostle' ye keep referring to?" I ask.

"He it is that guides back to God," Bartlett says.

"He's one of us?" I ask.

"Aye, he is," Bartlett says. "But he is *more*! He can endure the Sun!"

"What?" I cry.

"That's impossible," Sarah says emphatically.

"How?" Carl asks.

"It's the power of God!" Bartlett says.

That twitching eye of his is really distracting!

"Impossible," Sarah reiterates, and then she turns toward Carl. "So, tell me, my *Captain*: why haven't you tested *him* as you tested *me*? Why should we put *any* stock in *any* drivel that *he* says? None of us can endure the Sun. How do you know if he's a real Penitent?"

"She called ye 'Cap'n'?" Bartlett says, turning to Carl and scrutinizing him with one eye closed. Again, I'm reminded of an eighteenth-century pirate. Perhaps that is exactly what Bartlett used to be.

Carl shoots Sarah a look of profound annoyance. He turns back to our host and says, "I'm not in charge here. Sarah just joined our little family tonight. She doesn't even like me all that much."

"Nothing personal," she snarks back.

"OK," Carl says, "she just . . . resents men in general, then."

"Aye," Bartlett says with a nod. "I see." He gives Sarah a less than friendly look, his eyebrows lowered.

"But she's right," I say. "We do have a test . . . of sorts. So far, nae but Penitents have been able to pass it."

"Why should I submit to any test of yours?" he asks, his voice becoming surly again.

"Because we need to know if we can trust you," my husband replies.

"Trust *me?*" The shorter man retorts in anger. "How do I know if I can trust *ye?*" He makes a sweeping gesture in our direction. "Ye, who come here, claiming to be Penitents, but ye come armed with swords? I've been fooled before this!"

"Fooled?" I say in alarm. "By whom? Are Lilith's agents already here?"

His eyes grow huge. I see real fear in his face. "No, no, lady!" he says in a calming tone. "I meant . . . long ago." *There's that twitch again. It must be a nervous tick. He's probably nae even aware of it.*

"Very well," he growls. "If it's trust ye be wanting, I'll do my best to earn it." He shakes his shoulders and rolls his neck, like an athlete preparing for a feat of strength. "Give me your test."

Carl stands. "It's simple," he says. "Fly without wings. We don't need them to fly. Just imagine yourself flying without wings and . . . fly."

"That's impossible," Bartlett says with a sneer. "Carl, is it?"

"That's right," Carl replies. He lifts into the air about a foot, wingless.

Bartlett curses, his bearded jaw dropping, as he stares at Carl.

Carl settles to the floor. "Do it," he says.

Still muttering curses under his breath, Bartlett lifts into the air about a half a foot or so, white wings beating furiously, but insubstantially at the air.

"It's impossible," Bartlett says glaring at Carl.

Sarah mutters a very unladylike oath. "See? This rotter convinces Penitents to starve themselves, but he's no Penitent himself. *You* killed the Master here," she says to Carl. "I say we force him to tell us what we need to know and then . . ."

"*Ye* slew the Master of Salt Lake City?" Bartlett cries. "*Ye* are the Breaker?"

Carl winces in annoyance. "How many of these blasted *titles* are you people going to give me?"

Still floating in the air, his wings beating, Bartlett says, "What other . . . titles do ye have?"

"Never mind," Carl says through tight lips. "Concentrate on making the wings go away." His hand tightens visibly on the hilt of his sword.

"*Ye* be the Breaker?" Bartlett says with a shocking intensity.

"Aye, he is that," I reply.

Bartlett glances at me and then focuses on Carl, and his eyes bore into my husband's eyes.

Then the wings are gone.

Bartlett glares at Carl, and his expression is one of fierceness.

He drops to the floor lightly, and he extends a hand toward Carl. "I'm very pleased to make your acquaintance."

I dinnae ken how Carl can stare intently back at the man while his eye twitches like that! I would have to look away, myself.

"Yeah," Carl says, taking Bartlett's hand and shaking it. "Welcome to our little band."

He did nae call us a 'family,' as we did with Rolf. A 'band.' Carl is nae ready to fully accept this man. He's holding back.

"Now, Bartlett," Carl says, motioning the stout little man to sit again, "tell us about the Congregation and this vampire Apostle who can endure the Sun."

Chapter 11

A BARN. 'Tis a great and *bonnie* barn, to be sure, but 'tis a barn all the same. Michael had a mansion for his "temple," but the Congregation meets in a barn.

When I was a lass, barns had walls made of stones, loosely fit to allow for ventilation and to allow the smell of dung and urine to escape. But many modern barns are used to house farm machinery instead of livestock. Such is the case with this barn. It has walls that are solid and would block the deadly rays of the Sun. 'Tis painted white, trimmed with green.

And next to the barn is a modest farmhouse. 'Tis small, but appears to be well maintained. Though 'tis nae a mansion.

This is where the Apostle lives.

Bartlett has led us here. He phoned ahead, of course, but the so-called Apostle agreed to meet with us . . . especially after the former sea captain informed him that we were the fabled "Breakers."

Bartlett's own tale is a sad one.

"I was the captain of a slave ship," he told us. "It was common practice for the female cargo to be tied up and ravaged by the crew. For my part, I didn't indulge, but one young woman caught my eye. I pitied her and . . . it changed me. I couldn't sell her when we reached Jamaica. I kept her for myself. I was . . . besotted."

His eyes took on a faraway look. "Her name was Nabila." He blinked as if he suddenly remembered that we were there. "Eventually, I freed her and . . . married her." He swallowed hard. "But she didn't love me in return. No, she fell in love with a vampire, the Master of a Cult. He Converted her. In turn, she Converted me. I did it to be with her, ye understand. But then I learned she'd made me a cuckold."

Bartlett's jaw worked as he ground his teeth. "In a jealous rage, I killed her." A tear fell from his eye. "I . . . mourned her, nonetheless. I mourn her still."

He looked at me. "I despised what I had become. I've sought release from this hell ever since. I've sought forgiveness. I . . . want to believe there's hope I'll find Nabila . . . on the other side."

I cannae help but pity him.

We have Bartlett and Sarah in tow. I'm tasked with watching Sarah, and my husband is keeping charge over Bartlett. Bartlett (I cannae bring myself to call him Isaiah) wanted to bring his cutlass. He seemed adamant on the point, but when Carl said he would be more comfortable if our new acquaintance left his sword behind, Bartlett immediately and unconditionally conceded.

I cannae fault Carl for his caution. I found it easy to trust Rolf. His repentance seems absolute. 'Tis harder for me to trust Sarah, but 'tis far easier to trust her (or, at the very least, to *consider* trusting her) than it is for me to put my faith in Mr. Bartlett. More than likely, 'tis his eye's twitching from time to time that unnerves me. I vow 'twould make me daft if I were to watch it overlong.

We alight on the lawn in front of the farmhouse. The Moon is nearly to the full, so there's plenty of light. To our vampiric eyes, enhanced by the Seed, things are as sharp as they would be at noonday to a mortal.

There are the usual scents of a farm that's nae longer a *working* farm, but more of a residence. I smell the scent of the simple full-sized van (with heavily tinted windows, of course) parked in front of the house. There's also the scent of rich but rocky soil gone fallow and mud left over from the winter snows. From the house, there's a strong scent of wood smoke coming from the chimney.

And there's the stench of the neighboring swine farm. It comes and goes. I would imagine that on some nights, depending on which way the wind is blowing, that smell could be overwhelming. Mercifully, tonight is nae one of those nights.

We approach the homey-looking house on foot, Bartlett in front, followed closely by my Carl, Sarah, and me walking abreast behind them. Once again, we approach with our blades sheathed, but with hands firmly on the hilts of our weapons.

I want to keep an open mind about the Apostle and the Congregation. Surely they are misguided, but they may very well be sincere. I'm pretty certain that Carl and I are the only Mormon vampires in history, and when ye dinnae have the fulness of the gospel . . . well, ye must grope in the dark and find your way the best ye can. It's nae the first time in history that people have gone earnestly but tragically astray in their quest to know God and seek redemption.

I picture Sarah in her quest to find God during her century as a nun. If the other good sisters had even suspected . . . I suppose that in many ways it was a perfect disguise, especially in the days before SPF-50. She could remain cloistered away from the Sun behind stone walls, and when she *did* have to venture briefly out in the daylight, she could do so hidden by an all-covering habit. And, on a cord about her neck, she would have worn the very symbol that, had someone suspected her, would have "proven" to all and sundry that she could nae be the Daughter of Lilith she actually was. She would be free to Hunt the guilty in the wee hours of the night.

And still, in all those years, she did nae find God.

I spent the better part of two centuries looking for Him in every cathedral, mosque, synagogue, temple, chapel, shrine, and ring of standing stones I encountered in my travels around Europe, Asia, and Africa. 'Twas nae until I traveled to southern Utah eighty years ago and came to the temple in St. George that I found a place that was truly holy.

And I could nae so much as touch the white outer walls of the temple with my hand or set a foot on the stair. I had found the House of God at last, but I was barred from any contact with the Divine. Still I knew that I had found precisely where I needed to be.

And so I settled among the Mormons.

And here I've stayed. Here I've, at long last, found love and redemption, if nae a cure to vampirism. Nae, that *cure* will come only when the Prophecy is fulfilled, Lilith is slain, and my beloved and I . . . and every other vampire, Penitent or nae . . . are dead. Then Carl and I will see God. Then I will meet my sister-wife, Sharon, my husband's first wife. That should be . . . an interesting meeting, to say the least. Then Carl and I will be together for eternity.

The door opens, and a warm light floods toward us. A tall, very thin vampire, judging by his scent, is silhouetted in the opening.

"God's light shine upon you, Isaiah," the tall man says, grasping Bartlett's outstretched arm. His accent has a hint of Germanic or Nordic to it.

"God's light guide you home, Paul," Bartlett replies. It sounds like a ritualistic greeting to me.

Paul extends a hand and takes Bartlett by the forearm. The shorter man clasps Paul just shy of the elbow as well.

"I brought them," Bartlett says.

"Yes," Paul says with a smile, "I see."

The so-called Apostle looks up at us, and focusing on Carl, he releases Bartlett's arm and extends both of his hands in an inviting gesture. "Welcome, honored guests, to my home!"

He steps back, holding the door open, and motioning to us to enter. I can see him more clearly now. His face is gaunt, his cheeks hollow. He looks as though he has nae Fed often enough of late. He is so thin that I listen to his heart and breathing, fearing that he may be near collapse. But nae, his heartbeat is steady and strong and his breathing robust.

With his meticulously combed blonde hair and sunken but intense blue eyes, he reminds me a wee bit of Rolf, though he has the look of a Norseman about him. He's dressed in a turtleneck sweater and jeans, with well-used work boots on his feet.

As we enter the house, I note that Paul is unarmed.

We're in a cozy living room, simply yet tastefully furnished, with a welcoming fire burning merrily on the hearth. An ancient, though well-maintained, Viking broadsword and a Seax knife with Nordic runes etched on the blade hang above the mantle. Above them is a silver crucifix with an emaciated Christ fixed upon it. 'Tis large, but nae so large as to be ostentatious. There's a wide picture window, heavily curtained, of course. Beyond this room, I can see a small dining room with a table and four chairs. There is a laptop computer on the table with Bartlett's website plainly visible on the screen.

Paul closes the door behind us and turns to us, focusing his gaze on Carl. We turn so that we're standing roughly in a circle. Carl's grip on his sword hilt is tense. I try to appear more relaxed, but my hand also does nae leave the hilt of my weapon.

"So," Carl says, "you're the Apostle?"

Paul inclines his head in a slight nod. "I'm as God wills me to be." He lifts his head and says, "And you're the Breakers?"

"If you say so," Carl replies. There is an edge to his voice. His distrust is obvious. Carl told me once that he'd met more than his share of dishonest ministers. A vampire cleric would seem doubly dubious to him. "It's not a title we've ever applied to ourselves. If you mean, are we the ones who destroyed the Cult here? Then, yes, that's us."

Paul nods several times. I see a flash in his eyes. I cannae tell if he's pleased or nae.

'Twould seem my dear husband is nae big on diplomacy this night. 'Tis understandable, given that we're surrounded by vampires we dinnae know, and his experiences with our kind (excepting for his dear wife, of course) have been horrific . . . until recently. 'Tis time for me to take the initiative on manners. But is it nae *always* the way? Men are the warriors and women the peacemakers? Or it may be that 'tis best for Paul to think of me as less deadly than I truly can be. Let him think of Carl as the more dangerous of us two.

"I'm Moira," I say, drawing Paul's bright, sunken eyes to myself for the first time. "And this is my husband Carl." I gesture toward Carl and then toward Sarah. "And this is Sarah, my Teacher from long ago."

"And I'm Paul, but you know that already." He turns his gaze back to Carl, and he extends a hand. For a few seconds they stare into each other's eyes, and the tension grows.

Honestly, laddie! Make nice!

Then Carl takes Paul's thin hand and shakes it, nae warmly, but firmly. Neither man looks away. They continue to take each other's measure like two opponents before a battle.

"You were a warrior once, were you not?" Paul says.

"U.S. Air Force," Carl says, his tone cautious and even.

"I thought as much," says Paul, at last releasing Carl's hand. "I've been a warrior many times."

"Brother Paul?" Bartlett says, causing the other men to turn and look at him.

"Yes, Isaiah?" Paul says lifting an eyebrow.

"I . . . ah . . . that is . . . I brought them. I . . ."

"Of course, Isaiah," Paul says. "You have *duties* to attend to. You should get back to them."

Bartlett's shoulders sag visibly. "Of course," he says and bows his head, his eye twitching.

"Bartlett," Carl says firmly, stopping the old mariner as he turns to go, "remember what I said."

"Aye," Bartlett says, nodding once, and then, with one last glance at Paul, he turns and exits the house, closing the door behind himself. I hear him take to the air, and there is nae sound of wings.

"And what would that be?" Paul asks.

"What?" Carl says, nae taking his meaning.

"What did you say to Isaiah?" the gaunt man asks.

"I told him I wouldn't tolerate killing."

"I see," Paul says with a nod. "You are the guardian of this place? Of Utah?"

"If that's what it takes," Carl said. "I will take down any vampire who kills a mortal."

"Isaiah doesn't kill. Isaiah wouldn't kill. He is a true Penitent, a servant of God."

"He looks well Fed," Carl says. "Unlike you."

"Isaiah is a special case. His mission requires him to maintain his strength. And, he is not truly ready to . . . purify himself. Each in his own time."

"But he asks the rest of us to starve ourselves to death?" Sarah demands. If she were nae so pale from lack of Feeding (and she will need to Feed again very soon), she would be an angry red.

"Yes," Paul says. "Sarah, is it?"

"Just answer the bloody question!" she says through clenched teeth. "Why are you demanding that we starve when Bartlett is the picture of health?"

"I'll be happy to answer your questions," Paul says, "but might we sit?" He motions toward the sofas.

Carl and Sarah dinnae move, so I take them both gently by the arms and nudge them in the direction of the couches. We sit, and Carl and I place our sheathed swords across our laps. Paul sits on the loveseat.

"You won't need those here," Paul says.

"That has yet to be determined," my husband says as he tightens his grip on the hilt.

"As you wish," says the self-proclaimed Apostle.

"Well?" Sarah demands.

"As I said, Isaiah is not ready. His repentance is not absolute. But, thanks to him, our little community is gathering. He *started* all this." He pauses. "Well, actually, *you* started all this, didn't you? But Isaiah is the one who brought us together."

"Why is he telling us to starve ourselves to achieve this sodding Sanctification?" Sarah presses. "I've been in agony for weeks and it's all for *nothing!*"

Paul nods. "Of course. Human blood is what corrupts us. God forbids the consumption of it. Genesis chapter nine, verse four says, 'But flesh with the life thereof, which is the blood thereof, shall ye not eat.' We must cleanse ourselves of our addiction to human blood. Only then are we ready to meet God."

"Well, you're not dead," Sarah says angrily. "You look like you've missed a few meals, but you're certainly not dying."

"No, I'm not," he agrees.

"Then how are you surviving?" she presses.

"I, too, am not yet ready to meet God," he replies.

"So, you tell others to starve themselves to death while you go about saying, 'Do as I say, not as I do'?" Her rage is making her tremble.

"I help others to cleanse themselves of the corruption of human blood so they may ready themselves to accept the Blessing of God. He has revealed unto me how we may survive without the consumption of human blood."

"What're you saying?" Carl asks, stunned. "You've found a way to survive without blood?"

I'm shocked as well, but something in what he said is tickling at the back of my brain. "Ye keep saying, '*human* blood,'" I say. "Ye dinnae mean the blood of beasts. We all know we can receive nae nourishment from the blood of beasts. 'Tis part of the Curse."

"That is precisely what I mean," he replies evenly.

"So many of us have *tried* to survive on animal blood. *I* tried and starved nigh to death."

"Not just any beasts," he says with a thin, knowing smile. "Special beasts that are a Blessing from God. Swine, to be exact."

Sarah snorts in derision. "You're mad! I, myself, have tried pig blood and cow blood and chicken blood. It doesn't *work!*"

"Yes," he says, and his eyes are shining, "but these are *genetically enhanced* pigs. I've spent the last two decades tinkering with their genetic code so they can produce blood that is genetically similar to human blood. Just this year, God gave me a vision and showed me the way. It isn't perfect. As you can see, I'm not the *picture* of health, but the Blessing *is* enough to *sustain* us."

Sarah utters an oath such as would've made Bartlett proud.

"Bull," says Carl simply and less colorfully.

I place a hand on his thigh. "I dinnae know, laddie. Pigs are very close to humans genetically. We've been doing transplants with pig tissue, such as heart valves, for years. South Korean scientists are cloning and breeding pigs whose organs are lacking the gene that triggers rejection. They hope to produce organs suitable for human transplant. 'Tis *conceivable* that he could have found an imperfect substitute."

"You mean we could be . . . free?" Carl says, and there is hope in his eyes.

"'Tis still blood, laddie," I say. "Technically, the scripture forbids the consumption of all blood."

"But at least it's not *human*," he says.

"Will you two knock it off?" Sarah snaps. We both look at her. "You're doing it *again*! He could be lying to you. For all you know, he could have been sent here by Lilith."

We stare at her for a moment, nae catching her meaning.

"*Test* him!" she cries in exasperation.

"Ach! I'm so sorry!" I say. "Ye're right, of course."

"Sarah," Carl says, "I owe you an apology."

"Later, you bloody man," she says. "Just test him and find out if he's full of . . ."

"Excuse me," Paul says, interrupting her. "What are you talking about?"

"We have a test of sorts," Carl replies. "We use it to assess the sincerity of self-proclaimed Penitents."

"How do you know it's reliable?" Paul asks, obviously intrigued.

"Actually," I say, "we dinnae know for certain. The only person who has failed was undeniably evil. It may be that she was an anomaly. Your man Bartlett passed, and frankly, he . . ." I let my voice trail off. I'm nae prepared to say that he gives me the willies.

"Interesting," Paul says. "Isaiah *is* a special case. Very well. Test me."

"Simple," Carl says. "Fly without wings."

He blinks.

Carl is nae offering the usual explanation as to how we dinnae need wings to fly. He really does nae trust Paul.

I cannae say that I do either.

Still, without the explanation, 'twould seem he is setting Paul up to fail.

"You can do that?" he asks, narrowing his eyes, looking at Carl with that same appraising stare, like one warrior taking the measure of another.

"Yes," Carl says, but says nae more than that.

"Men!" Sarah snarls, and she lifts into the air directly from the sofa. She has nae wings, and they dinnae even flicker.

Good for you, lassie!

"Fascinating," Paul says, staring at her.

Sarah drops back to the sofa. "Now, get on with it," she says and crosses her arms defiantly.

"Very well," Paul replies. He closes his eyes and stands up slowly. He gently lifts into the air and floats there.

Without wings. Nae even a flicker.

Carl grips my hand.

Paul opens his eyes and alights on the floor. Then he sits, leans forward, and says to Sarah, "Satisfied?"

"Not hardly," she mutters, but says nae more.

"How about you?" he says, turning his gaze to Carl.

I can feel a slight tremor in my beloved's hand. This has shaken him. 'Tis obvious to me he's worried that our test is unreliable.

It troubles me as well. *Deeply.*

How do we know if we can trust *any* of them?

Dear merciful Father in Heaven, help us to discern the truth!

"Show us this wonder blood," Carl says.

"I'll test it," Sarah says. "I'm famished." She does nae sound happy about it.

"Ah," Paul says, rising, "that's the problem. It doesn't quite work that way."

"What do ye mean?" I ask.

"Well, it only works once you've Sanctified yourself," he says. "That is why you were told to come fasting. You've obviously Fed, though inadequately, in the recent past. Unless you're cleansed, you can't absorb enough nutrition."

"Of course not!" she snarls.

"You literally have to break your addiction," he says, his expression sad. "Until you do, I can't spare any. There are so many of us, and our supply is limited. But what we have, we share among those who can benefit from it."

"I was really hoping to take a sample for testing," I say.

"I'm sorry," Paul replies. "I wish I could oblige you."

"How many of you are there?" Carl says.

Is Carl hoping to get the numbers of the enemy?

"Not including Isaiah (who doesn't meet with us), we're one hundred and twenty-one in number. That includes myself."

"One hundred and . . . ," I start to say, but I cannae wrap my brain around it. *How can there be so many? So many seeking redemption.* It should fill me with hope, but instead I feel a chill in my gut.

". . . twenty-one," he finishes for me, nodding.

"And you can all sustain yourselves with this enhanced pig blood?" Carl asks, stunned.

"The Blessing," Paul replies. "Yes, we do. So you see why I can't spare any samples. We own and run the nearby pig farm that you couldn't have helped but notice when you arrived."

I wrinkle my nose. "Aye, we did."

A hundred and twenty-one!

"And are your numbers growing?" Carl asks.

"Not so much anymore," Paul says, shaking his head sadly. "We may have found all or most of those who are coming. Or perhaps, they are being intercepted. And some are not able to reach Sanctification. "

"Or perhaps they starved to death waiting for you," Sarah says. "I fell out of the sky tonight waiting for you to find me."

"I'm truly sorry," he says. "I can't search the skies every night. Tonight, I had to attend to the Harvest."

"Ye had to bleed the pigs?" I ask.

"That's right."

"What happens to those who cannae achieve Sanctification?" I ask.

"Ah," he says, a note of profound sorrow in his voice, "*those* we comfort as they transition from this life."

"Meaning they die?" I ask.

"Yes," he replies, "but we comfort them in their final hours."

"How many have died in this way?" Sarah asks. The anger is still burning in her eyes.

"Seventeen," Paul says, and his eyes well with tears.

"And how do ye comfort them?" I ask quietly.

A tear spills from one sunken eye and rolls down a hollow cheek. "We hold a vigil and pray with them and for them until they pass. It is a solemn and sacred time." He falls silent.

I want to know more about the pig blood.

"I'm intrigued. Might we have just a *taste* of the . . . Blessing?" I ask. *Maybe I can discern something from the taste and smell.*

He hesitates a moment and then says, "I'll give you each a sip of my dinner."

He walks out of the living room, through the dining room, and into the kitchen. I hear the sound of a refrigerator opening and closing, something pouring. I can smell the blood. It does nae smell quite right, but still the scent is inviting. Again the refrigerator opens and closes, and then Paul returns.

He is bearing a golden chalice. 'Tis nae ornate, but it *is* gold. As he approaches, we stand. He presents the chalice to Carl.

"Just a sip, if you please," he says. "That must sustain me for days."

Carl takes the cup and sips a wee bit. Then he hands the cup to me.

I sniff the blood. Again, I note that it does nae smell right. I've tasted the blood of swine before, in the time when I tried and failed to survive by consuming animal blood. I remember the taste well, even after all these years. I take a small sip and savor it in my mouth. It is nae cold yet. *At least the part of his story about bleeding the pigs must be true.* It tastes . . . like pig, but there is a hint of something more.

Could it be true? Could this actually sustain us? Nae more Hunting? I want so badly to believe it!

How I wish I could analyze it!

I hand the cup to Sarah. She puts it to her lips and tastes it. Then she hands the chalice back to Paul. "It tastes . . . I could almost believe it," she says.

"As I told you," Paul reiterates, "it won't work for you unless you're Sanctified first. Otherwise, it won't provide enough nutrition." He looks at

Sarah. "There really is a purpose behind the fasting. Otherwise, you would arrive here, and we would have no way to Feed you."

Sarah's reply is a low grunt.

"I hope you'll forgive me, but I'm famished," Paul says and drains the chalice. He places the chalice on the table and then returns to sit again on the loveseat.

"And ye have been developing this strain of pigs for twenty years?" I ask.

"That's correct."

"Here? In Utah?"

"Not here. I *was* located in Colorado. I moved myself and my farm here only six months ago . . . when I discovered Isaiah's website and learned of the Breaking. That's when I relocated to this place."

"And then ye formed the Congregation?" I ask.

"I met Isaiah and urged him to encourage Penitents to gather here. We formed a group."

"Who gave you authority to create a church?" Carl says. There is suppressed anger in his voice.

"It's not a church," Paul says calmly. "It's just a gathering of sinners. That's the very definition of a congregation."

"But you presume to call yourself 'Apostle,'" my husband counters.

"An apostle is, by definition, 'one who is sent out.' In other words, an apostle is a messenger. God sent me to deliver a message to those of our kind who seek redemption. He gave me a vision and showed me the way to free us from our addiction to human blood. If others follow me, it is because of that."

"Bartlett fed us a load of tripe about you being able to endure the Sun," Sarah says.

Ach! I cannae believe that skipped my mind until now! "Aye, he said it was a sign from God."

"Ah," he says, "*that*." He smiles. "It's another of God's gifts to me. I'm to use it only to help others believe. It's like the signs God gave Moses to convince hardhearted Pharaoh to liberate Moses' brothers and sisters from bondage. I'm to use it to help my brothers and sisters free themselves from Lilith and her unholy Covenant.

"I can't pass for a mortal in the daylight. I simply can endure the Sun. It's something you just have to see to understand." He pauses. "I invite you to attend our worship service," he continues. "We meet on Saturday night. On Sunday morning I will walk in the Light."

"Why not show us at dawn?" Carl asks.

"I don't want to get stuck here all day," Sarah says.

"Dinnae worry," I say to her, "we can return with our van, cloaks, and sunscreen before then. We can get you safely to . . . wherever it is you're staying afterward. Where *are* you staying? Do you have a hotel?"

"Yes," she says, and then she turns to Paul. "So, show us at dawn."

Paul shakes his head. "It's very draining. No, you'll have to wait till Sunday morning. Besides, the sign that God has given is not to gratify unbelievers. And, frankly, I really don't think I've convinced you. If you join us for the worship service, you will see. Tonight is Monday night, so that would be in five nights. Prayers and the Blessing begin at three in the morning."

I look at my husband, and he nods.

"We'll be here," I say. "We'll observe. Nae more."

"If they're coming, I'll be with them," Sarah says.

Paul nods. "Excellent. You will be welcome. We'll see if we can help you embrace the Light.

"Now," he continues, "if I may, I've answered your questions . . . or at least some of them. I'm simply *dying* to know about the Breaking."

Before we approached Bartlett tonight, the three of us agreed we would nae mention the fact that Carl is the Unwilling or anything else about the Prophecy. I *want* to believe Paul has found a viable substitute for human blood, but beyond that, I cannae bring myself to trust him with that much of the truth.

"It's simple enough," Carl says. "I'm a Penitent. When I learned that the Master of the Cult in Salt Lake City planned on Converting four Chosen into new vampires all at once, I had to stop him. I couldn't allow the deaths of even more mortals. So I killed the Master and his two wives. That made *me* the Master of the Cult. I had no *use* for the Cult, so I dissolved it. End of story."

Paul looks dubious. "It can't be that simple. One word from the Master, and you would have been bound to obey him."

"Moira and I made a surprise attack. He was dead before he knew what hit him. The sight of a vampire flying without wings unnerved him," Carl says.

That's near enough to the truth, laddie!

Paul shakes his head. "But . . . once you became the Master, you could *not* have defied Lilith's command that you must never dissolve a Cult. You *know* that. So, how did you *do* it?"

That really is the crux of the matter, is it nae?

Paul is staring at Carl with an intensity . . . a hunger that's unsettling. He desires this bit of knowledge more than anything. Why? Is he just curious? Or is it something more sinister?

"Because," I interject, "God is all powerful. He is more powerful than Lilith or even Lucifer himself. We've devoted our lives to God . . . made our covenants with God. His covenants override any previous vows we may have made. He has forgiven us . . . redeemed us. He has freed us from Lilith's power. We obey nae Master but Christ." I smile at Carl. "My own dear husband showed me that."

Paul looks at me, and the doubt in his sunken eyes is plain to see. "It can't be," he says, shaking his head a wee bit. "That can't be it."

"Surely," I say, "ye dinnae mean to deny the power of God."

Paul opens his mouth and then shuts it. "No," he says. "You're correct, of course. God is omnipotent." He nods and looks thoughtful. Then his head snaps up, and he looks at Sarah. "You are her Teacher?"

"Yes," she answers slowly.

"Did you have a Master?"

"I killed him to gain my freedom."

"So, *you're* a Master. You are *her* Master!" he says, pointing at me.

"Yes," Sarah replies.

"Command her to do something!" he says. "I mean, please command her. I have to know if she can really disobey you."

"Slap your husband!" she says to me.

I smile and say, "Nae."

"Incredible!" he says, his eyes burning. "This changes *everything!*"

I notice that Sarah is trembling. Suddenly she springs into the air, wings beating furiously. In a flash she flies straight through the curtained window, shattering the glass.

From far away and fading fast I hear Sarah cry, *"Get out! Get out now!"*

Carl grabs hold of my arm, and before I ken what's happening, he lifts me up, and we're flying out the ruined window after her.

I catch one glimpse of Paul's face before we're swallowed up by the night. He looks furious.

Carl flies through the night air as fast he can, dragging me behind him. His sword is drawn.

"Laddie," I say, "ye're hurting me. I can fly on my own."

He releases me, and blood begins to flow back into the rest of my arm from where his iron grip had been like a tourniquet. He glances back to insure that we're nae being followed. I draw my own sword as we continue to fly away from the farm as fast as we can.

"I'm sorry, my love," he says. "Do you see her?"

I scan the sky looking for Sarah. It takes a moment, but I spot her, racing away. 'Tis hard to miss the wings.

"Sarah!" I scream after her.

She glances back and, seeing us, wheels around and stops. She hovers, waiting for us.

She remains stationary, and as we approach, her wings flicker for a bit and then disappear altogether.

As we close on her, we slow our approach. She's looking past us intently. *She's looking for Paul.* She's shaking with fright.

"Sarah," I say, "what in the . . ."

"When he told me to command you," she says, a quaver in her voice, "I couldn't stop myself!"

"'Tis fine," I say, "ye . . ."

"*No, it's not!*" she screams at me. "I couldn't stop myself because I was *forced* to obey him! He's an *agent* of Lilith! He's one of her Enforcers!"

Chapter 12

E VERYONE, back to back!" Carl commands urgently. We wheel around in the air. I'm facing toward the farmhouse.

"Scan the skies!" he says. "Look above and below."

"I'm sorry I ran," Sarah says from behind me. "It was the only thing I could do. If I'd stayed . . ."

"Dinnae trouble yourself about it," I say.

"Any sign of pursuit?" Carl asks.

"Nae," I say, "but we're miles away now."

"Let's get out of here!" Sarah says. "Why aren't we going to ground?"

"We have the high ground here," Carl says, "so to speak. Never yield the high ground. And, besides, we might not see him coming from below." He pulls out his cell phone. 'Tis already open. He puts it to his ear. "Did you copy all of that?" he says into it.

"Every word." I can hear Rolf's voice coming from the phone.

"What's your position?" Carl asks.

"I'm still above the farmhouse," Rolf replies. "He hasn't moved."

"Get over here ASAP," Carl orders.

"On my way," Rolf replies.

"We've got your six." Carl snaps his phone shut.

We've got your back, I translate from Carl's pilotspeak in my head.

"I had Rolf follow us after he located Bartlett through the Internet," he says.

I can see Rolf hurtling toward us at high speed. "I see him," I say.

Rolf pulls up in front of Carl. He has his sword with him, but it's sheathed, strapped to his back.

"Any sign of him?" Rolf asks. He's looking at Carl, but *I'm* the one facing the farmhouse. He still thinks of Carl as the "commander." Well, I suppose he is . . . in the air. 'Tis his element to be sure.

"Nae as yet," I say.

"Good thing," Rolf replies. "I can't be sure unless I get a look at him, but I'm pretty certain I know him. I'd recognize his voice anywhere. I'm fairly positive that was Günther, my Teacher . . . and there isn't a more dangerous vampire on the planet."

"So why is he calling himself 'Paul'?" I ask.

"Because that's his name: Günther Paul Müller. I think he added the middle and last name when patronymics went out of fashion. He was a Saxon warrior before his Conversion. He has fought in every major war in Europe for the past eleven hundred years, usually on the winning side. The Nazi's were one of the more notable exceptions, but Hitler seemed invincible for so long . . ."

"Later," Carl says. "What makes him 'the most dangerous vampire on the planet'?"

"Most of our kind give *in* to our urges. Günther is the most disciplined man I've ever met. From what I gathered, he passed the 'wings test'?"

"Aye. Now we dinnae know *who* we can trust."

"Well," Rolf says, "you said it might have to do with discipline . . . and Günther *epitomizes* that." He pauses. "I hope you still can trust *me*."

"We'll have to do what everyone else has to," Carl says, "rely on our instincts."

"And the Spirit," I add. "I've felt good about ye since the beginning." I give him a wee smile then turn my attention back toward the farmhouse. Still nae sign of Paul.

"Where does that leave *me*?" Sarah asks from behind me, bitterness and hurt in her voice.

"You've had opportunities to run, and you haven't," Carl says. "Uh . . . I mean . . . other than when you fled the farmhouse in order to warn us, that is. You've had opportunities to *betray* us, and you haven't. And you may very well have saved our hides back there. You're not the sweetest person I've ever met . . . at least not to me . . . actually I don't know anybody sweeter than Moira . . . you know what I mean . . . Anyway, I'm inclined to trust you."

Sarah snorts. "It's not the most ringing endorsement I've ever heard, but I'll take it." She pauses. "And . . . for what it's worth . . . I'm sorry. I haven't been able to trust a man in . . . well, a *long* time."

"And, for what's it worth," I say, "my heart tells me ye are sincere."

Rolf clears his throat and then glances over his shoulder toward the farmhouse. He looks back at me and cocks his head toward Sarah.

"Aye, laddie," I say to him. "Forgive me. Rolf, this is Sarah. Sarah, Rolf."

Rolf circles around us and then hovers in front of her. I risk a glance back and see that he is extending his hand.

"Hello, Sarah," he says.

"Yeah," she says. "Sorry. This is all a bit much to take in after nearly a millennium of protecting women against you blighters. I . . . well, it's nice to make your acquaintance." I can hear her taking his hand. "I don't think I've ever said that before. I didn't learn drawing-room etiquette as a whore, and I haven't had much use for it in my life as a vampire."

"He's coming!" I cry. I can see him rising into the night sky from the farmhouse. He's just a dot to me from this distance, but it cannae be anything else. "He's alone."

"Rolf," my husband commands, "take Sarah and get out of here! Get out of *earshot*. If one of us calls you and the first word you hear is not . . . uh . . . 'taco,' hang up immediately. That'll be our 'all clear.'"

Rolf nods.

"And get her Fed," I say. *Ach! There 'tis again! The need to Hunt! The need to feast on evil blood! What's wrong with me?*

"Go! Now!" Carl says.

I hear them flying away behind us. I'm nae taking my eyes off the man approaching us, though. He seems to be moving at a *cautious* speed. Floating beside me, Carl turns and stares off in the same direction that I do.

I need something to take my mind away from the horrible hunger I'm feeling. Anything.

"'Taco?'" I say.

"Part of one of my old call signs back when I flew T-38s. I was in a hurry. I had to come up with *something!*"

I snort. "'Taco !'"

"You still have a tally?" he says, reverting to his pilotspeak. *Can you still see him?* I translate.

"Aye, laddie. Twelve o'clock low, but climbing." *Did I just say that? Now I'm doing it too!*

"Tally ho," he says.

I see him, he means.

We hold our drawn swords at the ready.

"Keep your eyes on him," Carl says. "I'm going to make sure they got away."

"Aye, laddie."

From the corner of my eye, I see Carl spin around. "They're bugging out to the south," he says. "I can barely see them. If we can hold the enemy here for just a little bit, they'll be safe."

"Then that's what we'll have to do," I say. "He's taking his time, though." Paul is moving slowly. "He wants us to see him."

"Roger. I'm checking for other bandits," Carl says as he spins around beside me, scanning the skies for anyone else approaching us from another direction. "No joy."

"What's that mean again?" I say. I don't know all his jargon.

"I can't see any other targets," he translates. "You keep him in sight. I'll keep watching for threats." He fishes in the pocket of his coat. "Here," he says, handing me a small metal bottle with a valve at the top and a small translucent plastic oxygen mask attached to it by a thin tube. There are straps attached to the mask to hold it in place over a person's head. "Just in case. Now put it away."

I stuff the emergency oxygen bottle into the pocket of my own long coat. Carl used one of these to defeat Michael a year ago by pursuing him higher and higher until Michael could nae breathe, could nae get enough oxygen in the thin air. Michael became hypoxic and then Carl, who was breathing from his bottle, slew him.

I can see the ersatz "Apostle" clearly now. He's wingless and has his arms high in the air in a gesture of surrender. His hands are empty.

He could still have a sword at his back.

"You handle him," Carl says. "As you keep pointing out, you're better with a blade. I'll watch for . . . trouble." He moves a little behind and above me, maybe ten feet up and behind so he can get a better vantage point. "I've got your six."

"Aye, laddie," I say, keeping my gaze fixed on Paul. "I love ye, ye dear, silly man, perverting the King's English as only an American military pilot can."

"I love you too, Moira," he says back. "We'll come through this all right. The Prophecy, you know."

"Were ye nae the one who said we could nae be certain the Prophecy meant *we* would live to kill Lilith? That we had to remain *valiant*?"

"OK, OK. Focus on the task at hand, pretty lady."

"Aye, bonnie laddie."

Paul halts a hundred yards away. "I'm sorry," he calls out to us. We can hear him perfectly, of course. "I didn't mean to do that. I'm really angry with myself. I just got so excited. You don't know what this means to me. You're *free*! I try so hard to make sure that everything I say is in the form of a request, because I know what . . . what my voice, my *status* can make others do. You got Sarah away, did you? Well, I don't blame you. But, please believe me when I say I mean you no harm."

He pauses.

"I'm unarmed," he continues after a moment. "May I approach?"

"Turn around and show me your back!" I say.

He does so. I see nae weapon hidden there.

"Turn around and pull out your pockets," I tell him.

He turns around, floating in the air and pulls his pockets inside out. He is nae hiding anything there.

"Ye may approach," I say, "but slowly. Keep your hands open and in sight. One false move and I'll run ye through afore I remove your head."

Nae taking my eyes off the approaching demon, I say to my beloved, "Still clear?"

"No joy," Carl replies.

When Paul is ten yards away, he halts again, keeping a comfortable distance. He's really trying to appear unthreatening.

"Thank you," he says.

"Give me your full name," I say, my sword held at the ready in front of my chest.

He blinks. "What?"

"Ye heard me," I say.

He nods. "Günther Paul Müller, although I was born Günner Polsson. I changed it to fit the times."

"Aye, we know who and what ye are. And we know why ye are here. Go home to your mistress and tell her and her minions that they are persona non grata in Utah."

Müller bites his lower lip and nods. "You know who and what I *was*. I've not served Lilith for more than half a century. I was an Enforcer, ordained by Lilith herself. I was the eldest and chief among her Enforcers. I've murdered hundreds of thousands to feed my hunger. I've executed more than a thousand of our own kind at Lilith's command. I've slain countless mortals in battle over the centuries. I've done great evil in my long life. I was the very vilest of sinners."

He bows his head for a moment and then looks at me directly. His eyes appear profoundly sad.

"That is who I was. But I'm not that man anymore. I'm trying to serve the Lord. I cannot escape my status as an Enforcer. I'm normally very careful to avoid commanding anyone, for I know I'd be robbing them of their free will. I desire only to return to God and stand before Him and rely on His mercy after having done all that I can to repent of a millennium of blood and sin."

He glances pointedly at Carl, but I dinnae shift my focus: I keep my gaze directed at Müller.

"Obviously," Müller says, looking back at me, "I haven't achieved what the two of *you* have, but I've given my life to God. And He has shown me how I and others like me can be redeemed."

"What was your turning point?" Carl asks from behind and above me.

Müller looks up at Carl and asks, "My turning point?"

"What happened that made you want to change after a thousand years of murder?" Carl says.

I dinnae think Müller notices the hint of sarcasm in my husband's voice.

"Ah," Müller says. "Very well. It was toward the end of the Second World War, after the Normandy invasion . . . what you call 'D-Day.' I fought on the side of Germany, my ancient homeland. I was an assassin in the SS. I received orders to kill Winston Churchill. We had intelligence that Churchill would be in Belgium at a secret meeting with Field Marshal Montgomery in an effort to get Montgomery to advance more rapidly to the south. The Americans were becoming impatient with Montgomery's caution. The Russians suspected that the Americans and the British were holding back to allow the Soviet Union to expend men and materiel on the eastern front."

Did Churchill meet with Monty in Belgium? I dinnae remember any secret meeting. WW II is more Carl's fascination than mine. It seems like a silly detail for Müller to fabricate.

Maybe 'tis true.

"My assignment came from Reichsführer Himmler himself. Himmler knew what I was, and he knew I could fly into Belgium on my own, but he had other ideas. I was to make the assassination appear to be carried out by the Russians. This would drive a wedge between the Soviets and their uneasy allies, the British and the Americans."

Carl questioned the historic military details of Rolf's story. Why is he nae asking questions of Müller? Is it because he finds everything about Müller unbelievable? This part, at least sounds credible to me.

"The plan was to fly a captured Soviet A-7 glider towed behind a captured Li-2 transport plane from the east into Belgium (as if it were coming from the Russian front). The transport crew, the glider pilot, and I would be wearing Russian uniforms. It was essential that the glider be identified by the British in order to implicate the Soviets, so the pilot and I would land just before sunset. I would kill my pilot immediately after landing so he could not be captured and interrogated. Then I would emerge as soon as I could be safe from the Sun's rays, kill Churchill (and perhaps Montgomery if circumstances allowed), ensure that I was seen in my Russian uniform, and then make good my escape.

"All of this required me to travel in the glider during daylight. All the glider's windows were painted black, except in the cockpit. The transport aircraft developed engine problems and released the glider's tow cable early. We were forced to land far from our target and behind the British lines. I was trapped in the glider until sunset.

"When British troops approached the glider, my idiot pilot opened fire. The English returned fire, and the pilot was killed. Worse for me, the gunfire shattered the blackened windows. The rays of the setting Sun streamed in."

My idiot pilot? That does nae sound like humble servant of God.

He continues, wiping sweat from his brow, "A thrown grenade destroyed much of the fuselage. I pressed myself into the shadows of the wreckage to protect myself from the Sun. I used our ability to blend into the shadows to try to escape detection by the lone soldier who entered the glider in order to look for survivors. There was so little room in the shadows for me to hide, and the soldier noticed the patch of unnatural darkness. He panicked and fired his weapon into it and into me. Worse still, his gunfire shattered another blackened window, and the Sunlight hit me full in the face.

"That's when it happened."

He pauses.

Is he pausing for dramatic effect? His story seems believable so far. Is he pausing because we're coming to the part of the story that we may find harder to accept?

"Instead of bursting into flames, I found myself enveloped in a bright and blinding light. I could hear the Englishman cry out and then scramble away.

"I, myself, could see nothing but the light."

What? This makes nae sense! Where would the light come from?

"And then there was a voice. It was a kind voice, soft and still. It said, 'Günther, my son. Cease from killing. Emerge from thy world of darkness and embrace the light. Behold, I show you a better way.'"

This sounds a wee bit too familiar, like the real *apostle Paul in the New Testament, only Paul was nae a monster like Müller. Is that why Müller goes by the name of Paul now?*

"And, as I stood there, wrapped in blinding light that protected me from the Sun, there came into my mind the knowledge of the Blessing, how I would, in time, develop a way for our kind to Feed . . . without taking human life. And then the voice came again and said, 'Now, go thy way and sin no more. Teach my word to others who have ears to hear and wish also to be free from sin, who wish to return to the light.'"

He pauses again. His gaunt face looks transported, as if in ecstasy. "And then the voice left me. But the light did not. It stayed with me for some time and kept me safe. And then it vanished, and I found myself in darkness once more. The Sun had set, and the English had fled.

"I was exhausted. I fled to find the nearest shelter I could, a barn for pigs. There I rested and regained my strength through that night and the next day."

Pigs! I dinnae think I believe his story about talking to God . . . but could *he have discovered an alternative to human blood?*

"And from that day until this I've labored to save my fellow Penitents. I gave up killing. I Hunted, of course, as a Penitent, preying on the guilty, but I didn't kill. I fled Europe and came to America, where I began my research to fulfill the promise of the Blessing. And now I've achieved it. I'm free from the need to consume human blood, and I'm helping others find their way back to God."

"Nice story," Carl says. "But there are a few problems with it."

"Yes?" Müller says.

"For one thing, Churchill never met with Montgomery in Belgium."

"I'm sure you're correct," Müller says. "Our intelligence was very likely faulty, and those were desperate times for the Reich."

"For another thing," I add, "your story sounds a wee bit familiar. I've heard it before, *Paul.*"

"It does sound a lot like the story of Saul on the road to Damascus," my husband says. *I can tell by the way the volume of his voice fluctuates that he's still scanning the skies for "bogies."*

"God works in mysterious ways," Müller says.

I nod. "Aye, but Saul was merely zealously misguided before his conversion to Christianity. He was nae evil incarnate. And God did nae call him as an apostle on the spot. He only called Saul to repentance. "

"In other words," Carl says, "We're having a hard time believing God would send a serial murderer as a messenger."

"I see," says Müller. "Let me ask you this: who better to send to vampires than one of their own? Are Penitents really going to listen to a mortal?"

"How long have ye been in Utah?" I say. "Six months, ye say? Ye dinnae understand the Mormons here." *Take care, lassie! Dinnae reveal too much now!* "They send out their missionaries at the tender age of nineteen, and they send them to foreign lands. And people of all ages and lands *listen* to them!"

"The argument could then be made," Müller says, "that the Lord sends *unlikely* messengers, doesn't He?"

He suddenly wobbles in the air. He shakes his head as if to clear it. "Forgive me," he says, "but the Blessing doesn't provide enough nutrition for me to sustain flight for this long . . ." He wobbles again and then plummets toward the ground.

I dive after him. It's nae that I actually *believe* him, but I'm nae prepared to let him die in such a way. 'Tis nae in my nature.

"I've got your six," Carl says. I can hear him following me as I accelerate toward Müller. I find it comforting to know he supports me in this. I dinnae think Carl could let even an unarmed *enemy* fall to his death without lifting a finger to help him. In all likelihood, Müller would survive the fall, even from this height, but I cannae just let him fall.

The "Apostle" is tumbling below me like a rag doll. And the ground is getting very near.

I close on him and match his speed. I catch hold of his shirt and arrest his spinning. Then I slip my arm under his armpits and around his chest and hold him close. I pull up and start to climb again. I keep my sword in my free hand.

Immediately Carl is at my side. "Here," he says. "Let me take him."

I shoot him a look of amusement and annoyance. "Laddie, I'm perfectly capable . . ."

"I'm not just trying to be a gentleman," he says, taking the limp Müller from me and draping him over his shoulder. "You *are* better with a sword. The best I've ever seen."

"Ah, laddie, flattery will get *ye* everywhere."

And there is that lopsided smile and lovely twinkle in his blue eyes.

Just as we land in front of the farmhouse, with its shattered picture window, Müller begins to stir. His eyes flutter open, and he looks around, obviously confused. From his position, hanging over Carl's shoulder, I imagine he cannae see much more than the back of Carl's shirt.

With a start and a jerk, he frees himself from Carl's hold and stands in front of us.

"It's OK," Carl says. "You're home." That's what he says, but he draws his sword again immediately.

Müller looks about wildly for a moment and, seeing where he is, shudders and visibly takes control of himself.

"Forgive me," he says in a strained voice. "I pushed myself too hard. Unfortunately, I need to Feed again. I need to take more of the precious Blessing. I hope you'll join us on Saturday night, but you must . . . excuse me right now."

He turns and walks shakily through the door, and shuts it behind himself. The thick curtains of the shattered picture window flutter in the disturbed air. I can hear Müller stagger across the floor. Now I can hear the refrigerator open and close. Müller is drinking greedily.

The scent of the pig blood fills our nostrils, and I notice again the *oddness* of it. And there is the sense, almost the *certainty* that it holds nourishment. Obviously, Müller is deriving nourishment from it. How I wish I had just a wee sample to test!

Carl tugs at my arm and cocks his head toward the sky behind us. I nod, and we rise into the night.

We fly south, putting miles between us and the farmhouse. Carl signals to me, and I take up the Number Two formation position. We make frequent turns to "check six."

When we're safely away and out of earshot, even for our kind, I ask, "D'ye believe any of what he said?"

"Yes," he replies, "I believe *some* of it."

"What part?"

"Oh, I believe his story about the botched assassination in Belgium right up until the point where he says he was enveloped in light. I don't believe for one second that God spoke to him. If He *did*, He would have called him to repentance and sent him to find someone with the priesthood (like He did with Saul), *not* call him as a messenger of some kind. I believe he discovered *some* way to protect himself from the Sun for brief periods, but the rest is all lies. The rest is bull."

"Aye. The parallel to Paul is nae so good. Paul was a sincere zealot, nae a serial killer. The Lord sent angels to Alma the Younger, Laman, Lemuel, and other wicked men, but it was to tell them to stop what they were doing. And," I say, "it did nae *feel* right."

"My thoughts exactly," Carl says. "He reminds me of every smarmy, crooked minister I've ever met in my life . . . and I've met some doozies! I've told you about that Korean minister who acted like he wanted to beat me to death so he could send me to Hell and then, later, told me in private and in English that it was all just part of the *show*?"

I laugh. "Aye, only about a score or more times in the past year!"

"Sorry," he says sheepishly. "It's a good story."

"What about the *blood*?" I ask. *Ach, why do I feel so hungry all of a sudden? 'Tis hard to think of anything else! 'Tis as if I can still smell it!*

"I don't know *what* to think about that," he says. "It tasted . . . almost like it *could* be true . . . but I don't buy the idea that God showed him how to do it."

Ach! I can smell it! How? It's maddening! Stand fast, lassie!

"I know what ye mean," I say. "I *do* wish I could have gotten a sample of it, even a *wee* sample! I could have gotten it tested! What I would nae *give* for one!"

"What's it worth to you?" he says.

"What? How? Ye've got one?"

"May . . . be," he says with a mischievous grin. "What's it worth to you?"

"I'll love ye forever and ever!" I say.

"You already promised me that."

I punch his shoulder, nae *too* hard. "What more could ye ask for?" I say in mock anger.

He rubs his shoulder. "Ow! Well, when you put it *that* way . . ." He stops rubbing his shoulder and reaches to his collar. He grabs it with his thumb and forefinger and pulls it slightly toward me.

I can see a small spot of red, about the size of a dime.

"I 'accidently' spilled a drop. Is it enough, you think?"

I throw myself in his arms and smother him with kisses.

"Oh, aye, 'twill be enough, ye clever, clever man!"

Chapter 13

T ACO."

Carl is speaking into his cell phone. We're sitting on the large stone near Ben's grave.

"Thank God!" I hear Rolf's voice exclaim back through the phone.

I cannae help but giggle. "Taco!" I say and snort with laughter.

"I *heard* that!" Rolf says.

"So did *I*," says Sarah, her voice more distant through the phone.

"You're all right," Rolf says. "Without the two of you . . ."

Carl grimaces. He *hates* the idea that he is seen as some sort of messianic figure. "You do realize that, if we succeed, we're all going to die, right?" he says.

"'Yea, though I walk through the valley of the shadow of death I will fear no evil,'" Rolf quotes, but there is something odd about his voice. That's it: his slight German accent is gone. In fact, if anything, it sounds like a Texas accent, almost like how Carl sounds when he uses pilotspeak.

"I'm willing to lay down my life and trust in God," he continues, "just like Lamoni's people did in your Book of Mormon. I've been reading it. I found a copy in my room."

"Did you get Sarah Fed?" Carl asks.

Blood! Evil blood! I'm actually salivating at the thought of the blood of someone truly evil! Why is this happening?

Father, give me strength!

"Yes," he replies. "And you might be interested to know, judging by the way she reacted, I would say she's surprised and genuinely touched that you asked. *You* and not your wife." He pauses. "OK, now she's glowering at me. That's more like the Sarah we've come to know and love . . . in the past few hours."

I had been about to ask about Sarah myself, but Carl beat me to it.

Well done, laddie!

"Good," Carl says. "Let's rendezvous at . . ."

"Not tonight," Rolf interrupts him. "I'm beat and so is Sarah." Suddenly his Texas accent is even thicker. *Why?* "I think we're going to check into a hotel and rest." *Why not just go to her hotel or yours, Rolf?* "Besides, there's a late night rerun of *The Treasure of Sierra Madre* on cable tonight. You know what a fan *I am* of movies from the old silver screen in con*text*." *Why is he talking that way? He's emphasizing the wrong syllables.* "After that, they're showing *The*

Caine Mutiny, and *We're No Angels*."

"Roger that," Carl says, and his voice *sounds* cheerful, but his countenance is grim.

I dinnae ken *what* they are talking about. So far as I know, Rolf has never discussed his taste in movies with either of us. And the way he was speaking! 'Twas just so odd.

"Good-night," Rolf says. "We'll *chat* later."

"Enjoy your movie night," Carl says and closes the phone.

"What in the world?" I ask.

"He was speaking in code," he says.

"Ye worked out a code?" I ask. "Then why use 'taco' of all things?"

He smiles. "No, I'm not that clever. It's Rolf who was the clever one. He made up the code on the spot."

I look at him in confusion. "I dinnae ken . . ."

"It's a common technique used since the Viet Nam War and, to a lesser extent, in the Korean War. You say something obviously false, but only the two of you would know it's false. That alerts the other party that you're trying to communicate something. Everything else is meant to convey a message."

"What was the message?" I ask.

"The important thing is they're being followed."

"Nae!" I cry. "Are *we* being followed? Have ye seen anything?"

"No," he says slowly. "I think we're still in the clear. I also suggest we don't go home tonight. Let's go get your car."

"As ye say, laddie, but ye will explain to me what ye gathered from Rolf's message?"

"Actually, I haven't worked it all out. You'll have to help me with that," he says. "But let's get moving."

We lift into the air. Carl takes the lead position, and I slide into the Number Two slot. He heads toward the city and Memory Grove Park, where my car is located.

We continue making turns to "check six" as we go, making sure nobody is following us. It appears we are, as my husband says, "in the clear."

"So," I say, "was he using that accent to alert us?"

"That would be my guess," he says. "He would assume the person or persons trailing them wouldn't know who he was or what his voice normally sounds like. So that was the first clue, but, to be honest, I didn't notice it right away."

"I noticed quick enough that there was something different about his voice, but I could nae say what . . . at least nae at first. Was there anything significant to the accent he chose?"

"I can't be sure," Carl says, "but I don't think so."

"Could it have anything to do with the accent ye, yourself, use when flying?"

"What?" he says, glancing back at me, looking genuinely perplexed. "What accent?"

I grin back at him. "Dearie, ye are completely unaware, are ye nae?"

"What are you talking about?"

I giggle. *I'm more nigh three centuries old, and this darling man makes me act like a blushing lass! Well, technically, I'm only seventeen.* "When ye fly, ye sound like ye were born and raised in Texas, laddie!"

"I *do* not!" he cries. "*Do* I?"

I nod. "Aye, laddie, ye *do*."

"I never realized . . . but . . . OK . . . uh, so back to the message." He turns his head to focus on the sky and the route. "I guess that makes sense. He must have been trying to emphasize combat aviation terminology. The obvious lie was . . ."

"'Twas about him being a big fan of the silver screen! He never said anything like that before."

"Exactly. For all I know he *might* be a big fan of black-and-white movies, but we both know he never mentioned it. And the movie he mentioned was *The Treasure of Sierra Madre.* I've never seen it, but it was a Humphrey Bogart movie, wasn't it?"

"Bogey!" I say excitedly. "That's how ye knew he was being followed."

"Roger that," he says, confirming my guess.

"And that particular movie involves *bandits*!" I say.

"I didn't know that, but it makes sense. He was probably counting on you overhearing."

"Is that a crack about my age, *laddie*?"

"Not at all: just your *experience*, pretty lady, who is younger than I am . . . technically."

"OK, so we know he was being followed. What does the rest of it mean?"

"Well, he emphasized the words 'I am' and the last syllable in 'context.' I'm pretty sure he meant he would send me an instant message or a text message when he thought it was safe. Even if he's followed, the bandit or bandits can't overhear the contents of a text message."

"Brilliant," I say.

"Not too shabby, no," he replies. "But I don't get the part about *The Cain Mutiny* or *We're No Angels.*"

"I can help with that," I say. "They're both Bogart movies, as well. *The Caine Mutiny* is about an obsessive sea captain and *We're No Angels* . . . well I think the important thing there is the lack of wings."

"Bartlett," he says simply.

"Aye. What of the part about the hotel?"

"I think it means just that: they're going to check into some neutral place so they don't lead the enemy back to their own hotels . . . or to our house for that matter (not that either of them knows where that is)."

"The 'enemy,'" I say sadly. "Is that what he is now? I did nae like him, but I hoped . . ."

"I think we need to treat anyone associated with Paul and his Congregation as the enemy," he says.

"Aye, ye're probably right."

We fly on toward the car in silence for bit.

"Carl," I say, "why are we moving so slowly? I mean, isn't this the speed we use when we're just a 'flying cap' as ye say?"

He laughs as he starts another scanning turn to check behind us. "Am I really that bad?" He does nae wait for an answer. "And it's 'flying CAP' not 'a flying cap.' It's an acronym . . . I know. I know. *Another* one!" He chuckles at himself. "It stands for Combat Air Patrol. It means, basically, 'patrolling the sky.' When you're 'flying CAP,' you're not trying to go anywhere too fast; you're just looking for bandits. And there is the fact that a fast-mover is easier to spot from a distance because it catches your attention. So, since we're high up . . . and we don't want to be seen . . . and we want to make sure nobody's following us . . ." He lets his voice trail off, sure that I understand now.

I suppose I do.

"So what's the plan, Red Leader?" I say, using a *Star Wars* reference that both annoys and tickles him.

"First, get your car with its supply of emergency daylight clothing and sunscreen so, wherever we go, we're prepared for the Sun. Second, I know you've got blood in the car. I could smell it. And I'm starving."

"What?" I say. "Ye Fed this morning before leaving for work. Ye should be good for *days!*"

He shakes his head. "I know. I *should* be just fine . . . but lately . . . it seems like I'm *always* starving. It's getting harder and harder not to just go Hunting. It's hard to think of anything sometimes but evil blood."

I freeze right where I am, hovering in the air.

In a moment, he notices I'm nae at his side, and he rushes back to me. He takes my hands in his and looks into my shocked eyes with concern. "What? What did I say?"

I swallow hard, my mouth suddenly dry. "Carl, how long have ye been like this?"

"What? What is it? Is it bad? Is it some sort of vampire disease or something?"

"There's nae disease that can harm us, laddie," I say. "But I've been experiencing the same thing."

Now shock widens his blue eyes.

"How long," I say, "have ye been feeling this way?"

"I don't know," he says. "Maybe a month . . . maybe less. It's been slowly getting worse. I suppose it started about the same time as the dreams."

"DREAMS?" I cry. 'Tis nearly a shriek! "Ye're having *dreams*?"

"Ouch," he says and looks down at his hands.

I look down and release his hands quickly. I was squeezing them so hard I must have broken several bones.

I take his dear hands in mine again, gently this time, and raise them to my lips and kiss them as the Seed quickly repairs them. "I'm so sorry! I'm so sorry, my love!" I sob over and over.

He pulls my hands to his lips with his own now-restored hands. He kisses them and kisses me, kisses my eyelids. "It's all right, love," he says, his voice soothing. "I'm fine."

I nod. "I'm sorry . . . 'tis just that I've been dreaming too."

"OK," he says, obviously missing the point.

"Vampires dinnae dream," I reply.

"What do you mean?" he asks. Then his jaw drops. "Wait a minute! I really *don't* remember dreaming since . . . since my Conversion . . . at least not until recently. I didn't know we don't dream."

"Well," I say, "we're nae *supposed* to dream."

"But that night, over a year ago, the night you got trapped in my house and you had to spend the night and I had to sleep on the couch . . . that night you said, 'Sweet dreams' . . ."

"Ach, that was just an expression."

"I had no idea," he says. "So what does it mean . . . that we're dreaming again?"

"Laddie, what are ye dreaming about?" I ask. "Is there a crucifixion, a man in a white robe?"

"Yes! I've had that nightmare twice! I'm the one getting crucified! I get burned by the Sun!"

I feel a chill down to my very bones.

"How is this possible?" I ask. "I've had the same dream, nae twice, but more than a *dozen* times!" *Only twice! 'Tis nae fair, but I would nae wish this upon anyone, much less the man I love!* "How can we be having the same dream, nae to mention us *dreaming* at all?"

"I don't know. I didn't even know we weren't supposed to be dreaming."

"So, ye've had nae dreams before about a month ago?"

"Not that I remember."

"Have ye had the dream about Ben?"

"Ben? No. What's your dream?"

"I relive Ben's death . . . but with horrific details that did nae happen."

"I'm sorry, Moira," he says. He takes me in his arms.

I had nae realized that I'm crying again. All the pain, the terror of the dream is back at this moment. Carl lets me sob into his shoulder.

"Why didn't you tell me?" he whispers.

"Ye were Sleeping . . . peacefully, I thought, when I was awakened by my dreams. I did nae want to wake ye . . . nae that I *could* have. Even though I would wake screaming, ye did nae move a muscle."

"I'm so sorry," he coos. "The two times I had the crucifixion dream, *I* woke screaming too, but *you* were Sleeping like . . . well, like a vampire."

He strokes my hair for a bit. It is so comforting to be held like this . . . by this man. *How I love him!*

Abruptly he pushes me away.

"Crap!" he cries and looks about wildly. "We could be surrounded for all we know!"

We both scan the skies for a few moments.

"No joy," says Carl. "How 'bout you?"

"I dinnae see anyone, either."

We look about a moment longer and then I say, "Let's get to the car."

"Roger," he says and immediately sets off in that direction, still scanning the skies and resuming the relaxed speed we were moving at before he mentioned his hunger and the dreams . . .

As we fly, we compare notes on the crucifixion dream. The details vary, but the essentials are the same. We're being crucified. The man in white with the Sun emblem on his chest. The others in white robes chanting. The spear piercing our sides. The Sun rises and we burst into flame. Through burning lips we quote the last mortal words of Jesus.

As we land and approach my car, I ask, "Ye said ye dreamt the crucifixion dream only twice. Are there any others?"

"Yeah, but nothing so gruesome as your dream about Ben."

Carl opens my door for me, and I get in. He hurries around and jumps in the passenger side.

"No, my recurring dream is weird," he says, "but can we eat first?"

I nod and reach behind me to retrieve my bag. I'm salivating, and my fangs have extended. *At least I'm nae alone in this. Nae longer alone. I was alone for so long!*

I retrieve two bags of blood and give one to Carl. We both shake our bags to remix the blood. I bite into a corner of mine and suck out the sweet, salty blood that I should nae *need*, but I *want* so badly. By the time I look over at Carl, he's finished with his as well. I take his empty bag and put both bags in the sadly depleted briefcase.

"Like I said: it's weird," Carl says as I turn around. "I'm sitting in a classroom. It's like Sunday School, only nobody's dressed up. There's a professor. At least I *think* he's a professor. That's how I see him in the dream. And we're discussing the Book of Mormon of all things. Sometimes, it's the Bible, but it's always the scriptures or church history. Only . . . it doesn't feel like an academic class. There's some discussion, but very little debate. Kinda like . . . a gospel essentials class."

"That does nae sound so strange," I comment.

"Well, that's not the weird part," he comments. He turns in his seat a little so he can look at me more directly. "What's weird is the fact that he's mortal . . . the professor, I mean. I can smell him, and I know he's mortal, and he smells delicious, but not in an evil way."

"That still sounds fairly mundane, laddie."

"Right," he replies. "Everyone else in the room is a vampire."

"Ah," I say. "Interesting. A classroom of vampires being taught about spiritual things by a mortal."

I start the car and pull away from the curb.

"Where're we headed?" he asks.

"We still have some hours until daylight. We cannae go home, ye say (and I agree), so I want to get that blood sample analyzed."

"And where are we going to get it analyzed?"

"I have a friend . . . an old friend . . . who should be able to help. So we're going to head south. In the meantime, ye're going to need to change your shirt so we can give my friend that sample." I motion toward the back seat. "Be a dearie and fetch the emergency clothes from the boot."

It's my habit to buy only cars that have access to the boot from within the car. I cannae know when I might be forced to hide in the boot of the car in an emergency. We keep a suitcase of emergency clothes, coats, hats, gloves, sunglasses, and sunscreen, one in my car and one in Carl's minivan for just such an occasion as this, when we might nae be able to return home. We both have work in the morning and will need clean clothes. Carl, of course, will need *protective* clothing as well. He's wearing his long coat, but he does nae have the rest of his safeguards. I'll have to drop him off at work in the morning. He can't go retrieve the van from home.

Carl climbs into the rear of the car and releases the latch at the top of the back seat to get access to the boot space. As he does so, he says with obvious amusement in his voice, "First of all, it's called a 'trunk' in this country, not a 'boot.' And second of all," he continues in a tone that is mockingly serious, "*how* old a friend?"

"Ah, laddie, ye know ye love me for my Old World charm," I say with a grin. "And, I'll have ye know that the boot used to be the space on the end of a carriage where the coachman rode. 'Twas only later, when it was used for storage and then replaced by an actual trunk at the back of an automobile, that ye started calling it a 'trunk.'

"And," I continue, "ye know very well that, after Donald, I loved nae other man till I met ye. Ye have nae cause to be jealous . . . though I dinnae mind it at all. I taught him in Primary long ago. He teaches microbiology and molecular biology at BYU. He'll be able to tell us what type of blood that sample is. His name is Sammy Gallagher. Dr. Sam Gallagher, Ph.D., I should say. I'm afraid we're going to have to wake the laddie or we'll nae get to work on time."

Carl sets the shirt with the precious sample in a wad between the two front seats and then climbs back into the passenger seat, just finishing the buttoning of his spare shirt. It's wrinkled, but it'll have to do.

"You don't have to worry about me. I can be late. All we're doing is waiting on approval from the hardware manufacturer on the game we just submitted. So we're not all that busy. Can't you take a day off if you need to?"

"'Twouldn't be a good idea anyway, so soon after our trip to Florida, but Winnie's in the hospital, and I was her surgeon tonight. I need to check on her."

"Winnie *Morrison?*" he says.

"Aye. She had a bad fall yesterday."

"Wow! She *hates* you. She hates me too. But she *really* hates you."

"Aye, laddie. If anything, saving her life did nae improve her opinion of me. It only made her more bitter."

A tear spills from my eye.

Carl reaches over and catches it, wipes it away from my cheek. "Why does it bother you so much? She's a bitter old woman who drove her own husband away. She simply takes it out on you so she doesn't have to look at herself to find the cause of her own misery."

I open my mouth to speak, but he continues.

"And don't give me that crap about her blaming you for her husband leaving her. It's not your fault and you know it."

"Aye, laddie, I ken 'tis nae my fault, but 'tis such a burden to carry when someone is miserable and lays the blame at your feet. I *want* to help her, but I cannae do *anything* except watch her destroy herself." *Did I just say too much? I cannae betray Winnie's secret. 'Tis nae my place.*

"I know," he says, wiping away another tear. "So, how bad was it?"

"Bad enough. Her body will heal, if she gives it a chance. We saved her life, but I dinnae know if she has the *will* to live." *I should nae be saying that much!*

Carl's phone beeps. He pulls it out.

"It's a text from Rolf," he says.

"What does he say?"

I glance over at Carl, and he's grinning.

"What?" I ask.

"Taco," he says.

That makes me smile, as well. "I guess they're safe," I say.

"Well, at least for now." He starts pushing buttons. "You know," he says as he texts back to Rolf, "before my Conversion, I was never very proficient at this . . . texting, I mean. It took me too long to do anything. Now . . . it's easy. It's almost faster than talking."

"So what does he say?" I ask again.

"They're safe. They're sharing a room at the Plaza Inn. They plan to get another room as soon as the Sun is up. Then Rolf is going to let Sarah Sleep while he stands watch."

He pauses and looks up at me. "Do you think Sarah will let him? Watch over her, I mean?"

"I dinnae know, laddie. Ask him."

"I will." He rapidly enters the question into his phone and then continues to read Rolf's messages. "It *was* Bartlett following them. Bartlett didn't approach . . . just followed. Rolf wants to know if we can obtain a weapon for Sarah. I'll tell him we'll try."

"I have an idea where we could get one, laddie."

"I'll tell him." He sends the message. His phone beeps as a response comes in. "He says, yes, Sarah will let him stand guard." He looks up at me. "Wow! That's a *lot* of trust!"

"Well, she *is* exhausted, and 'tis the only practical thing. 'Tis nae as if he'll be able to wake her halfway through the day."

"Right. She'll be sleeping like . . . well, uh, the undead."

I frown at him. I *hate* that inaccurate word! He doesn't notice my expression. He's intent on his phone.

He sends another message. "I told him we have a sample of Müller's pig blood, and we're going to get it analyzed. We'll get in touch with him after that. The new safe word is . . . 'basket' and the duress word is . . . 'hyper.'"

"What's a 'duress word,' Carl?" I ask. *The 'safe word' must mean 'all clear' like 'taco' did.* I barely suppress a giggle.

"A duress word is something you slip into a conversation to let someone know you're under duress, meaning you're being forced to do or say something."

"What if ye say both words?"

"You assume duress. It's safest. If someone uses the duress word, you have to assume there's danger."

"What a depressing way of looking at the world."

"I'm afraid, my love, this is the world we live in. We have to be very careful.

"Oh," he says, "and be *very* careful not to use either word by accident."

"What if it just slips in? 'Tis a common word."

"That's the whole point. The duress word *has* to sound casual, so as not to alert the enemy."

"What if you dinnae use the 'safe word' *and* ye dinnae use the 'duress word'?"

"It means you're not under duress, but you may not be free to talk. It implies caution, perhaps danger, but not duress."

"I see," I say. *At least* I think *I do.*

"If I were still in the Air Force, I wouldn't be comfortable using open communications like cell phones and texting. Actually, I'm still not *comfortable* with it, but we're improvising. You use what you've got when you're surrounded by the enemy."

"Is that how it is?" I ask. "Surrounded?"

"We have to assume we are. There's Lilith's bogus 'Apostle' and Bartlett. I don't know how many more. How many of Müller's one hundred and twenty do you think are under his direct control . . . his slaves?"

"Maybe none of them are," I say, "but it does nae matter in the end. All he has to do is command them, and they have nae choice but to obey him."

"So he has an army of a hundred and twenty . . . plus Bartlett.

"I really don't get him," he continues. "What's his motivation for doing all this, for being in league with Müller? He obviously isn't drinking the pig blood, and he isn't pretending to be a holy man."

"I dinnae know, but I *believe* his story. I think he was telling the truth . . . at least so far as he was able."

"Yeah, I think we have to assume Müller's exercising some level of control over him."

"Aye, he does nae seem to be overly religious, but he *did* speak of Müller with awe. Did ye notice, though, that he could nae fly without wings at first?"

"Moira, we know our 'wings test' is worthless," Carl says sadly.

"Nae foolproof, I'll grant ye, but maybe nae so worthless as ye say."

"What do you mean?"

"What I mean is, Bartlett could nae do it at first."

"That's not surprising."

"But he could nae do it at all, not at first. The wings did nae even flicker until something changed, and suddenly they were just *gone*. With me, it did nae happen all at once like that. It was the same with Rolf and Sarah. How was it with you and with . . . Ben?"

"The same," he says slowly. "With Bartlett it was 'impossible,' as he said. Until what? What happened and they just vanished?"

"'Twas when I confirmed to him that *ye* were the 'Breaker.'"

"You're right! But why?"

"Laddie, 'twas the same as when you told Rebecca to 'shut up' after killing Michael (and thereby becoming the Master of the Cult). She could nae speak nae matter how much she wanted to. 'Twas nae only Bartlett's wings, dearie, 'twas his whole demeanor. 'Twas as if he *had* to make us believe him. What if . . . What if Müller had commanded Bartlett to do whatever it took to win the confidence of the 'Breaker,' should he encounter him or her?"

"You know . . . that sounds right. Yeah! When you were under Michael's control, you couldn't get up off his bed. I couldn't even *lift* you. You did whatever it took to stay where he commanded you to stay."

"Take off your clothes, my dear," Michael drawled, as he leered at me. But there was nae lust in those eyes, only hatred and contempt. "But do it slow. I want to enjoy every minute of this."

I had to obey him. I had nae choice! But what did it matter? I'd just put a sword through my husband's heart!

Carl! *I screamed in my head.* Forgive me! Dinnae abandon me!

"Now, lie down on the bed," Michael commanded.

I struggled to resist him, but I could nae. I lay down on the bed and tried with all my might to flee, but my body would nae obey me.

"What's your name?"

Dinnae answer him! Resist, if only that much!

"Moira," I said through clenched teeth.

"No, I don't think so," he said. "Your name is Benjamin *now. You took him from me, so now* you're *gonna be my little niggah boy."*

Carl! Please! Dinnae leave me here!

In my mind, I cried out from the depths of my soul, Oh, merciful Father in Heaven! Dinnae forsake me now! Dinnae let me be . . . *raped* again! Nae again!

"I'm gonna treat you just like I treated Benjamin," Michael drawled on. "You're mine, now. I own you. And I'm gonna show you just what that means as soon as I deal with Rebecca." He wagged a finger at me. "Now you just lie right there and don't you move and don't you make a sound, not unless I or one of my wives says you can. I'll be back, but I promise not to return until I'm really *angry."*

With that, he turned and walked out of his bedroom.

And I was alone.

I could nae move. I could nae cry out. I could only lie helpless, waiting . . . waiting to be raped again.

"Aye, Carl, my love," I say, "I remember it very well. When ye came to rescue me and tried to lift me from the bed, I could nae move a muscle, but I was forcing myself to fly down into the bed to prevent ye from lifting me up."

Carl nods. "So Bartlett is under Müller's control. He's not just a disciple."

"Aye, he's a slave. Or so 'twould appear. Most likely Bartlett knows precisely what Müller is."

"Speaking of which," Carl says, "why *did* we let Müller go?"

"'Speaking of *whom* . . .'" I say absently.

"*You're* correcting *my* English?" Carl says with a grin. "*You?*"

"There is nary a thing amiss with my English," I say, mock indignation infusing my voice. I square my shoulders and lift my chin haughtily. "I'm speaking a perfectly acceptable dialect of the King's English."

"Well, so am *I*," he says. "It's called 'Uh-mar-i-can.'"

"More like 'Utahn,'" I say and flash him a smile.

"Seriously, though," he says, his tone instantly grave, "why did we just let him go?"

"Could ye have killed him when he was like that, laddie? Or let him fall?"

"The fall wouldn't have killed him . . . probably."

"From that height?" I muse. "It could have. It depends on how and on what he lands. If he struck his head hard enough, it would burst open. His internal organs could have been pulverized, even liquefied. His abdomen could have exploded. The Seed can repair virtually anything, but it cannae gather what's scattered about."

"All right! All right!" he says, raising his hands in protest. "That's gruesome enough."

"Sorry, laddie! That's just the physician talking."

He is silent for a moment.

"No," he says finally.

"Nae, what?" I say.

"No, I couldn't let him die . . . or kill him when he was . . . you know . . . unarmed and defenseless. And we weren't sure *what* he's doing. We have no *proof* that he's killing anybody . . . anymore.

"Argh!" he says angrily. "I *hate* this world of vampire justice. Who made the two of *us* judge, jury, and executioner?" His voice drops to a whisper. "I don't feel qualified . . . or worthy. Who am *I* to judge?"

I laugh once bitterly. "If *any* of us is worthy to judge vampires, 'twould be ye, lad. Ye, who have nae killed for blood. Ye, who are Unwilling." I swallow once and then I say softly, "'Twould nae be me."

He places his large but gentle hand on my thigh. "Moira," he says, "the past is forgiven. You've been washed clean in the blood of Christ. 'Though your sins be as scarlet . . .'"

"The past shapes who I am," I say, and a tear falls from my eye.

"Who you are," he says, "is the sweetest, purest, kindest soul I've ever met."

"Who murdered seventy-two men," I say. "I ken that I've been redeemed . . . but 'tis a part of me. 'Tis part of what brought me here."

"To *me*," he says and gently squeezes my leg.

I look over at him, tears streaming down my face. I see his lopsided smile and his bonnie blue eyes, and I cannae help but grin myself.

"Besides," I say, turning my attention back to the highway, "ye are nae judge and jury. Ye are simply defending your city. That makes ye a guardian, a knight."

"And that makes *you* my lady fair . . . who just happens to be able to kick my butt when it comes to actual sword fighting."

"And ye best nae forget it, laddie!"

Chapter 14

KILL HIM! Plunge your fangs into his throat and drain him! Drain him of his sweet evil blood!

The prey stands with his delicious blood pulsing in his veins, pumped by a heart pounding with his terror. He's holding a knife to the throat of a frightened lass (a college student, most likely), barefoot on the cold pavement and dressed in pajama pants and a T-shirt. He holds her in front of his own worthless carcass, using her as a human shield.

Kill him! Rip out his throat, and let his sweet life gush into your waiting mouth!

Many students leave their apartment doors unlocked as roommates come and go at all hours. This evil man must have found such a door available to him and taken this hapless lass from her bed in the wee hours of the morning.

And now he's *mine*.

Now he knows true *terror*.

Carl and I were forced to park south of the BYU campus. The shortest route to Sammy Gallagher's office led us through this student apartment complex. And that was when we smelled the nigh irresistible ambrosia of the blood of someone truly evil.

At any other time, under these circumstances, I would say something like, "I'm a Daughter of Lilith and ye, ye pathetic little defiler of helpless women, ye are my prey." That's what I *would* say.

But nae *this* night.

This night I simply growl deep in my throat, and the sound is like the guttural snarl of some demon from the infernal pit.

This night I dinnae want to show him the error of his ways.

This night I simply want to kill him, consume him, and then rend his corpse limb from worthless limb.

I'm dimly aware that Carl is growling inarticulately at my side. I dinnae care.

The prey is *mine*.

The man's lips move wordlessly. I hear a scream beginning to rise in his throat with its delicious throbbing veins. The knife trembles in his hand. It makes a little cut in the lassie's throat. I see her blood. I smell her blood.

'Tis *maddening*.

In an instant, I'm upon him. I rip the knife from his hand and toss it aside. I dinnae care where it lands. The lassie drops from my sight. I dinnae care. All I want is the evil blood.

I sink my fangs into the prey's neck, and the blood, flavored with the exquisite sweetness of pure malevolence, floods my mouth. I drink it greedily.

It has ne'er tasted so sweet!

Carl is beside me. "Save me some," he snarls.

The homicidal rage erupting inside me threatens to turn itself on Carl. *He's mine! His blood is* mine! *Dinnae touch* him!

What is happening to me? Would I lash out at Carl . . . harm *Carl . . . over this pathetic dreg of humanity?*

With a supreme effort, I wrench my lips free of the prey's neck and stagger away from him. Carl lunges in and latches on to drink.

"Do . . . nae . . . kill . . . him," I manage to force myself to say. *Kill him! Rend him! Drain him! He's* MINE!

Trembling, Carl pulls back for a moment from the source of the indescribable sweetness, then licks the wound to close and heal it with the Seed in his saliva. Then he drops the filthy man-shaped maggot to the concrete walkway. The prey moans and raises his hands to Carl and then to me, his eyes wordlessly begging us to take more.

Take it all!

Hold fast, lassie! Stop this now!

I'm wracked with a sudden chill. *Father, forgive me!*

I could have killed *him!* Perhaps, if nae for Carl, I *would* have.

The lassie! The victim!

She has backed herself into the doorway of an apartment, and she's crouching there, cowering. She stares at both of us in horror.

Carl stands over the wretched waste of human flesh that was our prey. My husband is breathing raggedly, his chest heaving. To my eye, he's struggling as much as I was to keep from killing the human garbage lying on the ground.

"Laddie," I say through clenched teeth, my fangs still extended, "ye see to the vermin, and I'll see to the victim."

Carl nods. He bends down and lifts the would-be rapist (and ye can be sure he's done this afore) from the ground. I can hear the horrid man pleading with Carl, nae to spare him, but to take more of his blood.

His evil blood! Take it all!

I force myself to turn my attention to the traumatized figure hunkering against the door. She's too horror-struck to flee or even to scream. She holds her hands before her face, trying to ward me away.

And there is the blood trickling down her neck onto her T-shirt. It's nae but a wee flow, but 'tis so frightfully hard to resist all the same.

Collect yourself, Moira MacDonald Morgan! That's the victim *before ye! Dinnae traumatize her further!*

I take a deep breath and force my fangs to retract.

I can do this!

"There, there, lassie," I coo. "I'll nae harm ye. Dinnae be afeared."

I extend a hand to smooth her hair from her face, but she flinches. She has nae place to go, nae retreat. I manage to lay my hand gently on the side of her head, and I stroke her blonde hair.

"Ye're safe, now," I say. I lick the fingers of my other hand and quickly smear my Seed-laden saliva over her small wound. It seals closed almost instantly.

There is blood on my fingers. *How I want to lick them clean!*

"There, dearie," I say to her with a smile, "all better now."

I can hear Carl Persuading the useless monster to confess his sins to the police and to never again hurt another living soul in his worthless life. I try to ignore them . . . to block them out.

"Ye'll be fine, lassie," I say. "Here. Let me look ye over. I'm a doctor."

"You're a monster," she whispers, her eyes staring into mine.

"Aye, lassie, that I am. But, I'm a *nice* monster. We saved ye from that pile of garbage over there." I stare back into her eyes. "Please, lass, let us help ye." I'm nae using Persuasion. I want her to just *believe* me . . . to trust me.

She gives me a wee nod.

"What's your name, dearie?"

"Candice."

"Where do ye live, Candice?"

She extends a trembling hand and points off to my left, toward other apartment doors.

"Let me help ye up," I say, offering a hand, the one with blood on it. "Can ye stand?"

She shakes her head.

"That's all right, dearie," I say, and I scoop her up in my arms. I stand and turn around with her.

Carl has finished with her attacker. The prey is curled in a fetal ball on the ground, sobbing. "I'm so sorry!" he says over and over again between wracking sobs.

"I'll stay here with him," Carl says, obviously having taken control of himself. "Call the police. Don't use *your* phone. Hurry. We don't have that much time left before . . ." He lets his voice trail off.

"Daylight," the lassie in my arms (Candice) whispers.

Clever girl.

"I know what you are," she says, nae looking at me. "I've read *Twi* . . ."

"Dinnae say it!" I hiss. "I *hate* that book!"

She flinches away a bit.

"I'm sorry, lassie," I say, softening my tone, "but I really do hate that book."

From where I'm standing now, still holding her, I can see that the door to one of the apartments is wide open. I carry Candice inside. I set her down on the hideous canvas-covered couch. She looks at me in panic and tries to clutch at me. *And a moment ago she was calling me a "monster."*

"Now stay there, lassie," I say. "Ye're in shock. I'm just going to fetch ye a wee bit of water."

I turn away and hurry into the small kitchen. The blood on my fingers, Candice's blood, rivets my attention for a moment. I rush to the sink and rinse it from my hand and then stare at the red-tinged water as it rushes down the drain . . . out of reach.

I would venture to guess that there are six girls living in this apartment. The kitchen is so small! The smell of rotting food in the trash under the sink assails my nose. At least there are nae unwashed dishes in the sink. Now, if this were an apartment for men . . . *Best to stay focused, lassie!* I find a plastic tumbler in a cupboard and fill it with water from the tap. Then I hurry back to the wee living room.

"Here, lassie, drink this down."

She takes the tumbler and drains it with trembling hands. I take the plastic drinking glass back from her and set it on the coffee table (that will ne'er be used for that beverage at *this* university). I'd better treat Candice for shock. I gently help her to lie down on the sofa, and I elevate her feet and place them over the arm of the couch. I find a throw blanket on the floor and spread it over her.

"I need to call the police, dearie. May I use your phone?"

She nods.

"I'll be right back," I say.

I hurry into the kitchen, where there is a common phone. I dial nine-one-one and give the dispatcher a terse description of the events, leaving out any mention of Carl and myself. I even think to use my best imitation of a "Utah" accent. Hopefully, they'll think I'm just some Good Samaritan, who does nae want to be identified or "get involved."

Then I hurry back to Candice on her couch. I kneel beside her and ask, "Did he hurt ye, lassie?"

"No," she whispers, "he was rough . . . and he scared me. I thought I was going to die."

"Well, ye are safe now."

She is silent for a bit as I give her a cursory check for injuries. She should be fine . . . physically. Emotionally? Even though the prey did nae actually rape her, the trauma of a *near* rape can be almost as devastating.

We really need to get away from here, but she looks as if she wants to ask me something. I cannae just leave her like this.

"Thank you . . . for saving me," she says quietly.

"I'm just grateful we were here to do it," I say. "But, lassie, please . . .

when ye talk to the police . . . will ye leave out the part about *who* rescued ye? Just say it was . . . two strangers. That's true enough. And try nae to describe us. Will ye do that?"

She looks at me as tears fill her eyes. She nods. "But," she says softly, "please tell me one thing?"

"If I can," I say cautiously.

"Why do you hate *Twili* . . ." she says, but stops short of saying the book's name when she sees my stern look of caution. "Is it because it's not . . . realistic?"

"Realistic?" I snort. "'Tis a fantasy, nae more. 'Tis nae more unrealistic than any other fiction about . . . our kind."

"Then what is it?"

"After all ye've been through tonight, *this* is what ye ask?"

"I *love* those books," she says. *Perhaps 'tis the shock that is speaking.*

"Well, my *problem* with them is the depiction of a young woman who is willing to give up *everything* . . . to become a serial *murderer* even . . . so long as she can be with the boy she loves. I know it turns out well in the end, but 'tis a *terrible* message for teenage lassies, do ye nae see? 'Tis so hard for teenagers to stay *moral* and clearheaded about love as it is, and to say 'tis worth *any* sacrifice, betraying *any* principle, even *murdering* to be with the one ye love . . . well, I think that's a bit *scary*."

She stares at me dumbfounded for a second and suddenly she giggles.

"*You* think *that's* . . . SCARY?" she says.

I'm glad she can find something to laugh about after all she's experienced this night. At least 'tis nae just hysterics . . . I hope.

"Maybe," I say, "'tis a wee bit *ironic*."

"Is the other one . . ." she says glancing in Carl's direction, ". . . is he your . . ."

"My husband," I say, "sealed to me in the Temple of God." *Now why did I say that?*

She gasps. "The *Ogden* Temple?"

My eyes widen. "How did ye . . . ?"

"You're the 'Ogden Angels'! You saved those two temple workers last year!"

Ach! Nae again!

I open my mouth to respond, but stop as I hear sirens approaching.

Time to go!

"Candice," I say, "the police are approaching. Ye cannae hear them yet, but *I* can. We'd best be on our way."

She looks at me in panic.

"Dinnae worry, lassie," I try to reassure her. "I'll lock the door after I leave and *that* piece of filth out there . . . he'll nae hurt another living soul again. He'll nae come near ye. He'll *wait* for the police."

The poor lassie shakes her head in mute protest, her eyes wide with panic.

"*And*," I add, "we'll nae leave until the police have him in hand. We just have to get out of *sight*. I promise. We'll be right outside. Will ye trust me? Please?"

She looks about suddenly. She can hear the sirens now.

"Go!" she hisses.

I take her hand and squeeze it briefly, and then I exit the apartment, twisting the doorknob to lock the door as I leave.

"I don't want to *rush* you," Carl says, still standing over the prey (with his luscious, evil blood still pulsing weakly in his veins), "but we gotta go, pretty lady. She OK?" he says, pointing his chin quickly in Candice's direction.

I nod. "Aye, as well as can be expected. I promised we'd stay around, but out of sight, until the police arrived."

"Which is *now*," Carl says, quickly retrieving the bag containing his shirt with the spot of pig blood on it. He takes my hand, and we both lift into the air just as the first police cruiser pulls into the parking lot.

I took at least a quart from him and still *I want more!*

I look down and watch an officer secure Candice's attacker as another police cruiser arrives. They will take care of things from here.

"How can I still be *hungry*?" Carl hisses.

"Ye as well?" I ask.

He nods.

"I want nothing more than to go back and finish him," he says.

"Carl, what is *happening* to us? *Dreams* . . . and this nigh unbearable *hunger* . . . even when we're already *sated*?"

"Moira, you know more about this . . . life . . . than *I* do."

"This . . . this is far beyond my ken."

We're out of sight of the police now. I pull down on Carl's hand, and we descend, landing in a dark spot between two pools of light near the McDonald Building, which houses the University's Office of Information Technology. We'll go the rest of the way on foot.

We walk in silence for a short distance, and I can tell by the way Carl catches his breath that he wants to say something but cannae quite bring himself to articulate it. Finally, he takes a deep breath and then whispers, "I almost killed him."

"I as well, laddie," I say quietly. "I've nae been so close to losing all control since . . . since Edna."

The night Carl and I defended the Ogden Temple from a gang of thugs. The night I used the Seed in my saliva to Heal the compound fracture in Edna's leg. The night it took all my will to keep from killing Edna's attackers.

The night I was finally able to touch the temple walls.

Carl squeezes my hand. "For a second," he says, "I was ready to shove you out of the way to get to him. I could have . . . I think I was capable of . . . hurting *you*." If his voice was a whisper before, now, it would only be audible to the Seed-enhanced ears of a vampire. He is looking only at the ground.

And he's chewing at his lower lip the way he does when he's struggling to keep his emotions in check.

I stop him and put my arms around his neck. I kiss him gently and put my lips to his ear. "Ye could ne'er do that, my love. Nae matter what the . . . temptation. 'Tis nae in your nature. And had the situation been reversed . . . well, then 'twould be *me* struggling and overcoming the very same urges."

He takes my face gently in his hands and wipes away the tears that are now falling freely from *my* eyes. He kisses each eyelid in turn, kisses my lips tenderly, and then enfolds me in his arms and holds me close.

There's nae time for this, but I dinnae trouble myself about it. We *need* this moment. I will *nae* lose this man that I love so very, very dearly.

"Whatever it is . . ." he says, a hitch in his voice, "whatever this new *danger* is . . . we'll overcome it. We'll face it together."

"And," I add, "with God's help, we'll beat it."

I hug him tightly and say, "We'd best be off. Sammy's waiting. And the Sun'll rise whether we're ready or nae."

He breaks the embrace, winks at me, and, taking my hand, begins to walk briskly toward the Widtsoe Biology and Agriculture Building.

Chapter 15

WHAT AM I LOOKING FOR, specifically?" Sammy says as he stares intently at the spot of blood on the rumpled shirt in his hands. Sammy is a balding man with sparse blonde hair framing an otherwise boyish face. I look at the tweed-jacketed man, and I still see the precocious, towheaded, seven-year-old laddie I taught more than three decades ago.

We're sitting in Sammy's (I mean *Professor Gallagher's*) office. 'Tis, of course, a mess. Books are everywhere. I see the obligatory tomes on biology, but there are also volumes of fantasy, science fiction, and horror. (I note with a wee smile that he has Mr. Stoker's amusing *Dracula*, a book that shaped the modern popular conception of our kind more than anything else.) There is also a small collection of resin statues or figures from science-fiction and fantasy movies. I see a set of scriptures open to Moses. I find what I'd expect to see strewn about any office, but there's nary a microscope or any other instrument such as I'd expect to see in the office of a professor of microbiology and molecular biology.

"What I need to know, laddie, is the *species*," I say. "I dinnae want to say more than that, since I dinnae want to prejudice ye."

"You mean," he says, looking up at me in surprise, "you don't know what it is?"

"Truth be told, I . . . cannae be sure."

"Oh, OK," he says slowly. "Without a general idea . . . it could take longer."

"How long?" Carl asks.

"Possibly hours, but definitely today. If I knew what I was looking for . . . Is it yours?"

It takes me a second to realize that he said this last to Carl.

Carl says, "No."

"Why would ye ask that, Sammy? I'm sorry. *Sam?*" I say.

"It's OK, Moira," he says with a grin, "I don't know how I'd handle it if you stopped calling me 'Sammy.' I think my wife would be jealous if you stopped treating me like one of your little Primary 'bairns.' I have to remind her how much older you are than me.

"Speaking of which," he continues with a sheepish smile, "the reason I asked your husband, 'Is it yours?' is because I really meant to ask . . . I mean,

I know it's like . . . taboo . . . a forbidden subject . . . What I mean is . . . is he . . . you know . . . like . . . *you?* I mean, is he . . . you know . . . does he have the . . . *virus?*"

"The *virus?*" I say. *He means the* Seed!

"Yeah," he says, obviously screwing up his courage. The words come spilling out like a flood, a flood that he must've been holding back for a very, very long time. "Those blood samples you've brought me to analyze over the years . . . you never told me where they came from, but I've always assumed that they were *yours*. You never offered explanations, and I never asked questions. I mean . . . it was *you*. I don't know how *anybody* turns down a request from Moira MacDonald. I know that *I* never could."

I can feel my face reddening.

"Anyway," he continues, "you asked me to look for anything *abnormal* without being really *specific*. And I never found *anything* abnormal *except* for the virus. And it seemed like you expected that when I reported it."

And here I thought I'd been so clever!

"But, I kept digging," he continues quickly. "I ran a lot more tests than you asked for. I was intrigued," he says a wee bit defensively. "I learned that all the samples seem to have come from the same person, a woman, and, of course, they all contained the dead virus. That virus was something I could never identify . . . something *unique*."

I should've known a bright lad would suspect something.

"One time," he says, "you brought me a sample that was very fresh. It was still *warm*. (You must have drawn it in the hall right before you came into my office.) And it contained the *live* virus."

I had taken the sample in the ladies' room just before I met him that time.

"The virus didn't live long," he continues quickly. "I mean, it should have just gone dormant, but instead it *died*. Not like any virus I've ever seen. I mean, we've retrieved *bacteria* from the lens of one of the lunar probes, Surveyor 3 . . . a NASA tech sneezed on the camera lens before it was launched into space . . . and the camera was retrieved by the Apollo 12 astronauts and brought back to Earth . . . and after years in the vacuum and exposure to solar radiation on the lunar surface . . . the bacteria became *active* again when it warmed up in a normal atmosphere. It was still *alive*."

He gestures excitedly with his hands. "And a *virus* is usually a lot tougher than bacteria. But *this* virus dies within minutes. I mean, it can't seem to survive outside the host . . . but that's not all there is to it, is there? Is there?"

He does nae wait for a reply. "The next time you called and told me that you were bringing me a sample, I brought my cat from home." He grimaces. "(My wife would *kill* me if she knew.) And . . . I've never, *ever* heard of you being *sick*. I figured it would *probably* be safe. Anyway, *please* don't tell my wife about that!"

I dinnae like where this is going at all.

"So," he says, "right after you left the sample with me, I ran it through a Chamberland filter to isolate the virus, then injected a saline solution containing the live virus into the cat."

"Sammy!" I cry. "Ye did nae!"

He lowers his eyes sheepishly. "Sorry, but I did. I needed a live host to keep the virus alive. Once I injected it, the cat immediately began acting . . . well . . . happy . . . like he was having the best *scratch* of his life while rolling around in catnip and being fed tuna. After a few minutes he stopped acting that way."

Poor puss!

"The virus must have reproduced at an *amazing* rate to spread throughout his system like that and produce that effect, but then it . . . I mean the *virus* . . . died. (Don't worry: the cat's fine.) So, it can't survive outside the host, but not just *any* host can sustain it. It can't survive outside of *you*. So, other than my little experiment with the cat, all I've *ever* been able to do is to study the *dead* virus . . . and I could never learn much from that. But the virus *is* what makes you . . . *immortal*, isn't it?"

I stare at him dumbfounded. *What can I say to all that?*

"So," he says to Carl, catching his breath at last, "are you . . ." he points at me, ". . . like Moira?"

I shoot Carl a warning look, but he's nae looking my way.

"Yeah," Carl says, "I am."

"Carl!" I cry.

"*What?*" he says. "I'm not bound to keep the Great Secret. I never was."

"But I've kept *my* secret for half a century in that ward," I say.

"What's 'the Great Secret?'" Sammy asks, but then he shakes his head. "Never mind that for now," he says, raising a halting hand. "Don't worry about it. I figured this out on my own," Sammy says. "You trusted me enough to bring me those samples to analyze. I knew this meant *something*. You've kept in touch with me over the years. I mean, *nobody* really talked about it, but *everybody* has to question it a little . . . how you never aged, I mean. It's like we just *wanted* to believe that it was simply your unnamed 'medical condition.' But nobody ever wanted to question sweet, pretty Sister MacDonald. So . . . we didn't talk about it . . . much."

He shrugs sheepishly. "When I was a teenager, my theory was that you were a translated being . . . like the Apostle John in The New Testament or the Three Nephites in the Book of Mormon . . . you know . . . who remain in the flesh, serving the Lord until the His Second Coming. *Now*, I don't know *what* you are, except that I know you don't age. Not a single day. I shouldn't ask, but . . ."

The cat is out of the bag, as they say.

"I was born in 1739," I say.

"Wow!" Sammy says incredulously. "I mean, I *suspected*, but . . . *wow!* I never thought you'd be *that* old! I mean . . . *look* at you! You could be one of my undergrads!"

He stares at Carl expectantly.

Carl laughs and glances quickly at me before turning back to Sammy and says, "I was born in the year of our Lord one thousand nine hundred and seventy-four."

"*Wow!*" Sammy says again, his face full of wonder. I dinnae think he realizes that Carl is having fun with him. "One thousand nine hundred and . . ." His expression shifts from wonder to annoyance to puzzlement. "Wait a minute! You're only . . . but you look *older*! I thought you *must* be *way* older than Moira! I figured you . . . immortals like you . . . must age really slow or not at all, but you *look* older!"

"Sammy," I say shooting Carl a look of mock annoyance, "I stopped aging when I was a mere lass of seventeen."

"Then why . . ." Sammy begins, but trails off. I almost can *see* the wheels turning in his mind. He always was a bright lad. He leans back in his chair behind his desk. "Obviously *you*, Carl, stopped aging at a different point in your life. You *do* appear to be older, but you must have stopped aging *recently*." He touches the fingertips of his two hands together and places the thumbs under his chin and his tented fingers above his nose. He stares intently at Carl over his fingers. "Less than five years ago, I'd guess."

Carl smiles. "Good guess. Actually, it's just over a year ago."

"Wow!" Sammy makes that one syllable sound as if it were two as he rolls it around his mouth. He drops his hands to the desk. "So how did you become infected . . . and why does it only seem to work on you . . . or the two of you? Are there *others* like you?"

"Laddie," I say, "that is really a discussion for another time . . . and I *do* promise to answer your questions. But both Carl and I must . . . be going. We'll chat about it tonight when ye call with the results of your tests."

Sammy thrusts out his lower lip. *He's pouting!* 'Tis just as he did so many years ago when he was a wee lad.

"OK," he says and nods. "I'll be patient until then."

He slaps his head. "You've really got to get going, don't you? I forgot all about your *sun* allergy! I suppose you've got it too, don't you?" He looks at Carl.

"That's right," Carl says.

"I *wish* I could test the virus and see if it is photoreactive!"

"It is," I say. "I've exposed it to direct sunlight and it is *highly* reactive: Any sample containing the live virus bursts into flame. Even samples long infused with the dead virus are highly flammable."

"Fascinating!" he says, tenting his hands again and placing them around his nose and chin as he did before. He stares at the two of us.

We rise to go. Sammy stands as well and lifts Carl's blood-spotted, crumpled shirt in both hands. "I'll get right on this, and I'll call you as soon as I know anything. OK?"

"My thanks, laddie!" I say and extend my hand to shake his in farewell. He's about to take mine, when there's a knock at the door.

Sammy looks past me and says, "Yes?"

The door opens, and a man with slightly graying, close-cropped hair and a pleasant face pokes his head in and says, "Hey, Sam. Are we still on for racquetball this morning? I called your cell, and your wife answered and said you'd already left, but you'd forgotten your gym clothes and, apparently, your phone."

"Tony!" Sammy says, slapping his forehead again. "I totally spaced it! Something came up. I can't. I've got to do a favor for an old friend." He points at me.

The newcomer steps into the office. He's wearing khakis and a plaid dress shirt with a tie. He's got a gym bag slung over one shoulder. He extends a hand to me and says, "Hi, old friend of Sam's. I'm Tony Lupescu."

Somewhat flustered, Sammy says, "Moira, Carl, this is Dr. Anton Lupescu. He teaches ancient scripture here. Tony, this is Dr. Moira MacDonald . . . I mean, Moira *Morgan*. And this is her husband Carl. I've known Moira since I was a kid. She was my Primary . . . uh, I mean, I knew her when I was a kid in Primary."

I take Tony's hand and say, "How very nice to meet ye, Dr. Lupescu. The name is Romanian, is it nae?"

"Yes, it is. And call me Tony," he says with a genuine smile. There is nae trace of any European accent. He turns to Carl. "Tony Lupescu," he says offering his hand to Carl.

"Carl Morgan," Carl responds, taking his hand.

"I usually play racquetball with Sam here a couple of times a week before classes, but never *this* early."

"How come you're here before the sun's up, Tony?" Sammy asks.

"Oh, I just finished an early-morning meeting with Dr. Corelli," Tony says.

"I don't know Dr. Corelli," Sammy says.

"He teaches European history. He's a visiting prof, here just for the year," Tony explains. "A very early riser."

"Well, it was nice to meet you, Tony," Carl says, "but We have to get going."

"I'll call you with the results," Sammy says.

"Thanks, Sammy," I say.

We turn to go, but there is nae a lot of room in the wee office, so we cannae sidle past Tony all that easily. He's nae moving. Instead he's looking at me intently. *Why?*

Suddenly, he jerks as if startled.

"I'm sorry," he says, stepping aside. "Lost in thought."

As we pass him and step out of the office door, Tony touches my arm, stopping me.

"Forgive me," he says, "I know it's kinda personal . . ."

I turn my head to look at him.

He continues, ". . . but you look too young to be a childhood friend of Sam's."

"Why, thank ye," I say and give him a smile, but I'm nae pleased. It makes me horribly uncomfortable when people comment on or question my age. The way he's looking at me is giving me the willies. And I've had enough of that for one night.

"They really have to go," Sammy says.

"No," Tony continues, shaking his head slightly, "that's not what I mean. You look like a *co-ed.*"

"*Tony!*" Sammy says, shock and indignation plain on his face.

Tony visibly shakes himself. "Oh, gosh! I'm sorry. That was . . . rude. Forgive me."

"Ye're forgiven," I say. *I'm nae so sure I like this man.*

"And you're an *old* friend of Sam's, right? You've lived in Utah for a *while,* right?"

He's asking very pointed questions. What's he driving at?

"Aye, I've been here for ages," I reply.

"And you're up in Ogden, you say?"

"We didn't say," Carl says pointedly. "And we really have to go."

We said nary a thing about Ogden.

"Right," Tony says. "You need to go. And quick! The sun'll be rising soon."

My breath catches. *This mortal knows what we are.*

Carl scowls beside me.

"Tony," Sammy says, obviously puzzled, "what's going on?"

A smile spreads across Tony's face.

"It's OK," he says to Carl and me. "I'm a *friend.* I'm on your side. And I'm honored . . . *very* honored to meet the Breakers."

Chapter 16

WOULD SOMEBODY *please* tell me what's going on here?" Sammy cries. "What are you talking about? It's like everyone is speaking in code, and I'm the only one who doesn't have a decoder ring!"

Lupescu knows what we are! This mortal knows who we are! He mentioned Ogden, and he knows we're the so-called 'Breakers'!

"Who *are* you?" Carl says, clearly angry, to Lupescu. "How do you . . ."

". . . know who and what you are?" Lupescu says, still grinning like a wolf.

"Aye. Explain yourself!"

"Well, *somebody* better explain *something*!" Sammy demands.

"OK," Lupescu says, the grin slackening, but nae entirely disappearing. "I'm . . . *affiliated* with a group of . . . your kind that has been gathering here over the last few months."

"You mean the Congregation?" Carl says, nearly snarling.

"No!" Lupescu says. "Oh, Heavens, no!"

"Then what?" I say.

"Not the Congregation," he replies. "No way! I think something really *bad* is going on up there. And before you ask, I'm not talking about your traditional *Cult*, either. Nothing like that! We call our group the . . . you know . . . *Stake*. Kind of a play on words. It's sort of funny . . . OK, maybe not so funny. If you've been following the web traffic about the *gathering* here, surely you've heard of the . . . uh . . . *Stake*." He makes a quick, but meaningful glance in Sammy's direction. *He's trying to be cryptic for Sammy's sake.*

Carl and I exchange a hurried look, and then we both nod.

"We've heard of it," Carl says. "We assumed it was different names for the same group."

"No," Lupescu replies, shaking his head. "Two very different groups with, I think, two very different goals. I'm pretty sure Paul is enslaving his followers . . . or *worse* . . . and all I'm doing is simply trying to . . ."

A loud noise stops Lupescu mid sentence. Sammy has slammed a large book down onto his desk.

"WILL SOMEBODY *PLEASE* tell me what's going on?" he demands.

"Forgive me, Sam," Lupescu says with a grimace. "This really isn't fair to you." He points at Carl and me and says, "But they *really* have to go. I'll explain it to you once they're gone. I really meant to recruit you into this anyway. We need your expertise. But we have to let them go."

He turns to us and pulls a card out of his wallet. He offers it to Carl, who takes it. Both Carl and I look at it. It says simply, "The Vampire Stake," and it lists a phone number and an e-mail address.

"Please call me," Lupescu says. "I really need to talk to you. *We* really need you. My people are *terrified*, especially with Paul in the area. We've lost a couple of good people recently to Paul and his Congregation. We need to know how you *freed* yourselves . . . from Lilith's control."

"How do ye know *any* of this?" I say in wonder. "Who *are* ye?"

"Me?" he says. "I'm just someone who has studied your *condition* or at least the *stories* of people like you for a *long* time. Well, not long by *your* standards, but most of my life. I'm just trying to help those who are attempting to find their way back."

He's emphasizing certain words to convey special meaning to Carl and me without letting Sammy in on the fact that he's talking about vampires.

"You sound a lot like Müller," Carl says.

Aye, he does.

"Müller?" Lupescu says, confused.

"Paul," I say.

"Oh," Lupescu says, his eyes widening. "No, we . . . the Stake, that is . . . just *meet*. We talk. We discuss. I'm teaching them the gospel."

"It was *YOU!*" Carl exclaims.

"What d'ye mean, laddie?" I say, looking at Carl.

"From my dream!" he says. "He's the professor from my dream!"

I gasp. I note that Lupescu gasps as well.

"Your *dream?*" Lupescu says. "You don't dream!"

"We're nae *supposed* to dream," I say.

"But I've dreamt about *you* repeatedly," Carl says.

"OK. You guys are really freaking me out!" This comes from Sammy.

Carl, Lupescu, and I turn in Sammy's direction. I catch a glimpse of the sky outside a window. 'Tis beginning to lighten!

"Carl," I say, "we must go *now!*" I grab his hand and we flee. "Call me, Sammy!" I yell over my shoulder. "We'll talk."

"Don't forget to call *me!*" Lupescu says. "We *need* you!"

As we run toward the building exit, we're hurriedly applying sunscreen from the tubes we keep in our individual long coats. A young woman passes us in the hallway and stares at us. We must present a comical sight as we smear cream over all our exposed or potentially exposed skin.

I screw the top onto my homemade sunscreen just as Carl finishes applying his own sunscreen. I stuff the tube into my coat pocket. I reach into the neck of my coat and pull out the hood I had specially sewn into it and pull it low over my face. Next come the gloves from my pockets. Now the sunglasses. I look at Carl and see that he has prepared himself in like fashion. *Too bad he does nae have his cowboy hat anymore. I think it makes him look* rugged. *I know* he *thought it just made him look silly.*

We've reached the exit. The sky looks dangerously bright. We plunge outside. We probably have nae more than a handful of minutes to reach the safety of our car.

'Tis nae enough.

There are a number of people about, walking to early morning classes. So flying is out of the question.

We *will* be exposed to the light.

We start to run . . . nae at the speed that we're capable of, but at a speed that mortals will nae think is . . . superhuman.

The first deadly rays of the Sun begin to stream o'er the mountains as we reach Candice's apartment complex. The quickest route to the car involves going through the complex.

It has become a full-blown crime scene.

There are three police cruisers in the parking lot, and there is also an unmarked car with a small flashing light on top. The whole area where the attack took place is taped off. One police officer is keeping guard over the taped-off area. Another is questioning a witness. *There was a witness? What did she see?* A third officer seems to be watching over everything, controlling the area.

The would-be rapist is naewhere to be seen. He has already been taken away, I suppose.

We slow to a walk. We cannae afford to attract attention. We can try to keep to the shadows, but the Sun is peeking over the mountains now.

Where's Candice?

Ah, there she is. She's sitting in the unmarked car, talking with what appears to be a plainclothes detective. She glances at us, and her eyes widen in recognition and shock.

She's wondering how we're able to be out in the daylight. Maybe she expects us to sparkle.

How I do hate *that book!*

If there were nobody to observe us, we could be at my car in seconds, but 'twill take us another minute or so to get to safety at this pace. So long as we can escape notice or delays, our protection should last that long.

I hope.

I dig into my purse for my car key. Best to have it ready for . . .

"It's *them!*"

The voice is that of the lass who was being questioned by the police officer. She takes a few quick steps in our direction. She stops and points at the two of us and says, "They're the ones! They're the *vampires*! I saw them!"

Ach! This is bad. This is very, very bad. She must have seen the attack and our part in stopping it.

We quicken our pace a wee bit.

The policeman has followed the lass who is still pointing at us. He comes to stand beside her and says, "Are you sure? How can you tell? Did you get a look at their faces?"

"No, but I recognize the coats they're wearing," she replies.

We keep on walking. Twenty yards and we'll be around the corner and out of sight, if nae out of the Sun. Then perhaps we can move more quickly. We cannae risk being detained.

"Hold on, you two!" the officer calls to us. "I need to talk to you."

My first instinct is to run, but Carl grabs my hand and we halt.

"We cannae stay in the light much longer, laddie," I whisper so only he can hear.

"I know," he replies just as softly, "but we can't afford to draw more attention by having him detain or follow us."

"And how much more attention will we draw when we burst into flame?" I reply.

Slowly we turn toward the officer. We cannae reasonably get into the shade. So we pull our hoods low and turn so our faces are hidden by the shadows. We both remove our sunglasses. We need to be able to make eye contact with him to use Persuasion.

As the policeman approaches us he says, "There was an incident here about forty-five minutes ago. A young woman was taken from her bed at knifepoint."

"How awful!" I say, doing my best to sound horrified. I'm nae much for acting. "Is she OK?"

"Yes," he says, nae betraying emotion, "she's fine. She was rescued, she says, by a couple of Good Samaritans . . . a man and a woman. A witness has identified the two of you as being involved."

"What?" Carl says. "You mean she thinks we attacked the victim?"

"No, she says you attacked the *suspect*. She says . . ." and now he looks a wee bit embarrassed ". . . that you drank his blood. She says you're . . . vampires."

I finally manage to fix him with my stare. "Officer, you know how ridiculous that sounds," I say in a low, but imperious voice. "You need to let us go."

He hesitates and blinks a few times, but I can feel the Persuasion does nae take hold. He must be very strong-willed.

What are we going to do? My legs already feel hot in my jeans.

"No," he says slowly, and somewhat suspiciously, "I need to ask you a few questions."

"It sounds like your witness has seen one too many bad movies," Carl says. "Besides, we're out in the daylight . . ."

There is a sudden scream from behind the officer. He turns to see the source.

So does everyone else.

A very quick glance reveals that 'tis Candice, still sitting in the unmarked car. I think she's trying to give us a chance to get away.

Clever lassie! My thanks to ye!

And that's all the opening we need. Carl takes my hand, as we both replace our sunglasses and wheel about. We run, this time at full vampiric speed.

We dash out of the parking lot and turn to put the building between us and the mortals. This takes us less than a second and a half. It takes us another three seconds to reach our car and the safety of our tinted windows.

I'm about to start the car when Carl says, "Hold on a second. Let him give up looking for us. We don't want him to notice the car driving away and take down your license plate."

We watch the corner of the apartment building. Sure enough, the officer comes into view. He scans the streets and, seeing nary a sign of us, turns and heads back to the scene of the crime.

Why did he give up so easily? I dinnae ken enough about police procedure to hazard a guess.

I wait a few seconds more to be sure, and then I start the car. We both breathe a sigh of relief as we pull away from the curb.

"Did you touch anything in the apartment?" Carl asks abruptly.

"Aye, laddie, I did," I reply. "The phone, the kitchen faucet, a plastic tumbler."

"Tumbler?" he says puzzled.

"A tall plastic drinking glass," I reply with mock annoyance. "Honestly! *Men!* Ye dinnae ken anything!"

He chuckles. Then his expression becomes sober. "Well," he says, "they may not look for fingerprints in those areas. *Hopefully* not."

"Well, my fingerprints should nae be on file anywhere. I've endeavored to avoid that type of thing all my life."

"I'm sure you have. Still . . ."

"Still, we would nae want that to come back and haunt us, now, would we? 'Ogden' is bad enough!"

"Uh-huh."

"I did nae touch the faucet with my fingertips, so that would be clean. The tumbler would nae take a good print with its rougher surface. The phone now . . . that could be a problem."

"Well," he says, sighing, "there's nothing we can do about it now except leave it in the Lord's hands. Hopefully, the police will disregard the witness's account of vampires."

"Aye, laddie. We could use a break. We dinnae need more attention right now."

"Wouldn't your prints be on file at the hospital?"

I smirk. "They *should* be. *Somehow*, I dinnae e'er quite make it down to personnel to get that taken care of. I've even had the HR clerk track me down with a pad and ink in hand, but for some reason she left without accomplishing her task."

"'For some reason?'"

"Aye, poor lass got confused as to why she was there."

"Right," he says and grins.

As I pull onto the freeway, Carl says, "What are we going to do about Dr. Lupescu? It really freaked me out when it became obvious that he knows all about us."

"Aye, it gave me the willies as well."

"You said that his name was Romanian. Isn't that where Dracula is supposed to be from?"

"Aye, Vlad Tepesh, Vlad the Impaler, Vlad Dracula (his name means 'son of the dragon') was a voivode, a prince of Wallachia in the fifteenth century. Wallachia is part of modern-day Romania. It included Transylvania. And, aye, there is a Castle Dracula in Transylvania."

"Really? Wow." He pauses. "He wasn't one of *us*, was he?"

"Ach, nae! He was a mass murderer, though. He was about as evil as they come, to be sure, but he was nae a vampire. We have Mr. Stoker's silly wee novel to thank for that, as well as for the rubbish that most people believe about us."

"Did you ever meet him?"

"Meet whom? Stoker?"

He nods.

"Nae, although I could have. I was in Washington, DC, when Stoker and the famous actor he managed, Henry Irving, visited the White House during the tenure of Teddy Roosevelt. But I did ne'er make a point of it. He, Stoker, was a bit of a philanderer and I've nae stomach for men (or women) of that sort. Although, now that ye mention it, 'twould have been amusing to let him try to make a pass at me and then scare the Devil right out of him. That way he would ne'er have gone near another woman, other than his wife, again."

Carl chuckles. "That would have made a great story."

I sigh. "Aye. Opportunities lost and all that."

"What were you doing in Washington, DC?" he asks.

"'Twas in 1902. I was there to see a display of relics on loan to the Smithsonian Institution. 'Twas purported to include a nail from the True Cross, a piece of wood from the Ark of Noah, and the head from the Spear of Longinus. I was searching for anything truly holy at the time. I had been attending medical lectures in Philadelphia when I heard that the relics were going to be there."

"What's the Spear of Longinus?"

"Supposedly 'twas the spear that Joshua carried at the Battle of Jericho and, much later, the spear that pierced the side of Christ on the cross. Longinus was the name of the Roman centurion who thrust the spear into the Lord's side. There are at least three relics that are purported to be the actual spearhead, and this was nae one of the three. But I had to go and see."

"So did you get to see the relics?"

"'Twas difficult. Sunscreen was nae invented until 1938. I had to rely on the heavy clothing customary at the time, with the large hats. I usually wore a wide hat with a heavy veil such as would later be popular with ladies riding in early automobiles. The Smithsonian relied heavily on natural lighting in those days. But I braved the day to approach the holy. I was disappointed, though. The spear had gone missing and was nae to be found. The nail looked old, but was probably nae more than a few centuries in age. The wood fragment did nae look like much. And neither of them *felt* holy."

"Not like the temple," he says.

"Aye, 'twas nae like the temple. I felt the holiness of the temple in St. George the moment I stepped onto the grounds. Nae, at the time I went to see the relics, I was still under the impression that *things* had power. I did nae understand that the true power comes from the priesthood or the actual presence of the Divine."

"Anyway," he says slowly, obviously changing the subject, "we were talking about Lupescu."

"Aye, laddie. We were."

"It was creepy," Carl says. "He seems to know so much. But *why*? Why does he creep us out so much? I mean, he wasn't *evil*."

"I think perhaps 'twas just the combination of him knowing so much and there being nae time to really find out what he's all about."

"If he's Romanian, do you think he has some obsession with vampires? Surely he doesn't want to *become* one. That can't be it, can it?"

"He doesn't seem like the type," I reply.

"Oh, and what type would *that* be, sweet, wholesome Moira, love of my life, or at least my immortality?"

"I was nae so pure when I sought out Conversion at Sarah's hand. But, nae, he seemed just very . . . *friendly*."

"Yeah," Carl agrees. "He seemed like a nice guy. He was just talking about really awful stuff as if . . ." He looks like he's searching for a word.

". . . as if he just found the Holy Grail," I finish for him.

"Yeah," he says and nods in agreement. "Maybe it's just a scholarly obsession."

"But, laddie, ye said that in your dream he was *teaching* a classroom full of vampires. And *he* said that he was teaching them the gospel."

"That fits with my dream. Maybe he's telling the truth."

"To what end?" I ask. "With the exception of ye, the prophesied Unwilling, all of our kind are murderers. Most are murders many, many times over. Ye know 'twould take abject repentance and a special clearance from the President of the Church to allow any of them to be baptized. In my own case, I spent more than two centuries in my search for redemption."

"I don't know," Carl says, placing a hand on my thigh. "But, it reminds me a little of the sons of Mosiah in the Book of Mormon. They went to preach to their enemies, a 'bloodthirsty' people. They helped save many, many souls, including Lamoni and his father, two very wicked men with a lot of blood on their hands."

"I know what ye mean, laddie. I'm nae saying that they should nae be *taught*. I'm merely saying that I cannae imagine that . . . well, that the Prophet is going to grant clearances in every case or in *any* case. There just is nae enough time. "

"Do you remember," Carl asks, "the people of Anti-Nephi-Lehi?"

In the Book of Mormon, Lamoni and many of his people repented, and then his father the king and many of his people repented. They buried their weapons and covenanted never to take another life. The king (Lamoni's father) gave up the throne and changed his name to Anti-Nephi-Lehi. He completely rejected his heritage and submitted himself to the will of God.

"Aye, laddie, I remember."

"But not *everybody* was converted," he continues. "Do you remember when the new king sent soldiers against the converts?"

When the soldiers came against the people of God, the converts bowed themselves down to the earth and prayed. They would nae defend themselves because they'd made a covenant with God. More than a thousand men, women, and children were slaughtered. But then, many of the soldiers laid down their arms and joined the converts, even at the cost of their own lives.

I nod. "Aye, laddie. I think I see what ye're getting at: ye're saying 'tis ne'er too late to begin yer repentance."

"I don't know what'll happen." He sighs. "I don't know how sincere *any* of these Penitents are. And if they're anything like Bartlett . . . I just don't know. If they're like Rolf . . ."

"Speaking of Rolf," I say, "we should check in with him and Sarah."

"Sounds good," he replies, pulling out his cell phone. He begins texting. Soon enough there is a beep, and he reads Rolf's response. "'Basket,'" he reads out loud. "That's the safe word. He thinks we need to have two safe words so that both sides can inform the other that all is clear."

"That's sounds wise," I say. "What do ye think?"

"Way ahead of you, sweetheart. The new safe words are 'willow' and 'aspirin.'"

I chuckle. *At least they're related.*

"I *thought* you'd like that," Carl says with a smile. "Did you ever use willow bark to make a pain-killer?"

"That I did, laddie," I say with a smile. "Long ago."

"The duress word is 'fishing.'" He texts a bit more. "He reminds me about getting a weapon for Sarah. He says she's Sleeping."

"I know a decent swordsmith," I say. "I'll call him once I get to work. He should have something that would suit. He'll even deliver it, if I ask."

"How do you know a *swordsmith?*" he asks in wonder. "I mean, I know you've been around here a long time, but why would you seek out a swordsmith when you already had weapons enough for you *and* me?"

"I'm a swordmaster. Remember, laddie? Actually, I'm old-fashioned enough to prefer the term 'swordmistress.' Swordcraft is an art form that I appreciate. I have weapons sufficient for myself, but I've been the patron for a blacksmith-turned-swordsmith up in Hooper for decades, as I was with his father before him. I want to see the art preserved, particularly when it comes to Scottish weapons."

"When you say, 'patron,' do you mean you subsidize his work?"

"Aye, laddie. Ye know I've laid aside a wee bit of money over the years."

"'A wee bit?' You gave away a million bucks last year anonymously."

"*We* gave it away. Ye consented to it."

"Yeah," he says with a shake of his head. "I should've figured you might've accumulated some wealth over the centuries, but I had *no* idea."

"My expenses have been low."

He snorts. "I'll say." He sighs. "It's amazing how much you save when you don't pay for food and your home has been paid off for more than half a century."

"Get their room number," I say, and Carl immediately begins to text the question. "Tell him I'll arrange a delivery today."

The phone beeps again, and Carl reads, "Four-two-seven." He begins to send another, longer message. "I'm going to fill Rolf in on what we learned tonight." Carl enters his messages with vampiric speed.

"Ask him if *he* has been dreaming and if *he* is experiencing abnormal hunger," I say, dreading the answer.

After a few rapid exchanges, Carl says, "No, he hasn't, but his reaction to the fact that *we're* experiencing both is what you'd expect: shock and concern. And he isn't offering any theories either."

After a few more exchanges, he closes his phone. "OK. He'll check in with me after Sarah wakes up."

"So 'tis only the two of us experiencing this."

"So far as we know," he replies. "What makes *us* unique?"

"I ken what makes *ye* unique. Ye're the Unwilling. But is that what makes ye susceptible to dreams and such? And what about *me?* What makes *me* different . . . and susceptible?"

He strokes my thigh gently. "I know what makes you unique and special. You are the purest soul I've ever met."

"What about your Sharon?"

"Sharon was . . . *is* special and practically perfect in her own way." He is silent for a wee bit. "I think that's part of the reason why God took her and Lucy and April and Joseph home: she was needed on the other side." He pauses and then affectionately squeezes my leg. I lay a hand atop his. "And," he says slowly, "it seems that God has a mission for you and me that required some . . . *changes* in my life. I have to trust that He knows what He's doing."

Carl turns his hand over. I place my hand in his. He lifts it to his lips. "I love you."

"And I love ye, ye dear, sweet man."

My phone rings, ruining the moment. I fish it out of my purse and look at it.

"It's Sammy," I say out loud.

This is going to be interesting. How did Sammy react to what Lupescu told him?

I open my phone and say, "Hello, Sammy."

I can hear him breathing, but otherwise there is silence on the other end.

"Sammy?" I say.

"How could you?" he says, clearly upset.

"Sammy, I . . ."

"How could you not have *told* me?"

"Ye have to understand, laddie, I . . ."

"This is like the coolest thing *EVER!*"

"*What?*"

"My Primary teacher is a *vampire!*"

Well, at least he is nae angry.

"The mysterious and beautiful Sister MacDonald turns out to be one of the undead!" he says. He sounds positively giddy!

Carl smiles and shakes his head in amusement.

"I'm nae *undead*," I say. *I hate *that term!* "I'm very much alive."

"Sun allergy! Right! Oh, my aching butt!"

"Sammy, let me explain . . ."

"Oh, Tony filled me in. He explained a *lot* to me. Now I see everything in a different light. Does the bishop know?"

"Aye, laddie, he knows. They've all known for more than half a century. I had to have special permission to be baptized."

"Yeah," he says (and I can almost *hear* him grinning), "Tony said that would have been necessary. From the First Presidency, no less! But," he says, and his voice is suddenly serious, "you haven't killed anyone in a while, right?"

"I've nae taken a life in two and a half centuries."

"Did they all deserve to die?"

I'm silent as the grave for a moment.

"I'm sorry. That's . . . none of my business, is it?" he says.

"Laddie, 'twas a time of war. They did horrible things to me and my family and the man I was to marry. I cannae say they *deserved* to die. All I can say is that after centuries of repentance, God has forgiven me. I can say nae more than that."

"What about your husband, Carl? How many has he killed?"

"Sammy, my dear, sweet Carl has nae taken a mortal life as a vampire. He is unique."

"Never?"

"Nae, he didn't even *want* to become a vampire."

"That's not possible. Tony says you have to *choose* to become a . . ."

There is an audible gasp on the other end of the line, but it does nae come from Sammy. The gasp was too quiet. It was someone else there with him. *Lupescu?* There is suddenly a lot of noise, almost as if Sammy dropped the phone.

"Carl is the *Unwilling?*" The voice on the phone is Lupescu's.

Carl's head snaps toward me.

Ach! Nae! I've done it again! I do very well at keeping my own secrets, but nae at keeping Carl's.

"The Unwilling . . . from the Curse?" Lupescu says, his voice breathless with excitement. "And *you're* the *Penitent!* And you married in the temple, right? This changes *everything!*"

Chapter 17

PLEASE, OH, *PLEASE*! You've *got* to meet with us!" Lupescu is pleading with me over the phone.

"How do ye know *any* of this?" I cry. "Even if the vampires in your group are truly Penitent, they are nae free to speak of the Great Secret. 'Tis one of the greatest prohibitions Lilith has made."

"*You're* talking about it," he says.

"Aye, but I'm free of Lilith's control."

"That's *right*!" he says, as if that explains everything. "You two are the *Breakers*! You've shown that your kind *can* break free! That's why they're all coming here: to find out how you did it. You've given them hope . . . hope like they've never had! Most of them were *suicidal* not that long ago."

"But, from what ye are saying, Dr. Lupescu, it sounds as if they're all still bound by their Oaths and by the Covenant. Surely none of *them* revealed the Great Secret to ye."

"Tony. Please call me Tony. Can I call you Moira?" He does nae pause for me to reply. "Of *course* none of them revealed it. I discovered it myself. Vampires . . . or the study of vampire lore, rather . . . has been an avocation of mine for most of my life."

"Why? Because ye're Romanian?"

"There is *that*, yes, but it's in my blood, you could say. My great-great-grandfather was a vampire."

"Really?" Carl says to me. "I know you said it's possible, but . . ."

"Do ye mean to tell me, Tony," I say, "that your great-great-grandfather *became* a vampire or that he sired your ancestor *as* a vampire?"

"Oh, he was a vampire, all right, but he was a Penitent. He fell in love with and married my great-great-grandmother, who was mortal, obviously. It happened in Romania a long time ago . . . well, not so long ago by your standards. After he met her, he lived as sinless a life as he could. He stayed with her and loved her and cared for her and was true to her until she died at the ripe old age of a hundred and seven. It was a very romantic story."

Ah, if 'twere true, 'twould be very romantic indeed. I can just picture a young-looking man caring for and loving his aged, white-haired sweetheart till her dying day.

"After she died, he disappeared. The story goes that he knelt at her graveside and exposed himself to the Sun with a prayer for redemption on his lips. It was a family tradition to tell the story and show where the heat of his passing charred and cracked her gravestone."

"But how do ye know about the Curse?"

"I was getting to that. Before he died, he wrote it all down in my great-great-grandmother's Bible. That's how I know about the Curse. He wrote it there. In Latin. And nobody in the family could read Latin. Heck, most of the family couldn't read at all."

Writing it down in a dead language without the express intention to show it to a mortal would nae violate Lilith's command, I suppose.

"We all knew the stories of great-great-grandfather in my family, how he never aged, how he avoided the Sun, how he never ate or drank . . . how he died. In Romanian folklore, *strigoi* and *moroi* . . . vampires, you know . . . aren't always monsters, you see. On occasion, they're protectors.

"So, in our family, we assumed he was a vampire, but nobody in my family could read Latin, so nobody knew what he wrote. Perhaps he intended it that way to avoid Lilith's prohibition. We took it to a priest once, but he told us to burn the Bible because it contained blasphemies.

"My parents moved to the States before I was born. And, when I attended college, I studied Latin just so I could translate it. So now I know . . . and I've learned a lot more since."

"How did ye meet so many vampires, much less become their teacher?"

"Well, it started with Dr. Lorenzo Corelli. He was the *very early riser* I was meeting with this morning before I showed up at Sam's office. Do you remember?"

"Vaguely," I say. "Ye said something about a Dr. Corelli."

"Well, he was the first vampire I met. It was about six months ago. He's a visiting professor teaching European history. The first time I met him I was struck with the weirdest sense of déjà vu. I was sure I'd seen him before. It really bugged me. I felt like it was really *important* that I remember *where* I knew him from."

He pauses for a tick. *A dramatic pause?*

"Once I woke up in the middle of the night," he continues, "and couldn't get back to sleep. So I started thumbing through a Renaissance art book. I minored in art history, you see. So, I was looking at a fresco called 'The School of Athens' by Raphael, because it's a favorite of mine. I wrote a research paper on it in college."

Another pause.

"And that's when I saw him," he says. "Dr. Corelli was a dead ringer for one of the students in the foreground of the painting! Of course, with my family history, I immediately leaped to a conclusion: Corelli must have been one of Raphael's models! He must be a vampire! He teaches in the Joseph F. Smith Building on campus, and that building has its own underground parking lot. His classroom is in the basement. His office is on the shaded north side of the inner courtyard. He could spend the whole day inside and never see the Sun."

Wouldn't that be convenient!

"So," Lupescu continues, "I was determined to investigate. I'd never met an actual vampire. I had to know if my suspicions and theories were correct. So, I struck up an acquaintance with him. It was easy. He seemed to take to me right away. I kept inviting him to lunch and kept bringing cookies or cornbread that my wife had baked. He never accepted either an invitation or food, of course. I sat in on a few of his lectures. He's very popular with his students. He's able to describe history as if he had been there. Maybe he *was*."

Aye.

"Anyway," Lupescu says, "he and I got along really well. As much as I wanted to learn from him, he was also a great listener. He seemed genuinely interested in me and my family. He's been like an uncle to my kids. He's really a gentle soul. He hasn't told me much about his background . . . the way he was before he became a Penitent, but Lorenzo Corelli wouldn't harm a fly."

He gasps. "Oh my heck! Did I just make a Hitchcock reference?" he says. "Wow! Hope that wasn't Freudian!"

"If ye suspected he was a vampire," I say, "why on earth would ye approach him? Do ye wish to die before your time? And to expose your children to him!"

"Well," he said, "he's great with children. Like I said, he's a really gentle soul. And I didn't take him to meet my family until I was sure of what he was and that he was no longer a danger to anyone. And there was just that *connection* there . . . like we'd known each other all our lives."

He hesitates. "And, I approached him . . . if for no other reason than because there were students to protect. But that wasn't my motivation . . . not really. I just wanted to *learn*! I hunger for *knowledge* the way *you* hunger for blood. Just think of what someone like *you* could teach us mortals! You've *lived* history!"

"We've lived in the shadows!" I say with disgust. "We spend our lives in an endless quest to sate our basest hungers. We're nae *wiser* for the centuries we've lived. We're parasites at best and serial killers at worst!"

"But there's something *noble* about you Penitents! Everything you say is true, of course, but *you've* turned your back on evil and, in spite of your . . . *needs* and urges, you have resolved to repent, *even if there is no hope.*

"But," he continues, excited, "I believe there *is* hope! You and your husband . . . I can't believe I've met the Unwilling and the Penitent . . . you've been sealed in the temple of God. You've overcome everything!"

"What we've overcome," I say, "we've done with the help of God. And we must endure to the end as everyone else must. We can fall just as anybody can."

"But you're 'the Unwilling and the Penitent . . . joined in the House of God'! You *can't* fall! Adam's Prophecy . . ."

Sitting beside me, Carl shakes his head vehemently. "We almost fell last night!" he growls.

"We had a very close call last night on our way to meet with Sammy," I say.

"What do you mean?" Lupescu says, the alarm clear in his voice.

"We nearly killed someone. I came closer last night than I have in centuries. Carl had a similar reaction. It's becoming nigh impossible to control our . . . urges of late."

I pause. "We . . . *can* fall."

"But, if *you* fall . . ." Lupescu's voice falters.

"God will call someone else," I say.

Carl gives my thigh a gentle squeeze.

How I love him! I lived for centuries without him, but now . . . I cannae imagine life without him. And, if we succeed and fulfill the Prophecy . . . well, then we will have eternity together. If we fail . . . Nae! I cannae consider the alternative.

There is silence on the phone, except for Lupescu's quiet breathing.

"Please," he says, his voice nigh a whisper, "meet with us. We can help each other."

I glance at Carl and raise an eyebrow. He nods.

"When and where do ye meet?"

Lupescu sighs in profound relief.

◢ ◢ ◢

"They won't let me leave."

Winnie is lying on her bed in the ICU. She's glaring at me, and the loathing that emanates from her face is like a venomous fog filling the room. Her voice is still hoarse, but 'tis nae making the horrid hollow sound it was last night.

"Winnie," I say as gently as I can, "your injuries were too severe. We'll be moving ye out of the ICU this morning, if all goes well, but ye'll nae be able to care for yourself at all for a few days. After that, ye'll be in a wheelchair for a wee bit. Is there anyone ye can stay with or who can stay with ye for a while?"

"They won't let me leave," she repeats. "My sister's coming. She could take care of me, but they won't let me leave for seventy-two hours on *your orders*!" Her raspy tone carries all the vitriol that it would if 'twere her normal, bitter voice.

"Ah, Winnie," I say, shaking my head sadly. "'Tis true. I cannae let ye go until we can be sure that ye dinnae pose a danger to yourself."

"You can't keep me here!"

"Actually, I can. Ye're on a seventy-two hour psychiatric hold."

She flinches at the implications of the word.

"Ye attempted to kill yourself. I'm bound by law and ethics to keep ye under observation for three days so that we can be certain that ye dinnae try to harm yourself again."

She stares daggers of hatred at me, and her breathing quickens. *She's trying to find something particularly nasty to say to me.*

"It will nae make ye feel better," I say.

That stops her. She looks at me in shock and confusion.

I place a hand over hers. She flinches, but does nae, or perhaps, can nae move her hand away.

I continue, "It will nae take away the pain to say something horrible to me. Ye will still be just as miserable as ye were before, except that ye will add a wee bit of guilt to the burden your soul is already laboring under."

Winnie's jaw trembles.

"And whatever it was that drove ye to suicide," I say, a bit more forcefully, "will still be there, gnawing at ye. Once I've lifted the suicide watch and released ye into the care of your sister, ye'll still be haunted by whatever demons ye had before. Eventually, ye're going to have to banish those demons or else someday ye *will* succeed in killing yourself, and there is nary a thing I can do to stop ye."

"You could drop dead," she says, averting her eyes. "You're the only demon who haunts me."

The way things are going, Winnie, I may nae survive the week.

"That would nae solve your problems."

"*You're* my problem. It's all because of *you*." She nearly spits that last pronoun at me. "It's because of *you* my Heber left me."

He left ye because ye drove him away with your jealousies and your constant nagging and sniping. Ye cannae see that because ye would have to admit that ye were at fault, when it's so much easier to blame someone else.

"Winnie, there was ne'er anything between Heber and me. I doubt we said two words to each other that were nae the usual pleasantries exchanged in church. To me he was ever 'Brother Morrison' and nae more."

"He couldn't take his eyes off you!" she croaks like some huge, bloated toad. "None of the men could! None of them *can*! A woman your age! How old are you . . . you . . . you *witch*?"

I shake my head. "Old enough to know that ye dinnae really want the answer. Ye only need someone to blame. And ye'll ne'er be happy until ye . . ."

"HAPPY?" It comes out as a hoarse shriek. "You *stole* my only chance for happiness! He's gone! Gone! And he's never . . . coming . . . back!" Her massive body is wracked with pathetic, heaving sobs.

"Heber left more than two decades ago, Winnie." *What is she going on about? Surely, this cannae be what drove her to suicide.*

"He's getting married again!" she chokes out between sobs. "He wanted a . . . *clearance* . . . so he can marry some . . . *redheaded SLUT* he met . . . in

Idaho! He wants to . . . get married in the . . . temple again! I refused, but . . . since I didn't have . . . *cause*, he got his clearance . . . anyway!"

"Winnie," I say astonished, "is that why ye . . ."

"The letter from his bishop came yesterday!" she wails. "And it's all . . . your . . . fault!"

"Winnie, I . . ."

"Why can't you just . . . *age* like everyone else? What did you do? Sell your . . . soul to the Devil, you bi . . ."

"Winnie, trust me when I say, ye dinnae want to be in my . . . condition." *Although ye very nearly have the right of it.*

"You *enticed* . . . my Heber. It's not fair. You . . . are so . . . *pretty*! It's not natural! How many times . . . have you . . . had surgery?"

This is pointless. I feel anger rising in me. Winnie has nae provoked me to anger before, but I'm *sick* of this.

"I have the face I was born with. I've nae done a thing to it."

"Lying *whore*!" she spits.

My anger boils up. I *must* keep it in check!

"And do ye want to know what my *face* has got me, Winnie?" I say in a voice as icy as an arctic tomb. "I'll tell ye. I was *raped* by forty-five men. *Forty . . . five.* 'Twas so brutal, I very nearly died. Did I entice *them*? Was *that* my fault? They murdered my father and my mother, but they raped me. Then they left me for dead. Would I *had* died! That's what my *beauty* has got me."

Winnie stares up at me. She looks me in the eye, and her expression is unreadable at first. Then, suddenly, I see the hatred fill her eyes like bile and she screws up her face with all the venom she can muster and says, "You *deserved* . . ."

"How *dare* ye!" I hiss. "Do ye think I or *any* woman deserves to be *raped*? Nae. Even a wicked, bitter she-toad like you does nae *deserve* to be raped." I feel the rage building in me like roaring flame stoked by the bellows of all the years of hatred and poison endured at this foul woman's hands. "How *evil* do ye have to be to . . . to . . ."

Winnie recoils in horror. Why? Because of my words?

Nae! My fangs are extended!

What have I done?

"What *are* you?" she gasps.

Was I . . . was I about to . . . kill her?

What have I done?

I clamp my mouth shut, and with a great force of will I retract my fangs. I suck air in through my nose in a desperate attempt to calm myself.

"Winnie," I say in a shaking whisper, "I'm so sorry . . ."

"Help!" It's barely a wee whisper. 'Tis all she can manage in her fright. "Help! Somebody help me!" In a moment she'll find her voice again. She gropes for the call button.

Chapter 18

"I NEARLY KILLED Winnie Morrison!" I blurt into my cell phone.

"What?" Carl says in alarm.

I'm sitting in my office, still trembling with shock at what I almost did.

"She was goading me, and I got so angry," I say. "I lost control, and she saw my fangs."

"Wow. Did you *deal* with it?"

"Did I use Persuasion? Aye, I did. I very nearly commanded her to be nice to people. I thought about it, but I did nae do it."

"Tempting, I know."

"Aye, but 'twould nae be right. I just made her forget the fangs. I lost my temper. That's all she remembers."

"I'd've thought Winnie would be strong-willed enough to resist."

"Winnie is stubborn, aye, but she's nae strong of mind. And it could nae have hurt that she is on pain-killers. That would have weakened any resistance."

"So, why do you think you lost it with her?" he asks. "She's goaded you before. Many times, in fact."

"I told her that I had been raped, raped by forty-five men, and she said I *deserved* it."

He's silent for a moment and then says, "Nobody's that spiteful . . . are they?"

"I guess Winnie is," I say, "but I was already losing my temper afore that."

"OK," he says. "So what is it? Here's what we know: we're always hungry. *I'm* hungry again. Are you?"

"Aye, as hard as that is to believe. By the by, I've disposed of the rest of our supply from last night. It'd spent too long without adequate refrigeration. I'll be able to get some more today, but it will nae be as much as we seem to need right now. There will be more later in the week. And we'll need to give some to Rolf and Sarah."

"It'll have to do. So we have abnormal hunger . . . dreams . . . your anger."

"Are ye making one of your lists?"

Carl makes lists when he is trying to connect ideas and figure things out. Such a list helped him figure out how we fly, how we're able to lift heavy objects, and so on.

"Of course," he says. He's grinning right now, I'd wager.

"Have ye experienced a loss of control with your anger?"

"Not yet, but I'm gonna be on the lookout for it. What else have we got? For the list, I mean? What else is out of the norm?"

"Vampires," I say slowly.

"What do you mean?"

"We have a higher concentration of vampires in one area than either of us has ever experienced afore," I say. "The Congregation has a hundred and twenty-one vampires, plus Bartlett, plus Rolf and Sarah, plus the two of us. That's a hundred and twenty-six vampires . . . plus however many are in Lupescu's group . . . all in one area. Michael's Cult numbered only four, and with the two of us, six is the most ye have ever known. *I've* ne'er known more."

"And," Carl says, "it seems like our . . . *symptoms* started *after* the Penitents began to gather. I don't know how big the so-called Vampire Stake is, but Müller's people arrive starving and are constantly underfed thereafter."

"It has to be connected," I say.

"Yeah. Has your friend Sammy called with the test results on that sample of the 'Blessing'?"

"On the pig blood? Nae. I thought for sure he'd have called by now."

My phone beeps. "Hold a tick," I say. I look at the incoming call. " 'Tis Sammy! Speak of the Devil! I'll call ye back."

"Go! Later! I love you!" Carl says and hangs up before I can say anything in farewell. I tap the button to answer Sammy's call.

"Aye, Sammy. What have ye learned?"

"I've learned that my favorite Primary teacher is Elvira, Mistress of the Dark. How cool is that?"

"About the blood, laddie?" I say, trying nae to sound annoyed at the lad.

"Right," he says, and it sounds as if he discerned my annoyance, because he's all business now. "Well, I'm sorry it took me a while. It was pretty confusing. I found markers for both *sus domestica* and *homo sapiens*. That's the common domestic pig and human."

Could it be? Blood that is close enough to human to be a viable substitute?

"Both pig and human, ye say? At the same time?"

"Well . . . yeah. That's what I said."

"So, 'tis some type of genetically engineered pig with human markers?"

"You know as well as I do that, as unlikely as that is, you wouldn't get results like these, Moira."

Nae, 'twould nae be the precise markers for both species. "But ye said . . . 'twas both pig and human at the same time."

"Like a chimera?" he says.

"Aye."

"No way. There was overlap on the common markers. That's all."

"Ye mean 'tis a *mixed* sample?"

"Yeah. There's pig blood mixed with some human blood."

"Ye mean like somebody poured it into a mixing bowl and stirred blood from a pig and blood from a human together?"

"Yeah. That's right. If you could get me a larger sample, I could run more precise tests with antibodies to be sure."

"Nae, laddie. I dinnae think I'll have access to another sample anytime soon."

"So . . ." he says, "what does it mean?"

"It means that Paul's so-called Blessing is nae but a fraud." *He's nae just bleeding pigs; he's bleeding humans as well. He's keeping his followers on the verge of starvation by telling them they're consuming God's "Blessing," when in fact they are simply feeding off mortals the same as they were before. I never liked or trusted Paul, but part of me dearly wanted to* believe *that somehow the "Blessing" could be real!*

"What are you talking about? Who's Paul? And what's the 'blessing'?"

"Paul is an extremely evil and dangerous vampire," I reply. *He's so disciplined that he's keeping* himself *on the verge of starvation to perpetrate the fraud. As* Rolf *said,* very *disciplined indeed.* "And the so-called Blessing is pig blood . . . ordinary pig blood . . . mixed with some human blood. He's been passing it off to his followers, an army of Penitents . . . d'ye know what Penitents are?"

"Yeah. Tony said that they're *good* vampires who won't kill. Like you."

"That's oversimplifying, but 'tis close enough for the moment. Anyway, Paul's been passing this mixed blood off to his army of Penitents as genetically engineered pig blood that's a substitute for human blood."

"I thought that was impossible. Tony said you must consume *human* blood to survive."

"Precisely, laddie. He's convinced them they have to kick their addiction, so to speak, to human blood. What he's really doing is slowly starving them to death, while making them totally and exclusively dependent on *him* to supply their only source of nutrition. 'Tis diabolical." *And I wanted so badly to believe it!*

"Wow," he says slowly. "I'm not sure I understand all of it, but . . . Is it really like an addiction? That would totally *suck*. No pun intended."

"'Tis nae an addiction. We consume human blood and we live. If we dinnae consume it, we starve. But I cannae explain it all to ye now. It'll have to wait."

"Are you going to meet with Tony's group?"

"Aye. We've agreed to be there tonight at eight."

"Cool. I'll be there too. I'm *so* geeked-out right now!"

"Laddie, I dinnae like the idea of ye being in a room, surrounded by vampires. I've known ye since ye were a wee lad and . . . I just dinnae like it. Besides, this is serious and deadly business, ye know."

"Yeah, but we're on the *Lord's* side, right? There's that Curse that Tony kept talking about . . . that prophecy. It says you're going to win, right?"

"Aye, Sammy. It says that we . . . or someone else *like* us . . . will *eventually* win, but it also says that when we do, we—all the vampires, the evil and the Penitent, are all going to die."

"That doesn't sound like a happy ending."

"Nae, laddie. There is nae happy ending for us . . . nae in *this* life, at least."

"And when the time comes," he says, "you're willing, the both of you, to lay down your lives . . ."

". . . to rid the world of the plague of our kind?" I say. "Aye, I hope and pray that, when the time comes, I'll have the courage to do just that."

Merciful Father in Heaven, help me have the courage to do what's right. Give me the courage to give up this life that is now become so sweet for the hope of a better one. But, truth be told, I'm nae so anxious to let this life go. If we could have just a wee bit longer, Carl and I . . . Ach! "Lord, I believe; help thou mine unbelief."

I thank Sammy for his assistance and then hang up.

I need to call Carl and tell him the results. I start to dial, but I'm interrupted by my office phone.

"Dr. Morgan?" the receptionist's voice says through the speaker. I don't recognize his voice. He must be new. He sounds young.

"Aye?" I reply.

"Dr. Morgan?" he says again.

"Aye?" I repeat louder this time.

"Dr. Morgan?" he says.

Ach! This is irritating! I have important things to attend to, and the lad is being obtuse.

"Can ye nae hear me, laddie?"

"Oh," he says, "you're there! All, I heard was someone saying, 'I,' over and over."

"*Yesss?*" I hiss through clenched teeth.

"There's someone at Reception to see you. A Mr. Duncan Bell? He says he has a package for you. Actually, it looks like two packages. Says he wants to give them to you in person. Can you come down to Reception?"

"What's your name, laddie?"

"Stuart, ma'am."

"Well, Stuart," I say. "Ye're *new* here, are ye nae?"

"Yes, Dr. Morgan. New at Reception anyway. I used to work in the . . ."

"Fine, Stuart," I say, cutting him off. "The first thing ye need to know is I have an allergy to sunlight, so I dinnae e'er come down to Reception. And the second thing ye need to know is that 'aye' is spelled 'a-y-e' and it means 'yes,' as in 'aye, aye, captain!'"

"Sorry, captain . . . I mean, *doctor*." His tone is hurt, apologetic.

"'Tis all right, Stuart." *Why was I so rude to the lad? Is it because I'm hungry* again? *Hungry* still? "Ye meant nae offense. I was rude. Please forgive me."

"Sure, doctor," he says, his tone brightening. "What do you want me to do?"

"Could ye have someone escort him up to my office?"

"Right away, Dr. Morgan. I'll send him up with a courier."

"Thank ye, Stuart." I hang up.

I'll have to do something nice for Stuart. I wish I could bake him some cookies, but I cannae cook. I cannae abide the smell of cooking. And I could nae taste them to see if they were even *edible*. The least I can do is to apologize in person.

I'll do that after Mr. Bell delivers his package. I'll just have to take care to avoid the Sun coming in through the windows.

Maybe there'll be clouds.

It bothers me greatly that I'm having so much difficulty controlling my urges lately. I need to speak to Carl and see if his lists have yielded any insights, anything to help me regain control.

I quickly dial Carl on my cell. He answers on the first ring. "What did you learn?" he asks.

"'Tis a fraud. Simply pig blood mixed with human blood."

"I *knew* it was too good to be true!" he replies, anger heating his voice. "I mean, I *wanted* it to be real. I *wanted* there to be *some* alternative . . ."

"The question is, laddie, what are we going to do about it?"

"We don't know what we're up against," he replies. "I suspect Bartlett is under Müller's control."

"I agree."

"And we don't know how many of the other hundred and twenty followers are slaves and how many are just true *believers*. Of the two, true believers are the most dangerous. A slave will find ways to resist . . . if he can. A true believer, who sees Müller as his only chance for salvation, will do anything to serve him."

"Aye, a fanatic can be truly dangerous."

"But, we need to do *something*. Somehow, Müller's getting a huge amount of human blood to produce his 'Blessing' and that needs to be stopped."

"And," I say, "we need to find some way to free his followers from his control."

"Yep. Why haven't we seen any sign of vampiric activity, Penitent or otherwise, around the area, if there are so many vampires here? The 'Blessing' is bogus, so where is the *human* blood coming from?"

"That is a good question, laddie, and I dinnae know the answer." I pause a wee bit. "Have ye had any epiphanies about our hunger and our . . . other difficulties lately?"

"Nothing earth shattering. I *do* think it has something to do with being in relatively close proximity to so many starving vampires."

"Meaning what?"

"Meaning . . . I don't know what yet. I don't think we have enough pieces of the puzzle. But I've got a question," he continues. "Rebecca told me once that Michael . . ."

"Hold that thought, laddie!" I say as I hear footsteps approaching. "I've got a visitor. I love ye. Bye!"

"I love you too. Bye!" He hangs up and so do I.

There's a knock at the office door. Outside the door, I can hear two hearts pumping lovely, delicious blood. 'Tis nae *evil* blood, but all the same . . .

Stop it!

That would be Mr. Bell and his courier escort.

"Aye, come in," I say.

A young courier, Alice, as I recall her name, opens the door a bit and sticks her head in. "Dr. Morgan? A Mr. Bell to see you."

"Aye, Alice, I'm expecting him."

She opens the door the rest of the way and motions Duncan Bell inside. "Do you want me to wait here for him, doctor?"

"Nae, lassie. I'll walk him out." *I need to apologize to Stuart anyway.* "Thank, ye."

"No problem, Dr. Morgan," she says and walks away, leaving Duncan Bell and his *two* long packages with me.

"Mr. Bell," I say, smiling and trying to ignore the throbbing in his strong neck, "thank ye for coming so quickly."

"For you, Miss MacDonald, anything," he says, acting a wee bit shy. "You know that."

"'Tis Mrs. Morgan now," I gently remind him.

"Right," he says. "Mrs. Morgan. Your . . . patronage is deeply appreciated."

"And I appreciate your talent, laddie," I reply. "Let's see what ye brought me." I nod toward the two items wrapped in brown paper.

He sets both parcels down on my desk. Then he unwraps. I see a glint of steel and smell the scents of leather, wood, and oil. I can detect the faint odor of the smithy smoke about him too, though, to be sure. There's the scent of the soap he used to clean up with before coming.

Focus on those scents, lassie! Nae the perfume of his blood!

Having pushed the paper aside, he reveals a beautifully wrought broadsword with a nice fuller running down the middle of the blade. The long groove of the fuller, called a 'blood groove' by some, makes the blade lighter and stronger. The quillions are made of brass, and they slope down toward the blade in the Scottish fashion. The wooden handle is wrapped in brown leather, and the sword is balanced by a large brass pommel, polished so bright it might be mistaken for gold. Still sitting in the brown paper is a fine scabbard of leather-wrapped wood, trimmed with brass.

He takes a bit of oilcloth from a pocket and wraps it about the blade. He lifts the sword in this manner, by the blade, his skin nae touching the steel, and presents it to me, pommel first.

"Here's the broadsword you asked for, Mrs. Morgan."

I wrap my right hand around the handle and take the sword gently from him.

"'Tis a beautiful piece, Duncan," I say. "I've nae seen a better."

I turn away from him and slowly rotate my wrist to swing the blade in a horizontal figure eight. "The balance is excellent!" I point the blade toward the ceiling and strike the pommel with the flat of my free hand. I can feel the vibration traveling through the entire weapon. "And the steel is nicely tempered. Ye have done very well, Duncan! 'Tis a fine blade!"

"Thank you, ma'am," he says, blushing. It makes my mouth water to look at him, so I look back at the sword. *I hope Sarah appreciates it.*

"Laddie, I've known ye since ye were a wee lad and your father's apprentice. Could ye nae call me 'Moira'?"

"If you insist," he replies, "but it feels weird calling someone by their first name who knew my father when *he* was young."

"There ye go, commenting on my advanced age, laddie!" I say with a smile. "The next thing I know, ye'll be calling me 'Granny Moira'!"

"Never that, Mrs. . . . uh . . . Moira."

"How much do I owe ye, lad?"

"Not a *dime*, ma'am!"

"But, laddie, from a discerning buyer, this piece would fetch five hundred dollars, maybe more!"

"Which is only a fraction of what you contribute each year to keep our smithy alive," he replies. "Ma'am . . . Moira, please accept this as my thanks for keeping us going for decades."

"I'm nae but a patron of the arts," I say. "Yours is only too rare a talent in this day and age."

"Then, please accept the sword with my thanks," he says and nods his head deferentially.

"Aye, Master Bell, I will." I nod to him as well, in mock formality.

He reaches for the second package and begins to unwrap it.

"What's this?" I ask.

"My father wanted you to have it," he says. "Before he passed on, he fashioned it especially for you. He called it his 'masterpiece.'"

I lay the broadsword down next to its scabbard and then watch with rising anticipation as he exposes his late father's gift.

Once again, I smell the leather, the wood, and the metal, but I dinnae see the glint of steel. I see only a shining blackness. Soon he carefully draws from the paper an object of ebony beauty.

The blade is black as midnight, galvanized by heat, except where the single edge has been sharpened. It is polished to a mirror finish. It has three short fullers near the hilt. There is a black steel basket, wrought of interwoven bands of galvanized black steel, around the handle. The pommel is black as well, shaped traditionally like the head of a cat.

He presents the weapon to me, pommel first. "Please accept this with my father's gratitude," he says smiling.

"A schiavona!" I cry. "I've ne'er seen the like!" I take the sword in my hand. I turn the magnum opus over and gaze at it in wonder.

"So, you like it?" Duncan says.

"Oh, aye, very much indeed."

He beams at me.

"Laddie, there is nae a finer blade in all the world!"

"That would have meant the world to my dad." He gestures at the scabbard lying in the paper. "Take a look at the scabbard too, please."

I look. I lift it up with my left hand. It is, of course, wood, wrapped in leather with blackened steel accents. The leather has been embossed on both sides. It says, "PER MARE PER TERRAS" on one side and "MANU FORTI" on the other.

"'By sea, by land' and 'by a strong hand,'" I translate from the Latin.

"My father says that those are the clan mottos of Clan MacDonald and Clan MacKay," Duncan says. "He told me to ask you why he should have used the motto of Clan MacKay. Sometimes he liked to be cryptic and keep me guessing, so I thought he was just playing with me. I told him as much, but he said that he honestly didn't know and that I should ask *you* when the time came."

Suddenly, I cannae keep back the tears. "The original name of Clan MacKay was Clan Morgan. By marriage, I now belong to Clan MacKay." I look up at him in time to see him discreetly brush a tear from his eye. "Laddie, why are ye just now giving this precious gift to me and nae when your father was still alive?"

"He made me promise to hold it for you until you asked me to bring you a sword. He told me that someday you would, though you never, ever had in the past. I asked him if he meant that you would ask for *this* sword, and he told me no. He said that this one was special. He said that I should bring you something I had made, but I should give you this one at the same time. He also gave me a letter to give to you when you asked for a sword."

"Aye?"

He reaches into his shirt pocket and hands me an envelope. "Here. He wanted me to make sure you read this."

I take the envelope. 'Tis addressed simply to "Moira." I open it. I unfold a couple of sheets of paper, handwritten, and I read:

Dear Miss MacDonald,

I hope you're pleased with the schiavona. I wanted to thank you for all the years of supporting my smithy. You have allowed me and my son after me to do what we love.

I know you have your reasons for "promoting the art of Scottish swordcraft" as you put it, but you never, ever commissioned, purchased, or received a single weapon from me or my son. So, I wanted to make you something to show my gratitude.

I set out to make a claymore, one of the greatswords that were once outlawed because they gave the clan chiefs too much power. I thought it would be a fitting tribute to a great lady. I created three of them before I gave up. They just didn't seem quite right. I couldn't manage to make something that matched what was in my head.

After finishing the third sword, I looked at it, and though it was a fine piece, I was disgusted. It just wasn't right! It didn't say "thank you" the way I wanted it to.

So I lay down on the couch and stewed for a while. Eventually I fell asleep. Then I had a dream. An unusually vivid dream.

In the dream, I saw myself working in my smithy. Usually, when I see myself in a dream, I see myself as a young man. This time, though, I was old, as I am now. I was making the basket of a sword. I had already made the blade. It was single edged, which was not my usual style. It was also galvanized to a deep black. The basket, too, looked different from what I was used to.

I watched my dream self as he worked, and he took no notice of me. After a while, I started looking around the smithy. On the wall I noticed pictures of swords that were black and had a basket similar to what I was making. Some of the pictures were captioned "Blackened Scottish Schiavona." I also saw sketches of the components for the sword I was making.

There was even a sketch of the scabbard with some words in Latin written above and below it, as if they were going to be written on either side of the scabbard. Now, I don't know Latin (being born and raised in Hooper, Utah), but I knew it WAS Latin.

And I remember saying to my dream self, "Why on earth would I make this particular sword?"

And then my dream self turned and spoke to me. "Because someday Moira MacDonald is going to need a sword. And it can't be the sword of her own vengeance. It must be the sword of the Lord's justice. It has to be as black as the night in which she lives, and it has to reflect the light of the moon and stars. Someday she will be fighting demons from within and without. Someday she will need to know that God will never abandon her. Someday she will ask for a sword, but not for herself. It will be for another. When she does, she will need this sword. She must arm herself with the sword of truth. And the truth will set her free."

And then I woke up. I wrote down the details of the dream. I'm not usually one to have dreams that mean anything. My wife, now, she used to have dreams, and I learned to pay attention to hers. But this one meant something, I was sure.

So I made the sword. It's the last one I'll ever make. I'll leave it with my son, Duncan. He'll get it to you when you ask him for a sword. I've never made a sword that would actually be used in real combat. I've got no idea how to make a sword to fight demons, but I believe that this is the sword the Lord commissioned for you.

God will never abandon you. Remember that with God, nothing is impossible.

Your brother,

William Bell

My hands tremble as I read the letter, and tears pour down my face. When I'm done, I look up at Duncan.

His face is filled with trepidation and concern. "Are you OK, Mrs. Morgan?"

"Do ye know what this letter says?"

"No, ma'am. I've been so curious, but he gave it to me sealed, and I never opened it."

I hand the letter to him, and he begins to read.

While he reads, I'm left to my own thoughts. It must not be the sword of *my* vengeance? My hanger? I took it from one of the English soldiers I killed long ago. That would be the sword of *my* vengeance, I suppose. So God wants me to wield *this* sword? How is it "the sword of truth"?

I pick it up and look at it more closely. *There! On the blade!* If I look at it with the light on it at just the right angle, I see what appears to be letters. The indentations are so subtle that they could be the marks of hammer blows from when it was forged. But now that I look, 'tis unmistakable. I check the other side. 'Tis the same. I see the same letters: "F-I-R-I-N-N." I feel a chill as I recall the word I've nae spoken for centuries . . . at least nae in my native tongue. "Firinn" is Gaelic for "truth."

"Mrs. Morgan . . . I mean, Moira?" Duncan Bell says. "What's going on here? What did my dad mean, you're going to need a sword? Fighting demons? Was my dad nuts?"

I take the letter back from him. "Nae, lad. He knew precisely what he was about. Or he knew well enough, at least."

"But . . . demons?" he says, wringing his hands.

"I cannae explain to ye just now, but suffice it to say, I will wield your father's sword against unholy monsters. I'm nae what I appear."

"I know," he says.

"What?"

"I know who and what you are."

If he mentions the temple in Ogden . . .

"The angels in Ogden, who protected the temple . . ."

Nae!

"According to the story, one of them had red hair and green eyes. And you don't look a day older than you did when I was a boy."

"I'm nae an angel, laddie," I say, shaking my head quickly.

"A translated being, then!"

"Nae, I'm . . . nae what ye think."

"But you're on a mission from God, right?"

"I suppose . . . I am, ye could say." His face brightens. "But I'm nae an angel. I'm . . ." I throw up my hands in frustration. "Ach! I cannae explain."

He opens his mouth to speak, then hesitates a tick. "OK. You can't explain. I can accept that. But you're going to use my father's sword to battle demons."

"Aye. That I will."

His face splits in a wide grin. "Cool," he says. "All his life, my dad made weapons that were objects of art. Cool to look at, but not good for anything else. Now his masterpiece is going to be used to slay demons! Wielded by an angel of God!"

"I'm nae an *angel*!"

"OK," he says, still grinning like that cat that ate the canary. "Whatever!"

I walk Duncan Bell close enough to the lobby so that he can find the rest of his way on his own. I, myself, stop off at the gift shop to pick up a card for Stuart. I have to pick one that is fairly generic and does nae mention "Get well." I wish I could find one that says, "I'm sorry I was such an arrogant ass. Please forgive me," but, sadly, nary a one is to be found. I write something similar to that on the card I select, address it to Stuart, and make my way toward the reception desk.

I'm in luck. There is nae any direct sunlight between me and the desk.

I'm so hungry!

Nae now! I cannae deal with this right now! I need to focus.

Focus on something else, lassie. Anything else!

I try to focus on the reception desk. 'Tis unmanned. Stuart is nae there. He cannae have left for more than a moment. I dinnae know what he looks like, but he'll be wearing a name tag at the very least.

I stand for a moment, looking for someone, anyone who might be Stuart when I'm overwhelmed by the honeyed scent of evil blood. I clamp my mouth shut and battle to keep my fangs and drool in check, but still I look about, my head snapping from side to side as I search for the source of the evil blood.

Kill! Feast! Rend!

There!

My head snaps toward the reception desk as a young man in a white shirt and tie comes walking toward it. He has a nametag on. For one wild second I think he looks like a Mormon missionary. But *he* is the source! *His* is the evil blood!

Behind my tightly closed lips I lose my battle. My fangs extend and drool begins to escape the corners of my mouth.

All my attention is focused on the young man with his sweet, sweet evil blood. With the perfect clarity of my Seed-enhanced senses, I take in every detail of his appearance. I see the black hair, the faint stains at the armpits of his white shirt, the brown eyes, the pink skin, the throbbing jugular, the nametag that says, "Stuart Hopkins."

And I advance on him.

Chapter 19

C OME WITH ME, Stuart," I say, using Persuasion. My lips are tight to hide my fangs. "Come with me *now*."

His expression is slack as he rises and follows me. I turn and head back toward my office. I force myself to keep moving, to keep my back turned to him. I *ken* that he is following me. I can hear his footsteps and the pounding of his evil blood.

I struggle to keep control of the volcanic rage erupting inside me and of the compulsion to kill him and drain him right now in plain view of everyone.

I'm waging a battle in my mind.

I keep telling myself that I'm merely trying to protect the hospital and the innocents here, but I ken that I'm deceiving myself. I keep telling myself that I only want to *question* him to find out what he has done that is so evil, that I will nae Feed, and then, after I've questioned him, I will send him off to the police to confess his crimes. I tell myself that my motives are pure, but they are nae pure. My motives are fiendish . . . demonic . . . homicidal.

My motives are *insane*.

I want his blood. I want it very badly. I want it so badly that I would give up *anything* to have it at the moment.

Anything?

Am I willing to give up all that the Lord has given me after two and a half centuries of abject repentance? I've found redemption, a purpose, and eternal *love*.

Carl! Ben!

Am I willing to give ye up to rid the world of this . . . monster?

He is a *monster*! He *has* to be!

Maybe Carl's right. Maybe this is nae my fault. Maybe it's caused somehow by all the starving vampires. 'Twould nae be my fault if I . . .

'Tis still my choice, outside stimulus or nae. *I* choose! *I* accept the consequences!

"*. . . not suffer you to be tempted above that ye are able . . .*"

I can resist this!

I cannae murder again! I cannae! I've made covenants in the temple! I waited so long!

Am I willing to give up Carl and Ben so soon just so I can taste Stuart's sweet blood? I dinnae even ken what he has done! I ken only that he is *evil . . . delicious . . . mouthwatering . . . irresistible . . .*

When did I stop walking? I suddenly find myself facing Stuart, watching the throbbing of the delicious nectar in his neck.

Nae my fault. He deserves it!

He must have done *something* worthy of death! Else his blood would nae cry unto me as it does, *screaming* for me to take it! And I've denied myself for so long! I *deserve* a kill . . . a *righteous* kill. He *deserves* to die! He deserves to die at *my* hand!

Ye cannae be judge, jury, and executioner, lassie!

Oh, but I can . . .

I am Death.

I am Hell.

I am a Daughter of Lilith, and I *will* have him!

But nae here. Must find somewhere private.

Swallowing a mouthful of saliva, I turn around and force myself to continue walking.

Find someplace private. And then . . . then he's mine!

A series of images flashes through my mind:

> Christ kneeling in Gethsemane, begging His Father to allow Him nae to drink the bitter cup . . .
>
> Nephi as he takes Laban's head . . .
>
> Myself as I kneel and receive the Ordination at Sarah's hand, my blood on her lips and her Seed-laden blood on mine . . .
>
> Carl as he kneels across from me in the Ogden Temple . . .
>
> Ben's severed head cradled in my arms . . .
>
> Myself draining Stuart's life, reveling in his sweet blood . . .
>
> My office door . . .

My office door?

I find myself standing before my office door. I cannae remember arriving here. In my fist I'm still holding the crumpled card that I bought for Stuart. I shove it into my pocket as I pull out my keys. I unlock the door, open it, and enter, my whole body trembling in anticipation of the Feast . . . in anticipation of the Kill.

I cannae remember wanting anything so badly in all my long life.

Stuart follows me in, and I lock the door behind him.

Did anyone see him enter my office?

Do I care?

I turn and face him. He stands there . . . waiting for me . . . smelling like fragrant Corruption . . . like the Devil, himself.

Drool spills from my mouth. My own heart is thundering in my chest.

I'm moments away from the sweet release from the agony of waiting!

I'm moments away from my own damnation.

This is my *Gethsemane. There is nae going back from this. Either I* pass *this test or I* fall *and* embrace *what I am.*

And what am I?

I am a Daughter of Lilith, and I exist to consume the wicked.

Stuart Hopkins, I am the Judgment of God. I am your *Judgment. I am your Damnation. Prepare to enter the Hellfire that awaits ye.*

I stare at the throbbing life force hammering in Stuart's neck. The sweetness of sin calls to me with all the might of the Mormon Tabernacle Choir singing the "Hallelujah Chorus."

I must choose.

And I choose.

I choose for all eternity.

Carl. I choose Carl.

And Ben.

And my God.

Tears spill from my eyes, mingling with the drool spilling from my mouth. The temptation's still there, but I can *fight* it. I can *conquer* it. Stuart's blood still sings to me, but I can . . . nae, I *will* resist it.

I wipe the drool from my face with a shaking hand.

Spittle continues to fill my mouth, but I swallow the bulk of it down. I cannae force my fangs to retract just yet . . . nae with my need to Feed unsated and the evil blood so near.

On legs that will barely support me, I lurch to my chair and collapse into it. I take the Sword of Truth in my quaking hand, and I stare at the ebony blade. I see my mouth reflected in the shining black steel. I stare at my fangs in the reflection as I will them to slowly retract.

"Stuart," I say, straining to force the words past my lips, "face me."

He turns. He looks at me, but his expression is blank, vacant. He is still firmly in my thrall.

"What have ye done? What is it ye have done that is so evil? What have ye done to make your blood *scream* your guilt to me?"

"I haven't done anything evil," he says without inflection.

"That's nae possible, Stuart. Ye have done *great* evil. What is it? Have ye murdered?"

"I do God's work," he says. "I collect the ghosts and send them back to God."

"Ghosts? What ghosts?"

"The runaways . . . the homeless . . . the junkies . . . those who are invisible . . . that nobody wants. But God wants them. He wants them back."

"And," I ask, "does nae anyone come alooking for them . . . these 'ghosts'?" I force myself to face him again, ignoring the percussion of his pulsing blood.

"I collect only those who are from out of town or out of state. They are the ones who are truly invisible."

"And where do ye find them, these 'ghosts?'"

"In alleys, under overpasses, in bus stations, in abandoned buildings. I find them wherever I can . . . wherever they haunt."

Haunt? That's an interesting choice of words.

"And what do ye *do* with them once ye collect them?" I ask. *Another serial killer.*

"I send them to God."

"How do ye send them to God?" I ask

"I give them to Him."

I do wish he would be more forthcoming rather than just answering the exact question I ask, but that is a consequence of the Persuasion.

"How do ye '*give* them to God'?" I ask.

"In the beginning, I gave them drugs or alcohol. Then I took them out to the West Desert, slit their throats . . . like you do with a lamb or a goat for a burnt offering, making them sacred to God . . . and then I buried them. But God spoke to me and told me that He had a higher purpose for the ghosts. He told me to deliver them to His angel."

All thought of evil blood and Feeding is driven from my mind as a chill grips my innards like the icy hand of Death.

"How do ye know 'twas an angel?" I ask in a whisper.

"He had great white wings, and he came down from the sky, and he spoke the word of God," he says.

"Does this angel have a name?"

"Yes."

"What is the angel's name, Stuart?"

"The Angel Isaiah."

◢ ◢ ◢

"'Tis most assuredly Bartlett," I say to Carl over my cell phone.

"How can you be sure?" he asks.

"Stuart described him to a T," I say, "right down to his beard, his manner of speaking, and the twitch in his right eye."

"OK. That sounds like Bartlett."

"An interesting detail I can't account for is the 'angel' had a halo of light around his head," I say. "But that could be just a product of Stuart's addled imagination."

"If you ask me," Carl says, "a halo would be no different than projecting wings. I think the wings have always been meant to deceive people into believing vampires are angels or gods."

"Ye may have the right of that as well, laddie," I say. "I've ne'er thought of it like that.

"Be that as it may," I continue, "he's been kidnapping 'ghosts,' as he calls them, for months and delivering them to Bartlett at the rate of two or three each week. Sometimes more."

"Which means Müller could have dozens of victims by now."

"Aye."

"And this guy, Stuart, may not be the only one supplying him," he says. "There could be other sick souls thinking they're doing God's will."

"I fear ye have the right of it again, laddie."

Carl pauses. "Why haven't we seen any mention in the news of people going missing . . . especially in these numbers . . . before?"

"Stuart said they were 'invisible,' meaning nobody took notice of them before their disappearance. Why would anyone pay attention to some junkie or drifter from out of the state? A few whores go missing — who's to notice? There is nae record of such a person . . . at least nae locally. Nobody around here knows them, so if they go missing . . . Well, ye dinnae notice the absence of something, or some*one*, ye were nae aware existed."

"'Ghosts.'"

"Aye, laddie."

"How does he know when and where to meet Bartlett so he can deliver the victims?"

"He calls Bartlett's cell phone."

"Cell phone? He didn't think it was strange that an 'angel' might have a cell phone? How does *that* make sense?"

"It does nae have to make sense in the twisted mind of a homicidal psychopath, with religious delusions. Stuart Hopkins thinks he's on a mission from God to rid the world of 'ghosts.'"

"Wow," Carl says. "What did you do with him?"

"I Persuaded him to return to the reception desk and dial nine-one-one and confess to all the original killings, the ones he did himself. I told him nae to mention the 'angel' or the subsequent victims. *We* must be the ones to deal with that. The police came and took him away just minutes ago. Dinnae worry, though: I watched and made sure he did as he was instructed, so he would nae be a danger to anyone else."

"Did you . . . *Feed*?" he asks. *Poor, Carl. He's suffering too.*

"I very nearly killed him, laddie, but, nae, I did nae Feed. I . . . wanted to . . . I wanted to so very, very badly . . . but I did nae Feed."

"How did you . . . *resist*?" His voice is barely a whisper.

"'Twas the hardest thing I've ever done, I think. It came down to a choice between his blood . . . and *ye*," I say. "I chose *ye*, Carl . . . ye and Ben. I dinnae ken why our urges are so much stronger now . . . and they're getting stronger by the day . . . but I believe I'll be able to face them now. And I believe I can face them and *conquer* them in the future . . . because I know what I *want*. And I *dinnae* want, I *cannae* want *anything* so much as I want *ye*, my love. And I want ye forever and ever . . . for time and all eternity."

Chapter 20

TWENTY-SIX.

That's how many Penitents are members of the "Vampire Stake." Lupescu assures us that they are all here. None of them would pass up a chance to meet the Breakers, let alone the Unwilling and the Penitent.

Müller has one hundred and twenty Penitents who follow him ... or perhaps are *enslaved* to him. If ye add in Müller, himself, and Bartlett, that's a total of a hundred and twenty-two vampires. Even if ye count Rolf, Sarah, Carl, and me among the Stake vampires, we're outnumbered more than four to one. How can we possibly face so many? And how can we possibly face so many without *harming* any of them? They are ... well, nae *innocent*, to be sure. None of us are. But they were deceived into following the wrong man in their quest for redemption.

Twenty-six. Well, 'tis more vampires than I've ever seen assembled in one place before. Ach, 'tis more vampires than I've met in my entire life.

And they are all staring at us.

After work, I picked up Carl from his place of employment. (They call it a "studio." Are video games a form of art? Seems a wee bit pretentious to me.) We chanced a trip to our safe house, being fairly certain that we were nae being followed. Neither of us had been able to shower in two days.

Our safe house is a nondescript, modest home in a younger neighborhood in the southwest quarter of the city. Well, "younger" is a relative term. 'Tis younger than our home. There, we picked up changes of clothes for Rolf and Sarah, as well as spare sunglasses and coats with hoods for the pair of them.

We also brought blood I had secured from the blood bank at the hospital so they could Feed. The blood called out to both of us, but despite our heightened urges, we knew we did nae really need to Feed. At least, in our heads we knew it. 'Twas still quite difficult to abstain and save the blood for Rolf and Sarah.

We drove to the hotel and took the protective clothing, the blood, and the sword up to their room. At the door, Carl knocked and spoke the safe word, "willow." Rolf answered with "aspirin" and then admitted us.

Sarah was Sleeping, of course. We gave Rolf two pints of blood so he could Feed, and we opened one of the remaining pints and smeared a bit of the blood under Sarah's nose. 'Twas enough to wake her. She consumed the rest of that bag and one other as well.

Then we presented her with the broadsword. She made a snide remark about it being Scottish, but I could ken that she was clearly pleased with the gift. By the way she handled the blade as she inspected it, I could tell she'd wielded a sword before this. I would have hazarded a guess, however, that she was nae a great swordswoman.

Sarah was close enough to my size to wear the clothes we provided, though she's a wee bit larger in the chest than I am, especially now that she's been Fed and restored to her normal state of health. She's rather plain of face, but she has a nice enough figure. More than once, I see Rolf stealing an appreciative glance.

Good luck with that, Rolf-laddie! Sarah'd sooner disembowel ye as give ye the time of day. On the other hand, she did trust ye enough to stand guard as she Slept. With our kind, that's a lot of trust.

The clothes we brought for Rolf were a different matter, given that he's both taller and more muscular than Carl. He selected a shirt, but retained the jeans he was wearing. "I've only worn them a few times, so they're still good," he said.

Men! Who can understand them?

Since 'twas still daylight after Sarah and Rolf had each showered and prepared themselves against the Sun, we proceeded south toward Provo in my car.

And here we are, surrounded by more vampires than I've ever seen in one place. They are a varied lot, these Penitents of the Vampire Stake. I count fifteen men and eleven women, most varying in apparent *biological* age from the teens to the midthirties. One young woman looks to be about fourteen or younger. There are nae older-looking vampires. Most Converts are chosen from among a vampire's lovers. I've never heard of an older mortal being chosen for Conversion.

The Stake Penitents come from all over the world. I see those of European, Indian, African, Middle Eastern, Native American, and Asian stock. To be sure, all of those races exist here in the United States, so they could all be Americans as well.

The four of us are armed, of course. Carl is wearing the dirk that belonged to my father, and the basket-hilted claymore that once belonged to my long-dead betrothed, Donald. Rolf has his bastard belted at his waist, and Sarah is holding her new broadsword in her hand. (I need to get her a sword belt.) And I have my schiavona at my side.

Nary a one of the others carries a weapon.

I dinnae know what Carl, Rolf, and Sarah are feeling at this moment, but I feel terribly awkward, as if I'm the only one wearing a formal gown at a casual dance.

And the way they are looking at us! Expressions range from awe to hope to suspicion.

We're in a classroom (or perhaps it is a conference room) on the third floor of the Joseph Smith Building on the BYU campus. Tony Lupescu is standing in front of the table at the head of the room, looking very smug. Sammy is seated at the end of that table with an expression of childlike awe on his face. *Ye should be terrified, laddie!* Everyone else in the room is a vampire. They are all seated in chairs facing us.

One of them, sitting toward the front, is the only one wearing a tie. He's also clean-shaven with his black hair in a fairly short cut. (Nae that a vampire has much choice in the matter; our hair remains at the length it was when we were Converted. And typically, men are required to shave as part of the ritual.) But with the tie and grooming, he's the only one of them who could pass for a BYU professor. He must be Professor Lorenzo Corelli, the first vampire Tony befriended. Corelli's one of those who looks on us with suspicion.

When did I start thinking of the mortal as 'Tony' again rather than 'Lupescu'? Does that mean I'm inclined to trust him now?

"Listen, Lorenzo," Tony says, his tone a wee bit distressed. "We've welcomed others before. Why all the suspicion now?"

Corelli strokes his chin like a man accustomed to wearing a beard. "We lost Constance and Ramón last week," he says in an accent that is a vague mixture of any number of European nationalities. "They went to spy on the Congregation and never returned. They haven't reported in, either. How do we know that these four," he points an accusing finger in our direction, "aren't some of the Apostle's thralls? Or, worse, his willing allies?"

Another vampire, a young-looking African woman, says in thickly accented English, "You say to us that these are the prophesied 'Unwilling and Peninent,' joined in 'the House of God,' but what *proof* do you have? For that matter, what proof do you have that they are the Breakers?"

There are murmurs from the others. Some are murmuring and nodding in agreement. Others are outraged. Others are fearful.

Sammy looks outraged. Tony looks worried.

"That's easy enough to prove," Carl says, lifting a calming hand, "assuming there's a Master among you. If you're a Master, command me."

All eyes turn toward the African woman. "Ghalyela?" Tony says, a smile returning to his face. "Make it a good one. Something *outrageous.*"

Ghalyela sits up, squares her shoulders, and says, "You . . . Carl, is it?"

Carl nods.

"Bow before me and kiss my foot," she says.

"I bow to no one except my God," he says, his lopsided grin spreading across his handsome face.

Ghalyela gasps. There are gasps from all around the room.

"And all my kisses are for my wife." He takes my hand and squeezes it.

Corelli's face is unreadable. He rises slowly to his feet.

"Think, people," he says. "This proves nothing."

"But, Lorenzo," Tony cries, "you said that no vampire could resist the command of a Master!"

Sammy looks confused.

"That's true for most of us," Corelli says, "but not for all of us. A Master is not subject to another Master."

Carl looks at him for a second and then nods. "Fine," he says. He points at Corelli and says, "Do the Macarena!"

"What?" Corelli says, mystified.

"It's a dance. Dance for me."

"I know what it . . . is . . ." Corelli's eyes widen as understanding dawns on him. He claps his hands together. "*Excellente!*" he cries and smiles a huge smile. "You . . . you're free!"

"Yeah," Carl says, "Moira and I both are." He raises my hand in his for a moment.

I smile at Corelli.

"And you," Corelli says, looking at me with obvious excitement, "you're the Penitent? *The* Penitent?"

I nod. "Aye."

"And you have been . . . *in the House of God?* The Mormon *temple?*"

"Aye, Carl and I were sealed together there last year."

"*Che bello!*" He turns around to the other vampires in the room. "Have any of you *tried* to enter one of their temples?"

Several hands are raised. Nearly half of them have tried.

"I have," he says. "I couldn't set *foot* inside the lobby. I couldn't so much as touch the stone of the outer walls!"

There are murmurs of agreement from those who raised their hands.

"Could *any* of you touch one? Enter one?" he asks.

There are a number who shake their heads. There are nae nods.

"I do not understand," Ghalyela says.

"You're new here," Corelli says to her, visibly enthusiastic.

She nods.

"We—all of us," he continues, making a sweeping gesture to indicate everyone in the room, "have come here seeking redemption, hope. After I met Tony and started taking his lessons, I wanted to *know* if he was right. It *felt* right, but I wanted to test it. I've been praying for centuries, but I never felt my prayers were heard. He tells us to *pray* to know if what he tells us is true. Mormons say that a lot, you'll find!" He says, winking at Tony.

"So," he continues, "I decided to see if there was something to it all. I tried to go to the temple. Not go *to* the temple, I mean . . . in the sense that a *Mormon* means, but just to see if there was anything different about it. I've been in the greatest cathedrals in Europe! But the temples here are *different*. They *feel* different! I couldn't set foot in one of the lobbies. I was *barred* somehow. I tried to touch a wall. I couldn't."

He turns back to me. "But *you!* The two of you have been *inside* and, what's more, you received the greatest sacrament of the Mormons. You were *married* there!"

"Aye." Turning to speak to the rest of the vampires, I say, "I *was* barred just like ye . . . like all of ye. 'Twas Carl. He showed me that I was . . . that I was *forgiven*. He was ne'er *barred*, as ye put it."

"Never?" Corelli says, looking at Carl with awe.

"I never consented to Conversion," Carl says. "I was . . . well, Unwilling."

"How was this possible?" Ghalyela asks in wonder.

Carl sighs. "OK," he says. "Have a seat. It's a long story."

◢ ◢ ◢

"And you," Corelli says, pointing to Rolf and Sarah, who are seated next to each other, "are you two . . . *free* as well?"

My husband has finished the tale of his Conversion and of the Breaking of the Cult. Many questions have been asked and answered. It has been hours.

Sammy is beginning to yawn.

"No," Sarah says, her eyes darkening, "far from it. We're just as vulnerable as the rest of you lot."

Rolf says, "I've read this Book of Mormon"—he glances at me when I raise an eyebrow—"cover to cover—and I really *hope* it's true. I *believe* it's true."

"Why do you not simply get baptized and receive whatever sacraments Carl and Moira have received?" Ghalyela asks. "Would you not then be *free?*"

"It's not that simple," Rolf says.

"It takes a clearance from the Prophet of the Lord," Tony says.

"We," Rolf says, gesturing around the room, "all of us are murderers." He looks quickly at Carl. "Except for Carl, of course. Murder is very hard to repent of."

"Carl I understand," Ghalyela replies. "Carl is unique. But, Moira received such a . . . clearance."

"Aye, that I did," I say. "I'd spent one hundred and eighty years in abject repentance. I'd nae killed in all that time. I'd . . . participated in the Church as much as I could while nae being baptized. I had a very wonderful, kind bishop who would nae give up on me. He knew what I was. *He* petitioned the Prophet on my behalf. It took months to receive my clearance. It was half a century after that before I was able to enter the temple. I'm nae saying that it cannae be done. 'Tis an individual thing. Each case has to be evaluated separately. I'm just saying it takes *time.*"

"Each of you is different," Tony says. "A few of you have been Penitents for centuries. Some of you only gave up killing a few months ago, after you heard about the Breaking. But *all* of you are new to the gospel. Even for *mortals* who have murdered, getting a clearance is very hard. It can take years, and it may not be granted at all. For *vampires* . . ."

"Then why are we *doing* this?" a man with the chiseled features and coloring of a Navajo says from the back of the room. "Why *bother* with *trying* to repent if there's no *time?*"

All eyes in the room are focused on him as he continues. "We, all of us are out of time. Here we have the fulfillment of the Curse practically upon us with the Unwilling and the Penitent *right here in the room*. You're saying they could kill Lilith and bring the Curse down upon the lot of us. Why not *give up* and just let the Sun end our torment? We have no hope for anything better, and we're all going to die soon anyway."

Once again, murmurs fill the room. Some of the vampires are nodding in agreement.

"What a bunch of bleating sheep!" says a voice. All eyes turn to Sarah. "Are you saying you didn't *choose* this life?"

There is dead silence.

Sarah steps forward from where she was standing near Rolf. "*I* chose this life! *You* did, as well. Every single one of you! Carl, here, is the only one who didn't. It was forced on him. But the *rest* of us? We all chose to slaughter mortals and drink their blood so we could have immortality or love or . . . *whatever! I* chose it! I could claim that I was seduced, but there are probably a lot of us who might claim that. We *knew* it was evil! We *knew* it was *unspeakably* vile! But we chose it anyway. We all had our reasons. Believe me, *I had mine.*"

She glares at them as if daring them to challenge her.

"Now," she continues, her voice angry, "you all act as if you don't *deserve* the damnation you chose! Well, I *deserve* mine."

"It's not that we don't *deserve* damnation, as you put it," the russet-skinned vampire replies, "it's just that, from what I'm hearing tonight, it sounds like there's no *point* in going on, if we can't be redeemed. It's all very well for Moira and Carl here: they're free of Lilith's power . . . or her *control*, at least. And from all appearances they have been forgiven. But I've got the lives of hundreds of white men on my conscience."

"And now *you* . . . ," he says, pointing at me, "you tell me that it took you *centuries* of repentance to receive your redemption. Lilith could show up tonight, and you could kill her and *then* where would we be? Dead and in Hell, that's where."

"And from what Carl has told *me*," Rolf interjects, "Dr. Lupescu has been teaching you about the Book of Mormon. Correct?"

There are nods from around the room.

"Well," he continues, "I've read it. There are many examples of evil men who repented. There's Alma, his son Alma, Ammon, Aaron, Omner, Himni, Amulek, and Zeezrom. There was Lamoni, his father Anti-Nephi-Lehi, and the Children of Ammon. *They* were all murderers. *They* deserved damnation, but they *changed*. They swore an oath never to kill again, and they were *forgiven*.

"But the *most important* . . . the most important of *all* were the Lamanite soldiers who were sent to kill the Children of Ammon. Many of the soldiers threw down their weapons and joined the Children of Ammon. They joined them in prayer, and some of the penitent soldiers were struck down."

He looks around the room.

"Well, don't you see?" he says, exasperated. "They were forgiven *even though they hadn't been baptized or been inside the temple or done anything!* God forgave them because their *desire* to repent was sincere. When they threw down their weapons and started praying, *they knew that they could be killed!* And some of them *were!* They were willing to lay down their lives to find God. They were 'out of time' and they *still* chose to meet God doing everything they could in the short time they had left, *even if it was only so much as to pray and beg for redemption!*"

"You see, Dezba," Tony says, addressing the Navajo vampire, "it doesn't end *here* in this life. If you're on the *path*, God can and *will* make up the difference."

"But," Dezba says, his voice breaking, "I've killed so many, not to mention all the other sins." A tear spills down his stoic face. "There's not enough forgiveness in the *world* for such as me."

"That's what *I* said," Rolf replies. "But Carl and Moira told me otherwise. I will follow them into *Hell*, if necessary, to find that forgiveness."

Rolf steps forward and stands in front of Carl. He stands facing the Stake vampires, and then he turns and faces Carl. Rolf pulls his sword from its sheath.

There is a collective gasp from the room. I'm about to pull my own blade to block him when Rolf abruptly kneels at Carl's feet.

He holds his sword by the handle in his right hand and lays the blade across his left. He bows his head and extends both hands with his weapon toward Carl.

"I may not live long enough to make the covenant of baptism with God, but I make this covenant before God right now. I swear fealty to *you*, Carl Morgan. You are God's chosen Unwilling, prophesied to lead us against Lilith and all of her Children. I'm not worthy to serve God, but I will serve you in His name. My life and my sword are yours to command in Jesus' name."

I look at Carl, and his face is a mask of horror.

"I'm not a Master," Carl says in a stricken voice.

Rolf looks up at him and says, "But I will serve you. You're my only hope."

"*Christ* is your only hope," Carl says. "I'm not Him. I'm not some messiah. There's only one Messiah. He's the only one who can redeem you."

"Yes," Rolf replies, his voice thick with emotion, "I know that, but you're God's chosen servant. And I *will* serve you. I will serve you in His name. I'm yours to . . ."

"Stop it!" Carl snaps.

Rolf cuts off speaking abruptly. His eyes are wide in surprise.

"Get up!" Carl barks.

Rolf quickly rises to his feet. He stares at Carl, and there is alarm in his expression.

"I'm sorry, Rolf," Carl says, his voice softer. He places a hand on the shoulder of the former Nazi. "It's all this talk of serving and following. It really, *really* bugs me."

"Laddie," I say to Carl, "*look* at him."

Carl looks at Rolf, really looks at him, and sees what I see. He sees the wonder and alarm and . . . something else.

"What?" Carl says.

"I have to obey you," Rolf says, his voice soft.

Carl shakes his head. "No, you don't."

"Yes, I *do*."

The horror returns to Carl's face. "NO!"

Rolf nods and a grin spreads across his face. "Yes! I'm *bound* to obey you!"

"NO! NO! *NO!*" Carl roars.

"Yes," Rolf says, once Carl has finished yelling at him. "You don't get it, do you, my Captain?" His smile is *huge!*

"Get what?" Carl replies. "That somehow I've become a Master again?"

"No," Rolf says. "You're not a Master. But I'm bound to serve you."

Carl opens his mouth to speak again, but Rolf raises a hand.

"Please," Rolf says, "let me try something. Trust me."

Carl nods grimly.

Rolf turns around and fixes his eyes on the African woman, Ghalyela. "You're a Master. Command me to do something."

She looks at him dubiously. "If he is your Master now," she says, indicating Carl, "you will not be required to obey *me*."

Someone snaps his fingers. I look over at the source of the sound. It's Tony, and he looks thrilled. "Pardon me," he says, fairly bouncing in his excitement, "but I'm not sure that's true. In fact, I'm fairly positive it's not."

All eyes turn to him.

"Well," he continues, "from what I've learned, any non-Master must obey any Master (or for that matter, their own Teacher if there is no Master), *unless* . . ." and he now pauses for dramatic effect, "*your* Master has commanded that you will obey no other Master but *him* . . . or her. Carl hasn't *done* that. So this may be a valid test of the hypothesis."

He's rubbing his hands together. He looks like a teacher warming to his subject. *That's an apt comparison in this case, I suppose.*

"What hypothesis?" Corelli asks.

"I don't think Carl *is* a Master," Tony says, shaking his finger at nobody in particular. "I think our Mr. Rolf is correct." He pauses and looks at Rolf.

"I don't think I ever got your last name."

"Oettinger," Rolf replies.

I cannae believe I never asked him that! Well I've known him for so short a time!

"It's a theory I have about the true nature of the Essence," Tony continues.

"The Essence?" Sammy pipes up. "That's the demonic component of what makes them vampires, right?"

"Yes, Sam," Tony says, looking at Sammy, but 'tis plain to see that he is really speaking to all of us. "The Seed is the biological component, and the Essence is the *spiritual* component. But I want you to think about it. The Seed and the Essence come from Satan, right?" There are nods from around the room, but he continues right on. "Satan may be *cunning*, but his knowledge is limited. He doesn't know how to *create* anything." He pauses and is visibly gratified to see the puzzled expressions on our faces.

"Satan only knows how to imitate and *corrupt*. He's not a genetic engineer. So how could he create the *Seed*?"

"He couldn't," Sammy says.

"*Precisely!*" Tony says, pointing at Sammy as he would to a student who had come to the right conclusion. "The Seed, or something like it, had to *already* exist. I need *your* expertise on this, Sam. I think that Satan imitated and corrupted something that already existed, but," he says, waving a hand dismissively, "we'll have to get back to that. I'll need you to do some research for me, Sam."

Sam nods. "Sure!"

"But back to the *Essence!*" Tony continues. "I think the Essence is a counterfeit for the Gift of the Holy Ghost. Once again, Satan can't create *anything*. He can only imitate and corrupt . . . and that, often poorly. The Holy Ghost's power can be felt by everyone, if they are open to it. The Essence can be felt only by those who have received it by ritual. (Which, might I point out, is conferred by a laying on of hands, just like the gift of the Holy Ghost.) The Holy Ghost inspires, testifies, and *entices* us to Christ. The Essence *forces* you to obey. That was always Satan's plan: to take away our agency, our free will. We make covenants with God, and it is up to *us* whether we will keep them or not. The Essence *forces* you to keep your vampire Covenants, specifically to obey Lilith and her Masters."

He makes a grand sweeping gesture at the vampires in the room. "You all gave up your free will when you Converted and received the Essence. All of you, except for Carl, that is."

He turns to face Carl. "*You* were never bound to obey because you *never surrendered your free will*."

He turns to Rolf. "*You* are bound to Carl because you pledged to obey him, and you did it of your own free will. And I think . . . I *hypothesize* that because you *voluntarily* chose to obey him and you did it in the name of Jesus . . .

well, the Essence will still enforce your covenant and that's bad . . . but I *hypothesize* that it will *trump* any other covenant you have made. And that's *good*."

We all stare at him.

"Well, go on," he says to Rolf. "See if Ghalyela can command you! Let's see if it works."

Rolf turns to Ghalyela again and bows. "Command me," he says.

She blinks for a wee tick and then says, "Dance for me."

We all stare at Rolf. He stands stock still for a tick and then he raises a foot. There is a collective groan from everyone.

He grins and says, "Just kidding!" as he sets his foot down again.

Now there is a collective sigh of relief.

Tony claps his hands. "Excellent!"

"But now," I say, "he's just bound to a different Master."

Carl flinches at the word.

"Yes," Rolf says, "but I'm sworn to obey a man whom I trust to never lead me astray."

"To never 'exercise unrighteous dominion,'" Tony says.

"Exactly," Rolf says.

Carl opens his mouth to speak, but Rolf interrupts him.

"More importantly," Rolf says, "I may be *bound* to you, but now I can follow you into *battle*."

"What do you mean?" Carl says.

"What I mean," Rolf answers, "is that *none* of us could have followed you to stop Müller and his abominable Congregation. We couldn't get within earshot of him. One word of command from Müller, and I'd have been helpless. I would have become a slave, a weapon in his hand. By swearing fealty to *you*, by entrusting my life to God, I'm *free*. At least, I'm as free as I can be for now. And I'll take that. It's better than living in constant fear that Lilith or one of her agents can appear and make me a slave again."

There is a low, visceral snarl from behind me. I turn and look at Sarah. She stamps her foot, cracking the floor tile beneath it.

"I *knew* it!" she growls. "I just *knew* it would come to this!"

She waves her sword, pointing it angrily at Carl, and then she stomps over and kneels in front of him.

She presents her sword to Carl just as Rolf did and says in an annoyed tone, "In the name of the Lord Jesus, I swear fealty to you, Carl Morgan, the Unwilling. I will serve you in His name. My life and my sword are yours to command."

Then she rises and faces him. "You won't let me down, will you?"

Carl's shoulders sag, and he sighs. "I promise you . . . I'll do my best."

"Fair enough," she says and turns away from him. She hastily wipes away a tear.

She stomps over to Rolf and says, "You bloody . . . *man!*" She makes the word sound like an epithet. *Perhaps it is to her.* She transfers her sword to her left hand and, with her right, she slaps his face so hard that I can hear his jaw break.

He cries out in pain. His hand goes to his jaw and he massages it as the Seed quickly knits it back together, all the while staring Sarah in the eye.

"I hate you," she says, glowering at him, "you and all your egotistical, domineering sex."

She reaches up quickly with her hand, the same one she used to slap him, and takes him by the back of his head and pulls his face down to hers. She plants a huge kiss on his lips.

He does nae have time to react.

She releases him and stands beside him. "Bloody man," she mutters.

Rolf looks shocked and stands frozen for a moment. Then a grin splits his face, and he reaches beside him for her hand.

She lets him take it.

He looks at me and then at Carl. Then he shrugs his shoulders and acts for all the world as if nary a thing of any significance has just happened.

For my part, I can only stare at them in stunned silence for a wee bit before I turn my attention back to Carl. Poor lad! He looks as flummoxed as I feel.

Corelli coughs politely. "I'm sure that something of great import just occurred," he says, glancing at Rolf and Sarah, "but I don't understand it, and I'm . . . not sure I want to."

He walks toward me and bows deeply. "Mrs. Morgan, might I borrow your sword?"

I pull the black blade from the sheath and offer it to him hilt first.

He takes it from me, bows low again, and then turns to Carl. He kneels and offers the weapon to him. Bowing his head, he says, "In the name of the Lord Jesus, I swear fealty to you, Carl Morgan, the Unwilling . . ."

One by one, they all come forward, kneel, and covenant, using my sword. The last to come forward is Dezba, the Navajo vampire.

At least I think he's Navajo.

As he kneels in front of Carl, holding my sword, he looks up at him and says, "All my life I've hated your people for what they did to mine. I need to let go of that hatred. It is what brought me to . . . this Hell of an existence. I ask for your forgiveness. Forgive me for my hatred." His voice quavers.

"I can't forgive you," Carl says. "You've done nothing to me. That has to come from God and those you've killed. I can't forgive you."

"I understand," Dezba says, his voice trembling, "but God is not here, and they are not here."

"My brother," Carl says, laying a hand on Dezba's shoulder, "I promise you that He can hear you. I can feel his Spirit here tonight."

Dezba lifts his face toward Heaven and says in a strong voice, "Oh, Great Father! Tony has said that *you're* the God of my fathers! I want to believe! Help me to believe! Forgive me for my sins! Forgive me for my hatred of my white brothers! Forgive me for the lives I've taken! Help me to find my way back to thee! In the name of Jesus Christ I ask this!"

He bows his head now, and presenting the sword toward Carl, he says, "In the name of the Lord Jesus, I swear fealty to you, Carl Morgan . . ."

Chapter 21

IT IS *GONE*! *Gone!*" Ghalyela cries, her richly accented voice filled with wonder. We turn to look at her. Her bright eyes are wide with awe and joy. "It is *gone*!" she cries again. "I cannot *believe* it!" She laughs. 'Tis a deep and hearty laugh of relief.

"What's gone?" Tony asks.

Ghalyela continues to laugh, and tears run down her beautiful black face.

I look at Carl. He shrugs and looks as perplexed.

We watch as she laughs. Eventually, her laughter dies down, and she sighs loud and long. She puts her head in her hands. "It is gone!" she says again. "*Twenty-seven years* and it is finally gone."

"What is it?" Tony presses again.

"The Calling," she replies, lifting her head and looking at him. "I'm a Master," she declares, as if that explains everything.

"I don't understand," Tony says. "What do you mean, 'the calling'?"

"Do you not know?" she asks, puzzled. "Are none of the rest of you Masters?"

She looks around the room, but nobody responds.

"I am," Sarah says after a wee pause. "I killed my Master. Technically, that makes me one."

"Were you Sealed to Lilith as her consort?" the black-skinned woman asks.

"No," Sarah replies in disgust.

We all know very well that Lilith takes every Master as her consort. Male or female makes nae difference. Sarah knows this as well as any of us. She taught it to me.

"That explains it," Ghalyela says, nodding. "Killing a Master makes you Master of the Cult, yes. Once you become a Master, Lilith will send an Enforcer to collect you and bring you back to her. She will seal you as her consort. She will have you for one night or longer . . . as long as she desires. And then you're bound to her forever. You are always at her Call. If she wants you, she will Call you. You will feel it in your mind, in your whole body. And you cannot resist. And it is always there, like an itch in the back of your mind that you cannot scratch."

"But you said something about 'twenty-seven years,'" Sarah says. "Is that how long you've been a Master?"

"No," Ghalyela replies, shaking her head, "I've been a Master for the better part of a century. Twenty-seven years is how long I've been on the run. All that time, the Call has been there."

"I don't understand," Carl says. "If you've been on the run, how have you resisted her Call?"

"I've not, precisely, been able to resist it," she replies. "Even before I fled, when Lilith would Call, I would send my first husband, Ngozi. He is only too happy to go in my stead. Lilith has female consorts, but she *prefers* men. She would accept my man as a substitute without question. He has carried on the charade since I left.

"If Lilith were to catch on and summon me specifically," she continues, "I would have been forced to go. I've lived in dread that she would Call me, ever since I desired to repent.

"But now," she says, clapping her hands, "I'm *free*! That niggling itch is gone! And she cannot Call me!"

"Rolf," Carl says, "you told us that Lilith was aware that I had killed Michael and that I had dissolved the Cult."

"That's correct," Rolf replies.

"How could she know?" Carl asks. "Is it something similar to the . . . link that she seems to have with her Masters?"

"It's the *Essence*," Tony says.

"How would *ye* know?" I say. "How would ye know *anything* about the Essence and what it really is . . . or even how it works?"

"OK," Tony says, blushing mouthwateringly, "I don't *know*. It just *feels* right. I've been studying this for a long time . . ."

"I've been *living* it for a long time."

"Yes," he replies going even more deliciously crimson, "I know you have, but . . . well, sometimes it takes an *outsider* to look at things objectively."

I nod. "Aye. I can see how that might be. 'Twas Carl who discovered how we're so abnormally strong, how we're able to fly with or without wings . . ."

There is another collective gasp from the room. Mortal and immortal alike stare at us.

"Fly . . . without wings?" This is from Lorenzo Corelli. "How is that possible?"

I sigh. *Time to explain it again.* "We dinnae need wings to fly," I say, trying to keep the annoyance out of my tone. "The wings themselves are simply mental or psychic projections. We project the wings because we think we *need* them."

I lift off the floor for a moment and hover there. "See? Nae wings." I drop back to the floor lightly.

"Incredible," Lorenzo whispers. There are similar expressions from around the room. Some of them are in languages that I dinnae know.

"Ye just have to . . . turn them off," I say. "It takes practice, but ye can do it simply by imagining yourself flying without them."

"We used to use it as a test of Penitence," Carl says. "We reasoned that it showed self-discipline, because unrepentant vampires were unable to do it . . . or so we thought. That is, we thought so until Müller and Bartlett were able to do it."

"Bartlett?" Ghalyela asks in confusion. "Who is that?"

"The 'Keeper,'" Rolf explains.

"The Internet site?" Ghalyela asks.

Rolf nods.

"Aye, he's Müller's slave," I say. "Müller has been using Bartlett to ensnare the Penitents who are gathering here."

"Of course he has," Corelli says. "That makes sense."

"We think Bartlett may have been sincere at first," Carl says, "but Müller found him and co-opted him and his website."

Corelli nods. "Yes, I see. That must have been when the posts about 'Sanctification' started. He's luring vampires here and making sure that, when they arrive, they are at his mercy."

"But why not just ensnare them with his command?" Sarah says. "He *is* one of Lilith's Enforcers, after all."

There are a few nods from around the room. 'Twould appear some did nae know Müller's position in Lilith's hierarchy.

Others look alarmed.

"Yes," Corelli says, nodding again, "that also makes sense. He's an Enforcer. So why not simply *enthrall* all of us? Why the deception of this false religion? Why the Congregation?"

"I assume ye know about the pig blood?" I ask.

"I filled them in on that before you arrived," Sammy says. He looks happy to have something to contribute.

"Because," Rolf says, as his handsome face darkens with understanding, "it's not enough to kill us or enslave us. He wants to *corrupt* us. He wants us to follow him voluntarily. If he can't do that, he'll kill us. But he wants zealots and true believers. It's like Hitler when he wanted to take over Austria. He could have simply invaded and conquered it militarily, but no, he wanted them to join him voluntarily through the Anschluss. He wanted them to join him because they *believed* in his horrific lies. He wanted them to give up their Jews of their own free will.

"It's like when each of us was Converted," he continues. "We were given an Offering. We didn't have to *murder* our Offering to complete our Conversion . . . *Carl* didn't kill his . . . but we weren't told that. We were told it was *necessary.*"

"So our damnation would be assured," I say.

Rolf nods sadly. "Yes."

"Well," Carl says, cocking his head, "in the immortal words of Yogi Berra, 'It ain't over till it's over.'"

"What?" Ghalyela asks. Her confusion is reflected in the faces of most of the vampires in the room.

"'Tis an American saying from a famous baseball coach," I say.

"Manager," Carl whispers, correcting me. He means it to be surreptitious, but, of course, all save the two mortals can hear him.

"*Manager*," I repeat with a quick a glance filled with mock annoyance. He winks at me.

"It means," I say, "that ye must never give up. Fight all the way till your last breath. The rest is in God's hands."

"All right," Corelli says, "you also mentioned an *understanding* of how our vampiric strength works."

"Right," Carl says. "You remember how Sarah slapped Rolf here a bit ago and broke his jaw? You all heard it." He glances at Tony and Sammy. "Well, maybe *you* two didn't hear it, but the rest of us did. She broke his jaw."

Carl rubs his own jaw, probably remembering the time I punched him and broke *his* jaw.

"Did you break any bones in your hand, Sarah?" Carl asks.

She shakes her head.

"No, of course not," Carl continues. "That should be impossible. When I was Converted, I gained about twenty pounds of extra bone and muscle mass, but that can't account for me being able to lift a car, for example. The strength has to come from somewhere else."

"The Essence," Tony says with assurance.

"No, I don't think so," counters Carl. "I think it's our minds. We're able to project wings, a darkness that helps to hide us, and so on. The Seed seems to have unlocked something in our minds. In the case of our physical strength, it's something called *tactile telekinesis*. We can lift or move objects that we're touching. I'm not sure what the limits are, but I can lift a car just as easily with one finger as I can with both hands. You just have to *believe* you can do it. It's what makes us fly. We fly because we think of our bodies moving through the air. We can't move objects that we *aren't* touching, but, if it's *connected* to us, we can move it."

"That explains a trick I learned long ago," Corelli says, nodding. "I discovered, quite by accident, that I could make my cloak hold still in the wind or billow behind me when there *wasn't* any wind." He shakes his finger at Carl enthusiastically. "*Yes*, Carl, I think you're right about this."

Neat trick. It would ne'er occur to me to try to manipulate objects that I was nae touching with my hands.

"OK," Carl says, "that theory seems to fit the facts."

"*Anyway*," Tony interjects, "as I was saying before I was so *rudely* interrupted . . ." He grins a big Cheshire Cat grin in Carl's direction.

Carl nods his head and grins back at him.

Tony nods and says, "The *Essence* seems to connect all of you together."

That's right. Before we got sidetracked, he was about to explain how Lilith's Calling works. At least he was about to explain his theory about it.

"The Essence allows Lilith to feel what is going on with her Children, I think," he continues. "It's my theory that's how she knew that the local Master, Michael, was dead. It was how she knew that the Cult was dissolved. I've spent some time pondering this since you told me about it . . . and I think the Essence is responsible for the two of you, Carl and Moira, having dreams."

"How so?" I ask.

"Wait just a minute!" Corelli cries. "You're having *dreams?*"

"Aye, that's right," I say.

Carl nods. "I've repeatedly dreamt of this *gathering* with many of you and *you* especially," he says, pointing at Tony. "Although, it was in a different room," he says, looking at our surroundings.

"We don't normally meet in this building," Tony says.

"Also," Carl continues, "there's a repeating dream where I'm being crucified and then burned by the Sun."

I nod and say, "I've had that particular dream myself many times."

"B-b-but," Corelli stammers, "we don't *dream!*"

"And *we* did nae dream, until a few months ago," I say. "It began after the Penitents started to arrive here in Utah."

"And that's when the hunger began too," Carl adds.

"What hunger?" Tony asks.

"An abnormally intense hunger," Carl replies. "We always feel like we're starving to death."

"The lure of evil blood is nigh unbearable," I say.

"Is anybody else experiencing dreams or abnormal hunger?" Tony asks the assembled vampires.

All of them shake their heads.

"That fits too!" Tony says, smiling happily.

"I'm *so* glad ye find our misery amusing!" I say with a wee touch of sarcasm. "It has been quite . . . difficult for the two of us to bear."

"Ah," he says. "Sorry." He pauses for just a tick and then he rubs his hands together in obvious glee. "But it fits! Don't you see?"

I shake my head. So does Carl.

"It's the *Essence!*" he says. "You're connected to all other vampires, but you're *free* of Lilith's control. That makes you different. I think it's like *feedback*, for lack of a better word. You're suddenly feeling all the *hunger* as all these other Penitents slowly starve themselves. You're *dreaming* because any large assembly of vampires in the area seems to force itself into your subconscious mind. In short, *you're* having to bear all the burdens of the Penitents around you."

He snaps his fingers and points at Carl. "It's like Christ bearing the burden of our sins in Gethsemane!"

"Will you *stop* with the *messianic* references?" Carl snarls. "I'm *not* some doggone vampire messiah!"

"No," Tony says, nae backing down, "you're not, but you're a *type* of Christ . . . like Moses, Noah, or Abraham."

"No, I'm *not*," Carl reiterates, his voice a hiss filled with danger.

I squeeze his hand to calm him.

"You don't realize what has happened, do you?" Tony says. "All of these people here, these vampires, are bound to you to the death! They're going to follow you into *Hell*, if need be, to destroy Lilith. They're all going to lay down their lives to end her reign on Earth. You two are the ones who are prophesied to stop her. You're going to sacrifice your *own* lives to do it. All their hopes are centered on you and the fulfilling of the Prophecy. If that isn't messianic, I don't know what is!"

"It's to *Christ!*" Carl protests. "They need to look to *Christ* and *no other!*"

"Of *course* we're looking to Christ," Sarah says. "*You* aren't going to redeem us of our sins; *He* is. You're simply the one who's showing us how to find our way back to Him."

Sammy says, "You're like the missionaries who go out and show lost and hopeless people that Christ is waiting to welcome them back with open arms. All they have to do is to repent, turn to Him, and serve Him."

The images of Elder Wallace, Elder Rasmussen, and Bishop Hettinger flash through my mind.

"You served a mission, didn't you, Carl?" Sammy asks.

"Yeah," my husband replies, his voice softer, the anger gone, "in Korea."

"Well, you remember," Sammy continues, "how you *mourned* for every single soul who wouldn't listen, especially those you *knew* were close to committing to baptism, but just couldn't bring themselves to give up cigarettes, coffee, or liquor . . . or sexual sin or whatever? Remember how you wept and *bled* inside for each of them? Well, that sounds like what you're feeling now. You can't wash away the sins of those around you, but you will still mourn with them and feel pain as they struggle to find their way. You're *not* messianic, but you're the one who's going to show them how to find the Savior."

"But I'm not strong enough or *good* enough," Carl replies.

"Nae," I say. I smile at him, and I'm nearly overwhelmed in this moment with my love for him. "Ye are nae *worthy* of the task, but were ye *strong* enough, *good* enough when the Lord called ye to Korea? Nae, ye were just a lad of nineteen. And ye went *anyway*, did ye nae? And the Lord sustained ye. He called ye. He helped ye then. And He will help ye now."

"He's going to help both of you," Sammy says. "You're as much a part of the prophecy as Carl is. You're the Penitent. Without you, he wouldn't be able to do any of this. You're both in this together."

"Aye, laddie," I say to Sammy. Then, to Carl I say with a smirk, "We're in it up to our necks for sure."

♦ ♦ ♦

"Why are you so sure we *need* a battle plan?" Martha asks. She is the vampire who appears to be barely fourteen, but is actually nearly two centuries old. Obviously she was Converted at a very young age. "Why can't we just leave the Congregation be?"

"We can't ignore them," Carl explains, "because Müller is corrupting those of our kind who truly want to repent, leading them down a false path, and he is murdering mortals. I don't need any other reason."

"But, even if you stop Müller here, the work of corruption and death is going to continue," Martha replies. "This is only one small corner of the world. Lilith's hand reaches everywhere."

"This is my *home*," my husband says, and in his eyes, there's a smoldering that is terrible to behold, "and I *will* defend it. And I will not let even *one* more mortal die at the hands of Müller if I can help it."

"Then why not attack now . . . tonight?" she counters.

I thought perhaps she was afraid to fight. Nae, she sounds almost eager. This lass has a fire in her that her apparent youth masks. I like her.

"Because we don't know what we're up against, for one thing. And because, Müller was eager to have us witness the next meeting of the Congregation. That's not going to be until Saturday night slash Sunday morning. It's Tuesday night. So that means he won't need to Feed his followers for four more nights. We've met him, and he is obviously keeping himself on the verge of starvation to promote the deception. He said he was 'bleeding the pigs' last night to produce his obscene 'Blessing.' So I think we have some time before he kills again. I'm not suggesting we wait until Saturday, but I think we have a night or two so we can lay our plans."

He looks around the room. "How many of you have weapons?" A few raise their hands. I note that Martha is one of them. "Obviously you don't have them here, but you have them at . . . well, wherever it is you're living right now?" Several more raise their hands.

"Six of you do not," he notes. "Those of you without weapons, can you *handle* one if we can supply you with one?" All six of them nod.

Carl turns to me. "Can your swordsmith friend supply six more weapons?"

"I would imagine so," I reply. "I could give someone my hanger as well." I'm surprised to realize that I dinnae mind the thought of getting rid of it. "I'll call him in the morning."

"Great," he says. "I'm calling a counsel of war tomorrow night, an hour after dusk. Will that work for everyone?"

There are nods and murmurs of assent from everyone, including the mortals.

"Cool," he says. "Everyone come prepared with your ideas. All ideas are welcome."

He looks at Tony. "Do you have everyone's number or some way to get ahold of everyone?"

"Yes," Tony replies with a grin. Then, perhaps realizing the gravity of what we're discussing, he adds, "We have a calling tree."

"I need a copy of it," Carl says.

My military man! He is assuming command!

"You'll have it," Tony replies with a nod.

"Make a copy for Rolf," Carl says, pointing at the German. "He's my second-in-command." He looks at me. "No offense, sweetheart."

I put up both hands. "Nae problem, laddie!" I smile at him. "Military tactics are nae my area of expertise."

"You will obey Rolf's orders . . . and Moira's as you would my own," he continues. Then, apparently realizing he'd just given a command, he grimaces. "No, scratch that! I didn't mean to put it that way!"

He looks both sheepish and annoyed. "Look, I'm not comfortable with this whole 'bound-to-obey' thing. You all chose to follow me . . . I get that . . . but I don't want you . . . obeying orders blindly. I need you all to be able to think for yourselves, especially in combat. I'm your leader and Rolf is my second, but . . ."

He throws up his hands in frustration. "Argh! This *sucks*! How do I give orders without making them . . . *commands* that you can't resist?"

"Ye could say, 'please,' laddie," I say with a wink.

"You've gotta be *kidding* me!" he cries. "What kind of a messed up army is this? Orders that start with 'please?'"

"Try it," says Rolf. "Make a request and see if I can disobey it."

"O . . . K," Carl says. "Would you *please* sit down?" he says to Rolf.

Rolf does nae move.

"Pretty please with a cherry on top?" Carl says with his bonnie lopsided grin.

"Well," Rolf replies, "since you ask so nicely . . . On second thought . . . Nope!"

"Cool," Carl says, his eyes shining. He turns to the rest of us. "OK, in the heat of battle, I might slip up, but I will try to make all of my orders sound like requests. But, *please* try to treat them like orders that you're not *bound* to obey."

"That sounds like a plan," Corelli says. He looks delighted.

"Uh, Carl," Rolf whispers. *Of course, everyone in the room can hear him . . . except for Tony and Sammy.*

"Yeah?" Carl says.

Rolf looks embarrassed, but he pushes on, "Are we about done here? Sarah and I need to go somewhere and . . . *talk*."

Carl chuckles. Sarah glowers at him.

"I'll bet you do," Carl says. "Go on. Get out of here."

Rolf and Sarah turn immediately to go.

"Oops!" Carl says. "I mean, *please* get out of here. The safe words are . . . how about 'Babylon' and 'Egypt'? Duress word is . . . 'tiger.'"

Rolf nods. "Got it. You better explain the concept to *them*," he says, indicating the rest of the people in the room.

"Will do," Carl replies.

Rolf and Sarah turn to go. They have been holding hands all this time.

"Oh!" Carl cries. He jumps up and calls after them.

They turn and Carl walks up to Rolf. He tries to whisper, but with this lot, 'twill do him nae good.

"Uh," he stammers, "just . . . remember that you're . . . uh . . . trying to live by *God's* law now."

"Are you trying to give us the 'sex talk,' *daddy*?" Rolf says with a mocking grin.

Carl fidgets and says, "Yeah. Sort of. I mean . . . you're sharing the same room and . . ."

Sarah gives him a look that would curdle new milk.

"We'll be *careful*," she says, enunciating each word. "I was a nun for a long time after I was a whore. I've been without a man for most of a millennium. I'll wait till I can have this one *legal*. He hasn't even asked me to marry him . . . yet."

Rolf's eyes go wide.

"Don't worry, though," she continues in a perilous tone. "He *will*."

Rolf laughs softly. There is a nervous edge to his laugh, though. Then his face splits in a wide grin.

Sarah turns to Rolf and pokes him hard in the chest with her finger. "And . . . we . . . *will* . . . wait!"

"Yes, *ma'am*," he says, grinning like the village idiot.

Carl turns back to the Stake vampires as Rolf and Sarah exit the room.

"Who'd have thought?" I say. "*Those* two?"

"I heard that!" Sarah's voice comes echoing from the hallway outside.

I smile to myself. *Love is strange. He's so bonnie and she's . . . well, she's nae beauty, and she's so . . . prickly. It cannae be her sweet demeanor.*

Carl clears his throat. "Safe words and duress words," he says. "This is what we use to authenticate communications . . ."

It has been a very long night. We've learned the stories and strengths of the various members of the Stake.

Martha was seduced and Converted when she was but a lass in her native Virginia, by a vampire who apparently had a taste for younger girls. She was barely fifteen (though she looks younger), and she was desperately in love. But he abandoned her for an even younger lass, whom he similarly corrupted. Betrayed and devastated, she wandered, surviving as a Renegade, avoiding other vampires. Those she did encounter invariably tried to bring her into their Cults and thus under their control. She became very adept at killing those who sought to enslave her. She loathed what she had become in the name of love. She wished for nothing more than genuine love, family, and children, which, of course, she can ne'er have. She will ne'er be a woman, and she's barely more than a child.

Ghalyela is a master of the Zulu iklawa, a short spear. She's nae a Zulu herself, but she learned it from her original Master, who *was* of that people. It was her encounter with Lilith, when Ghalyela was 'sealed' to Lilith as her consort, that drove her to seek for a way out of the path she had chosen.

Lilith, she told us, is incredibly seductive, indescribably beautiful, completely irresistible, but ultimately devoid of any human sentiment. She loves nobody. She cares for nobody. All vampires are her chattels. We're nae so much as children to her—merely toys to be played with on occasion and discarded when she is bored. Mortals are merely livestock to her. Ghalyela saw in Lilith the epitome of what she, herself, had become. Ghalyela would ne'er be more than a slave to a soulless monster. And so, eventually, she fled.

Dezba's weapon of choice is a U.S. Cavalry saber taken from a white soldier. He had spent the first few decades after his Conversion hunting white men, especially soldiers. That ended the night he witnessed an American soldier, mounted on horseback, drag the fresh carcass of a buffalo calf into a Blackfoot village filled with starving women and children.

Aye, each of them has a story, but we've yet to hear Corelli's. He has waited until the last. Tony and Sammy, being mortals and in need of sleep, were forced to leave a while ago.

"For me," Corelli begins, "it was *love* that turned me around. I had stopped killing long before I met Mara. But I had found no purpose and had decided to end my life, having lost all hope of redemption. As I was waiting for the Sun to take me with the dawn, Mara discovered me. She was picking mushrooms in the forest when she saw me burst into flame. She covered me with her cloak. She was about to shield me with her body, so I relented.

"She saved me. She recognized what I was, but she was unafraid. As we came to know each other, we fell in love. But she consented to marry me on the condition that I agreed to live a sinless life from then on. She never desired immortality for herself. She was a pure soul, very devout in her faith. But she loved me. She *believed* in me. We had many happy years together. I loved her all the days of her life."

He smiles wistfully. "I love her still."

He pauses for a tick. "When she passed at a ripe old age, I tried to end my life . . . to join her. I waited at her grave for the Sun to take me. As my flesh ignited, the flames scorched her tombstone. It cracked."

Scorched and cracked tombstone?

"Even as I was burning," he continues, "I thought that, if there was any hope of joining my Mara, suicide was not the answer. She was in Heaven. I could not join her there as a suicide. So I fled to the safe shadows of the trees, and once the Seed had healed me, I left that place, never to return.

"Now, Tony tells me that it may be possible for me to be sealed to her in your temple. I *live* for that day. If I die in battle, I've left written instructions behind for him to have this done for us after I'm gone."

He swallows hard. "Her name is Mara, and her name means 'bitter,' but to me she is all the sweetness that Heaven could offer."

I step forward and I put my arms around him. After a moment, he returns the hug.

"Does Tony *know*?" I ask after a bit, my arms still tight around him.

"No," he says, pulling out of the embrace. "I'm not ready to tell him. I honestly had no idea he was here when I came to teach at this University."

"Does Tony know *what*?" Carl asks.

"Lorenzo, here," I say, pointing to Corelli, "is Tony's great-great-grandfather."

It's after dawn when Carl and I finally are back on I-15, driving toward Salt Lake. Carl and I are having one of our rare arguments. Well, 'tis nae an *argument* so much as it is a *difference of opinion.*

"He's not *dead*, so the ordinance isn't binding," Carl points out.

"I ken that," I counter as I drive, "but Tony did nae ken that when he had the work done for Lorenzo and Mara. 'Twas done in good faith, so why should it nae be binding?"

"You can't do a proxy ordinance for a living person."

"But it has been done *already*. 'Twould be valid, d'ye nae think?"

"I *know* that Tony had the work done for Lorenzo, but Tony was working from bad information. As far as he knows, his great-great-grandfather is dead, burned to death at Mara's graveside, and he didn't even have the right *name*."

"Aye, Lorenzo said it troubled him greatly that Mara was sealed to 'Laurentiu Constantinescu.' Still, the Lord will eventually straighten it all out, will He nae?"

"I sure hope so," Carl says with a chuckle. "I've got an ancestor who is actually sealed to his grandmother because he was named John, his father was named John, and his grandfather was named John, and somebody made a mistake in the genealogy and submitted the names wrong! I had the sealings redone, of course, but it's a *mess*!"

"Aye, laddie." I laugh. "That's one to be straightened out in the Millennium for sure!"

"Yeah, we do our best and leave the rest up to the Lord."

"As we do in everything," I say and squeeze his hand affectionately.

"Anyway, since he's not dead, it can't be . . . ," he says, but he's cut off by his phone.

He pulls it out and says to me, "It's Rolf." I glance at him, and I can see he's frowning. "What's he doing making a voice call in the clear?"

Any of our kind could be listening.

Carl flips the phone open and puts it to his ear.

"Babylon," Sarah says, enunciating each syllable.

Why is she *calling and nae Rolf? Is Rolf Sleeping and* Sarah *standing watch?*

"Egypt," Carl growls in response, giving the other safe word. "Why are you calling in the clear like this?"

He's annoyed that she's nae taking security seriously, I suppose.

"I don't *text*," she snipes. "I'm going away for a while. I need to clear my head."

"What?" Carl says.

"Just shut up, you bloody *man*!" Sarah snaps. "Don't you say another *word*! Don't *tell* me what to *do*!"

Carl opens his mouth to say something, but she cuts him off.

"I'm sick to death of *men*!" she says, her voice full of vitriol. "*Animals* are better. I think I'll go hang out with the *tigers* in Africa! Stay away from me!"

The phone connection is severed abruptly. She must have hung up.

Carl looks at me, and our eyes lock.

My blood runs cold.

Sarah just used the duress *word.*

Chapter 22

THE BLOOD STREAMS out from the slash in my wrist and into the drinking glass. The pain from where I cut it with the edge of my black sword is brief, and the itch of healing begins immediately. The blood slows to a trickle and then ceases altogether. I lick the last of it off my wrist and hand the glass containing the half ounce or so of thick, crimson, delicious liquid to Carl.

Carl lifts Rolf up into a sitting position with one arm and holds the blood under Rolf's nose with his other hand. He shakes the Sleeping man. Vampire blood provides nae nourishment to our kind, but the aroma should be sufficiently sweet to awaken Rolf.

He inhales deeply, drinking in the scent of the blood and then his eyes pop open. In a flash, he is off the bed and on his feet, his sword, which an instant before had been lying beside him on the bed, in his hand. He quickly scans the room. He notes us, but he is looking desperately for someone else.

"Where's Sarah?" he cries in alarm. "She was here when I went to Sleep!"

"She's gone," Carl says, his voice terse and to the point. This is his *crisis* voice, his *military* voice. He's taking command.

"She called us and said that she was going away," I say, as gently as I can. "But she used the *duress* word. I fear she's been taken."

"Taken?" Rolf asks, his eyes widening with horror. "What do you mean?"

"Either Bartlett or Müller or both," Carl says. "She used the safe word, so she wanted us to know she was OK. But she used the duress word as well, so that means she couldn't speak freely."

"I have to go!" Rolf cries. "I have to find her!" He turns quickly toward the window and looks as if he's about to take flight.

Carl places a hand firmly on his shoulder. "Hold on a second!" he says. "It's daylight. You won't do her any good dead."

Rolf's face twists in agony. His shoulders sag in defeat. "What am I going to do?" He looks toward Heaven and whispers, "Vater, hilfe du mir! Hilfst meine Sarah!"

"Did you two have a fight?" I ask.

"Fight?" he says, looking at me. In spite of his worry, he looks as if I had just asked the most ridiculous question in the history of human speech. "No! Far from it. We almost had to take separate rooms to ... be *safe* ... you know. She told me to Sleep while she stood watch."

"I had to ask, laddie," I say. "'Tis because of what she said."

"What did she say?" he demands.

Carl answers, "She said she was going away and that she was 'sick of men.' She also said she was going to 'hang out with the *tigers* in Africa.' I think she was trying to tell us something. We've been analyzing her words all the way here."

"'Sick of *men*,'" I say, "*could* mean that there was more than one of them. And, although 'tiger' was the duress word, she specifically mentioned Africa." From his puzzled but anxious look I can tell that he does nae ken my meaning. "There are nae tigers in Africa, so she's going somewhere to be with animals that either dinnae exist or should nae be where they are. Either way, we think she meant the pig farm."

"Bottom line: we think the Congregation has her," Carl says, "but she tried to make it sound like she didn't want us to follow her . . . at least not right away."

"But she wanted you to know where she is, yes?" Rolf says, a glimmer of hope in his troubled eyes.

I nod slowly. "Aye, we think so."

"So, what's the plan?" Rolf demands, looking to Carl.

Carl hesitates for a tick.

"Tell me we have a plan," Rolf says in a low voice like a growl.

"Frankly . . ." my husband begins.

"We cannot just *sit* here!" Rolf cries.

"No," Carl says, "that's not it. It's just that . . . I'm still trying to figure out why Müller, or Bartlett, or whoever it was, didn't take *you*. And why take *Sarah* in the first place? Müller expects us to show up Saturday night for their meeting. So why try to force our hand early?"

"It was day when I went to Sleep," Rolf says, "and Sarah was still here with me. She sang me to Sleep. I had no idea she *could* sing. A century as a nun might teach you, I guess."

It's obvious to me he's trying to control his mounting panic. *He really loves her, as amazing as that seems.*

"Müller claims he can walk in the sunlight," Rolf continues. "Do you suppose . . ."

"Nae," I cut in, "even if that is *true* . . . and I'm nae saying it is . . . he said he could nae 'pass for a mortal' when he does it . . . *however* he does it . . . *if* he does it. And Sarah would still be vulnerable to the sunlight."

"Sarah used the safe words," Carl says, rubbing his chin. "Why would she do that if she was just going to use the duress word later?"

"Do ye suppose she's under Müller's power?" I ask Carl. "I ken that she swore fealty to ye, my love, but Müller's an Enforcer."

"I don't believe it. Not for a moment," Carl says. "God is more powerful than Satan. No, she's free of Lilith's control and therefore Müller's as well."

"But Müller doesn't know that!" Rolf says, his face lighting up. "He would assume that she's *totally* under his control!"

"That's why she told us to stay away!" Carl cries. "She's infiltrating the enemy!"

"You mean she went willingly?" Rolf looks anguished again. "She wouldn't do that! She wouldn't leave me unguarded!"

I lay a calming hand on his arm. "Laddie, what if she left ye so that she could *protect* ye?"

"What do you mean?" he asks.

"Well, what if she felt the only way to protect ye was to draw Müller and Bartlett (and who knows how many others) away from ye? She would nae have been able to rouse ye, so she drew them away, perhaps?"

"And she took it as an opportunity to gather some intelligence," Carl says. "She took your phone so she could report back to us."

"And maybe," I say, "she used the safe words because Müller would expect we would have some way to verify our communications were secure, so he would command her to make us believe she was doing this of her own free will. Müller did nae realize we had a backup plan. Sarah could be pretending to cooperate so she can put them off their guard. Nobody pays any mind to a slave."

"That still doesn't explain why they took her," Carl says.

"For the same reason *she* went with *them*," Rolf replies, "to gather intelligence. Müller thinks Sarah will tell him everything. I hope she is good enough to fool him and feed him enough false information while not giving herself away."

"She was a prostitute in her mortal life," I say, "and such women often can make a man believe anything."

Rolf's eyes flash dangerously and he snarls at my words.

"Ach, laddie!" I say in haste. "I did nae mean to imply. . ."

"No," Carl says, "but, if Müller commands it, she might think she has to comply or blow her cover."

"Müller wouldn't ask it," Rolf replies. "His tastes don't run that way."

And ye would know, laddie, since ye both were in the SS together . . . and he Converted ye.

"Oh, gross!" Carl says, his face twisting with disgust. "The better for Sarah, I guess."

"You mistake my meaning," Rolf says with a shake of his head and a grimace of distaste. "He prefers them *younger*. A *lot* younger."

"That's *sick!*" Carl says, looking even more disgusted.

"Either way," I put in, "she should be safe in *that* respect . . . for the moment."

"She hasn't been intimate with anyone for almost a thousand years," Rolf says. "I haven't been with anyone since . . . since I fled Germany during the War." He stares intently into my eyes. His gaze looks haunted. "We discussed this last night. We're going to wait until we can be married. Maybe one of your temple marriages isn't possible for us, at least for now, but we're going to be married—" his voice breaks, and his gaze drops to the floor "—if we live long enough."

"We'll save her," Carl says, and there is nary a shred of doubt to be heard in his voice. But in his eyes I see the truth.

Carl's afraid. He's afraid he cannae save her. These people, Rolf, Sarah, and the Stake vampires, have pledged themselves to him, and he thinks he has already failed them.

I stare right back at him, and I give him an encouraging smile. Firmly I say, "Aye, laddie, we will." Turning to Rolf, I say, "Dinnae fear. We'll save her."

Rolf nods, his face grim. A tear escapes the corner of his eye.

I ken how ye feel, laddie. I ken well the loneliness and the loss. 'Twas how I felt when I thought I had lost Carl after just finding him.

"But," Carl says, "we have to wait until nightfall or close to it." He's all business now, the commander again.

"Nightfall!" Rolf groans. He's fairly wringing his hands.

'Tis maddening to have someone ye care for in peril and to be so limited! *We possess such power, but 'tis all for naught when we cannae move freely.*

"Aside from the fact that Müller will be expecting us to launch a rescue attempt," Carl says, "we don't know the lay of the land, especially around the farm. As far as we know, the Congregation isn't assembling until Saturday, so we may have sufficient numbers to do whatever we need to. We just don't know how many vampires Müller has with him right now. He may be alone, or he may have guards, willing or otherwise."

Carl pulls out his phone. "First thing, we need to activate Tony's calling tree. Let's see how many vampires we can muster for a rescue mission."

In the end, we're able to contact only two of the Stake vampires. The rest are undoubtedly Sleeping, and nothing so mundane as a ringtone will rouse a vampire in our deathlike coma. Lorenzo Corelli and Martha will be the only two joining us.

Tony and Sammy volunteered . . . *volunteered* . . . to come, but 'twould be far too dangerous for them. The best they can do for us is to continue efforts at contacting the remaining Stake vampires.

The plan is to go scout out the pig farm as soon as the Sun dips behind the mountains. In the meantime, there is nothing to do except spend the day as best we can and hope that Sarah will contact us.

Since leaving Rolf alone would be a bad idea under the circumstances,

Carl will take the day off and stay here with him. They'll see about getting Rolf another cell phone, probably through the hotel concierge.

In the meantime, I will head off to work. I must check on Winnie. I dinnae *want* to see her, but I must. 'Tis my duty as her physician and my *obligation* since I very nearly murdered her yesterday.

I've saved many, many lives over the centuries, and I've delivered many, many bairns into this world, but 'twould all have been for naught if I'd killed Winnie Morrison. Nae matter the provocation, nae matter the compulsion, nae matter any outside pressure, 'twould be shedding innocent blood . . . innocent enough, anyway. She still might turn her life around someday, and I'd be robbing her of that chance.

And as hateful as she is in her heart, her sins dinnae compare to mine. Of our individual needs for the mercy of the Lord, mine is by far the greater.

"Where is Mrs. Morrison?" I ask the nurse at the psych ward desk. He looks up at me from his computer monitor and blinks several times. His name is Arlen, and he's a wee bit on the portly side. In his brown scrubs, he reminds me of an owl as he blinks. Nae, owls are reputed to be wise. Arlen simply looks puzzled.

"Yes, Dr. Morgan?" He looks confused. "How can I help you?"

"Winifred Morrison," I say. "Where is she? She's nae in the room she was assigned to yesterday."

"Winifred Morrison?" he asks. "What room would that be?"

"*That* one!" I say in exasperation, pointing two doors down. "I just checked. The room is empty. It has been cleaned. And her chart is missing. Where *is* she?"

He blinks at me again. Stupidly.

"Winifred Morrison?" he asks again. He looks completely befuddled by the name. And then suddenly his eyes brighten, as if a light has just been switched on. "Oh, yes! Mrs. Morrison!" He beams, pleased with himself. "She's been discharged."

"*Discharged?* Are ye *daft*, laddie? She was on a seventy-two-hour *suicide* watch!"

"Yes, Dr. Morgan," he says nonplussed, "she was released into the care of her brother this morning."

"That's impossible!" I say. *This makes nae sense!* I raise my hand with my index finger extended. "She's nae mobile." I extend a second finger, counting the reasons why Winnie should nae have been discharged. "She has nae brother." I extend a third finger and shake my hand in his face. "She cannae be released *without my order.*"

He blinks at me again. "Her brother took her away in a wheelchair. He told me that he was her brother. And you *did* order her release, Dr. Morgan."

"I did nae such thing, laddie." *This is ridiculous. The man is daft.*

"I have the order right here, Doctor."

I extend my hand toward him. "Show me the order."

My annoyance evaporates, and my blood runs icy cold as he hands me a blank piece of hospital stationery. "There's your signature right there," he says pointing at the empty page.

"Her brother," I say as I struggle to keep a tremor from my voice. "Did he give his name?"

"Yes, ma'am." He looks at the blank page as if he is reading the invisible words. "Here it is right here in the order. It says she is to be released into the care of her brother."

He looks up at me and continues to smile.

Nae an owl. Arlen looks like a puppy that has performed a trick. If he had a tail, he'd be wagging it.

And a chill grips my innards as I realize I know exactly what he's going to say.

He beams and says, "A Mr. Isaiah Bartlett."

◆ ◆ ◆

"Bartlett took Winnie," I say into the phone.

"What?" Carl says in shock.

"Bartlett took Winnie Morrison from the hospital. He did nae even try to hide it! He Persuaded a nurse and left his *name*."

"He wants you to come after him," Carl says. "Trying to split us up, maybe."

"I dinnae think so," I say. "According to the nurse he Persuaded, Bartlett mentioned taking Winnie to 'the farm.'"

"So he's deliberately trying to lure us up there. He's trying to provoke us," Carl says, his voice is calm. He's nae angry. Just trying to think it through.

"But why Winnie, of all people?" I ask.

"Because Müller knows you care about her," he replies.

Ach! The truth is I do care about her . . . as much as I might nae want to.

"But *how* does he know about her?" I ask.

"Stuart Hopkins, your receptionist at the hospital." That's Rolf's voice coming through the phone distantly. He can, of course, hear the whole conversation with his Seed-enhanced hearing. "Either Stuart didn't report in or Bartlett learned of his arrest on the news. If he did, it's not hard for a vampire to recognize an account of someone acting under Persuasion. Either way, Bartlett knows your name, and now he knows you're connected with the hospital. It's not that much of a stretch for someone with Bartlett's Internet skills to find out where you live and work. Once he had that, he could easily find someone you care about. Your husband told me about her. She's your patient, yes? And a neighbor? Who would be a more likely target than a woman who lives in your neighborhood and is your patient at the same time?"

'So," Carl says, "Bartlett and Müller want us to come. And most likely it's a trap."

"Of course, it is," Rolf says in the background. "Paul knows you suspect him. Lorenzo mentioned that at least two Stake vampires have gone missing, and he suspected the Congregation was behind their disappearances. Paul has to know about the Stake. He doesn't want you showing up with any troops behind you. He is trying to force you to act now without backup."

Rolf pauses for a tick and then says, "He may even have an agent among the Stake vampires. If I were in Paul's place, that's what *I* would do."

"Nae!" I say vehemently. "That's nae possible! They have all sworn fealty!"

"Yes, they have," Rolf says grimly. "I wonder what will happen with that."

"What d'ye mean?" I ask.

"I mean," Rolf continues, "*if* Paul has an agent among us and *if* he or she was under Paul's control, where will that agent's loyalty lie now?"

"And if they were a *willing* spy?" Carl asks.

"Then I doubt any oath of fealty sworn under false pretenses would be valid or binding," Rolf says.

"Meaning we could have a traitor in our midst," I say.

Carl nods. "And, if so, Müller knows . . . everything."

"And that *changes* everything," Rolf says. "If he knows that you two are the fulfillment of the Prophecy . . ."

"Then," I say, "his primary goal has changed. He's nae longer worried about simply *ensnaring* us. Now he must *destroy* us."

Chapter 23

THE AIR WHISTLES past my ears, and despite the fact that my hood is cinched down tight around my face, I'm *certain* it'll come undone at any moment and expose my skin to the sunlight. In point of fact, 'tis drawn so tight, only the goggles shielding my eyes are showing.

The hang glider above me shelters me from the direct rays of the Sun. The fabric of the wings has been painted sky blue, the better to block deadly light. The weight of the paint and the inflexibility it adds to the fabric renders the glider unsuitable for actual flying, of course, but *I'm* the one doing the flying, nae the glider. The three of us, Carl, Rolf, and I, each with our own glider, are just using the wretched things to protect us as we fly in *broad bloody DAYLIGHT!*

If I could see my hands through the thick leather gloves I'm wearing, I'm sure I'd see that my knuckles are white, as white as white can be, as I grip the control beam that extends below the frame of the glider. I dinnae ken what 'tis called and I dinnae care! I have to force myself nae to crush the aluminum tube in my hands.

It takes great care to maneuver the wings so that they keep me covered. And I have to take great pains to make sure that the rushing air does nae dislodge any article of my protective clothing, which covers every inch of my body.

Anyone who cared to really observe the three of us might notice that our three gliders dinnae move the way they should. Our hope is, though, that they will allow us to get close enough to Müller's swine farm to spy it out. If we're very lucky, we might learn where Sarah is located. 'Twould be highly unlikely, unless we hear her voice, though. We will nae *see* her. *She* would nae be so daft as to venture out into the light! Nae, only *we* would be so *harebrained* as to do *that!*

"Ye *do* ken that this is completely daft," I say. I'm trying to put a brave face on the whole situation, but, truth to tell, I've ne'er been so *terrified* in all my long life.

"That's what makes it so brilliant," Carl replies in a cocksure voice. There's nae trace of his "pilot accent." "They'll never expect us to approach by air in the middle of the afternoon."

I cannae see it, but I'm sure he's grinning from ear to ear, despite the danger. *Lunatic! Aye, lassie, but who's more the fool? The fool . . . or the fool who follows one?*

"Now keep in tight formation," Carl says, his flying accent thick as ever again, the cockiness gone. "Uh, that is . . . *please* keep in tight formation," he adds, chagrined. "Sorry, Rolf."

My poor husband! 'Tis so hard for him to try at once to be the military commander while nae giving a command that Rolf has nae choice but to obey. He has to give commands while making them sound *like requests.*

"Three," Rolf acknowledges, his voice curt, all business.

"Uh, two," I add in belated acknowledgement as well. *I should have been the one to acknowledge Carl's command first.* It should have gone like this: Carl gives a command and then I answer, "Two," and Rolf answers, "Three." This is the way my husband instructed the two of us to acknowledge his orders in the air. When it was just the two of us, just Carl and I, there was nae need, but Carl explained it was a quick way to signal acknowledgement. It must be a military thing, because Rolf takes to it well. And with the three of us flying in formation, especially in this ghastly situation, clear and precise communication is vital.

I slide in a wee bit closer so my right wingtip is about three feet to the left and three feet back from Carl's left wingtip. He calls this "fingertip formation." In spite of my terror, I feel a wee bit of pride that I'm holding position so well. I glance over at Rolf and see that he's holding his position, the Number Three position off Carl's right wing, fairly well, but he bobbles left and right, up and down, and forward and backward a wee bit. He is nae so stable as I am. I suppose those lessons in formation flying have paid off!

Being so close to one another means that, should something go amiss, the shelter of another glider will nae be far away. And there is so much that *can* go wrong!

Carl initiates a slow turn to the west. I manage to stay right with him, but Rolf has trouble adjusting in the turn. *Ye'll get it, Rolf-laddie!* Carl does nae intend to make a beeline straight from Farmington Peak, where we began this daft journey, to the farm. He wants us to appear to be nae more than sportsmen out for a lark.

From Farmington Peak to the farm? *If I were nae so terrified of the Sun at the moment, I might find that funny.*

I *do* have to admit, 'tis a brilliant plan. Brilliant and insane.

I purchased the gliders over the phone, but 'twas Tony Lupescu and Sammy who picked them up and carted them to Farmington Peak. There they assembled them and painted them before we arrived . . . painted them sky blue the better to camouflage them against the open sky. We, of course, had to secure sweat clothes and heavily tinted goggles for the "mission." Carl would have preferred to leave Rolf behind for this, but did nae have the heart to deny him. I dinnae think that anything short of an outright command from Carl would have restrained Rolf in any event. I left work early and picked up Carl and Rolf so we could go shopping for protective gear. Tony and Sammy had to "blow off" classes to secure, assemble, and prep the gliders for us.

"If you're intent on aerial surveillance," I asked Carl as we drove in my car from Rolf's hotel, "why nae use a helicopter or small airplane?"

"For stealth," Rolf answered from the back seat. "A helicopter or any type of powered aircraft would make a lot of noise."

"Right," Carl said. "I really doubt Müller will be looking for an airborne threat, but we want to do as little as possible to attract attention. It'll be bad enough if anyone watches closely and notices that the gliders aren't following the laws of aerodynamics."

"What d'ye mean, laddie?" I asked.

"Since we'll be using the gliders primarily to shield ourselves from the Sun, we'll be moving and positioning them accordingly," Carl explained. "In other words, the gliders won't necessarily bank left when we turn left and so on. If someone is watching closely, it's not hard to miss. It just looks wrong, *even if you don't understand* why *it's wrong. We'll have to make all our turns gradually so it's not so obvious."*

"What we'll have to *do," Rolf said, "is hope nobody at the farm or Müller's house looks up. It's not like Müller would be able to* do *anything if he* did *see us. At least . . ." His voice broke. "At least we're doing something!"*

Poor lad! Every minute that passed with Sarah in the clutches of the enemy was agony to him. He was nae considering the possibility that Müller could harm Sarah or Winnie in retaliation.

"We'll go armed," Carl said firmly, "but this is simply a reconnaissance mission."

"I know," Rolf said bleakly. "But the waiting is killing me!"

Indeed, it *should* feel good to be doing something, but right now my fright is nigh to driving me mad! I dinnae fear death so much as I fear the horror of burning in the Sun. 'Tis about as horrible a fate as I can imagine.

If that is what ye fear, lassie, then concentrate on making sure it does nae happen! Focus! Focus on what ye are about!

I check my Number Two position relative to Carl. I steal a quick glance at my sword . . . my ebony "sword of truth" in my belt to ensure it's still there. I make a quick scan of the sky to our right to look, nae for "bogies," but for aircraft that might pose a hazard for us.

I see no threats.

Still, the fear of the Sun above me dominates my thinking. *Focus, lassie!*

The farm and Müller's house and barn are situated next to each other on the southern slope of the mountain on the north side of Immigration Canyon. The plan is to approach the farm, house, and barn from the east through the canyon. We're hoping that Müller would expect any threat to come from the west, from Salt Lake City, or from the north, from Ogden (if he has heard of the "Ogden Angels").

We've nae revealed where our home is to any of the Stake vampires, and only Sammy knows where Carl and I live. It still boggles my brain that we might have a traitor in our midst. How else would Müller have known about Sarah's location? I suppose that they could have been followed, but then why would they take only Sarah and nae Rolf? And they would have to have known about the meeting last night to have followed them afterward. Who could it be? Lorenzo? Ghalyela? Martha? Dezba? One of the others? The repentance of each one of them seemed so sincere.

A horrible thought occurs to me. *What if 'twere Sammy or Tony?* Either could be under Persuasion. Or there could be a traitor vampire using Persuasion to get information out of either of them. But Sammy became associated with the group only last night. Surely if 'twere Sammy, he could have betrayed far more about me, at least. He's known me for decades. Tony, on the other hand, knows so little about us.

A traitor. It makes me ill just thinking about it.

As we complete our turn to the west, the Sun is directly in front of us. The shadow of my glider narrows with respect to my body. It becomes increasingly difficult to stay completely in its protective shadow. I angle the glider slightly down, and I pull my knees into my chest so that my body is nae so long. This barely keeps my feet in the shade. The boots I'm wearing probably afford the best protection anywhere on my body, but I'm so deathly afraid, I cannae help but keep them out of the light.

In truth, we're moving far faster than we should be to maintain the fiction of hang gliding, but the longer we stay in the air, the greater the danger. And the lower the Sun dips in the west, the less shadow the gliders provide, unless we were to angle them down to a ridiculous degree. *That* would look *very* wrong. So speed it is! *Anything that gets us back to the safety of the car as fast as possible!*

"Tally ho," Carl announces. *He's found the farm.* He points, and though I try to follow the direction he's pointing, I dinnae see where it is .

"Where?" Rolf asks.

"One o'clock, low," Carl replies. "Thirty degrees declination."

I look slightly to the right of straight ahead (the "one o'clock" position) and then down about thirty degrees.

"Tally," Rolf says. *That means that he sees it as well.*

Ah! There 'tis! I can see Müller's farmhouse and the barn where the Congregation assembles. The van with the tinted windows is parked in front, as it was on our first visit.

And there, just to the north, is the farm.

"I see it too," I say.

Carl adjusts our course slightly to the right, and I keep my position as Number Two nicely. Rolf wobbles, but stays in position too. Carl begins a gradual descent and we stay with him.

Now I take a closer look at the farm. I see a large pen with about a hundred or more swine cooling themselves in the mud. There's another barn on the farm itself, larger than the one near Müller's house. I can also see what looks like a long, narrow building. 'Tis probably a bunkhouse meant for farmhands.

Farmhands? I assumed that Müller worked alone here. Now that I recall, though, the farmhouse did have well-tended flower beds in front of it. Somehow, I cannae see Müller planting and weeding flowers. He must have workers there to tend to things. *Mortals or vampires? And how many?*

"We're going to descend for a closer look," Carl says. "Maybe we'll hear something. We can afford only one pass, so keep quiet, listen hard, and keep your eyes peeled!"

He starts his descent, and Rolf and I follow his lead. We continue until we're about a quarter mile away and five hundred feet above the farmhouse. Carl levels out, and we follow suit. We slow our speed to give us more "time-on-target," as Carl puts it.

Suddenly, the stench of the pig farm, so much more potent in the heat of the Sun, assails my nose. The smell makes my gorge rise.

Focus on something else, lassie!

I try to focus on the sounds coming from the farm. The swine are making a ruckus that is hard to ignore.

Ach! The stench!

Heartbeats! I can hear hearts beating. *Focus on that!* Breathing . . . both swine and human.

A bird calls. The wind rushes past my ears.

Even at our reduced speed, we'll soon be passing directly overhead. We dare nae make a second pass.

There's a voice. It's female, but harsh. I'm able to make out a string of foul words, and then I hear, "I said get out there and feed the hogs, you disgusting cow! Do it now and do it *quick*! *Move!*"

I know that voice! I know I've heard it before. I just cannae quite place it.

The door of the bunkhouse opens, and a woman staggers out. From this angle I cannae see her face, but I can tell that she is rail thin and has limp blonde hair. She heads toward the barn, but her gait is lifeless, as if she is ill.

The door of the bunkhouse opens again, this time slamming with great force against the wall. Whoever opened it is obviously angry. A young woman stomps out. She has black hair and is dressed all in black as well. She comes up quickly behind the first woman and gives her a violent kick from behind. The first woman goes sprawling face down in the mud near the pen. The woman in black is carrying what looks like a riding crop.

"I said be *quick*!" she screams as she begins to whip the fallen woman across the back with frenzied strokes. With each stroke she screams more profanities at her helpless victim, repeatedly calling her "cow." 'Tis *her* voice that I recognized, but still cannae place.

"Don't make me use the leash again!" she says and gives her victim one more stroke. "Now, get *up*!"

The thin woman struggles to rise to her knees.

By this time, we're directly overhead. I try to swivel my head to see more, but can risk only glimpses if I'm to stay in formation.

We're past the farm now.

I hear the woman with the whip yell, "The rest of you cattle, get out here and get this worthless cow out of my sight!"

Carl begins to climb and to pick up our speed.

How I wish there was something . . . anything I could do to help that poor woman. But now we must flee.

Suddenly I can hear a loud burst of heavy-metal music. I risk a quick glance again, and I see the woman in black opening a cell phone.

"Yes, Master," she says into the phone.

"What have I told you about abusing the livestock?" Müller's voice is faint coming from the phone. He must be safe in the shadows of the farmhouse as he watches the scene.

Carl steepens our climb dramatically and continues to accelerate. Still, we cannae go all that fast, because of these huge gliders. It's like trying to push a giant umbrella into a windstorm.

"I'm sorry, Master," says the young woman with the whip and the naggingly familiar voice. Now that she's nae screaming, my vague sense of familiarity is sharpened.

Who is *she?*

"If you bruise them," Müller says in a tone of gentle reproach, "blood is lost into the tissues, and that's blood I can't harvest."

The voices are fading behind us, but I can still hear them . . . faintly.

"You can *beat* the cattle," Müller continues, "but just not so hard. I recommend that you cut a length of rubber hose and use that. It hurts *exquisitely*, but it doesn't damage the tissue."

"Yes, Master," comes the reply. "It won't happen again."

"I'm certain it won't, Lucy," Müller says.

Lucy! Yes, I *do* know her! Lucy, whom I rescued from would-be rapists a year ago last Christmas Eve. Lucy, who rejected her chance to start over. Lucy, who found Michael's Cult and became one of his Chosen for Conversion . . . until Carl and I destroyed the Cult. And like a dog returning to her vomit, Lucy has found her way to Müller. 'Twould appear she's still intent on becoming a monster. She seems to have the requisite contempt for her fellow mortals.

So tragic.

So foolish.

So pathetic.

So utterly contemptible.

"What in Lilith's name?" Müller's voice comes faintly.

I glance back once more.

In a trice I take in the scene behind us. I see Lucy, looking back toward the farmhouse. The woman she was beating lies face down in the mire again.

A number of gaunt-looking people, men and women, are shambling in Lucy's direction. They all seem to be wearing collars about their necks. I see all this, but 'tis nae what rivets my attention.

Nae, 'tis the figure emerging from the farmhouse that fills me with shock and a terror. He seems to be glowing with a blinding light. *Is that Müller? Could it be he? Is that what he looks like when he 'walks in the sunlight?'*

"The devil appeared as an angel of light," the scripture says.

I glance back again quickly.

The bright figure is now airborne, with wings beating. He has a wicked-looking assault rifle in his hands.

And he's coming straight for us. Nae hampered as we are by huge gliders, he's closing rapidly!

"Laddie!" I hiss.

Carl glances back, does a double take, and cries, *"Incoming!"*

I feel the bullets rip into me before I hear the gunfire.

Pain!

The glider slips from my grasp as a second sweep of bullets explodes across my back, inside my chest. I feel my heart explode.

And I'm falling toward the ground.

The itch of the Seed healing overwhelms the pain, but I cannae focus enough to keep in the air.

I hear Rolf cry out in agony.

Carl! Where are ye?

Everything's going gray.

Nae blood going to my brain.

Nae oxygen.

Then my newly restored heart begins to beat again and my vision clears. As I tumble, I look desperately for Carl. I spot Rolf tumbling toward the ground, but I cannae see my husband! *Where is Carl?*

There he is! He's below me and falling fast.

"Carl!" I cry. *I have to get to him!*

Fire!

I'm on fire!

I scream in agony as flesh exposed to the Sun by the bullets that ripped through my clothes is now aflame. The fire spreads across my back. My clothes are on fire!

I'm on fire!

In my pain, I see two other flaming figures. *Carl! Rolf!*

Fire!

I'm on fire!

Another scream tears from my throat.

Blackness overwhelms me in its welcome, cold embrace.

Chapter 24

FIRE!

I'm on fire!

I'm crucified, nailed to a cross! I cannae move! I cannae fly away!

My burning lips move as the flesh melts away. My tongue is ablaze, yet it struggles to form words. Somehow, through the inferno, through the agony, I manage to croak out, "Father, into thy hands I commend my spirit."

I'm engulfed in my own personal bonfire. My body is the fuel. The Sun is the torch.

I'm in Hell.

I awake screaming.

The flames are gone.

'Twas just a dream, lassie! I was on fire! But nae crucified! We were hang gliding in broad daylight! We were attacked! Müller attacked us! He was glowing! Flying in the sunlight! I was on fire, but now I am . . . Where am I?

Carl! Where's Carl?

I'm lying on my back. I start to sit up . . .

Instantly, I feel pain in my neck, my wrists, and my ankles. Something slices into my neck, slicing through my windpipe.

As my scream transforms into a gurgle, I instinctively recoil from the pain. The Seed's Healing repairs my torn flesh. The itch is awful, but after the agony of immolation in my dream and of near decapitation upon waking, I welcome the Healing of the Seed.

Something sharp is binding my neck, wrists, and ankles. I'm on my back, bound by . . . whatever binds me to a long, flat table or platform. *A gurney perhaps? Nae, I'd smell the chrome.* I cannae feel anything through what remains of my gloves, but I can feel wood through the places where my clothes have been shot or burned away. *A table then.*

Now that the pain and the itch are gone, panic spreads through my whole frame. I begin to tremble, but I feel the keen edge of whatever binds me threaten to slice into me once more. So, I force myself to hold still.

Think, lassie! Dinnae panic!

Where am I? Focus on that!

Because of . . . my bonds, I cannae move my head. I can only look up to try to see where I am, what's going on around me.

'Tis a darkened room. I cannae see much of it save for the beams of the ceiling, but from the coolness, the dampness, I would guess that I'm in a cellar.

And the room has the *feel* of being large. Out of the corner of my eye, I can barely discern a window, high up on the wall to my right. It's been painted over to keep out the Sun. In spite of the paint, I can see that 'tis still light outside.

Carl? Where's my husband?

Panic grips me anew, but I try to focus on the sounds in the room. I can hear breathing, slow and very shallow, and hearts beating very slowly. I hear blood rushing in arteries and veins.

I'm nae alone!

"Carl?" I call out, softly, so as nae to slice my throat open again.

There is nae answer save the steady breathing.

I listen closely to it.

I recognize that sound! That dear, bonnie sound!

I've listened to it many times over the last year. 'Tis the sound of my dear, sweet, thrice-beloved husband as he Sleeps. To a mortal, he would appear dead, his breathing nae detectable, but *I* can hear him. *I can hear him!*

Carl's alive! And he's here!

Thank ye, God!

Tears stream from my eyes and spill down the sides of my face.

Carl is alive!

He's somewhere nearby . . . off to my left.

There is another breather, another Sleeper on my right. Another vampire. Rolf, most likely.

It has to be Rolf!

We're all alive! We're captives, but we're alive.

That's better than the alternative of being nae more than crumpled, smoldering bones lying who kens where on the slopes of the mountain.

If we're alive, we can find a way out of . . . this . . . *wherever* we are.

I have to believe we can escape. I cannae give in to despair!

I can hear other sounds as well.

There are people above us. I hear footsteps, breathing, hearts beating, too fast to be Sleepers. *Mortals or vampires?*

I can smell blood too. There is the faint scent of blood on my body, doubtless left over from when I was shot. Aye, 'tis vampire blood. Nae just my own, but Carl's and Rolf's as well. Nae enough to rouse us from Sleep, but there all the same.

I can smell mortal blood too. *Above us?*

Hunger clenches my stomach in a knot. Carl, Rolf, and I Fed on blood from the hospital just before our disastrous flight this afternoon . . . *I assume 'tis still the same day* . . . but my ravenous, unnatural hunger is back.

Blood! I need blood!

The hunger is all consuming!

Hold fast, lassie! Focus on what ye must do! Focus on the danger! Focus on saving your husband! And Rolf too. Ye must save him as well.

I try to clear my mind and ignore the maddening smell of blood by focusing on the other scents. There is the acrid odor of burnt cotton and nylon . . . other fabrics as well.

Our clothes. Our charred clothing.

Aye, lass. Focus on that.

I notice a rectangular shape high up on the wall before me. 'Tis a small television set sitting on a shelf. The cord dangles down and is plugged in at the wall below. Why a TV in *this* place? I see a couple of cables that run off to my left and out of my peripheral vision.

There's the scent of metal . . . steel. Aye, definitely steel. And leather.

And residue of metal polish! Our *swords* are here in the room!

Surely nae still attached to our belts? Nae, the scent of the metal polish comes from farther away . . . somewhere beyond where my feet lie bound to the table.

Bound by what?

I smell other steel. It smells different from the fine carbon steel of our swords. And 'tis much closer.

Our bonds! Our bonds must be made of metal. Sharp metal to cut so cruelly. Some kind of wire?

An image forms in my mind of the fence around a prison and the loops and coils of flat, sharp . . .

Razor wire!

We're bound with razor wire!

Would razor wire be strong enough to decapitate me if I pushed hard enough against it?

Maybe nae. *Most likely*, nae. 'Twould probably break before it cut all that deeply, but I'd probably cut off all blood flow to the brain before it did. I'd have razor wire embedded in my neck, and it might block my windpipe from Healing, or it could even block the flow of blood.

Headless or nae, I'd be just as dead.

Could I, perhaps, free an arm before it severed the hand from my wrist?

Perhaps.

I steel myself to try, nae relishing the thought of possibly losing my hand (temporarily), when I notice the sound of footsteps running on stairs.

Down the stairs.

Toward us.

I hear a door burst open and slam against the wall somewhere off to my left. Someone enters. Two someones, by the sound of it.

In my heart, I ken who the first must be, but, still, when the tall, gaunt figure of Günther Paul Müller with his sunken eyes and hollow cheeks steps into my field of view, I can barely suppress a shudder that could get me sliced open in a number of places.

Müller holds his Viking broadsword at the ready. He looks intrigued.

"How is this possible?" he asks, his blue eyes burning deep in their sunken sockets. "How are you awake?"

"I *told* you, Master!" Lucy says, still out of my field of vision, her voice filled with pride. "I *told* you I heard her scream."

He makes a tired, dismissive wave with his left hand, the one without the sword, and says in a patient, weary voice, "Yes, Lucy. You have done well. Now, go and fetch two of the others. And bring Uzis. All three of you. Go. Quickly."

"Yes, Master," she says, her tone somewhat deflated. I hear her turn and run up the stairs, shouting to others as she goes.

The "Apostle" looks exhausted as he stares into my eyes. "How are you awake?" He asks again. "You should be Sleeping until sunset."

I say nary a word.

"You're an enigma . . . a puzzle, Moira Morgan. A paradox," he continues. "Unfortunately, you're a paradox I don't have much time to fathom." He purses his lips and then puffs out his lower lip as if he's pouting. "I must confess, if I can't solve the puzzle before your execution in the morning, it will trouble me for centuries like a pebble in my shoe."

At the word "execution," I cannae suppress a flinch. My wrists suffer the most damage.

Am I truly afraid to die? Has this life become so dear to me that I would nae gladly trade it for Eternity with my husband, free from the curse of vampirism? Aye, of course I'm afraid. Everyone fears to die. Am I assured a place in the Kingdom of God if I fail to fulfill the Prophecy? Aye, God kens all. He kens that I've done my best. If I fail, another will take my place to fulfill it.

But still . . . I'm afraid.

Müller sees my flinching. He smiles. His emaciated face looks calm, almost beatific. "Yes, you and your husband will be executed at sunrise."

I cannae suppress another shudder at the thought of Carl's death. The razor wire slices into me again, my neck this time.

The pain is excruciating.

And frustrating. I cannae move at all without cutting myself.

"I may spare my old protégé," he says, nodding in Rolf's direction. "I'm curious to learn if he'll once again chose to be subject to the will of Lilith . . . subject to *me* after your husband is dead."

He knows about the oath that the Stake vampires swore! There is *a traitor!*

He must have seen the horror in my eyes. He nods. "Yes," he says, "I know everything. You are the Penitent, and your husband is the Unwilling prophesied in the Curse. And you're going to *fail*. That old fool, Adam, was wrong. He bet on the wrong side."

"Others," I choke out, "will rise up. The word of God *will* come to pass."

"Perhaps you're right," he says with a weary smile, "but I don't think you are. In any case, you'll never know. You won't live to see it. And what is pathetically sad, in your case, is that you will have *failed*. Your whole life will have been for nothing."

I hear footsteps on the stairs again. I hear three pairs of footsteps as they enter the room.

Müller looks up and away from me.

"We're here, Master." Lucy's voice sounds eager.

I can smell the metal, oil, and gunpowder. They brought the weapons.

And mortal blood. They're all three mortals. None of them particularly evil smelling, though. And that makes sense, as well. Anyone truly evil would be irresistible to a vampire. These mortals are nae truly *evil*. Needy, greedy, petty, gullible, desperate to please . . . but nae evil.

"Ah, Lucy," Müller says, "Well done. The three of you each take a position beside the head of one of these three. Lucy, I want you here with the woman."

Lucy comes into view and walks behind Müller. She continues around the table (or whatever it is I'm lying on) and approaches me from my right. She stops by my head and stands looking at her Master.

Müller looks to my left, my right, and then to Lucy. "Very good," he says. "Just so. Chamber a round and place the muzzle about an inch or so from the head of your target. Be careful not to rest the barrel directly against the head. A sudden movement on the captive's part could deflect your aim."

I hear the sound of three bolts being pulled back and released.

"Excellent," Müller says with a smile. "Very good, my disciples. Steven, your safety is on." I hear the switch being changed. "Now," Müller continues, "if your target makes any move to escape . . . any move at all, all three of you empty your clips into their heads. I assure you, it will empty the skull of any brain matter. Even if it *did* regenerate, there would be nothing left of *them*. No memories, no knowledge, no personality. Just a shell. But, I've never seen a vampire survive such a trauma. I've heard stories of vampires who were just mindless monsters, the revenants of human myth. I've always thought that these were vampires who had suffered severe brain damage. In any case, if you must fire, take out the entire head."

He cocks his head and looks thoughtful for a moment. Then he says, "On second thought, you might want to hold your weapons just a little higher and aim them downward. Wouldn't want any of my Chosen to be killed by friendly fire, now would we?"

Lucy does as she is told and holds her Uzi up higher as she aims it at my forehead.

"Very good," Müller says and smiles. "Now, Moira," he says to me. "May I call you Moira?"

I glare at him.

"Moira," he continues, unheeding, "I want to understand. What woke you?"

I focus my gaze on the ceiling. I will nae answer him a word. He plans to murder us. I will nae give him the satisfaction of answering his questions. If the only victory I can win here is to keep his curiosity unrequited, then so be it.

"You're not malnourished," he muses, "so the remote scent of prey wouldn't wake you. There are only trace amounts of blood from your wounds. I saw to that."

He sways a wee bit.

He sighs. "I really must sit down." He steps away and grabs a stool. He places the stool next to my table and sits wearily. "I'm going to have to consume more of the Blessing. I won't bring it down here. I don't want to wake your companions."

He pauses. Then he yawns. "Dear me! Excuse my rudeness. I really am exhausted. Flying *and* wrapping myself in the Glory at the same time! Really takes it out of me."

The "Glory"? Is that what he calls the glow that seems to have protected him from the Sun?

"But enough of my troubles," he says in a condescending tone. "Tell me about yourself. I mean, beyond what Sarah has told me."

Of course Sarah had to tell him something. Surely she isn't the traitor!

Is she?

"Tell me what woke you," he says. When I dinnae answer, he continues, "Surely you didn't wake *yourself* somehow."

"It sounded like she had a nightmare," Lucy suggests.

Müller waves dismissively again and says, "Ridiculous. We don't dream." He gazes at me intently. "But maybe . . . *you* do?"

I try very hard to show nae sign. I just stare at the ceiling.

"Impossible!" he says. "No!" Then his eyes go wide. "You *were* dreaming!"

I keep silent as the grave.

"First you break my Queen's control, and now you're dreaming?" He pauses. "What else is there?" he demands.

He waits as if I would respond to his demand. *He's so used to having everyone, mortal or immortal, obey him. This is truly beyond his ken.*

"Fine," he growls. "You won't answer?" He stands. "Not even to save your husband's life for a few more hours?"

He sees the fear in my eyes, and he smiles. Then he nods. "But, of course," he says, "I *need* his execution to be public." He taps the side of his nose with his index finger. "Perhaps someone else."

Rolf? He's going to murder Rolf? In panic, my eyes flicker to my right, in Rolf's direction.

Müller laughs softly. "No, if I kill my old student, it will be public as well." His expression darkens. "I need to demonstrate the high price of betrayal."

"So ye've dropped all pretense of being God's servant?" I say. *Maybe I should nae have spoken, but I'm nae answering his questions, either.*

"Ah," he says with a smirk, "found your voice, have you?"

When I dinnae respond, he says, "You think I'm referring to a *personal* betrayal? I meant the price of betraying *God*, of course. I'm on a *mission* from God. *A* god, anyway. Just not *your* god. Godde*ss*, actually."

He worships Lilith like a god? Why is that so surprising?

"No," he continues, glancing at Rolf, "I think I'll keep Herr Oettinger alive a tad longer."

I cannae help but breathe a sigh of relief.

"You'll talk to me, or I'll kill someone else that you *care* about," he says. He stands and walks over to the wall in front of me. He reaches up and turns on the TV.

An image comes into focus. It's the inside of a barn. There's a wee bit of sunlight shining between the slats of the walls. This is nae the decorative barn with its solid walls next to the farmhouse. This must be the barn on the farm itself. There's straw and tack and tools . . . the normal stuff ye would expect to see in a functioning barn.

Why is he showing me a barn?

I hear a sound coming from the television. Someone is sobbing softly.

Müller grunts in frustration . . . *or is it anger?* Looking directly at the TV, he says in a voice much louder than he has been using, "Carla, why am I looking at the wall? You must have bumped the camera! Fix it!"

"I'm sorry, Master," says a woman's voice from the TV.

How can this Carla hear us? 'Tis then I notice for the first time the camera perched atop the television. The camera appears to be focused on me.

The image on the TV screen swings wildly and comes to rest on an open stall in the barn. There is a large figure lying in the straw inside the stall. It's Winnie! The sobbing is hers. There is nae evidence of an IV drip, so she must nae be receiving her meds. She's probably in great pain. The casts are still on her legs, but there's blood soaking through her hospital gown where the sutures over her ribs would be. They must have ruptured.

"That's better," Müller says. A woman ("Carla," most likely) walks into view on the screen. She has her brown hair cropped very short, like a man's, and she's wearing blue jeans, work boots, and a flannel shirt with the sleeves ripped off. She has the biceps of a body builder. And she's carrying an Uzi.

"Yes, Master," the mannish-looking woman says into the camera.

"How's our little piggy?" Müller asks.

"Down to just sobbing, now," Carla says. "She was a bit noisier, but I gave her a good kick to the ribs and said she'd get more where that came from if she didn't shut it." She smiles a wicked grin.

She has rebroken Winnie's ribs and torn open her sutures! The vile brute!

"Carla," Müller says in a voice that is at once stern and bone weary,

"Stop abusing the stock! You're wasting precious blood!'"

Carla looks shocked and frightened. She stands there trembling, both hands gripping her weapon with white knuckles.

"If she bleeds out," Müller growls, "in Lilith's name, you'll be next!'"

"I'm so sorry, Master!" Carla cries and falls to her knees. "Forgive me!'"

Müller pays her no heed and turns back to me. "I'm going to have to go seal her wounds. I need her healthy. But, I'll drain her and then rip her limb from limb if you don't talk to me and tell me all I want to know.'"

He turns and heads out of my sight, toward the stairs. "When I return, you will confess *all*," he says, his voice trembling, nae with rage, but with exhaustion.

I hear him walk up the stairs, his steps slow and halting.

Maybe he'll collapse again as he did the night we first met him.

I listen carefully, and when I think he can nae longer hear me . . . *I hope he cannae hear me* . . . I say, "Lucy, I'm nae going to insult your intelligence by urging ye to help me, lassie. Ye've *made* your choice . . . it's nae too late to *change*, mind ye . . . but 'tis *your* choice.'"

"That's right," she retorts and launches into a stream of expletives that would probably make her Mormon mother faint. "I asked you *twice* to give me immortality, to make me *strong*, but you *refused! Now* who's the strong one, huh?'"

She taps my forehead with the stubby muzzle of her weapon. I cannae help but move my head. The razor wire slices into my neck. Again. The pain is brief, but each time I bleed, there's the chance that Carl and Rolf will awaken at the scent. And when they awaken, they are sure to make a move that might be interpreted as an attempt to escape. (Like as nae, 'twould be an attempt to escape.) I cannae let my dear husband die . . . nor Rolf . . . I have to keep us alive a wee bit longer if we're to have any hope of escape later.

"Aye, lassie," I say as soothingly as I can, "ye have all the power now. In fact, if I may *beg* a boon of ye . . . *please*, when the others awaken, dinnae kill them. Give them a chance to realize their circumstances. Give them a moment to adjust.'"

She sneers at me. "Listen, bi . . .'"

"Your Master would nae be pleased," I interrupt, "if ye kill us before he has a chance to enjoy our public executions.'"

She begins to curse at me again, but stops abruptly as she sees that my eye is riveted to the scene playing out on the television. On the screen, Müller enters the stall. He is fairly staggering. He sidesteps a shaft of light coming through the wall. He kneels at Winnie's side. Her moans of pain turn to shrieks of horror as she stares at Müller's face.

His fangs must be out.

Müller lifts Winnie's gown and rips away her bandages. He lowers his face to her wound. Soon her screaming fades, and she begins to moan in pleasure as the Seed speeds through her bloodstream. Müller does nae consume a lot of blood because he does nae take very long with her. His primary purpose is to heal her wounds and stop her bleeding. *He needs her alive to keep me in check . . . at least until dawn.*

Now he's back on his feet, a wee bit less weary than he was. He looks at the woman named Carla. She flinches at his gaze. "Don't abuse the livestock," he says in a low, menacing tone, "at least not in any way that wastes blood. Understood?"

"Yes, Master," Carla says and bows her head with its butch-cut hair.

Müller nods and turns about. He stands for a moment and seems to gather himself. Then he bows his head as if in prayer. I see him take a deep breath, and suddenly he's enveloped in light. He is aglow.

He's preparing to go out in the Sun once more.

Then the glow flickers, 'tis shining blindingly one instant, and then 'tis utterly black, then back again and . . .

Did I just see what I think I saw?

. . . it disappears entirely.

Müller wobbles on his feet and nearly falls, but then he catches himself. His hand passes through the shaft of sunlight, and he snatches the hand away. Tendrils of smoke rise from his hand.

Aye, it was! That's exactly *what I saw!*

He turns abruptly around, and pushing Carla's Uzi aside, he brusquely fastens his lips on her neck. Carla's head lolls in ecstasy as Müller takes her blood. Once again, he does nae take much, but he spends longer with Carla than he did with poor Winnie.

He does nae want to take too much lest he nae longer appear to be a half-starved ascetic in the eyes of his Congregation.

Just as abruptly as he took her, he roughly shoves Carla away. She falls on her rump and sits there a moment staring up at him with a gaze that can only be described as *worship*.

He turns again toward the direction from whence he entered the scene, and enveloping himself in light once more, he walks out of the view of the camera.

Aye, that's it! I ken precisely how he does it! Nae wonder 'tis so draining for him!

And I could do it, and I'd be expending only half *the energy that he's using!*

"Angel of light" indeed!

"What are you smiling at?" Lucy says. She turns her weapon to the side and raises it.

I can see the blow coming, but I can do nary a thing to stop it. I steel my neck to hold as still as possible.

She slams the metal submachine gun into the side of my head.

Razor wire slices deep into my neck as the impact of Lucy's weapon knocks my head to the side. In spite of the pain, I pull my head back. It missed my carotid, but the metal remains embedded in my neck.

I wriggle and bobble my head about trying desperately to dislodge it. *If I bleed too much, Carl and Rolf will awaken! And then Lucy's fellow guards will kill them!* I struggle to get the wire out of my flesh, but I cannae dislodge it.

I want it out!

The cruel metal slides out of my neck. *Did* I *do that? How did I get the razor wire out of my flesh?*

The itch of Healing overwhelms my senses, and 'tis hard to think clearly for a moment.

Did I make the wire move? Is that something I can use to free myself and Carl . . . and, of course, Rolf?

The itch of Healing barely subsides when I hear the "Apostle's" tread on the stairs.

He wants me to answer his questions. If I dinnae tell him what he wants to know, he'll kill Winnie. He'll nae kill Carl or Rolf when he has Winnie to hold over my head. I'll have to give him what he wants . . . or at the least . . . what he *thinks* he wants. *Be on your guard, lassie! He will nae be fooled easily. The best ye can hope for is to divulge as little as possible.*

Müller enters the room and my field of vision. His gait is steadier, and though he still looks gaunt, he does nae look as if Charon the Ferryman were about to carry him across the Styx at any moment. He dismisses Lucy and the other two mortal guards with a wave of his hand.

He has enough strength to look after three bound prisoners by himself.

He sits on the stool next to me and lays his sword across his lap. Without looking toward the TV or the camera, he says, "Carla?"

"Yes, Master," Carla replies through the television. She steps in front of the camera.

"I'm going to have a chat with our guests here," Müller says. "A *private* chat. I want you to turn off the sound on your TV there, but watch us close-ly. If Mrs. Morgan or either of the other two makes any aggressive move or if you think I'm in trouble, I want you to put a bullet through your little piggy's head. Do you understand?"

"Yes, Master," she replies. I can see her reach toward the camera.

"Carla," Müller says, "can you hear me?"

There is nae reply.

"Good," Müller says, addressing me for the first time since his return, though he has nae taken his eyes off mine. "Now we can talk privately.

"Tell me, Child," he says, "about the dreams."

"First I want your promise," I say, "that ye will nae kill us . . . at least nae until sunrise . . . and that ye will let Winnie go. She needs a hospital. She'll have a serious infection soon in that environment." I glance up at the TV where I can clearly see Winnie and Carla. The woman with the Uzi is watch-ing us intently. I can hear Winnie sobbing again as the effects of the Seed-induced euphoria have faded.

"You're in no position to bargain," Müller says. His voice is . . . clinical. He looks at me as if he were watching an interesting bacterium under a microscope. "But I'm not going to kill you if I don't have to. At least, I won't before your execution at dawn. So, if you don't force my hand, I'll let the three of you live that long.

"As for the sow in the barn," he continues with nae animosity in his voice, despite the inflammatory language, "if you cooperate, I will let her live until my work here is done. Then I will leave her here and make an anonymous call to your hospital so someone will come and collect her. Is that sufficient to secure your cooperation?"

"If she does nae receive medical attention in short order, she will nae survive more than a few days," I say.

"My dear Moira," Müller says with a grin, "once you and your husband are dead, executed in full view of this pathetic bunch of deluded religious fanatics, my work here *will* be done."

I shudder, and I receive a dozen cuts as payment for my lack of control.

"I was sent here to locate the Breakers," Müller says with a wee hint of smugness, "but I've done more than that. I've found and captured the Unwilling and the Penitent, 'joined in the House of God.' I'm going to execute them (you and your husband) in full view of the Penitents and crush forever any hope they had of breaking free of my Queen. I'm going to *nullify* the prophecy of God. Do you comprehend what that means?"

"Ye cannae do that."

"No? What is it that God said? If he were to lie, he would cease to be God? Well, so be it. Amen to that. I will make his word null and void, and then he'll cease to be God. And once I've done that, my Queen will reign forever. As it was at the dawn of time, so shall it be forever. Lilith will be supreme."

He means it. He really thinks he can thwart the will of God. Maybe I can use that arrogance against him. But first, there is something I'm dying to know.

"Why are we nae dead, the three of us? Why are we nae burned to ashes?" I ask.

He smiles a serene smile. "I caught the three of you as you fell. You saved me like that when first we met. I've returned the favor. I enveloped you in my own Glory and protected you from the light."

Ach! Of course! And he did nae save us to return any favor. He saved us so that he could execute us publicly and crush the hopes of the Penitents.

"About that 'Glory' . . . ," I start to say.

Müller clucks his tongue. "Moira, Moira, Moira," he says. "Surely you don't expect me to reveal all my secrets. I'm not some movie-serial villain driven by his own ego to explain all his plans to the captive hero . . . captive heroine, in your case. No, I'm a magician, and I'd be a fool to reveal my illusions. I'm truly sorry . . . well, not really sorry . . . but you'll have to go to your tragic death without all the answers you crave."

Nae a movie-serial villain? Ye're doing a fair imitation of one!

"So . . . tell me about the dreams," he asks.

I have to give him *something* to keep poor Winnie alive. I tell him of the dream about Ben. I dinnae mention the crucifixion dream. As I tell of the dream, I have to give him some details of Ben's story. I cannae help but cry as I speak of my lost boy.

Perhaps my tears help convince him that there is nae more to tell.

"What made you start to dream, I wonder?" he says, nae taking his eyes off me. His gaze never wavers. I've the feeling again as if I'm a fascinating lab rat and nae more.

"I dinnae know," I reply. "Perhaps the trauma of losing my only chance for a child of my own."

He purses his lips in thought. "Perhaps," he says. "When did the dreams start?"

"Right after Ben . . . died." This is the first lie I've told. I hope he accepts it. *I dinnae want him to make any connection between the arrival of the Penitents, Müller's own actions, and the start of my dreams. He'll know I held something back.*

He nods.

I try nae to breathe a sigh of relief.

"By the way," he says, "I know now that there is more to your story about the Breaking than you told me before. Your husband's unique nature had more to do with it. If he never put any stock in the Oath and the Covenant, then he never surrendered his will to Lilith and her Servants. I see no hand of God in this. It's just a case of someone being in the wrong place at the wrong time. It's an accident . . . one I will remedy in the morning."

"Do ye really think ye can thwart the will of God?" I say.

He laughs mirthlessly. "God's will is thwarted all the time, every day, as it has been since the day that old fool, Adam, ate the fruit in the garden. Yahweh or Jehovah or Allah or God (or whatever you want to call him) lost control that day. And on the day that Lilith made the Great Covenant and entered into the Great Secret with Lucifer, God's downfall was made certain. In his *arrogance*, your God made a prophecy that I'm about to invalidate. And when I do, God will cease to be God."

He grins wide. "I, Günther Paul Müller, Günner Polsson, bastard son of a Viking raider by rape . . . *I'm* about to *kill* God."

I look for any hint of madness in his eyes, but I dinnae find any sign. He is *rational*. He really believes what he says. He *believes* he can *do* it.

And his rationality makes his mad plan all the more chilling.

"And you, my dear Moira," he says with a smile devoid of malice, "you and your foolish husband will become the spear I'm going use to impale the heart of your God."

In the end, it does nae matter that he's *wrong*, that he cannae thwart the will of God, that he cannae *kill* God, as he says. It does nae matter that, once he kills *us*, others will rise to take our place, and the Prophecy *will* be fulfilled. None of it matters to *us*, because, in the end, Carl and I . . . and maybe Rolf . . . will be just as dead.

Chapter 25

"TACO."

'Tis barely a whisper, a whisper so soft as only a vampire would hear . . . a vampire in the same room, that is. I dinnae recognize the voice, and I cannae see the speaker. Whoever it is, she's off to my left.

Müller left and summoned someone else to guard us. From the scent, I could tell the newcomer was a vampire and female. Before he left the basement, Müller commanded the new guard to nae speak to us. Then Müller closed the door. I heard his weary tread as he stomped up the stairs. Then his footsteps faded from my hearing.

"Taco," she says again. "I know that word's been used . . . compromised, as Rolf would say, but it's all I bloody have! I'm trying to prove I'm on your side!"

"Sarah?" I whisper just as softly between lips I dare nae move perceptibly. *There are eyes watching me from the other side of the camera.*

"Yes," she replies. "It's Sarah." She pauses and then whispers, "I've got to stay out of the view of the camera. The microphone won't be able to pick up me whispering like this, but that sick ape, Carla . . . the one on the telly, would surely notice my lips moving. She heard 'the Master' tell me to keep silent. If I'm caught, it'll blow my cover, so to speak. So I'll stay here by the door."

I look up at the screen. Carla is pacing back and forth. Even as she walks, her eyes stay glued to the TV in the barn where she is watching the images of Carl, Rolf, and me looking for any excuse to put a bullet in Winnie's brain.

Why did it have to be Winnie of all people? Even if I manage to save her by some miracle, and the rest of us manage to survive past morning, she'll ken precisely what I am and nae amount of Persuasion will convince her otherwise. After what she's been through, I dinnae think I'd have the heart to Persuade her.

Stop thinking like that, lassie! Save her first. Worry about repercussions later.

"Sarah," I begin, but she cuts me off.

"Listen! I don't have much time! Someone else could come at any moment! Everyone here thinks I'm under Paul's control . . . even Müller himself (I hope). If I'm caught disobeying his command not to talk to you, I'll be right there with you . . . or dead! We have a traitor. I don't know who, but whoever it is has told Müller *everything*. They know about Carl and you . . . who you are."

"I know," I whisper.

"You do?" she says. "Bloody good! Don't expect rescue from the others . . . the Stake vampires. The traitor sent word to them that *Carl* gave orders to stay clear for at least forty-eight hours, or until they hear from him, you, or Rolf, whichever comes first."

So nae help is coming from the outside. We're alone. Well . . . nae alone, precisely. We can still pray.

"How do I know that *ye* are nae the traitor?" I ask. *I hope 'tis nae her . . . but I cannae be sure. I'm nae fond of Sarah, but I want her to succeed. I want her to find salvation.*

"You don't," she says, and the bitterness in her voice is so raw that I truly do feel for her. "You have no more reason to trust *me* than you do anyone else."

"What makes ye think that *Müller* trusts you?" I say.

"He trusts me," she says, "because I've obeyed all his commands without hesitation. At least so far."

"*All* his commands?" I ask. *If she's nae the traitor, she may still have had to commit a heinous act to remain above suspicion.*

"By that do you mean, did he command me to sleep with him?" she replies.

"Something like that," I whisper.

"I was ready to, you know," she says, and I can imagine her face flushing. "I think I would have done *anything* to save Rolf. When Müller and the others came to the hotel, I had to lead them away from Rolf. He was Sleeping. He was *vulnerable*. I had to save him."

She seems so besotted with him. Sarah, the hardened, third-generation whore, the obsessive, bitter Hunter of men, loves Rolf. 'Tis difficult to wrap my mind around. Is it too hard to believe? I'm certain that Rolf loves her.

"But, no," she continues. "Seems Müller is into *younger* women. *Much* younger."

I hear relief in her voice.

"What did he command ye to do?" I ask, nae wanting to hear the answer.

"There was little time, and so he decided to test me quickly. He had me attack one of the hotel housekeeping maids who was making up a nearby room. I took as little as I could, but I had to make it seem likely that she would die. So I Fed slowly. I *must* have fooled him. He let me take my sword."

I hear her pat the hilt at her side. *Either that proves Müller does trust her, or it means she's in league with him. Could she have been in league with him all along?*

"How did Müller capture you in the first place?" I ask.

"I heard a number of stealthy footsteps coming down the hall at the hotel," she replies. "I knew Rolf and I were in trouble, and I couldn't protect him against so many. So I went out to meet them.

"Müller was there, surrounded by five mortals: one man and four women. They, the mortals, were all armed with machine rifles. My only chance to save Rolf was to lead them away from him. I tried to act as if I was running away, but Müller told me to stop. So I pretended to be enthralled."

"What happened to the maid?"

"I let her see my fangs before I took her. She screamed once. *Loudly*. I took enough just to make her heart beat a bit too fast. As I Fed, I thrashed about and made an awful mess of the room. When I was finished, I left the door propped open with her in plain sight. Someone should have found her shortly after." She pauses a tick and then hisses, "I had to *convince* that foul 'Apostle.' I was *desperate!*"

This sounds plausible . . . barely. She could be speaking the truth. She could be.

Or she could have been Müller's spy all along. Sent to find "the Breakers."

"He plans to crucify you and leave you to the Sun at dawn," she whispers. "It's how he 'helps' those of his followers who can't adapt to slowly starving themselves. Actually, that's how *most* of his people end up. He convinces them it's the only way they can be redeemed."

"They cannae be so stupid," I say.

"They're *desperate*," she says. "They want redemption so badly they're willing to pay *any* price." She makes a small noise, a sort of huffing sound, that I assume must be a whispered bitter laugh. "I starved myself to the point that I fell out of the sky, and all based on nothing more than a *hope* suggested by a bloody website!"

Was it that . . . or was it all part of Müller's design? Was Sarah bait . . . a fishing lure being dragged through the night sky to catch us? Had she been bait again to lure us here so we could be executed in front of the Congregation? Had Müller known about me all along and used my Teacher to capture me?

I dinnae want to believe it, but maybe Sarah's the traitor.

"It doesn't matter, though, if they are willing or not," she continues. "Once the Congregation has its hold on someone and Müller is ready to execute that person, he can simply command them, and they'll allow themselves to be crucified. They come seeking redemption and hope, but all they find is death. He boasted to me that, as they're burning on the cross, unable to escape because he orders them to stay there, he forces them to repeat the Last Words of Christ. How vile is that?"

I cannae suppress a shudder. I receive many cuts as a result, but it chills me to the bone. *'Tis what I've been seeing in my dreams! I've been suffering, reliving the ritual executions of the Penitents!*

"Why would Müller tell ye all this?" I ask. *Unless, of course, ye've been his all along . . . But I heard Müller order her to keep silent. Does that nae prove she's able to defy him?*

"It's because he thinks I'm *bound* to him," she hisses. "He *knows* about the oaths we swore to Carl, but he thinks he's more powerful. You and Carl are the exceptions, but he thinks once he gets anyone else within the sound of his voice . . . well, he's certain he can control them."

As he's controlling ye, perhaps? It cannae be true! Can it?

"Listen," she says, "the Sun's almost set. Rolf and Carl are going to wake soon. *You* have to do the best you can to calm Carl so he doesn't hurt himself . . . or kill himself . . . or, *worse*, put me in a position where I'd be *expected* to kill him and thus blow the whole charade. You'll only have your voice to work with, but I'm going to stand over Rolf to try to calm him. If they make any move to escape . . . well, you know what I'm *supposed* to do. So, make it look and sound good, or we'll all be in this together. I mean, we bloody well *are* in this together, but . . . Oh, you *know* what I mean!"

Are we?

"I *was* planning on just freeing you," she whispers. "Your bloody weapons are right over there . . . But, Müller boasted about having a hostage, a friend of yours, one he'll kill if you try to make a move. He says she's held at gunpoint on the other side of that ruddy camera up there."

"She's nae a friend. She hates me above anyone on earth . . . excepting, that is, her own self . . . But I *do* care about her. I've got to do all I can to save her. She may nae be nice . . . she may be a vile, putrescent, pathetic pain in the posterior, but . . . she does nae deserve what's happening to her."

"I thought as much, but are you willing to sacrifice Carl to save her? Are you willing to sacrifice Rolf? And what of your *own* life?"

"Ask Carl or Rolf if they're willing to lay down their lives for a stranger," I say. "I think ye ken what their answer would be."

"Yeah," she whispers. "I do."

She moves into position at Rolf's side.

And we wait. We wait for the moment when we will feel the Death of the Light.

Minutes pass in a sluggish, sepulchral silence, broken only by the nigh imperceptible sounds of Sleeping vampires and Sarah's and my own breathing and heartbeats. It's torment to be lying here, helpless . . . nae knowing if Sarah can be trusted . . . nae knowing if we can possibly survive the coming of the dawn.

At last, darkness falls. I feel the surge of strength, the feeling of power which comes as the last deadly rays of the Sun disappear.

I hear the sudden intake of Carl's breath. Rolf gasps immediately afterward.

Instantly, they begin to thrash against their bonds, and the scent of spilt blood fills my nostrils.

Sarah is able to calm Rolf quite quickly, whispering to him, but Carl is another matter. He cannae see me. He does nae ken where he is or what's happened since he was shot.

"Carl!" I cry, nae longer needing to whisper. "It's Moira! Hold still, my dearie! Ye are bound with razor wire! I'm here! Oh, hold *still!*"

I hear the horrid sound of his flesh being torn as he continues to struggle.

"Please, Carl! Dinnae struggle! Hold fast!"

"Moira?" my dear husband says and ceases his struggling.

"Aye, my love! I'm here!"

"Sarah?" Rolf says.

She's trying to speak to him, but he's nae ready to comprehend her nigh inaudible whispers.

"Rolf," I cry to him, "listen to me! Hold fast! Dinnae move or ye'll cut yourself! Sarah cannae speak. Müller has captured all of us and she's under his control. He ordered her nae to speak to us, and to *kill* us should we try to escape."

Then I whisper quickly and quietly, "But, as ye can see, she's speaking to ye now. Listen to her. I *think* we can trust her."

"Of course we can trust her!" Rolf whispers back, taking his cue from me. He kens that someone is listening to anything we say out loud.

I hope ye have the right of it, laddie! I pray we can trust her.

"*Please* trust me," she whispers.

"Are you all right, sweetie?" Carl whispers.

"Aye, laddie," I whisper back. "I am. I'm a prisoner just as ye are, but I'm hale and sound."

"Rolf?" Carl says.

"I'm here, Carl," Rolf replies.

"Good," my husband whispers. "Moira, *report! Sitrep!*"

"*Situation report,*" *I translate in my head.*

Even though he's whispering, his tone takes on a military quality. He's the general taking command.

"That glowing man we saw?" I begin. "That was Müller . . ."

I tell them *most* everything I know, with Sarah throwing in details from time to time. She stays by Rolf's side, though. She never takes her right hand from the hilt of her sword. I dinnae ken if she's merely keeping up appearances or if she's truly ready to murder us. *I hate nae knowing what side she's on.*

Sarah fills in her side of the story as well.

Both Carl and Rolf ask questions, and I answer them as best I can. But one detail I leave out entirely. I dinnae mention what I've learned about Müller's ability to endure the Sun. *I cannae trust Sarah . . . at least nae as we stand now. I must nae reveal that bit of knowledge to her.* When asked about how Müller saved us after he shot us, I simply tell them I was nae coherent at the time.

"But we most definitely have a traitor in our midst. One of our new friends betrayed us."

Or perhaps it was our own Sarah.

"Who is it?" Rolf asks.

"I dinnae know," I reply.

"I have no idea, either," Sarah whispers. "I haven't been here that much longer than you three have. All I know is that whoever it is sent word back that the others are not to come here, at least not right now."

"OK," Carl says. "So, we're on our own. And, for the moment, we don't dare make a move without risking Winnie's life."

"How do we know Müller will keep his word?" Rolf asks. "He's probably going to kill her anyway."

"We don't know that he *will*," Carl responds. "He has no reason to. But he'll keep her alive for now. He needs *her* to control *us*."

"Aye, you're right," I whisper.

"That buys us some time," says Rolf.

"Roger that," Carl says. "We have the rest of the night to come up with a plan. What options do we have?"

"We're nae going to sacrifice Winnie," I say.

"No," Rolf replies, "she's innocent. At least more innocent than *we are*. Carl excepted, of course."

"Knock it off," Carl replies. "I mean, *please* knock it off."

"You know what I mean," Rolf says.

"Yeah," Carl says. "Sorry."

"As you said," Rolf says, "what *are* the options?"

"Your weapons are here in the room," Sarah says. "Not that they'll do you any good with you trussed up like this."

There is silence in the basement for a wee moment as we all try to come up with ideas for escape.

"I feel like Steve McQueen in *The Great Escape*, all tangled up in the barbed wire after crashing his motor cycle," Rolf says. "I love that movie, but I root for the Brits and the Yanks now."

Fifty men or so sacrificed their lives so a few could escape in the story. How many of us will die? Will any of us escape?

"I have an idea," I say, as a daft plan takes shape in my mind, "but I dinnae think ye're going to like it." *I certainly dinnae like it!*

"Let's hear it, my love," Carl says.

I'm nae sure how much I can or should say with Sarah in the room. How I wish I knew where she stands!

"What if we . . ."

I stop speaking when I hear footsteps on the stairs.

It's nae *Müller's* weary stomp. 'Tis someone new. The footfalls are lighter. Almost those of a child. Nae a child perhaps, but someone young and nae quite an adult. At the back of my mind, something nags at me. In my mind's eye, I see the corbie worrying a bit of burned flesh from my father's charred corpse. I cannae escape the feeling that I *know* who it is.

I cannae see Sarah, but I hear her off to my right as she turns to face the newcomer.

The door swings open, and someone enters the room.

I hear Sarah gasp.

"*You?*" Carl says out loud to a person I still cannae see. "*You* betrayed us?"

The newcomer with the light tread almost steps into my field of vision, tantalizingly close, but I still cannae see who it is. I *feel* more than see that 'tis a smaller figure. Definitely nae a child, but too small to be an adult. I catch the gleam of a drawn sword just at the fuzzy edge of my sight.

Nae a child, but nae quite an adult. And in that instant I recognize her. Nae, never *an adult.*

"Why?" Carl demands. "Why would you sell us out, Martha?"

Chapter 26

MARTHA IS THE TRAITOR.

"Sell you out?" she spits back at Carl in response. "I was never a part of your pathetic little band! Paul sent me to spy on the ridiculous *Stake*!" Her voice is a high-pitched trill now that she's angry. It serves only to emphasize how young she is . . . biologically. In reality, she's only a few decades younger that me.

"Oh, we're so sorry!" she says, mocking us. "We're so sorry we're a bunch of murdering vampires! We want to go back to being mortal!"

Her youthful face twists in a snarl. "Like you didn't all *choose* it!" she hisses. "You *all* knew what you were doing! And *don't* feed me that tripe about *Carl* being so blasted *innocent*! That's a steaming pile of horse droppings if ever I stepped in one! I don't know what your problem is, Carl Morgan the Unwilling, but I know you're not as lily-white as you claim."

"But you *saw*!" Rolf exclaims. "You saw that the rest of us were *free* as soon as we swore fealty to Carl! *All* of us were *free*!"

"So *free*!" she snaps, taking a few steps in Rolf's direction.

I can see her plainly now. She looks so very young. Born in an age when girls matured early, she looks as if she would have bloomed late regardless. If I did nae know her true biological age, I would have said she was thirteen at the most. Maybe twelve.

"Well, *I* wasn't free!" she screams. "I felt no *different*! I'm still as bound to Paul as I was the night I Awoke from my Conversion!"

"It was *Müller*!" I say as the realization hits me. "*Müller* seduced you! He was your Master!"

"Yes," she says, her face balling up in a childish fury. "I *love* him!" She stomps her foot and points her sword at me menacingly. "And *he* loves *me* again!"

"Why?" I say. *I ken that I should nae provoke her. She could kill me at any moment, but I cannae ken why she would go back to him.*

From Rolf's side, I hear Sarah hiss, "Why would you go back to such a fiend? He *used* you! He *left* you! What happened to the *other* child he tossed you over for?"

"That little *harlot*! Foul child *whore*!" Martha snarls. "I bashed her skull in with a hammer! She healed, of course, but she was *never* the same. She didn't remember who she was, much less how to speak, Feed, walk, or clean herself.

Or how to please a man."

She seems to collect herself. "Paul was *furious* with me," she continues in a darker, calmer tone. "I thought he'd take me back, but he told me to go. He threw me out and told me to never come back. He called me a wretched old hag. I tried *over* and *over* to get him to love me. Followed him for centuries. But he would never take me back."

She smiles. "Until now. Now he *loves* me again!"

"You make me *sick*!" Sarah hisses. "Women like you make me want to *vomit*! I spent nearly a *thousand* years trying to deliver you pathetic creatures from the male monsters who abused you. And you *always* crawl *back* to them! You were '*young* and in *love*'... I've heard that countless times. 'I'll *change* him. This time will be *different*.' No, it bloody well won't! He *used* you and tossed you out like so much *rubbish*! And he'll do it again! *You* are the 'horse droppings' that *he* stepped in and then scraped off his boot. I cannot fathom why you *pathetic* wretches go back to debauchers like that!"

"Because no one else will *have* me!" she screams. Tears spill from her eyes. "*Look* at me! I'm never going to be a *woman*! Only a *pedophile* would *want* me! Paul's the only one who *ever* loved me!" Her mouth contorts soundlessly as she struggles to give voice to her anguish.

And, in a voice that is softer and choked with all the self-loathing in the world, she says "And I've nowhere else to go." Tears stream down her face. "I'm *worthless* to anyone else."

"Ye are nae worthless to God," I say. "To Him, ye are *precious*."

"Will you *stop* with all that tripe about *God*?" she snarls back. "Where was *God* when I lost my innocence? Where was *God* when I was frozen forever into this *shapeless* child's body?"

I see her sword flash, and in an instant, the point is under my jaw, pressing into the soft flesh of the submental area. One thrust and she could impale my brain. *Twould be easier to sever the brainstem, but with her vampiric strength, punching through to brain would present nae challenge.*

How can I think in such clinical terms at a time like this?

"Why, in Lilith's name, would I want *God* to win? What have I to look forward to? If *you* succeed, I'm going to *die*. We're *all* going to *die*! And I'm going straight to *Hell*. If you fail, at least then I'll have someone who *loves* me, someone who *wants* me."

I dare nae say a word. If I were to move my jaw, her sword would slide right in.

"It's not too late, Martha," Carl says. "Remember the story of the Anti-Nephi-Le ..."

"If you say another wretched word to me about *God* or your *insipid* Book of Mormon," Martha says, her teeth clenched, her face a mask of abject misery, "I'll lobotomize your pretty wife. Do you understand me?"

"Yes," Carl says.

I hear the heartbeat before I see him, but suddenly Müller is behind Martha, one arm encircling her waist. *He must have flown without wings to have approached so stealthily. How much has he heard? He could hardly miss hearing Martha's shrill tirade. Did he hear anything from Sarah that would make him suspect her?*

"Now, now, my pretty little princess," he coos as he strokes her hair with his free hand. He's so much taller than she is. The top of her head comes only to his sternum. His eyes fix mine as he says to Martha, "Don't you fret, my sweet. You *know* how much I love you. You are the *only* one I love . . . the only one I've *ever* loved. And we'll be together forever now. Thanks to you. You have done well."

The point of her sword is nae longer pressing under my jaw. She drops it, and I hear it clang as it hits the floor and she turns to him. He lifts her off the ground and pulls her up to his face and kisses her.

She seems to melt in his embrace. I can hear her heartbeat and her breathing quicken. For the moment, she's oblivious to everything else in the room . . . in the world.

Müller's eyes, though, never leave mine, and they are nae loving, nae warm. His eyes are cold, cold as the tomb.

She's just a tool, a weapon and nothing more. When she is of nae use to him or he finds some other bonnie younger lassie to corrupt, he'll discard her again.

And at that moment, I'm filled with the chilling certainty that he will do far worse than discard her. When she has fulfilled her purpose . . . when *we're* dead . . . he'll *dispose* of her. Permanently.

We have till sunrise. I doubt that Martha . . . sad, pitiful, desperate little Martha . . . will survive to see another.

'Tis nae long before Carl's cell phone begins to ring. Müller sets Martha down and plucks the phone from what I assume is a table somewhere beyond my feet and out of my sight, like our weapons, and shows it to Martha.

She glances at the number and says, "Corelli."

Müller nods and says, "That will be all for now, my pet. Go to our bed and wait for me there. Keep it warm. I won't be long."

She giggles and leaves the basement, her tread light and swift.

The phone rings a few more times and goes silent.

Müller looks in Carl's direction and then in mine. He comes to a decision. "You, I think, Moira. You will call Corelli back. I trust you will be careful not to say anything to cause Carla there to dispose of your friend in the barn." He nods in the direction of the television. I can see Winnie whimpering in the stall. I can also see Carla pacing back and forth in front of it, all the while keeping her eyes on us. *She's single-minded, that one.*

"Now, Martha has told me your little troop has been instructed to take orders from any of the three of you. She also told me about the code words you use to authenticate your communications. 'Babylon' and 'Egypt,' I believe. You will use these, just as I had our Sarah use them when she called you. (Not that you stayed away.) She also told me about your duress word, 'tired.' You will, of course, *not* use that word . . . not if you want your friend to live."

Did he just say what I think he said? Is it possible that Martha misheard *the duress word? 'Tiger,' nae 'tired!' Or is he just testing me?*

"Did you hear that, Carla?" Müller says, louder for the sake of the microphone.

"Every word, Master," she replies through the TV.

"Mrs. Morgan must begin her phone call with the word 'Babylon' or 'Egypt.' If she does not, shoot our little piggy."

"Yes, Master."

"Also, Carla," Müller continues, "if at any time Mrs. Morgan utters the word 'tired,' you're to execute your prisoner."

"Yes, Master."

He does nae know! He has the wrong *word!*

"Now, Carla, please repeat that back to me. I want to make doubly sure you're clear on this. I don't want any more mistakes."

On the screen, Carla flinches and then nods. "The first word she says has to be 'Babylon' or 'Egypt,' otherwise I shoot the sow. If she uses the word, 'tired,' I get to shoot the sow."

"Very good, Carla," Müller says and turns his head to flash her a smile. "I knew I could trust you."

She beams at him through the screen.

He turns back to me. "Now, Moira, what I want you to tell Corelli is that the three of you are all right. Make that the four of you. Mention Sarah as well," he says with a nod. "Tell him the members of the 'Vampire Stake' are to stay away from this place . . . except for Corelli and Martha, of course."

He winks at me. It makes my stomach turn.

"You see," he continues, "Corelli had arranged to meet up with Martha shortly after nightfall. Tell Corelli that Martha will be delayed for a couple of hours"—he pauses and winks at me again—"but the rendezvous is to proceed as planned after that. (I want Corelli to be a witness to your execution, you see, and take word back to your pathetic little group of religious fanatics.) So, yes, I *will* spare him."

He smiles with mock magnanimity. "See, you've saved one of them already!" He laughs softly.

"Once you're dead," he continues, pleased with his joke, "and they have *proof* you're dead, despair will take the lot of them. I expect they'll all be dead within a month . . . or they'll return willingly to the fold."

He opens Carl's phone. "Are you clear on what you're to say?"

"Aye."

"Wait," Carl says. "Moira is many wonderful things, but she is a *terrible* actress. She may not sound convincing. Besides, Winnie Morrison, your prisoner, is important to me too. We go to church with her. Let *me* make the phone call. I can convince Corelli."

Müller hesitates and then nods. "Very well. Yes, I see the wisdom in what you say. Besides, if the pig's life is not incentive enough, I have your wife."

What's Carl up to? He's right: I'm a terrible liar. Does he think he can get a message to Corelli, one that Müller would not detect?

Müller presses the call button twice to call Lorenzo Corelli back and holds the phone to Carl's ear. The phone rings. Lorenzo's worried voice says, "Yes?"

"Babylon," Carl says distinctly.

"Egypt," Lorenzo replies. "Thank God you're all right!"

"We're fine," Carl replies. "We're all fine: Moira, Rolf, Sarah, and I."

"Thank God," Lorenzo says again. "When you didn't answer . . . well, without you and Moira, we're all lost."

"Yeah," Carl says, "that's true. We're the prophesied ones."

"Yes, you are."

Did Lorenzo notice Carl's uncharacteristic acceptance of his role in the Prophecy? He sounded almost arrogant.

"Anyway, Lorenzo, listen," Carl says. "I've spoken to Martha . . ."

"Yes, I got a message from her earlier . . ."

"Right," Carl continues, "listen up. You need to meet with her as planned, but give her a couple of hours. She's got some things to take care of. She'll give you further instructions when you meet. She's got some spirit, that little thing. She's a *tiger*, that one! I like her."

"Yes," Lorenzo says a little too slowly, "she *is* special."

At least he got the message . . . I hope . . . that Carl is 'under duress' and maybe, just maybe, that Martha is nae to be trusted.

"One more thing, Lorenzo," Carl says, his voice taking on the tone of command. "Tell the others to stay away from Müller's compound. Completely away. In fact, *tell them to get out of the state.* Do you understand?"

"Yes, sir. I understand and I will obey."

"I'll be in touch."

"Good-bye," Lorenzo says. I hear the electronic click as the call terminates on Corelli's end.

Carl has just given Lorenzo an order that Corelli is bound to obey. He has nae choice. Carl just sent away any hope of rescue from the Stake. Of course, ye did the right thing, laddie. Ye saved as many as ye could.

We're on our own now.

Müller pulls the phone away from Carl and snaps it shut. He scowls for a moment.

"A little embellishment, perhaps, but you did well enough. I didn't want the others out of the state, though, but no matter: I'll track them down. That is, if they don't destroy themselves first. You were just trying to protect your men, save as many as possible. I can respect that. It won't do you or them any good, but I respect your need to try."

Müller walks toward the place where I assume weapons are lying and replaces the cell phone.

He turns back toward Carl. "You're wrong, though," he says. "That crone upstairs, waiting for me in my bed, is no tigress. She's a mouse, a pathetic leach. But, I'll be rid of her soon enough. I just have to stomach her one more time."

"Sarah," he says, turning to her, "my homely little slave, you're on guard duty. If possible, keep them alive. They have an appointment in the morning with the Light, and I don't want them to miss it. If not, try to spare the Unwilling or his wife at least. We need one of them to make a good show. Herr Oettinger is expendable."

"Yes, Master," Sarah replies, her voice devoid of emotion.

Turning back to us, Müller spreads his hands wide and says, "Enjoy your stay. I hope you like the accommodations. Do try to relax. I want my star performers in top condition in the morning. And take heart. You're going to see God soon. Well, that is, if he still *exists*, once I'm done with you."

He turns to go, stops, turns back to us, and says, "What is it you Mormons are always saying? Ah, yes! 'God be with you till we meet again.'"

He laughs softly.

"Auf wiedersehen."

Till I see you again, he means.

Chapter 27

THEY COME IN THE WEE HOURS before dawn. More than a score of white-robed and hooded figures, vampires all, stream into the basement. Their appearance reminds me of cowled monks. They dinnae utter a word. They are silent save for the sound of their breathing and the beating of their hearts and the rustle of their robes.

Here and there I catch a glimpse of an exposed hand or a face veiled in shadow. They all look withered, emaciated.

I can hear Rolf's breath catch. He remembers well the horrors of Auschwitz. I've seen photographs and video of that atrocity, though I spent those years safely in Utah. These men and women are nae wasted to that degree, but they are *severely* malnourished. 'Tis a wonder some of them are mobile.

Müller has summoned his flock early, it seems. He does nae dare delay our executions until Saturday night when his Congregation would normally assemble. He *must* slay us in the morning. To delay even another day might somehow increase our chances of escape. Though, with Winnie a hostage on the other side of a closed TV circuit, I dinnae see how he thinks we could manage it. Müller is counting on our placing Winnie's life above our own. He's counting on our being willing to pay the ultimate price to save the life of an innocent mortal.

And he has us dead to rights.

I *love* Carl. I love him more than life itself. I *ache* for his touch. I love him for so many reasons, nae the least of which is because he is an *honorable* man. And I will nae *dishonor* him by sacrificing Winnie's life to save his. I'm certain he loves me beyond all reckoning . . . beyond all reason, though I cannae fathom why. And I'm equally as certain *he* would nae allow Winnie to die in *my* place.

We've known Rolf for such a short time, but I believe with all my heart that he would nae hesitate to lay down his own life for Winnie.

'Tis Sarah who concerns me. She said she'd have done *anything* . . . even bed Müller to save Rolf. Rolf extracted a promise from her that she would save the hostage (as he refers to Winnie). I just hope she holds to her promise. And if Sarah, my old Teacher, the Ancient One who Converted me, finds a way to rescue Winnie Morrison before Müller crucifies Carl, Rolf, and me, we might stand a chance of getting out of this with our skins. We *might* . . . if my daft plan works. But if Winnie is nae free, we dare nae make our move.

It all depends on Sarah. She looks to Carl and me to lead her to salvation, but *she* holds the key to saving *us*. I doubted her earlier, but now all our lives are in her hands. And doubts or nae, we can do naught but await her signal.

She's nae longer guarding us. She was relieved hours ago by Bartlett. He stands there just below the TV in a long white robe with his hood drawn back. His arms are folded across his chest. He holds his cutlass, in his right hand and he's resting the blade against his left shoulder. He watches as the figures in white surround Rolf. The expression on his face is profoundly sad. It has been so since Sarah left him alone with us.

Does he regret his part in all this?

He has spoken nary a word to us. Müller must have given the same injunction to *him* that he gave to Sarah earlier.

We tried, Carl and I did, to engage him in some sort of conversation. He would only stare at us with those haunted eyes.

At one point, I asked him about his long-dead wife. I saw tears in his eyes, but he still kept his silence.

For my part, I can easily believe that Bartlett truly wanted a way out of vampirism. I can believe that Müller ensnared him and enslaved him . . . that Bartlett is nae doing *any* of this voluntarily. I can *believe* that . . . and I *do* pity him . . . but I cannae make myself feel the slightest bit of empathy for him.

I cannae see what's happening with Rolf. I can only rely on my other senses. I hear sounds that might indicate physical exertion on the part of several people. *Are they restraining Rolf?* I hear metal slide against metal, and I hear Rolf cry out. And there is an unmistakable *snip*.

They're cutting his bonds! They're holding him down and cutting his restraints! The razor wire is slicing into his flesh as they do!

I can smell the blood!

I hear the process repeated again and again until all Rolf's bonds are cut.

Soon I see a mass of white-cloaked figures bearing Rolf away. One of them has a sword to Rolf's throat. But Rolf is nae struggling. *We're just going to have to play this out . . . at least until we can be certain that Winnie is safe.*

Rolf and his captors exit my field of vision, and soon I hear the tromp of the throng as they climb the stairs.

Nae sooner do I hear their footsteps begin to fade away than I hear the sound of another troop coming down the stairs. This time, when they enter our prison, they remain just at the edges of my vision on the left as they take my beloved husband.

"Carl!" I cry out to him.

"I'm still with you," he answers.

I hear the sounds of his bonds being cut. Carl snarls in pain.

"I . . ." My voice falters. *I feel so helpless! As ineffectual as a wee bairn screaming at the midwife to put him back in the safe, warm darkness!* "I love ye, laddie!"

Carl cries out in pain as the last of his bonds is cut and his dear flesh is sliced anew. "I know you do!" he cries. "I love you too, with all my heart and soul!"

Then they begin to carry him away. "No matter what happens, my love," he says, his voice calmer, "we'll be together on the other side. Just remember that!"

"Aye, laddie! Ye're mine!" *Mine and Sharon's.* "And I'm yours!"

"For time and all eternity," he says.

And then he is gone.

I'm all alone in this room . . . alone with Bartlett.

Why did they leave me for last?

Because, ye ninny, ye are the easiest to see in the TV.

I look at the screen.

Winnie has mercifully fallen asleep, although she whimpers and moans in her uneasy slumber. Her current guard is a man I've nae laid eyes on before. He looks more nervous, less cocksure than Carla.

Would he put a bullet in Winnie's brain?

Of course, he would. He is a Chosen disciple of Müller's. He wants to become a vampire. He craves immortality at the price of becoming a serial killer.

And now I hear the feet of those who have come to take me away. They're coming to take me to Golgotha.

If that be my Golgotha, the Place of the Skull, then this is my Gethsemane. I'm waiting for them to take me to be crucified.

I could flee.

I've nae doubt that I could overpower these emaciated Congregants. The hands of twenty cannae be brought to bear effectively all at once. They cannae all get purchase on my limbs. 'Twould be as if I were just fighting a handful of them. And they are all starving, at the end of their strength, having been Fed only with Müller's so called "Blessing." Surely, I could break free of them once my bonds are cut. My sword is somewhere in front of me, sitting on a table, most likely. Once I get my hand on it, they could nae stand against me.

I could flee. I could rescue my beloved Carl, and together we could flee this madhouse. We could hide from Lilith and her minions for eternity. We could abandon Winnie Morrison to her fate. I saved her life once. Is it nae now time to save my own? To save my husband's?

I could flee. I could fight.

My Master, my Lord . . . *He* waited in his Gethsemane. He waited, knowing they would take him and that he would die horribly. He had *already* paid for the sins of the world. Had he nae done enough? Could nae someone *else* complete the sacrifice? The great and atoning sacrifice? He had already endured unimaginable torment . . . to pay for *my* sins.

Yet He waited.

And He let them take Him.

And He endured to the end.

And I will allow them to take me, as well.

And I will be crucified to save another.

And so will Carl.

And so will Rolf.

Unless Sarah can rescue Winnie.

They descend on me like a flock of seagulls after a beached fish. Bony hands grip my arms and legs. Skeletal claws are placed on either side of my head. I'm surrounded in a sea of white.

I feel cold metal placed against my neck. Whatever it is, it slides down and is slipped under the razor wire wrapped about my throat. I cannae suppress a yelp of pain as the added pressure forces the sharp wire into my flesh. But then my neck is free, and the Seed rapidly heals my serrated skin. The procedure is repeated on each of my wrists and my ankles.

Whoever is cutting my bonds is nae too gentle: I receive deep cuts with each steel fetter severed.

If these are nae outright thralls, they must be true believers. Of course they are true believers, lassie! Why else would they endure the agony of glacially slow starvation?

At last I'm free of the cruel bonds, but deceptively strong bony hands hold me fast. A sword is placed to my throat, and then I'm lifted up and borne toward the door. After so many hours of being unable to move my head, I can finally look about me, but I cannae see much in the sea of hooded faces.

I do catch a fleeting glimpse of one robed, hooded figure who looks . . . thicker, healthier than the rest. I cannae be sure, but I think . . . I *hope* 'tis Sarah, come to play her first part in our desperate gambit.

She moves away from the mass of Müller's disciples. I think I hear the faint clink of metal on metal . . . of steel on steel. *Good lass!* Now, I hope nobody notices that our swords are missing.

I've lost sight of Bartlett in all this. I assume he's following us out, but I cannae say as I care *where* he is. I just hope he did nae notice Sarah.

My captors bear me out of the basement and up the stairs. I'm carried out into a room I recognize as the farmhouse kitchen. Then we're out a back door and into the night.

I could flee now. I'd have open sky. I could escape.

The stars are so beautiful. There is nary a cloud in the sky, and up here in the foothills, away from the lights of the city, the stars fill the sky as far as I can see.

I'm going to be crucified. I'm going to Golgotha. Like a lamb to the slaughter. And I cannae help but be amazed at the beauty of a sky full of stars.

At least they are nae forcing me to bear my own cross.

I'm carried into the large, well-painted, well-maintained barn. 'Tis *nae* the barn where Winnie is being held captive. I cannae see much besides the ceiling arcing above me, but I can hear and smell the occupants of the barn. There are many vampires here. They are nae cattle, like the poor souls in the functional barn on the nearby swine farm. Nae, they are Müller's willing (or perhaps unwilling) chattel.

There are so many of them.

Probably more than a hundred.

Probably more than a hundred and twenty.

Müller has summoned the entire Congregation, I'd guess.

And they are chanting.

There are so many of them, 'tis difficult to discern what they are saying.

As my captors lay me down on the ground, they also take up the chant.

'Tis nae the ground I'm lying on. 'Tis a great wooden cross. My captors spread my arms wide. Bony hands hold my arms and legs steady. Once again, a pair of emaciated hands hold my head still. *Why hold my head steady? They're nae going to drive a spike through my neck . . . so why?*

This is it, then. They are going to crucify me. I'll have spikes driven through my hands, wrists, and feet. Müller will nae be able to bind us in place with his command as he has others that he has crucified. After enduring the agony of the spikes being driven through our flesh, we should still be able to break free when the time comes . . . when Sarah signals that Winnie is safe.

They're going to crucify my beloved Carl too. And Rolf, as well. How I wish I could spare him . . . spare *both* of them the torture that is coming!

The sea of white parts slightly to admit another white-robed Congregant. But he does nae have spikes or a mallet in his hands.

'Tis more razor wire!

Müller intends that we shall nae escape.

The newcomer quickly binds my wrists and ankles to the cross. Then he encircles my neck. Many times.

That's it, then. I could pull my hands and feet free of the spikes, but the razor wire might well decapitate me.

"Moira?" 'Tis Carl's voice. He's to my left.

"I'm here, laddie."

"It's going to be all right," he says, and he almost sounds as if he believes it.

"Rolf?" he calls.

"I'm here, my captain," Rolf answers from farther to my left. His voice is calm. "I lay down my life to save another. It will have to be enough. I pray God it *will* be enough."

From the sound of it, Carl is in the center, Rolf on his left hand and I on his right.

Hands force my mouth open, and a rag is shoved roughly past my teeth, filling my mouth, silencing me. From the muted gagging sounds to my left, I assume the same has been done to Carl and Rolf.

Now that we're bound and gagged, the sea of white parts. With my neck secured as it is, I cannae see much more than I could before. I cannae see my dear Carl or Rolf.

The volume of the chanting increases. I still cannae make out the words. Maybe they're in a language beyond my ken.

Now, I cannae see *any* of the Congregants, but their voices are all around me. I try to focus on one voice so that I can make out the words. Focus on just one voice . . . any voice. *There!* 'Tis a male voice to my right.

I listen to that one voice, one of many, and suddenly the words are plain.

By blood thou art condemned.
By fire thou shalt be cleansed.
Though night thy prison be.
The Light shall set thee free.

The chant repeats. The same four lines over and over, the volume rising and falling.

And now I see him, the figure from my dreams.

Standing to my left and in front of where Carl must be is a man in a white robe with a golden Sun emblazoned on his breast. His hood conceals his face, but he can be nae other than Müller. In his right hand he holds the wooden mallet, in his left a large iron spike. At his waist is a pouch that sags as if it holds a great weight. More spikes, nae doubt.

He raises the spike and the mallet high above his head. The chanting ceases. Müller speaks in a loud, clear voice, sounding like a preacher projecting to his flock, "Children of the Sacred Fire! You have drunk of the Blessing of God tonight, and it has sustained your bodies and your souls!"

In unison, the assembled Congregation replies, *"We've drunk and we're filled!"*

"You are truly blessed!" Müller cries.

"We're truly blessed!" comes the reply.

"God has *blessed* you! God has *chosen* you! The glory of the Sun shall make you free!"

"We shall be free!"

"But not all!" Müller cries. "Not all will embrace the Light of the Sun and be free! Some cannot accept the Blessing, and they must be helped to transition from this life to the next!"

"The Light shall make them free!"

"The Light shall set the sinners free!"

"Praise the Light!"

"We have before us this night three who have sought to thwart the will of God!"

The Congregation is silent except for a few hushed gasps.

Müller has departed from the scripted ritual.

"They promote the fable of the 'Breaking'! We know that there was no such Breaking! But they do far worse than promote a false hope! They preach blasphemy! They presume to lay claim to the fulfillment of the Curse! *This* one," he cries, pointing at Carl, "claims the title of the Unwilling!"

This time the shared gasps from the assembled vampires are loud and universal.

"He *claims*," Müller continues, "that he did not *choose* this life of darkness and blood! He *claims* that it was *forced* on him! He lies! He *blasphemes*!"

There are murmurs from the crowd now. *Do they doubt him? Why is Müller laying all his cards on the table? Why tell them who we are?*

"And this *harlot*," he shouts, pointing the spike at me, "this thrice-damned *whore* claims to be the prophesied Penitent! Are we not all Penitents? Are we not all sinners who require the mercy of God?

"And yet they *presume* to make themselves *holy*! They *assume* the mantle of prophecy when they are the vilest of sinners and charlatans! And *this* one," he shouts, pointing in Rolf's direction with his mallet, "claims to be the Prophet of God! He claims that *he* was the one who married them, 'joined them' if you will, in the House of God!"

Where did he come up with that?

Out of whole cloth, lassie!

"Together, they have led other deluded Penitents astray from the *true* path to Salvation! They seek to lead them back to indulging in the blood of mortals! They say it is no sin! They seek to destroy you! They seek to pollute you again!"

Müller's voice drops to a more normal volume. "And for that, they must die by the Light."

Silence reigns for a moment, but then I hear a throat clearing off to my right.

"Master?" 'Tis a woman's timid voice.

"Yes, my daughter?" Müller replies.

"Master," the voice says, "could they be telling the truth? Could they be the fulfillment of the Curse?"

"Think, my child," Müller says with exaggerated patience. "Tina, isn't it?"

"Yes, Master."

"Think, Tina. Is it possible to become a vampire without choosing it?"

"N . . . no," is the halting reply. *She sounds young . . . young both in body and in spirit.*

"Well," Müller says with the air of an indulgent parent, "there you have it."

"B . . . b . . . but, Master," she says, "if the Curse is to be, you know, be-lieved . . . I mean, why does Lilith forbid the creation of an Unwilling vampire? If it's not *possible*, why *prohibit* it?"

"It is a myth," Müller replies, his tone kind and patient, "a lie perpetuated by your old Masters to keep you in fear."

"But, Master . . ." This is another voice. A man's this time.

"My children," Müller intones, raising his voice slightly, "now is not the time for this discussion. Time grows short. The sky is beginning to lighten."

I cannae see it . . . the barn doors are still closed . . . but I can *feel* the approach of dawn.

A few more voices begin to question, but Müller raises his own voice and begins the chant, "*By blood thou art condemned.*"

A chorus of voices takes up the chant, and all doubt is drowned in the ocean of ritual.

Müller lowers his arms and appears to bow his head in prayer.

Then he advances on Carl, and I can nae longer see him.

Brace yourself, laddie! Be brave! Oh, that I could bear the pain for ye!

The first blow of the mallet is answered with a roar of pain from my poor dearie! With each cruel blow, each horrid spike driven into my husband's dear flesh, Carl gives a muffled cry.

I scream too! I scream around the gag in my mouth! I cannae bear to hear him suffer so!

The chant around me swells in volume.

Dear Father! Help him to be strong, to endure what he must! Please, Father, dinnae let our sacrifice be in vain! Let Sarah get Winnie safely away! And, please, merciful Father, find a way to spare my dearie! Put all his pain on me! Let me bear it! And Rolf's pain, as well, Father! Save them!

There is a pause between blows as Müller moves and applies a new spike.

By the time Carl is silent except for his ragged muffled breathing, I've counted six spikes. That would be one in each foot, one in each palm of the hand, and one in each wrist.

My poor, poor laddie!

At the edges of my vision, I can see figures in white come forward. They must be assembling around Carl.

And then I see him.

My poor, poor husband is hanging from a cross as it is lifted up and carried by a mass of white-robed vampires . . . carried toward the front of the barn. Blood drips from his hands. And about his head . . . is that a crown of thorns?

Oh, Carl!

How was I ever brave or calm about this?

He passes from my sight again.

I hear the sound of the barn doors opening.

And shortly, there is the sound of the cross being lowered, as it was in my dream, into a hole in the ground. I hear the sound of impact as the cross comes to rest upright and then I hear a muffled cry from my dear husband as the spikes and the razor wire tear his flesh anew.

Carl! Ach, my poor, poor laddie!

Now Müller is standing in front of me. He did nae leave me to last this time.

Where is Sarah?

Father, help me be brave!

Müller kneels to my left. I cannae see him, except out of the corner of my eye.

The sharp point of the iron spike is now pressing down into my palm. Müller raises the mallet to strike.

He brings it down, and I feel the spike driven into the flesh of my hand, breaking bones as it goes. I scream in agony, my voice muffled by the gag in my mouth. A second blow of the mallet drives the iron farther into my hand and into the wood behind it.

I feel another spike placed against my wrist. The mallet is raised again. Once more I feel pain as the new spike is driven through my flesh.

The mallet strikes again, and I feel more flesh ripping, more bones breaking as my wrist is nailed to the wood behind it.

The process is repeated on my other hand and wrist. Then finally my feet are nailed to the wood.

Ach! 'Tis maddening, this combination of pain and the itch as the Seed struggles to repair the damage! But it cannae force the invading iron from my body.

The chanting increases in volume as the Congregants around me close in. Many hands grasp the wood of the cross and lift and me upright. The agony in my hands, wrists, and feet doubles and redoubles as the spikes began to bear the weight of my body. The razor wire is forced into my flesh as my body sags against it. Each jolt as I'm hoisted upright sends new bolts of pain thundering through my wounded flesh.

But now that I'm upright, I can see my dear Carl. His back is to me, and the cruel cross that bears him is between us. I see tremors pass through his body as he struggles against the pain and the itch.

I'm brought beside him, and he passes from my field of vision.

Suddenly I begin to drop and pitch forward as the cross is lowered into a hole in the ground. I scream again around the rag in my mouth as I feel the flesh rip once more.

I can hear the chanting fade away as the figures move back, behind and away from me. I dinnae care. I just want to be delivered from the pain. My breathing becomes increasingly labored as the unnatural position of my body pulls at my internal organs.

'Tis like my dream, but in my dream, I was bound by Müller's command. In this living nightmare, I'm bound by the razor wire and by Winnie's life. Either way, I'm helpless.

Sarah! Where are ye, lass?

Father! Help her! Help her save Winnie! Deliver us!

Now I hear Rolf's muffled cry of agony. *Poor laddie!*

Sarah! Hurry!

With every thud of the mallet, with every muffled cry from Rolf, it seems as if my wounds throb anew.

At last, the pounding is done, and Rolf is brought forward. His cross is dropped into the hole in the ground. I cannae see him. I can but look straight ahead. At least the pounding is done.

Now all that remains is the agony of our wounds, of the unnatural posture of our bodies, of the shortness of breath as our diaphragms cannae seem to pull in enough air . . .

. . . the agony of waiting for the dawn.

The sky is getting brighter now. The stars are gone. There is nae a cloud in the sky to shield us from the Sun's deadly light.

And the Sun'll be rising soon.

Müller walks out in front of us, the golden Sun emblem on his chest catching the light from the barn interior behind us. He nae longer bears a mallet, and his pouch of spikes is gone. Now he carries a spear. The head of the spear looks ancient. It looks like 'tis made of iron.

Müller holds the spear aloft.

In spite of my agony, I cannae take my eyes off the spearhead. It looks . . . familiar.

An image flashes in my mind. *My trip to Washington, DC to see a display of ancient artifacts, supposedly holy relics. The display had been broken into, and one of the artifacts was missing. But I had seen a photograph of it. This missing relic was . . .*

The Spearhead of Longinus!

Could it be? The spear that pierced the side of Christ? Müller was the one who robbed the museum? Müller *stole the relic?*

Müller walks forward, toward Carl. I cannae see what happens, but from the sounds, I can see it all in my mind's eye.

Müller thrusts the spear upward into Carl's side and through his diaphragm.

'Twill nae kill him, of course, but 'twill be more pain for my dearie to suffer through.

I hear Müller approach me before I see him. I look down, and there he stands, the spear pointed toward my innards.

He thrusts upward, and the ancient iron pierces my side, puncturing my diaphragm and deflating my lungs. It hurts. I cannae breathe. Then the Seed repairs it quickly, and my labored breathing resumes once again.

When I look down for Müller, he's gone. Then I hear the sound of Rolf being skewered. I hear the huff as his lungs deflate, then I hear him begin to breathe again.

That's it. The ritual is over. Now we just have to wait until the Sun rises and consumes us.

In some ways, 'twould be a relief. 'Twould be a release from all the cares of this world and my unnaturally long existence. In other ways . . .

Sarah! Please hurry!

She has failed. I need to face that now. We're going to die here. We're going to burn in the light of the Sun.

"Müller! Let them go!" a familiar voice shouts from above. *'Tis Lorenzo Co-relli!*

I turn my gaze upward, and I see Lorenzo descending from the east. He has nae wings, I note with a wee bit of pride. He has Martha held tightly to his chest with his left arm while he holds a falchion to her throat.

"Let them go, Müller, or I'll take her head off!" Corelli shouts. "Martha here tells me that she's your lover. So free my friends, or I'll kill her!"

Müller lets out a loud laugh. "That hag?" he yells. "You can have her. She's too old for my taste."

"*Paul!*" comes Martha's pitiful wail. "You said you loved me!"

"Kill her!" Müller commands. "Just shut her *up*!"

Lorenzo hovers in the air, and the look on his face is one of fear. He thought he had a bargaining chip with Martha. *He understood our message and took her hostage. He had nae idea Martha held nae value to the enemy.*

"I said, 'Kill her!'" Müller roars.

Lorenzo hesitates. He does nae know what to do.

"Kill her NOW!" Müller's voice sounds hysterical. I cannae see him, but he sounds *frightened*.

He has realized that he cannae command Corelli! He was so sure he would be able to command Lorenzo in spite of their oaths to Carl! He *doubts* himself! Maybe for the first time in a thousand years!

"*Paul!*" cries Martha. *"Please!"* She looks tormented. She staked all her hopes and dreams on this man, and he has cast her aside. Again.

"Shut up, you *old*, worthless pig!" Müller snarls, and Martha cuts off mid wail.

Her Master commands, and she has nae choice but to obey him.

There is a collective gasp from the Congregation. The charade is over. Müller has revealed himself. They know what he is now. They know that he is at the very least a Master. He's nae a holy man; he's a charlatan. And they also see that he cannae command Lorenzo.

"Kill her," Müller says. His voice is calm. Deadly.

And behind me I hear the rustle of more than a hundred pairs of wings. The Congregation takes flight and converges on Lorenzo and Martha.

"Keep *him* alive," Müller says. "Bring him to me."

There is a writhing storm cloud of white robes and white wings where Lorenzo and Martha used to be.

I hear the awful sound of flesh being rent, of bones breaking. In her last moments, Martha could nae even cry out because Müller had commanded her silence.

It begins to rain from that cloud. I see red drops and spraying streams of crimson.

And so passes Martha.

She gave up her innocence and her mortality for a man who had her torn to bloody bits when he tired of her.

When the cloud disperses and the Congregants retreat to the shelter of the barn, many of their white robes are splattered with gore and gobbets of tissue—all that remains of Martha.

A small group descends to land in front of Müller, who has now stepped into my sight. The hoods have fallen back from many of the Congregants' faces. They are hollow-eyed and hollow-cheeked, but the looks on their faces say far more than their emaciated features. They are crushed. They are defeated. They placed their hopes and their trust in this man, and he has betrayed them. They are right back where they started. They fled the Cults and Lilith's control, hoping to find a way back to God. Müller offered them a way. But he has destroyed them. He has nae only enslaved them again, he has slain their hopes.

Now there is only death or servitude for them. And they may nae be allowed to choose death.

In the midst of this small group is a struggling Lorenzo Corelli. He is covered in gore. They force him to stand before Müller.

"Turn him around so he can see the death of his hopes," he says.

They force Lorenzo to turn and face us.

"I'm sorry," he says. "I failed you." Tears stream down his face, making streaks in the blood.

In spite of the horrible mix of pain and itch I feel from the spikes, the razor wire, the cross, and the Seed's frustrated Healing, I'm overwhelmed with sympathy. I wish I could comfort him. But I cannae say a word around my gag.

"Watch, rebel," Müller says with a sneer, "and see what becomes of those who oppose my Queen."

He turns to those holding Lorenzo. "Come, slaves. Let us step back into the shadows. The Sun is almost here."

Müller and the vampires guarding Lorenzo retreat to the shadows on my right, and I can see them nae more. I catch one last glimpse of Lorenzo's face, streaked with blood and tears. 'Tis a mask of abject misery.

From the shadows, Müller cries, "Behold! The death of hope! Behold the death of the Unwilling and the Penitent, joined in the House of God! Behold the unraveling of the Curse! Behold the thwarting of the will of God! The casting down of the prophecy of Adam! Behold the DEATH of GOD!"

The Congregants behind me begin to shout and to wail.

"Be silent!" Müller commands.

They all fall silent. They have nae choice. They have nae agency to choose for themselves.

"Lucy!" he calls. "Go, child, and stand outside by the crosses."

I cannae see her, but I can smell her blood. And it has begun to smell truly, deliciously evil.

"Lucy," Müller says, "if I give the word, and *only* if I give the word, shoot them. Just in case they have somehow arranged an unlikely escape, I want to take no chances. I want you by my side. Remember to aim for the head."

"Yes, Master," she replies, and I can hear the bolt pulled back on a weapon, probably the Uzi she had earlier.

"Nothing is left to chance," Müller says.

He extends a hand toward a pavilion standing in the distance. "Do you see, my Queen?" he shouts. "I, your most faithful servant, present you with the ultimate victory."

"I see, Günner," comes a distant voice, just on the edge of hearing. The voice is melodic. 'Tis beautiful, seductive. I've nae heard the like in all my long life. "You have done well, husband, and you will be rewarded. At first, I questioned the need for these theatrics, but you have brought so many of my Children back to me. And you have arranged for the death of those my mad old grandfather foretold. You have ensured my reign for eternity. Yes, you have done well. For this, you shall be my First Consort."

I look in the direction from whence the voice came. In the growing light, I see a huge pavilion about a half-mile in front of me. That's where the voice came from. There is a huge black helicopter sitting beside it, the kind with twin rotors. Its windows are solid black, of course, except in the cockpit. And from within the shadows underneath the huge tent, I can barely make out figures moving.

Lilith is here.

She has come to watch our deaths.

She will nae have long to wait.

The sky is light now.

The first rays of the Sun reach through the dawn like the fiery fingers of doom. In moments they will touch me. In moments I will die.

In moments Rolf will die.

Carl will die.

We shall all be consumed by the flames.

'Twas all for naught.

Sarah has nae come.

And, strangely, in that last moment before the light strikes me, the words come unbidden to my mind, though I cannae utter them aloud, "Father, into thy hands I commend my spirit."

Chapter 28

I'M ON FIRE!
I hear a great wrenching and tearing sound to my right and then a great gust of wind strikes me.

For a moment the flames are fanned higher, but then shadow, *blessed shadow*, covers me, and the fire is gone. *Gone!*

The Healing itch of the Seed begins to restore my flesh. My hands, wrists, and feet are still in agony, but the fire is *gone*!

A gentle breeze cools my scorched and Healing flesh.

I can see the sunlight beyond the edges of the shadow, but I look to the east and see that the Sun itself is blocked from my sight by a large rectangular shape. It takes me a moment to understand what has happened, but then I see *her*.

Sarah!

She's flying, holding one of the great *barn doors* aloft. She must have ripped it from its hinges. She's using it to block the Sun!

The breeze gathers strength as it blows from the east, and Sarah struggles to hold the door in place.

"Winnie's safe!" she calls.

Winnie's safe!

Well, then, I've had enough of *this*! I concentrate hard on the gag in my mouth. *I want it out! NOW!* And with that thought, the gag flies out of my mouth.

Tactile telekinesis, lassie! Lorenzo was right. He said that he could make his cloak flap as if moved by the wind even on a still night. I can manipulate anything that I'm touching, even if 'tis nae with my hands!

"Now for it, laddies!" I cry! *And I hope my daft plan works!*

Through pain and the itch, I force myself to concentrate.

Darkness! Shadow! Project the shadow!

It takes me a tick, but I manage to conjure shadow, blackness, around myself. Soon I'm encased in the deep shadows that our kind can wrap ourselves in to escape mortal eyes. If I've guessed aright, 'twill block the Sun.

My theory is that Müller wraps himself in shadow first and then covers that with a projection of light. The "Glory" he calls it. But 'tis the shadow that shields him from the light. And I'm nae trying to conform it to the shape of my body as Müller does. Nae, I want a bonnie great *cloud* of it!

I can still see out of the mentally projected darkness, but 'tis difficult, even for our kind, to see into it.

"Lucy," Müller cries, "*fire!*"

Automatic gunfire erupts. Several bullets strike me across my abdomen. *I cry out in pain, but 'twill Heal. 'Tis Healing already! 'Tis my head I've got to worry about. I cannae take any shots to the brain. That and I have to worry about maintaining the shadow!*

Lucy cannae see us inside the immaterial cloud, but that will buy us only a few seconds. We have to act quickly.

Now I concentrate on the razor wire about my neck. I imagine it expanding, breaking. The wire separates and falls away. In moments, my wrists and ankles are free of the thrice-hated, bloody bonds too.

I wrench my right hand and wrist free of the spikes. It tears the flesh even more to pull it past the heads of the spikes, but that will be Healed as well, soon enough! Now my left hand and wrist. Now my feet.

I'm free! It worked!

I ignore the itch of the Seed's Healing as I turn to my left.

I cannae see Carl!

"Carl!" I scream.

"Beside you," he says. And he *is* right there. I can see him but dimly in the blackness. He squeezes my hand quickly and says, "I'll check on Rolf. You help Lorenzo."

Then he is gone.

Carl is alive!

Thank ye, Father! Oh, thank ye!

Carl is alive!

I've nae heard from Rolf. *Carl will attend to him. Ye have your orders, lassie. Attend to them!*

I wheel to my right. The gunfire stops abruptly, and I hear a woman's cry rising to a scream.

Lorenzo is in the sunlight, and he is ablaze. The wind has picked up considerably and is fanning his flames. He has wrapped his arms around Lucy. That's why she's screaming, and that's why the gunfire has ceased.

I rush to his side, fighting the rising wind all the way, and engulf him in my cloud of shadow. The flames are blown out almost instantly, save for the smoldering of his clothes, and he falls to the ground. He writhes there as the Seed begins to repair his ravaged body.

The scent of evil blood rams like one of Müller's spikes into my nostrils. 'Tis Lucy's blood, and now 'tis truly evil. It *reeks* of delicious violence and murder. So irresistibly sweet!

Focus, lassie! Think of Sarah! Think of Lorenzo and Rolf!

I reach down and lift Lorenzo into my arms. I fly up into the air with him. *But where to go? Where can I take him that he'll be safe?*

I can think of only one place. In the house where we were held prisoner . . . that hated basement.

It costs me precious seconds to get him there as I'm tossed about by the gale, but by then he is mostly Healed. I get my first real look at the room where I was held prisoner with Carl and Rolf. I barely note the three tables with their vile razor wire and the fourth table where our weapons *used* to be.

Nae, my eyes come to rest on the television. The man who *was* guarding Winnie before now lies bound, gagged, and unconscious in the stall that used to be Winnie's cell. From the rise and fall of his chest, I can see that he's still among the living.

Ye did well, Sarah!

"Stay here," I say to Lorenzo as he clambers to his feet. "At least until it's safe to leave."

"Wait!" he begins to say, extending a hand toward me, his sleeve a charred ruin, but I'm gone before he can get another word out. I have to get back to Carl! And Rolf and Sarah too!

I race into the sunlight with my cloud of shadow wrapped around me like some magical cloak of protection in a fairy story. The wind is howling now, and clouds are rolling in from the east.

When I reach the barn seconds later, all is bedlam.

The remaining door has been blown open by the wind and is banging thunderously against the side of the barn. And inside, in the dark recesses, there is a mass of bodies . . . a squirming, giant anthill of white robes, many of them now stained with blood and soot. Some of the vampires are airborne with flapping white wings, but most are on the ground. They are all struggling, fighting desperately to reach whatever is at the center of the writhing pile of bodies. They are screaming or crying or yelling, but 'tis nae coherent like the chant of the ritual. Nae, 'tis like the howling of a pack of wild dogs as they try to bring down the prey.

I can also see Lucy as she lies on the ground, screaming with the horrific pain of the third-degree burns she sustained when Lorenzo disarmed her.

I need to find Carl!

I cannae see him anywhere! I cannae see Rolf or Sarah either!

Where are they?

I can see the barn door that Sarah was holding aloft to shield us from the Sun. It lies on the ground about fifty yards outside the barn. 'Tis nae flat, but 'tis canted at an odd angle.

"Carl!" I cry. "Where are ye?"

There is nae answer, but how could anyone hear anything in all this howling din?

Is Carl in the center of that squirming, clawing madness?

Aye, he must be.

Where is Sarah? In there as well?

Sarah has the weapons!

Some of the howling Congregants who are trying to tear their way into the center ... some of them are wearing robes that are charred and burnt through while others' robes are still smoldering. Few seem unscorched. They show nae concern for their own safety and have nae taken care to stay out of the sunlight. They were probably commanded by Müller to kill Carl, Rolf, and Sarah, and they must obey, even at the cost of their own lives.

Müller! Where's Müller?

For that matter, where's Lilith? Still safe in her pavilion?

I hear the sound of flapping wings behind me. I wheel about just in time to avoid a slashing cutlass.

Bartlett!

Within my cloud of shadow, 'tis difficult to see anything, but Bartlett was ablaze when he flew in. He cannae see me, but he must have known to strike at the heart of the cloud. And Müller must nae have commanded him to remain silent as he burned like a torch in the wind.

His robe still smolders, the embers kept alive by that gusting wind, and I use the glow to locate him. I can just make out the shape of him by it. I put all my strength in a blow to his midsection. My fist sinks deep into his innards. 'Twill nae kill him, but that should put him out of commission for several precious seconds. I wrap my fingers around his intestines and pull a handful of his slimy innards out. I take him by the shoulders, and I toss him into the screaming mad mound of struggling vampires, his guts trailing him.

He is instantly swallowed up in that maelstrom of ripping, tearing flesh.

That should keep him busy for a bit.

Müller! I must find Müller!

Quickly, I scan around, above, and below me. I dinnae see him at the moment. If Carl, Rolf, and Sarah are at the heart of the writhing mob, and I'm sure they have to be, then I must find Müller. If I kill *him*, the Congregants will be free of his control. 'Twould be the quickest way to save them ... *all* of them, *including* the Congregants.

But, regardless of where Müller is, I'll need a weapon. I look down to find Bartlett's sword, but I cannae see it. *Did he manage to keep ahold of it as I tossed him away?*

Sarah had *our* weapons. She snuck them out of the basement under her robe. That was the metal-on-metal clink I heard earlier.

I look about for Müller once more and still cannae see him, but my eye lights on the barn door lying askew on the ground. Something is nae right there. A nameless fear grips my guts. I fly down to take a look.

The door is leaning up off the ground ... as if something is under it, keeping it from being blown flat. I swoop down into the welcome shade underneath it. Instantly, I let the shadow go since I cannae see anything clearly inside it and I'm sheltered by the door itself.

As soon as the mentally projected cloud disappears, I see her and my fear is nameless nae longer.

Sarah.

She's lying there like a broken doll, one that's been dropped from a great height. Müller's spear transfixes her heart. I pull it free, but I know as I do so that I cannae save her. It has been far too long.

She's gone.

I want to take her in my arms and hold her to my breast. But I cannae take the time. *I have to help Carl!*

Sarah, my Teacher, the Ancient One who Converted me so long ago . . . is gone. She was nine hundred and ninety-nine years old. She'll nae see a thousand. I cannae say we were friends or that I *liked* her all that much, but I mourn her all the same. She was trying to repent. She had even found *love* after all these centuries and . . .

Carl! Rolf! I need to save them!

Poor Rolf! Does he know?

If I'm to save them, I need to take down Müller. I need my sword!

I hastily pat Sarah's hip with my hand. 'Tis there under her robe.

I lift the robe and find both my schiavona and her broadsword inserted into her belt. She must have gotten Carl's and Rolf's weapons to them before . . . before she was killed.

At least the lads are nae unarmed under that mound of enthralled vampires.

I take my black sword of truth firmly in my hand. I envelop myself in shadow once more and fly out from under the massive door and back into the gale.

I race toward the barn. This time the wind's at my back, and it speeds me along.

The screaming, roiling mass of bodies is still there, bloodier than before. *They're tearing each other apart in their mad, compulsory efforts to get to the center . . . to get to Carl and Rolf.*

I see nae sign of Bartlett. *Did he escape that madness?*

Then something is tossed clear of the carnage. 'Tis a human head. Even in its bloody, mutilated state, I recognize Bartlett's bearded face.

That's that, then. I cannae say I'm sorry for my part in his death, but I'm sorry he's dead.

Where is Müller?

I spin about looking for him. *There!* He's bent over Lucy, and she's nae writhing anymore. He has dragged her into the barn's sheltering darkness.

Müller has Fed off her. He has consumed her.

He'll be at full strength now. Even from this angle, I can see the flesh on his cheeks rapidly filling out.

And he has his broadsword.

He rises to his feet, and Lucy's lifeless body rolls over and onto her face

. . . and is still.

Another waste. Another failure. All this death and carnage. And there is the man responsible.

Müller has nae looked my way. I could attack him from behind before he spies me, but, even with a monster as loathsome and foul as he is, even with Carl's and Rolf's lives on the line, I cannae bring myself to stab him in the back.

"Müller!" I cry in challenge.

He whirls about, sword raised, poised to counter mine. He stands in the shadows, so I land before him in the safety of the darkness and let my cloud go.

I need all my skill to best a warrior with more than a millennium of experience, and I dinnae need the distraction of trying to maintain my own portable shadow.

Our swords meet in a blinding flash of steel on steel. He's fast. And very good. I've nae met his equal before.

We keep to the ground and the shadows, and fight like demons. Thrust, parry, thrust, slash, counter. Neither of us tries anything elaborate. There is nae time, and this is a contest to the death between two evenly matched adversaries. In spite of my burning need to save Carl, I need to keep my focus. I let go of all emotion and enter the fluid dance of combat, letting my body move as it's been trained to do, keeping my eyes on my opponent's eyes. The eyes will telegraph his next move. I enter a state of consciousness devoid of passion.

If I'm to survive and conquer, I cannae fight as if every moment could bring death to Carl and Rolf. I have to shut off the part of me that wants so desperately to save them. That way lies my own death and then I cannae succor them.

I have to detach.

I must be "in the zone," as they say.

As my body fights, my mind analyzes. It's nae like some staged combat ye might see on the television or in the movies. As vampires, we both move so fast that only a high-speed camera could make aught of our movements. In a matter of a few seconds we've exchanged scores of blows. Neither of us gives the other an opening. I give a little ground, and then he gives a little ground, but we dinnae move more than a few yards from where the duel began.

He has an advantage over me with his height, and he frequently attacks from above. I, on the other hand, have learned to exploit the height of my opponents. He'll be just as disabled (momentarily) if I manage to strike him on the legs, hips, or groin. When I parry his blow from above, I can attack from below.

It's a dance, aye, but a deadly one in which one dancer slays the other.

I'm nae sure I can best him. He has Fed recently, and I've been through a long physical ordeal. Eventually he'll wear me down. But I cannae let this go on much longer in any event. I dinnae know how long Carl and Rolf can hold out against that mob. How many of the Congregants will they be forced to kill while I tarry here with Müller? How many of the Congregants will tear each other apart trying to get to their targets?

Can Müller afford to wait *me* out, though? He has much at stake here. Lilith watches from a distance. At least, I *think* she's in the pavilion. I did nae notice if the helicopter was still there or nae. Can the tent possibly remain standing in this gale? I dinnae think Müller can let this go on much longer either.

So, amidst the flurry and fluid chaos of swordplay, I try a different tack. It is a risk, for it will mean engaging him on two levels and dividing my attention between the fight and trying to distract him. I could very well end up distracting myself at a critical moment.

"I'm sure she'll be forgiving," I say casually while parrying a wicked slash. "Your grand ritual turned into quite a debacle, but I'm sure in her six thousand years she has learned to be patient and to overlook failure."

"I haven't failed," Müller says. From his tone, he could be discussing the weather, rather than discussing my death. "All I have to do is to kill *one* of you. Adam's prophecy fails, and God still ceases to be God. I would prefer it were your husband, but you'll do."

He makes a lunging thrust that I dinnae parry as well as I should. It catches my charred sleeve near the shoulder. *That was too close, lassie.* Watch yourself. Ye're getting fatigued. This cannae go on much longer. I need an edge. I need to create a distraction.

I open my mouth to speak again . . .

BOOM!

A peal of thunder distracts *both* of us. We each jump back a step.

Out of the corner of my eye I can see that the sky has clouded over completely. I see distant flashes of lightning and some nae so distant.

At least we dinnae have to worry about the Sun for the time being.

Müller lunges at me again, thinking to catch me off guard. I parry his blade upward and then manage to continue the motion around and down to catch him across the chest.

First blood.

He snarls and jumps back.

I cannae press my advantage, though. He's too fast.

Then a voice, melodious, richly *female* intrudes into my awareness. I dinnae catch the words, but the voice can only belong to *her*.

Müller hears it too.

Our battle continues unabated, but Müller makes more mistakes. I'm able to draw more blood, and yet I'm nae able to deliver a crippling or killing blow.

BOOM!

Another crack of thunder startles us.

Lilith speaks again, but her voice is drowned out by the thunder.

And then they come. More than a score of them. With Lorenzo Corelli at the lead.

The cavalry is here.

Or, more accurately, the Stake vampires.

Corelli carries a simple claw hammer as his only weapon, but many of the rest are well armed. Most, but nae all. Some are armed only with baseball bats, golf clubs, one with a shovel. Some have wings. Others are wingless.

And they dive toward the mob of Congregants.

Müller sees it too. He presses his attack.

I take a sword thrust to the thigh. It severs my femoral artery. 'Twould be lethal to a mortal, but nae to me.

However it *does* slow me down . . . for a few critical seconds.

Ignore the pain. Ignore the itch.

Dinnae think about Carl. If ye die, ye cannae save him.

I barely parry Müller's beheading stroke, though his blade nearly severs my ear.

"Günner," the voice calls again. 'Tis beautiful and hypnotic, but it carries an obvious note of disappointment. "Günner, my Son. You have failed me. You know the penalty for failure, but death is too good for such a . . . disaster."

The detached part of my brain registers what is going on to my left as my body continues to fight. The Stake vampires are laying waste to the Congregants. They have thinned them down, and they have done so without killing any of them.

Ghalyela is a marvel to behold. With her two short spears, she keeps delivering crippling blows, a severed hamstring here, a severed wrist tendon there. She delivers blows that take the weakened Congregants out of the fight for half a minute at a time. Corelli lays about him with the hammer, breaking bones, but avoiding skulls. They're outnumbered, but I'm sure that Carl and Rolf are still fighting from within.

It looks like more than a third of the robed figures are out of commission (temporarily) at any given time. Some are dead, having been torn apart by their fellows as they try to get to the center . . . to Carl and Rolf.

Ach! Müller's sword! In my gut!

I strike at his head, but catch him with only the flat of my blackened blade.

Still, it makes him pull back, withdrawing his blade from my abdomen.

I place my left hand over the wound to keep my guts from spilling out before the Seed can finish its work.

"No, Günner," the voice says, louder this time. *Closer?* "For this failure, you're stripped of your rank and position. You are a Master no longer. You are no longer my Enforcer. You are nothing."

Müller howls! 'Tis the essence of anguish and loss, the howl of the damned soul who has forfeited his very reason for living.

"You are banished from my sight forever," says the honeyed voice, so like a caress. "If you ever see my face again, you will claw your own eyes out and then take your own life. Now leave me."

Müller turns and takes to the air, wailing as he flies.

I dinnae care where he goes. Nae even a wee bit. For behind me, the madness has stopped. I turn to see that the Congregants have all collapsed on the ground. Nary a one of them is fighting any longer. The Stake vampires stand watching, ready to resume the fight, but are staying their hands. Müller's command is nae longer in effect so the Congregation has nae reason to go on fighting.

I dinnae care a fig.

I have eyes for only one person.

Carl.

He's drenched in blood. He stands panting, his sword hanging limply in his hand, but he's *alive*! I barely notice Rolf leaning on his blade beside him.

"Carl!" I leap into the air to fly to him, but he points wearily behind me.

"After him," he croaks. "Don't let him get away. He's out for revenge now. He'll slaughter mortals. Go. Defend the city."

All I want to do right now is fly to Carl and be held in his arms and smother him with kisses till neither of us can breathe, but, instead, I wheel around and fly out of the barn after Müller.

Carl is alive!

Thank ye, Father! Carl is alive!

Now to stop Müller.

Chapter 29

THE FIRST THING I notice as I race after Müller is that the pavilion sheltering Lilith from the Sun is *closer*. 'Tis *much* closer. I can see more than a score of people moving about under there. *Her guards or retainers must have carried it closer so she could hear and be heard above the wind. I can picture them moving it like a huge palanquin shading a Middle Eastern sultan. They must've had a devil of a time getting' it here in this gale . . . Nae. Probably nae so much trouble as all that: those holding onto the poles could move it easily about as they willed. Our kind can manipulate anything we touch . . . even if we're unaware of how we're doing it.*

The second thing I notice is that the helicopter, although it has nae moved from its original location, is sitting with its twin rotors revolving. *She's ready to flee if she feels threatened. She would nae risk her own safety to settle Müller's mess.*

Carl, Rolf, and the Stake will have to deal with that. Carl has the right of it: Müller's out for blood. He's out for revenge.

Once I'm clear of the barn and have gained sufficient altitude, I quickly scan the dark, brooding skies for Müller. I cannae see hide nor hair of him.

Which way would he have gone?

If he's out for revenge, he'll be after Winnie. Sarah would have taken her to the nearest hospital emergency room. I was adamant on that point. Winnie must be safe. The nearest ER would be the U of U Hospital. *Would Müller know that?* Surely he would at least know she'd need medical attention, and large hospitals are nae so hard to spot from the air with their medical helipads. He may nae know the exact hospital or its location, but he'd know to head toward Salt Lake City.

I fly like a bullet toward University Hill. I quickly accelerate to the speed at which I can barely breathe. I can fly nae faster and remain conscious. I look frantically ahead, but still cannae detect any sign of Müller. And to complicate matters, the lightning flashes, the thunder booms, and the clouds burst. Pouring rain drenches my torn, burnt clothing. It limits my visibility. I cannae see more than a hundred yards ahead of me, even with my Seed-enhanced vision.

The lightning flashes again, and a great crash of thunder nigh deafens me.

This is stupid. I cannae see much in this rain, and I really dinnae know where Müller has gone. I could be flying in the wrong direction for all I know.

I come to a dead stop in the air. I hover there trying to clear my head.

The wind and the rain buffet me, but I ignore them and let myself drift.

Father in Heaven, show me where to go. Help me stop this fiend.

That's rich: a monster praying for strength to stop another monster.

Ach! I need to find Müller!

I hear a woman's bloodcurdling scream. It comes from behind and below me.

I spin around and, like a falcon, I power-dive in the direction of the sound. I cannae see the source, but I fly on through the driving rain.

She screams again, but this time the scream's cut short.

A school bus?

There, on the road below me, I see a bus. 'Tis painted blue and white. I'm certain the scream came from there. The rear door, on the opposite end of the long vehicle, stands open to the howling wind and the driving rain.

In two wee seconds I'm through the door and inside.

Müller is there, and he's Feeding.

He's Feeding on Winnie Morrison.

Though I cannae see the face of the enormous woman lolling in the right-front passenger seat, I can tell 'Tis Winnie from her girth, her bloodied and filthy hospital gown, and her smell.

Müller is leaning over her, his right side to me, drinking greedily at her neck.

With his left arm, Müller holds Sammy Gallagher aloft by the neck. Müller's hand is clamped around Sammy's neck, and Sammy is struggling and beating and kicking at Müller. Müller seems oblivious to Sammy's efforts. Sammy is turning a disturbing shade of blue. Müller's sword lies in the aisle. He does nae need it against these two mortals.

I thrust my sword between Müller's ribs and into his heart.

Müller drops Sammy to the floor of the bus. Sammy lies there gasping and choking.

I yank Müller roughly off Winnie. His weight throws me off balance, and I strike my elbow on a bus seat. The schiavona is wrenched from my grasp.

Müller pulls the sword from his side, but is unable to hold onto it, letting it fall to the floor.

I release him as I dive for my weapon.

Müller dives for his. He's sluggish with his heart just beginning to pump blood again, but he's between me and the mortals.

He spins in the aisle to face me, sword at the ready, though 'tis an awkward stance we both assume in these tight quarters.

Right now I wish I had a cutlass or even a dirk for fighting where I can barely move.

Sammy chokes and sputters behind Müller. His breathing is nae right.

"You have a choice," Müller says, his eyes on mine. His face is gaunt nae longer. 'Tis a strong face, one free of remorse or pity . . . the face of a murderer . . . or, rather, an executioner. "You can kill me or you can save your friends," he says, his voice calm and cold. "Clumsy me. I seem to have crushed his windpipe. I guess I don't remember how strong I am when I've had a good meal."

I return his gaze. He can read my decision in my eyes.

Decision? 'Tis nae decision for there was ne'er any choice.

"Excellent," he says and flies past me, parrying my sword thrust. He continues out the back door and is gone.

I rush past Winnie. Her heart's beating steady enough. Müller did nae have time to take much from her.

Sammy thrashes weakly on the floor near the driver's seat at the front of the bus. He claws at his throat.

I bat his hands away and quickly probe his neck with my fingers.

Müller told the truth.

He'll be dead soon. The only way to save him is with the Seed.

Quickly, I take him in my arms like a wee bairn, but instead of feeding this bairn, I'm going to Feed from him. My fangs extend, and I bite into his neck near the damaged windpipe.

Blood! Sweet blood floods into my eager mouth.

I take maybe a pint. 'Tis hard to keep my mind focused on what I'm about because I'm so *hungry! The projected hunger of the Congregation is so strong!* Sammy's breathing eases as the Seed, pumped throughout his body by his strong heart, repairs his trachea.

Blood! So sweet! I want it ALL!

Trembling, I pull my lips away from his neck and lick the wound to seal it. With shaking hands, I lay him down and turn my attention to Winnie.

Her round face has a look of pure ecstasy from the effects of the Seed. Her heart is steady. She'll live. In fact, she'll probably heal all the faster because of the Feeding.

"Thank you." Sammy's voice is raspy, but his breathing is near normal.

I turn my face in his direction. He's starting to sit up.

"Thank you for saving us," he says, his eyes wide. "Wow! I feel good. I feel . . . groovy."

"That's the Seed, laddie," I say with a sad smile. "It'll wear off soon."

"Does it *have* to?" he says, smiling. "I feel *great!*"

"Aye, laddie," I say. "Can ye drive?"

"Yeah," he says, shaking his head to clear it. "Just give me a minute." He smiles. "You know, I never did drugs, but that . . . *Seed* stuff is really something!"

"Sammy," I say, "focus. Focus on me."

"Yeah," he nods and looks into my eyes. "Have I ever told you how beautiful you are? *Stunning! Breathtaking!*"

"Laddie!"

"Sorry," he says, shaking his head again. "Don't tell my wife I said that."

"Get Winnie to LDS Hospital and ye have a deal."

"Groovy," he says and begins to stand up and climb into the driver's seat.

"Laddie, did Müller say anything that would tell ye whither he's headed?"

Now firmly in the driver's seat and reaching for the ignition key, Sammy says, "He kept asking me who you *love*. He said he wants to destroy everything you love because you cut him off from his beloved queen . . . or something like that. I couldn't help answering him. I'm sorry. He looked me in the eye and I . . . couldn't stop myself."

"That's all right, Sammy. It's called Persuasion. Most mortals cannae resist it."

He nods and starts the bus. The engine chugs to life.

"What did you tell him?" I ask.

"I told him that you love your husband, of course. That made him really mad. That made me sad. I *wanted* so desperately to please him. I'm so sorry . . ."

"Laddie! Focus!"

"OK. Then I told him . . . *me*." He turns his head and looks at me sheepishly. "I said, 'Moira loves *everybody*!' He didn't like that either. Then he asked who the most important person in the world was to you, besides your husband and me. I had to think about it for a second. I couldn't come up with anyone. He got really pissed then and he demanded, 'there must be someone she'd follow to the death or give her life for!' And then the words of that Primary song came to me. You know—" Sammy begins to sing "—'Follow the prophet. Follow the prophet.'" He looks embarrassed. "So I said, 'Maybe the prophet, the President of the Church.' That seemed to make him happy. 'That'll do,' he said.

"That's when he grabbed me by the neck with one hand and held me up like a rag doll. He bit Winnie on the neck, and then you came . . . And you know the rest."

"Get Winnie to the hospital," I say. "I have work to do."

"Sorry, Moira," he says.

"'Tis nae your fault, laddie," I say and fly out into the tempest again.

I shut the rear door behind myself and turn and head west.

As I fly, I cannae help but wonder at the arrogance of the man.

Müller thought he could murder God. When he failed and lost his position and his Queen, he sought revenge. But the President of the Church? What kind of corny movie-serial villain does he think he is? He cannae kill God, so he goes after the prophet?

Nae, he's just going after someone he thinks matters most to me. He's just out to hurt me.

Does the prophet need *my protection?*

Probably nae.

Most assuredly nae.
Does Müller even know where to find him?

I *dinnae know where to find that dear old man. The Church Office Building? The Administration Building? I dinnae know where his office is . . . or even if he'd be there at this hour.*

I *really doubt Müller has any idea, except, perhaps, to go to Temple Square. And he could do great damage there.*

By the time I reach Temple Square, Müller is hovering twenty feet or so above the three eastern spires of the great granite temple, his wings beating fiercely. He's holding a young sister missionary aloft. He's shouting at the people on the ground. Temple Square would be about to open to the public, but the gates are still shut.

"Where is he?" Müller demands. "Where is your prophet? Tell me where he is, or I'll impale this little thing on the spires of your temple!"

The poor young woman is terrified, but she does nae dare fight back. If he were to drop her, she'd fall to her death. The flag sticker on her name badge identifies her home country as Japan.

Müller has nae noticed me, so intent is he on the crowd of sisters and older missionary couples on the ground. They're screaming and pointing at Müller.

I pull up into a steep loop to avoid Müller's detection, crest the top, and dive for the lassie. I snatch her from Müller's grasp before he sees me coming.

Hastily, I deposit her on the grassy mall between the Tabernacle and the North Visitor's Center. Then, without a word, I turn hard round to face the enraged Müller.

We fly straight at each other. Our swords meet in a deafening crash like a metallic thunderclap as we very nearly collide over the temple's western spires.

I enter the "zone" again. I push all my emotions, my passions, my fears, my doubts, my grief for Sarah, my anxiety for Carl and the others facing Lilith and her guards . . . I hide all of that away in the dark recesses of my mind and I . . . *detach.*

And we fight.

Aerial sword fighting is nae like combat on the ground where ye can gain leverage with your feet. In the air, ye fly at your opponent at high speed and exchange nae more than one or two blows before ye have passed him and are turning and maneuvering for the next pass.

And turn and maneuver we do. I doubt we leave the Temple Square airspace, but we're all over it. After our exchange above the temple, the next blows occur when we're above the Assembly Hall, then the Tabernacle, then the temple annex, then the temple again.

With every clash, the crowd of missionaries and those gathered outside the gates scream in unison. What a sight we must be! Two flying beings, fighting with swords in the air above Temple Square while the storm rages with lightning and thunder: one of us with wings, wearing a long white, though blood-stained, robe ... one of us wingless, wearing tattered and scorched black, like some punk comic-book superheroine. If ye were a non-Mormon, ye'd think that *he'd* be the angel. To the Mormons ... well I dinnae know *what* they'd make of it, since angels have nae wings.

Does that make me *the angel?*

As we were before, we're evenly matched once again. We've both Fed, and so we're at peak strength. I'm more skilled and faster with the blade, but Müller has more physical power.

After nearly fifty passes, neither of us has drawn blood.

This cannae go on forever. There are more and more innocents on the ground watching us. They are in danger.

And who could resist *such a sight as this?*

On my next pass, this time over the freestanding tower of the Nauvoo Bell, I feint with a slash from the left and try to catch him across the neck as he passes. He is fooled by the feint and misses his stroke, but still manages to parry my slash.

And he gets a fistful of my hair.

Suddenly my head's hauled back sharply, and I lose control of my flying.

For a moment, I cannae tell which way is up.

I barely manage to counter a slash at my face.

I yank my head away, and a large chunk of my hair comes off in Müller's hand. I speed away to get some distance from my enemy.

I quickly orient myself relative to the horizon and pull up sharply through the rain into the beginning of a loop over the reflecting pool to the east of Temple Square.

Its surface is like a raging sea in miniature, broken and tossed by the rain and the gale.

Müller follows me, but he's caught off guard by the tightness of my loop. He tries to match mine, but undershoots. He flies below me, and suddenly I'm behind him.

Check your six, Adolf!

I pour on the speed and catch him with a wicked thrust that skewers his right thigh. I twist my blade, and arterial blood sprays through the gash in his robe.

Müller yells in pain and crashes to the ground just inside the temple fence. He lands in the space in front of the temple's eastern wall. Before I can reach him, he's on his feet and limping quickly up the steps to the leftmost of the great eastern doors of the temple.

The lower half of his robe is drenched in blood.

Oddly, he still has the handful of my wet, red hair in his left hand. He's holding it like some talisman or rosary.

His sword is still in his right hand, but nearly a foot of the blade is missing. The broken-off end of the blade lies in a shallow puddle before the temple. It must have broken when he crashed to the ground.

He puts the hand with my wet, bedraggled hair on the knob of the eastern door. Müller turns that knob and, though I hear the old lock of the door break as he forces it to turn, the door will nae open when he pulls at it.

I cannae help but watch in fascination as he tries to force the door open, first with his fingers and then using his broken sword as a lever.

He roars in frustration and then turns to face me, holding his foreshortened weapon at the ready.

I alight on the ground and walk slowly toward him through the driving rain, my weapon at my side.

"Ye *do* know, Müller," I say, my voice calm in contrast to the storm raging around us, "that I've been *inside* that temple and other temples like it." My voice is soft, calm. I doubt a mortal could hear it above the storm. But *Müller* does. "I'm nae barred from entering any House of God, now. My husband and I really *were* sealed together in the Ogden Temple . . . 'joined in the House of God,' as the Prophecy says. For eight decades, I used to come here nearly every night and stand . . . just over there . . ." I point my sword at the corner off to the left where I spent countless hours. "I stood there night after night and tried to just *touch* the walls with my hand. But I could nae do it, nae matter how hard I tried."

Müller glares at me, hatred and . . . *Is that* fear *I see?* . . . *fear* in his eyes. He looks like a caged beast. And like a caged beast, he does nae comprehend the truth of . . . of anything.

"Ye see, Müller, false Apostle of a fabricated faith, I *knew* it was a holy place, and so I could nae touch it. 'Twas Carl who showed me that it was *me*, myself . . . I was nae *allowing* myself to touch it. 'Twas a mental block because I felt *unworthy*. In spite of all my repentance, I did nae truly *believe* I could be redeemed."

I note, out of the corner of my eye, that a small crowd has gathered on the other side of the temple fence. They're watching our every move.

"But here ye are, Müller," I continue as I halt at the base of the steps and look up at him. "Ye are standing on the very steps. Ye've put your hand on the door, something I could nae do for the better part of a century. And do ye know *why*?"

He says nothing. He just continues to glare at me.

"'Tis because ye have nae *understanding* of what is holy anymore. Ye abandoned God so long ago. Ye have murdered countless mortals. Ye have seduced and corrupted young girls and done all manner of unspeakable evil for centuries. God's Spirit has 'ceased striving' with ye. Ye have nae concept of the *truth*. So, when ye touch something truly *holy*, ye cannae discern it. Ye are *dead* inside already. And, try as ye might, ye cannae *force* your way in. There is only *one* Way into the Kingdom of God. And that Way is Je . . .''

Müller snarls like a wild beast and lunges at me from atop the steps.

I bring up my sword to defend myself.

Nae! 'Tis a feint! He's flying above me.

Müller is past me and speeding away.

Stupid! Ye are a ninny, lassie! Ye should ha' taken him while ye had him cornered!

Nae. I would nae slay him on the very steps of the temple of God!

I take to the air and follow him.

Müller heads straight over the temple annex and past the wall of the Square. He flies like a great white-winged bird toward the huge Conference Center across the street. I pursue him, but I cannae reach him before he crashes through one of the great glass doors.

I fly through the ruined door and into the huge foyer of the Conference Center with its interior fountains, escalators and art galleries. He throws open one of the great wooden doors leading into the auditorium itself. He enters, and I follow him in.

Nary a one of the twenty-one thousand seats on the floor and the two levels of freestanding balconies are occupied. There is nae a single column in all this massive hall. 'Tis entirely open with all those red seats facing the choir loft and the massive pipes of the organ which tower at the back of the space. At the center of the high ceiling are catwalks, theatrical lights, speakers, and dangling microphone wires. 'Tis a massive open space, the largest performance hall of its kind.

I cannae see Müller.

Where is he?

"Do you know how long I've had this sword?" His voice echoes around the room. I cannae locate the source. He could be anywhere.

"More than a thousand years! I took it from some nameless Viking when I drank his blood and slaughtered his entire village. He probably wasn't my father, but he'd do. The sword was *mine*! I've wielded it in *thousands* of battles!"

I hover in the center of that great space, midway between the catwalks, lights, and speakers above and the rows of seats beneath. I wheel about, looking above, below, all around me.

My arm brushes against something in the middle of the air. 'Tis one of the two long microphone wires that hang from the center of the ceiling and extend more than halfway toward the floor.

"Now it's broken!" he roars. His voice echoes from everywhere. You've stolen *everything* from me! I'm *BANISHED*! I can never look on the face of my Queen again! I can never worship at her feet again, never bask in her glory! She'll never take me to her bed again! She was my *WORLD!*"

With those words still echoing, I hear another sound . . . the rush of air . . . *above me!*

He's falling straight at me from a catwalk! The suddenness and ferocity of his attack almost costs me my head. If 'twere nae for the shortness of his blade, he'd have sliced clean through my neck. His blade still manages to cut deeply into the flesh on one side, barely missing my jugular.

Where is he now?

Through a haze of blood, pain, and itch, I look about for him.

His blade bites deeply into my side!

I wheel about and barely block a chop to my sword arm.

I try to follow him with my eyes, but my dripping hair gets in the way.

The sudden loss of blood to the brain does nae help, either.

I catch sight of him as he turns toward me. He's over the choir loft, in front of the great organ pipes. He climbs up toward the center to attack from above. He maneuvers to avoid the forest of microphone wires hanging there.

The wires!

There's a nigh-invisible wire hanging nearby, one of two dangling over the congregation seats. I place myself right in front of the wire and hover there. I hold my sword in front of me. My left hand is occupied, holding the Healing wound in my side.

'Twould nae do at all to have my guts falling out before I can Heal. How attractive would that be?

I've lost so much blood . . . hard to think. I'll be right as rain in moments . . . but I dinnae have moments *to waste.*

Focus, lassie, or ye're dead.

I hold my position, using my obvious wounded state to lure him in. Müller flies straight at me, his broken sword raised to strike. I feint as if to parry his blow, but dodge to the right at the last moment. I grab hold of his robe and swing him around into the hanging wire. It whips about him, ensnaring him. For an instant he looks confused as if he does nae ken what's holding him. His wings wink out as he thrashes.

I thrust my sword through his heart.

He wriggles for a second longer, like a coney in a snare or a condemned man hanging from a gallows. Then he goes slack, and the light in his eyes fades. Though Müller's lifeless hand has gone limp, the clump of my wet hair still remains wrapped around his fingers.

The broken sword falls from his other hand. I make nae attempt to catch it; I need to make certain he's dead by holding my ebony blade in his heart. His ruined weapon seems to fall slowly until it clatters uselessly on the floor, somehow missing the seats below us. *The sound is like the tinkling of brass.* That weapon was used to slay hundreds of thousands. Now it's fit for nae but the junk heap.

I cautiously pull my sword from his chest, watching him all the while for any sign of life. While I wait, hovering there, holding my sword at the ready, I cannae help but pat the back of my head. Now that my side is Healed, I check my hair. *How like a woman!* The hair has grown back, of course . . . back to the length it was day I was Converted. It *always* grows back. The Seed prevents it from ever growing longer . . . or remaining shorter. *I never need a haircut, but I cannae change the length. Like the rest of my body, my hair is frozen, unchanging.*

When I'm satisfied that Müller is truly gone to his eternal damnation, I untangle his body from the microphone wire. I'm sure he could easily have broken or cut the wire and escaped, but he did nae understand what had happened to him.

If he had known the truth, it would have made him free.

Instead, my sword, with the Gaelic word for truth on the blade, has made the *world* free from one of its true horrors.

But Lilith remains.

Carl!

I must get back to Carl! And to Rolf and the others!

Poor Rolf!

With Müller's carcass under one arm, my sword in the other hand, I settle to the floor. I lay him down in the aisle momentarily so that I can retrieve the remnant of his sword. I thrust my own sword and Müller's broken one into my belt, gather up Müller's remains, and fly out of the auditorium.

I don't dare go back for the shard of Müller's sword that broke off in front of the temple. I'll have to leave it as one more mystery . . . tangible evidence of the battle of two "angels" over Temple Square.

The broken glass door has attracted attention. A small group of elderly missionaries has gathered around it. *I'm lucky . . . nae blessed is more like it . . . that none of them entered the auditorium while Müller and I were in there.* I fly toward a different, less crowded door. I dinnae think anyone notices me. As I exit the Conference Center with my burden, I decide to send the Church an anonymous donation to pay for damages.

Now that I'm back out in the storm, I start to climb into the air. I hear a soft, high-pitched, and heavily accented voice cry, "*Arigato gozaimasu!* Thank you, God's angel!"

I look back toward the voice, and I see the little Japanese sister missionary. She's standing in the driving rain, her missionary companion dutifully at her side, still on the grassy area where I left her. She's waving frantically at me. I shift Müller's bulk to my left arm so I can wave back.

Standing next to her is an elderly couple, a man and a woman. They're Temple Square missionaries as well.

And I recognize them.

'Tis Fred and Edna Spencer. They're the couple Carl and I rescued from thugs that night last year in front of the Ogden Temple. *I guess they accepted a mission call to Temple Square.* Dear old Fred pulls something from inside his raincoat and holds it up, somewhat surreptitiously, so that I can see it.

He's holding the nigh foot-long shard of Müller's blade.

He wiggles it a wee bit to make sure I've seen it and then stuffs it inside his raincoat. He pats his coat, then nods and winks at me. *What a dear, sweet man!*

I nod and smile. Then I fly into the raging tempest with my gruesome cargo.

I must get back to Carl!

Please, Father in Heaven, spare him!

Chapter 30

CARNAGE.

I don't know what I expected to find when I returned. I had conjured up fantasies in my head of Carl flying up to meet me in the air, me dumping Müller's body unceremoniously, and as I rush into the arms of my husband and smother him with kisses, him carrying me off to our home, which we have nae seen in days . . .

I knew that there would be some deaths . . . 'twas the site of a battle after all . . . but this . . . this is beyond anything I imagined.

'Tis a sea of red. Blood—vampire blood, but blood all the same—is everywhere. There is scarcely an inch of the barn walls that is nae splattered with the stuff. And the floor . . . the floor is awash in it. There are scores of bodies, most of them headless, bodiless heads, and thousands of *fragments* of bodies strewn about.

And I feel nae sign of the abnormal hunger I've been wrestling with for a while now. 'Tis . . . gone. I suppose that means that the Congregants are all dead or are nae starving themselves any longer.

The vast majority of the corpses are wearing the tatters of the once-white, now gore-stained robes of the Congregants. Most, aye, but nae all. Clearly some of *our* people fell here as well.

Lilith's pavilion lies abandoned on the ground about a hundred yards or so to the east. 'Tis flattened except for when a gust of wind lifts up a corner of it from time to time. The helicopter is naewhere to be seen.

So Lilith is nae longer here.

Is Carl *here . . . among the dead? Are his remains scattered like so much rubbish?*

I can see only one living soul.

And 'tis nae Carl.

'Tis Rolf.

He's kneeling in a pool of blood and offal, rocking back and forth, cradling a body in his arms. His black clothing is torn and caked with gore. I can barely hear his plaintive wail above the wind and the sound of the rain on the roof. In fact, his cry is wordless, barely distinguishable from that of the storm outside.

I realize that I'm still carrying Müller's carcass. I drop it to the ground. It lands on the blood-soaked floor with a wet, squishing thud. *May I never lay eyes on him again.* I pull his broken sword from my belt and drop it beside him.

I call Rolf's name as I fly to his side. He looks in my direction, but that is the only acknowledgement I receive. He goes back to his mourning.

'Tis Sarah he holds in his arms. *Of course, 'tis Sarah.*

I touch his shoulder gently, but remain inches off the ground for I'm loathe to set foot in the blood. He does nae look at me.

"Rolf, laddie." Tears pour down my cheeks to mix with the water that streams from my hair. "I'm so sorry."

He looks up at me, but he says nary a word. He just continues his keening wail. *He's nae even calling her name.* His tears have made rivulets in the blood that coats his face.

"Rolf," I say again. His eyes look into mine. The pain written there is as plain as an epitaph. He is grief incarnate. The loss of Sarah, her death is his entire existence.

I let myself settle in the red pool and kneel at his side. I wrap my arms around him and hold him. He continues to rock and wail, but he places his head on my shoulder.

And together we weep.

I need to find Carl, but Rolf's need is here, *now.*

"Rolf," I say after a minute when I can bear it nae longer. My voice catches in my throat, "Where's Carl?"

Rolf says nothing. He continues his inarticulate keening.

"Laddie," I say, barely able to force the words past my lips, "is he . . . here?" I cannae bring myself to give voice to my fears.

He continues his wailing.

"Rolf," I say, "*please* tell me . . ."

I hear footsteps behind me, squelching in the red mud of the barn floor.

Instantly, I'm on my feet, my sword at the ready.

A man, mortal by the scent of him, jumps back from the edge of the barn entrance, the side with the missing door . . . the door that Sarah ripped from its hinges so she could shield us from the Sun. The man raises his hands in a warding gesture. I cannae see his face clearly at first. But then he speaks, and I recognize the voice . . . and, aye, now the *face* of Tony Lupescu.

"I don't think he can understand you, much less answer you," he says.

I lower my sword, and Tony lowers his hands.

"Where's Carl?" I demand.

"Gone," he says.

The word pierces my heart like the iron point of Müller's spear. Misery and pain and loss such as I've ne'er known well up inside me like a flood. I drop my sword and fall to my knees in the blood beside Rolf.

"*CARL!*" His name rips from my throat, and I throw back my head and begin to wail. Rolf's lament and mine join in a duet of unspeakable grief.

I understand now. My grief is beyond words.

Tony's voice tries to penetrate my anguish, but I will nae let him in. What words can comfort me now? I've lost my heart, my soul.

"MOIRA!" Tony takes my head in his hands and yells into my face. "Not dead!"

"What?" I can barely speak.

"He's not dead," Tony says again. "At least he wasn't when he flew out of here."

"Carl's nae dead?" *His words make nae sense.* I turn my face to him. "But ye said . . ."

"I said he was gone," he says. "I'm sorry. I should have chosen my words better, but . . ."

I jump to my feet and, grabbing him with a hand under each of his arms, lift him up like a wee bairn. "Carl's *alive*?"

"Whoa!" Tony cries in alarm. "Y-yeah! At least he was ten minutes ago. He and the others took off after Lilith. I hope they're all right." He looks about, naked fear in his casting eyes. "C-c-can you put me down now?"

I pull Tony to my chest and hug him and shake him in my joy.

Carl's ALIVE!

Then the full import of his words seeps into my brain, and as it does, horror replaces my joy and steals my breath away. I hold Tony at arm's length and look him in the eye. "He went after Lilith?"

"Yes, he and the survivors flew after her when she took off in her helicopter."

"And they have nae returned?" *Obviously, they have nae returned!*

"No, and I'm worried *sick* about them." A look of pain twists his face. "Moira! My ribs!"

I loosen my grip and let him go.

He grimaces and places his hands in his armpits.

"Laddie," I say, "I'm sorry."

"I don't think anything's broken," he says through clenched teeth.

"Let me take a look," I say. "I'm a doctor."

"OK," he says, but he eyes me warily.

I help him pull off his rain-soaked polo shirt.

"Raise your arms," I say.

He lifts them over his head with a grunt of pain.

If they have nae returned . . . they could all be . . .

I look at the flesh where my hands had been digging into his sides. I probe it with my fingers.

"Ye're going to have some painful deep-tissue bruising, but I dinnae think I broke anything."

He cocks his head and smiles at me.

"I'll live, then," he says. "I'm just not going to *enjoy* life for a while. Is that it?"

I continue gently probing his injuries when I hear, "Honestly, Tony! I leave you alone with my wife for *ten* minutes and already you've got your shirt off."

My head snaps toward the sound of that blessed voice.

Carl!

My dear laddie and a handful of the Stake vampires come floating in from the storm.

Instantly, I'm in his arms, and the two us are flying out into the rain. I smother him with kisses, and he holds me like nothing in this world or the next could possibly separate us again.

Nae words.

I cannae give utterance to my joy. As unspeakable as was my grief when I thought I'd lost him, so also is my joy, the *fierceness* of my love for this man.

We just float in the air and let the rain wash over us like a baptism. It washes all the grief, all the pain of the past day and night away. *Has it been only a day? Nae matter. We have all eternity to spend in love. And I swear I will ne'er leave his side again!*

We remain like that for a short time, hovering high in the air, basking in the warmth of our love while the rain and the wind chill us and blow us about. I dinnae care. I'm so happy.

Carl's alive!

Eventually, hard reality intrudes on my thoughts.

"Carl," I say at last, my head resting on his chest, "who did we lose?"

"Too many," he says into my sopping wet hair. "Only five of the Stake vampires survived."

"*Five?*" I cry. I try to remember who returned with Carl, but I cannae picture them in my mind. Carl was the only one I had eyes for.

I pull my head back and look into his blue eyes.

"Yeah," he says. "Lorenzo's still with us. A few others."

"Ghalyela?"

He shakes his head.

"Dezba?"

He shakes his head again.

He lists the names of four other vampires. They are names that I can barely recall.

"And we lost Sarah," he says.

"I know," I reply.

"And something's wrong with Rolf."

"What d'ye mean?"

"I think he took a bullet or two in the brain when we were still nailed to our crosses. I know it regenerates, but . . . well, he doesn't seem to understand *language* anymore. He can't form words or understand anything you say. He can still fight. Oh, boy, can he fight! But you can't communicate with him. He doesn't even gesture or . . . anything. But when he saw Sarah, he knew her. I don't think he ever realized we had left after that."

Now I understand Rolf's wordless wailing. Lucy's bullets must have damaged at least the Broca's and Wernicke's areas of Rolf's brain. As Carl said, the tissue regenerates, but the knowledge is gone.

"Do you think he can learn to communicate again?" Carl asks.

Lightning flashes.

"Aye, most likely," I reply, "but 'twill take some time. He'll be like a newborn bairn. Someone will have to teach him. Someone will have to be with him constantly to monitor what he does. We dinnae ken what else he's lost. He could be a danger to himself and to others."

Thunder booms.

"What happened with Müller?" Carl asks.

"He's dead. What happened with Lilith?"

"She retreated. She came to watch an execution, not to fight a battle."

"What about the Congregation?" I ask. "Were there any survivors?"

"About a dozen or so."

"A dozen? I thought they were all dead. Well, a dozen is better than none."

"Not really," he says, and his voice has a grim edge to it. "Lilith offered to let them rejoin her if they did it of their own free will. About a dozen took her up on that offer."

"What happened to the rest?" I ask, nae wanting to hear the answer and fairly certain I know it already.

"She commanded them to tear each other to pieces and then kill themselves. It took less than a minute. There were no survivors. And they took a number of our people with them. The Stake vampires, to a man, tried to stop them. We tried to hold them apart, but they turned on us. They had no choice, I suppose; they had to obey and remove any *obstacles* that got in the way of that obedience. Ghalyela fell almost immediately. One of them nearly ripped my head off trying to get to the man I was restraining. Lorenzo lost an arm. Retrieving and reattaching it probably took him out of the thick of things just long enough to save his life. Others weren't so lucky. By the time each of us was able to contain our man . . . to hold him and prevent him from hurting himself or someone else, we'd lost seven of our own."

"Seven?" I exclaim. "But what happened to the rest?"

"Speaking of the rest," he says, "we'd best be heading back. I don't want them to think we've run off."

"I wish we *could* just run off." *How I wish we could just run away, but our friends—the ones still alive, at least—they need us.*

"Later, my love."

We reluctantly, lingeringly pull out of our embrace. Carl takes my hand. Together we fly back in the direction of the barn. We're nae moving all that quickly. I think Carl needs to tell me more before we get back to the others.

He just needed to get moving. He cannae remain still when there's work to be done.

"Just after we got control of the remaining members of the Congregation, that was when the farmhands, Müller's Chosen, showed up. There were eleven of them, and they came in with Uzis blazing. I don't know who told them to do it. Maybe it was a backup plan that Müller had . . . some order that he gave last night . . . or maybe it was *their* idea. I don't know.

"Anyway, when they came in shooting, we spun ourselves around . . ." His voice breaks. "Every single one of our people tried to shield his struggling captive with his own body. They were willing to lay down their own lives for the people who were still trying to kill them . . ." He chokes.

"Ye were, too, laddie," I say. "Ye protected your man, did ye nae?"

"Yeah, for all the good it did. After they shot the twenty of us *and* our prisoners down, the farmhands dropped their guns and came in with machetes and axes and beheaded all of them before they could recover. The Congregation people were just too weak. They never had a chance. But the Chosen got six of our people too. That's when Dezba fell. The man he died protecting was a *white man*, by the way."

He says nae more for a bit. We fly into the barn and out of the rain. The wind has eased up a bit, but the rain is as hard as ever.

Rolf is still kneeling on the floor, rocking Sarah's body. He's now silent . . . nae more of that pitiable inarticulate cry, but he stares at her and weeps. His tears fall on her face.

The five remaining Stake vampires have begun the grisly task of gathering up the bodies, heads, and other body parts. They are piling them up in the center of the floor. They're going to have to be burned, I suppose. Bodies that have been long suffused with the Seed burn very easily and very hotly. Even the bones do. And we simply can't leave them for the authorities to find. The blood will burn as well.

Tony Lupescu is helping out along with the vampires. He takes Müller's corpse by the ankles and begins to drag it toward the pile. He's having a hard time of it. Müller was a large man. Suddenly, Rolf is at his side. He grunts inarticulately at Tony, and although he forms nae words, his meaning is clear. Tony drops Müller and backs away.

Rolf lifts the corpse high above him and hurls it at the pile. He then stares at it for a few seconds before he turns and hurries back to Sarah's body. He gathers her up in his arms and takes her to one of the walls. There he sits back down and holds her to himself. He kisses her dead face, and he ignores the others as they perform their ghastly work.

I observe as Tony tries to lift another body. One leg of the corpse comes off in his hand. He stares at it for a moment as if he cannae understand what has happened. Then he drops it. He drops to his knees and retches.

"What happened to the Chosen?" I ask.

Carl barks out a bitter laugh. "They got what they deserved, I guess."

I look at him for a bit. *What does he mean by that?* And then it hits me. They had become murderers. *Evil blood.*

"Say that none of *our* people . . ." I say.

"Nope," he says, and shakes his head. "We were all too busy Healing to do anything about it, even if we had wanted to.

"By the way, my *hunger* . . . at least the abnormal hunger, is gone," he says. "How about you?"

I nod. "I think it passed when the Congregants died."

"Makes sense," he says. "We didn't kill the mortals. No, that was when Lilith's people came. There were eleven of them. I suppose they were all Enforcers. It fits that Lilith would have twelve Enforcers. With Müller gone, that leaves eleven. They swooped out from under that tent-thing of hers and they consumed and slaughtered all the farmhands. While they were Feeding, I saw that there were still a number of people under that tent. They had automatic weapons. I could see that much. *She* was still in the center of it all, but I couldn't see her clearly. Once the Enforcers had finished with the Chosen, they came after us."

He shakes his head wearily. "At this point, there were fourteen of us left, but not all of us had recovered and not all of us could find our weapons. Some had dropped them while trying to save, I mean, *restrain* the Congregation. We fought hard, especially Rolf, but, in the end, nine more of us were dead and four of hers were too."

He pauses. "That's when *she* finally showed herself."

"Lilith?" I ask.

He nods. "She said, 'Stop!' in that *voice* of hers. I mean, I've never felt *compelled* to obey any vampire, but there is something about her voice that just makes you *want* to obey her, makes you want to *please* her. It was . . . well, like nothing I've ever experienced before.

"So we *did* stop for a second. All of us. Except for Rolf. He beheaded his man. Then he looked around for someone else to fight. But then he saw her, and he just stared. Like the rest of us."

"Why?" I ask. "Why did ye just stare at her?"

"Well, frankly, because I'd never seen anything like her. She was . . . beautiful. *Beyond* beautiful. I mean, it's hard to describe, but looking at her was as if you were seeing . . . *perfection.*"

It makes me intensely uncomfortable to hear my husband describe another woman, even Lilith, as "beyond beautiful." I know the stories . . . from poor Sarah . . . so I know the effect she's said to have on people, but . . .

Off to my right, I hear Tony cough. "Uh, excuse me for butting in, but I think I understand what was going on."

"What do you mean?" Carl asks.

"Well . . . Lilith is two generations from Adam and Eve, right?" He actually rubs his hands together, the academic warming to his subject. "So, she was born before mankind degenerated physically and genetically. I mean, Adam and Eve were perfect human specimens, right? Created in the image of God, right? I would guess she was born before her father was cursed. So she would be very close to human perfection. Of *course* she's beautiful! She's Eve's granddaughter!"

"No, there was more to it," Carl interjects. "When she looked at me . . . she . . . *changed*. She looked like . . . well, she looked like *you*, Moira. And sometimes she looked like . . . well, Sharon. Sharon with wings, that is."

"She looked like my wife," Tony says. "I mean, my wife never looked that . . . perfect, but she looked like some *idealized* version of my wife. Only, my wife looks more . . . *wholesome*."

"Yeah," Carl says. "That's a good way of putting it."

So she's more beautiful, but I'm more wholesome?

"Anyway," Carl continues, "there she was, wings flapping in the air, right above that barn door out there." He points to the place where I found Sarah.

"I think she mistook our initial reactions for obedience," Carl continues, "because she said, 'Enough of this. All of you, come to me.' The Enforcers turned and flew to kneel before her. When *we* didn't come forward with them . . . although some of the Stake folks *did* take a step forward before stopping themselves . . . she looked *shocked*. Then she looked *afraid*."

"I don't think anyone has disobeyed her in six thousand years," Tony says.

"Rolf went forward, though," Carl continues. "Only, he wasn't going to see *her*. I *think* that's when he realized where Sarah was . . . or, rather, where her body was.

"Lilith didn't notice him. He slipped under the door apparently unobserved by her or her minions. One moment he was under there and the next moment there was a spear poking out through Lilith's stomach. Rolf had come up behind her with Sarah under one arm and Müller's spear in the other hand."

Grinning fiercely, Carl says. "Rolf had run her through. She screamed, and then she said something I didn't catch."

"I did," Tony says, interrupting. "She said, '*Benim ha-Ahman! Mishphatu Phosferno sher lif! Thakhati peni, sporanot caperno!*'" Tony's eyes are fairly glowing. He looks *excited*. "Maybe I got part of it wrong, but I'm pretty sure that's what she said. Believe me, it's *etched* in my mind! I'll never forget it! I don't know exactly what it *means*, but I'm *certain* it was pure *Adamic*! You know, the *first* language . . . the language of Adam!"

How could he possibly remember it word for word like that?

"Yeah . . ." Carl says, drawing out the word. "Well, whatever it was, I'm pretty sure it wasn't meant to be *polite*. Anyway, she pulled the spear out and tossed it away. Then she turned around to see who had *dared* to harm her, but Rolf was long gone with Sarah. He had flown back behind the rest of us.

That's when the helicopter arrived. It set down twenty yards from the barn. The rear loading ramp slammed down, and the remaining Enforcers grabbed Lilith like a bunch of Secret Service agents with the President of the United States, and they carried her inside. I caught a glimpse of the interior before they got her in there. I saw seven or so mortals with automatic weapons and the Congregation members who had rejoined her. And there were a bunch of mortals in there trussed up and lying on the floor."

He pauses again. "They were probably Müller's 'livestock.'" His tone is bitter. "An in-flight *meal* for the ride home.

"So, when the chopper took off, that's when we all moved . . . everybody except Rolf, that is . . . and we took off after her. Somehow, though, the chopper accelerated almost as fast as we did. A Chinook like that tops out at about a hundred and seventy knots. My guess is the vampires within helped it fly and accelerate by *lifting* it from inside, otherwise we would have caught up with it easily.

"We followed as long as we could, but eventually it was able to fly faster than we were able to . . . and still *breathe*. We pushed as hard as we could, but we had to give up finally.

"Bottom line: she got away." He stares intently in the direction of the dark sky beyond the mountains. "She got away, and it was all for *nothing*."

"What d'ye mean, laddie?" I say. "'All for nothing'?"

"All these people . . . dead. All they wanted was to be free . . . to repent. And they all died . . . *horribly*. And, the Stake . . . they trusted me."

He clenches his teeth. "And I let them down."

"Nae, laddie," I say. "Carl, dearie, ye did all ye could to save them. Ye sent them out of the state . . . Wait! How could they *possibly* be here when they were *ordered* to leave the state and to stay *completely* away from Müller's compound?"

"Corelli!" Carl barks, turning abruptly in the direction of those gathering the corpses. "Get over here!"

Lorenzo instantly rushes over to us. "Yes, Carl?" he says. He's exhausted. And he knows he's in trouble.

"I gave you a *direct order*!" Carl's face flushes with anger. "How in the world did you manage to disobey it? *Why* did you disobey it?"

"Why?" Lorenzo says, shaking his head in amazement. "Because you're the Unwilling and the Chosen! Without you, we're all *lost*! And, Signori," he says, holding both blood-soaked hands up in a warding gesture, "don't you *dare* chastise me for that! *All* of us, all our people, *knew* what they had to do. They gladly laid down their lives to protect you. You are the symbol of our hope for redemption . . . through Jesus, yes, I know. They laid down their lives just like those Lamanite soldiers did in the Book of Mormon." His face and his tone are suddenly very angry. "So don't you *dare* dishonor their memories and their sacrifice!"

He stares Carl in the eye, and for a moment, I think Carl might strike him. Then Carl bows his head and says, "*How* did you disobey? I thought you were *bound* to follow my commands."

"My dear Captain," Lorenzo says, his anger melting away and a weary smile spreading across his blood-streaked face, "I *never* disobeyed you. I *can't* disobey you. I followed your orders to the letter. To the *letter*."

"I don't get it," Carl says.

I dinnae 'get it' either.

"You've never been bound by a Master's command," Lorenzo says, "so you wouldn't understand. You've never been a *slave* like that. After a while, you find that there are ways to obey the letter of the law and still find loopholes.

"In this case, they left the state, as ordered. It's about sixty miles as the crow . . . or, in this case, the *vampire* flies to the nearest border. That only takes about twenty minutes at top speed. Once they had fulfilled your order, they turned around and came back."

Lorenzo taps a finger to his temple. "Now, staying away from 'Müller's compound' . . . *that* took a bit longer. You can thank your friend Sam from BYU for helping us out with that one. He found a reference on the Internet to a patent application for a polymer-based adhesive called 'Müller's compound.' So we figured that, as long as they stayed away from a polymer-based adhesive created by a man named Müller, we were safe. Besides, nobody in their right mind would classify this *farm* as either a compound or a polymer-based adhesive. But, just in case, they all agreed to steer clear of any barrels of glue they might encounter up here."

He smiles, but Carl's having none of it. Carl opens his mouth to say something, probably something he might regret. Then he snaps it shut again. Then he nods and slaps Lorenzo lightly on the shoulder. "Good thinking, soldier."

"I'll do better than *that*," I say. I step forward and plant a kiss on his cheek. "Thank you, Lorenzo."

He nods, and he blushes, although 'tis hard to see it under all the gore on his face.

A cell phone rings. 'Tis Tony's.

I wonder what happened to ours. Most likely they were confiscated by Müller when he captured us.

"This is Tony Lupescu," he says as he answers it.

"Tony, it's Sam," I hear Sammy's voice say. "Tell Moira that Winnie is at LDS Hospital and I'm on my way back up there with the bus. And, uh, Tony? I think the back door handle is busted. I think Müller nearly ripped it off when he broke in here."

"That's OK, Sam," Tony says. "I know a guy who can fix stuff like that before the coach even knows about it." He winks at me.

Why would he wink at me? He's a strange duck.

Tony steps away from us so he can continue his conversation with Sammy.

I, however, turn to Lorenzo.

"Why on Earth," I say, "did you bring *those* two up here? They could have been *killed!*" Now, I *feel like* slapping *him and nae so lightly as Carl did!* "He's your great-great-grandson, for heaven's sake!"

Lorenzo looks a little embarrassed. "Actually, it took us all night to figure out how to get around the 'Müller's compound' thing. We *assumed* that we would find a loophole, but nothing was forthcoming. In the meantime, Tony and Sam managed to borrow a BYU Athletics bus (from the women's volleyball team, I think) and we started up here. We needed a way to stay out of the Sun and still be close by until we figured out how to get around your order. Tony drove, and Sam spent time on his cell phone searching the Internet for a way around your order. He kept searching for a possible *place* name that might fit, but then he stumbled on the patent application instead. We covered the windows to protect ourselves, but we needed a mortal to actually *drive* the thing because none of us could man the driver's seat and sit in the sunlight."

"And they would have had to tie me up to keep me away," Tony says, returning to us after his phone call. "There was no *way* I was going to miss an opportunity to *learn* something! I heard *Adamic* spoken today! Do you know what that *means?*"

"Ye could have been *killed*, laddie," I say. "Nae amount of knowledge is worth that! Your life's too short to risk it so foolishly."

"Life's short anyway, especially *mine* compared to *yours*," Tony replies. "If you risk nothing, you lose nothing, but you gain less."

Behind me, I hear Rolf begin his keening wail again. We all look over at him. He rocks Sarah in his arms. Rolf has lost so much this day.

"Aye, laddie," I say, turning to Lorenzo. I look him straight in the eye. "Life *is* short. And nae matter *how* long or short it is, 'tis all we have: one lifetime. Ye should spend it with the ones ye love. Dinnae waste a chance to tell them that ye love them."

Lorenzo looks intently into my eyes. His suddenly become full of tears. He nods.

I reach out and take him by the hand. Then I turn to Tony.

"Tony," I say, "there is someone here I'd like ye to meet. I'd like to introduce ye to your great-great-grandfather."

Chapter 31

THE RAIN LASTS all day and well into the night, though the wind dies down to nothing, and the rain slackens a bit in the late afternoon. The sky remains overcast. 'Tis as if God sent the storm to help us.

Perhaps He did.

Carl and I check the functional barn to see if the Chosen who'd been left to guard Winnie, the one whom Sarah had trussed up, is still there. All we find are his severed bonds. I suppose he was among the Chosen who attacked Carl and the others before being slaughtered by the Enforcers.

We *do* find shackles in the stalls. Those cruel fetters had been used to bind the "livestock," the "ghosts" that Stuart Hopkins (and perhaps, others) had captured for Müller and Bartlett. Those poor souls were most likely dead by now, taken away in Lilith's helicopter and consumed.

Carl and I gather up the personal effects of the farmhands. We also collect the white robes and the weapons we find in the bunkhouse and in Müller's farmhouse. We do our best to remove any clue as to what really went on up here. There'll be difficult enough questions to deal with in the days ahead without leaving physical evidence for the authorities.

The firearms we crush. The bullets we bury. The swords we keep.

Ye cannae have too many swords.

There's some discussion about keeping some of the guns, but in the end we decide the "sword of truth" is the type of weapon the Lord wants us to use to "fight demons."

We burn the bodies of the dead, except for Sarah and the other identifiable members of the Stake, inside the barn. To the fire, we add the items Carl and I have gathered, as well as the three huge crosses. In less than an hour, the corpses are gone, including those of the dead mortals. The fire is so hot, it consumes most of the ash as well. Even the blood on the floor catches fire. Being mostly vampire blood, so long infused with the Seed, it too burns white-hot . . . so hot, in fact, that it turns the earth of the barn floor to a sea of glass. The barn itself is completely destroyed in spite of the rain.

Carl, Rolf, Tony, Sammy, Lorenzo, and I, along with the other four surviving members of "The Vampire Stake," bury Sarah and the others next to Ben on the mountainside. 'Tis the evening of the same day, the day that so many of our friends had died, but these burials could nae wait. Rolf insists on digging Sarah's grave himself. He carves her stone. 'Tis a small thing, her gravestone, but he carves a single rose and an image of the Salt Lake Temple on it. He's incapable of carving her name and he'll nae allow anyone else to help him. Still, 'tis lovely and surprisingly detailed. Nae, "surprisingly" is nae the word. 'Twould be much more accurate to say, "lovingly."

I sing two songs for the dead: "I Stand All Amazed" and "Amazing Grace." 'Tis all I can do to finish the second one. Of the dead, I knew Sarah the best. And I'm surprised to find that I not only mourn her, but I love her as well.

Carl, Tony, and Sammy take turns dedicating the graves as we all stand in the slackening rain. We save Sarah's for last. When Carl finishes with her grave, Rolf comes up to him. Rolf makes several inarticulate sounds and looks at Carl anxiously. Carl shakes his head to show his lack of comprehension, so Rolf turns to me.

The poor lad looks frantic.

"He knows it's time to go," I say. "He does nae ken how to communicate with us, but he wants something very, very badly."

To Rolf, I say, "I dinnae understand ye, laddie." *If he could at least gesture* . . . "I dinnae know what ye want."

Then it dawns on me. I *do* know what he wants!

"Sarah," I say. "Sa-rah."

Rolf's lips work, but nae sound comes out. Then, with obvious difficulty, he repeats, "Sa-rah."

"Aye, laddie. Sarah." I burst into tears. I wrap my arms around him, and he puts his head on my shoulder. He slowly encircles me with his arms. He sobs and repeats her name over and over. 'Tis the only word he knows, his entire vocabulary. But for now, 'tis sufficient.

When at last he releases me, he smiles. 'Tis a sad smile, but 'tis all he had to give as his thanks. He kneels beside Sarah's grave and kisses her small stone. "Sa-rah," he says. Then he stands.

He's ready to leave.

As we fly away from that solemn, sacred place, Lorenzo carries Tony in his arms, and Rolf carries Sammy. The other four follow them as we part ways, Carl and I to the west for home, and the rest of them southwest to Provo. Lorenzo's rented home is large enough, he insists, to house them all. They agree that they're safer together for now. And Sammy's positively giddy at the possibility of more vampire blood to test.

Tony received the revelation of his true relationship with Lorenzo with unabashed joy. He'd always felt a connection with the man. At last he understood why. Tony looked like a child on Christmas morn. "I've got to explain everything to my wife!" he cried. "You're going to be a big part of our lives, now! You've got to tell me all about my great-great-grandmother Mara!"

Lorenzo volunteered for the task of caring for Rolf. He vowed to teach him to speak and read and write again. "My German is flawless, but I'll teach him English first," he assured us. "We're going to need him to understand English in the battle to come."

The battle to come, I thought. *The battle that, win or lose, will end in our deaths.*

I squeeze Carl's hand as we fly.

"We can't stay here much longer," he says. "I don't know how long we have, but she knows we're coming."

There's nae doubt as to who "she" is.

"We *hurt* her," he continues. "I don't think that's happened for a very long time."

"She'll be more dangerous now," I say. "The cornered and wounded bear is the most deadly."

"Yep, but she'll have to regroup. Even wounded and exhausted as we were, we managed to take out five of her inner circle. And she knows now that we *exist*. I'm not sure how much she believed Müller's claim that he had captured the Unwilling and the Penitent, but she's sure to believe it now."

"Aye, especially after she's seen us defy her. She saw that with her own eyes."

"It looked like it really scared her too. I doubt *that's* happened in a long time, either."

We fly in silence for a bit, lost in our gloomy thoughts.

"I think we've got a little while to rest and plan," Carl says, breaking the silence. "I think we've got a little more time to be . . . together."

"We've got longer than that, laddie. We've got all of eternity. Ye're nae getting away from me *that* easily!" I'm trying to lift our spirits, but my attempt falls flat.

"'Easily'?" His expression is grim. "You mean, 'easily,' as in *dying*?" He chuckles softly. "Maybe death would be easier than what we've got to face right now."

"Aye, perhaps, but I will nae face it until I've had a bath, a change of clothes, and a bag of blood from the ice box."

"Sounds like a plan." He pauses. "I love you, Moira MacDonald Morgan. You know that, right?"

"Aye, that I do. And I love ye, laddie, with all my heart."

And with that, we fly on through the rain toward home.

So, cleaned, Fed, and dressed in fresh clothing, we go to face Winnie Morrison.

'Tis near the end of visiting hours. So much has happened the last night and day, 'tis hard to believe this is the evening of the same day on which we were crucified and forced to face the Sun, the same day on which Sarah and so many others had died. And as horrific as that was, I think I dread the coming encounter at least as much, or perhaps more than I did facing the coming of the dawn.

Carl has come with me for support, but, at the last moment, I ask him to wait for me in the waiting room on the hospital ward. As much as I ache . . . nae, almost panic . . . at the thought of being separated from him for even a moment with so little time left to us, I realize I need to face this *alone*.

Before entering her room at LDS Hospital, I check Winnie's chart. Her vitals are all good . . . or at least as good as or better than should be expected for a woman of her age and condition. Physically, she should expect to recover. But what of her mind? She tried to take her own life. And after her experiences in the last day and a half, what'll be left of her already fragile psyche? How much does she remember? Her chart contains nae notes concerning delusions (such as stories about vampires).

I ask the nurse on duty about her, and she informs me that Mrs. Morrison is resting comfortably. She tells me, however, that Mrs. Morrison has asked for *me* a number of times since being admitted.

I knock softly at Winnie's door, but there's nae answer. So I let myself in.

The lights are dim, set for sleeping. The TV's off. Winnie's eyes are closed. If 'twere nae for the rate of her pulse and breathing, ye might think she was sleeping.

Looking at her in the dark, lying there on her bed, with monitor wires and IV tubes connected to her, I'm reminded of a huge, bloated spider, waiting in her web to pounce on the fly foolish enough to enter her domain. The way I feel, 'tis an apt analogy. Nae so long before, I came close to draining her of life. But now she has the power to wrap me up in her web, so to speak, and drain away the life I've built here in Utah.

Ach, 'twill nae matter in the end. Carl and I both feel we have weeks left at most. Perhaps only days. Still, I'm loath to say good-bye to the home, the ward, the hospital, the friends, and the colleagues that I've cherished for more than half a century.

"Hello, Winnie," I say.

"You're one of those *things*, aren't you?" Her voice is confident, in control. 'Tis nae so much a question as it is a demand.

She holds all the power, and she knows it.

"I dinnae mean to be coy, Winnie," I say, "but what d'ye mean?"

"You know what I mean, *Moira*. You're one of those *vampire*-things."

"I was nae sure what ye remembered, what ye saw. And believe me when I say, I did nae want to traumatize ye any further. I'm so very sorry that ye became entangled in all this."

"So, am I *safe* here? Are they gone?"

"Aye, they're gone. We fought them off." *And we paid a high price too.*

She looks at me, and her wee beady eyes seem to bore into mine.

"How old are you, really?" she asks.

Winnie ne'er was one for subtlety.

"I'm two hundred and seventy, give or take."

She smirks. "How old were you when you stopped aging?"

"Seventeen."

She looks at me with her mouth agape.

"We matured earlier back then. I was nigh an old maid."

She shakes her head. "All these years, I thought you were a witch or you must've had facelift after facelift. And the truth was so much worse. You're no witch. You're a *monster*." She lets that hang in the air for a while.

I keep my silence.

"Does the bishop know?" she asks after a bit.

"Aye, they've *all* known. I had to have a special clearance to be baptized."

"Special clearance? From where?"

"The First Presidency."

"They . . . *knew?*"

"Aye, for more than fifty years."

"And they let you be *baptized?* How many people have you murdered?"

"Until today, I've nae killed another human being in more than two and a half centuries. Today . . . I killed a man . . . one of *my* kind. He was going to slaughter innocents. I had nae choice."

I pause a moment and then add quietly, "He tried to kill *you*."

She says nothing for a wee bit and seems to be trying to make up her mind about something. "All these years I've hated you and tried to find a way to ruin you, but nobody would listen to me. I told them there was something *unnatural* about you . . . about your *looks*."

"I was born this way. It has nothing to do with . . ."

She rolled her eyes and said, "Yeah, yeah. That Isaiah guy, the one who took me from the hospital . . . he was no movie star. Ugly as an old stump. You'd think he'd shave that stupid beard! Who's he trying to look like? Brigham Young?"

"He is as he was when he . . . when he became one of my kind," I said. "We cannae change much about the way we look. He could shave it, but it'd grow right back to the same length immediately. I cannae cut my *own* hair or even straighten or curl it."

"You make me *sick!*" she says, her tone bitter. "You know that? What *normal* woman stands a chance against *you?* That Carl of yours . . . is *he* like you?"

"Aye, but nae so old. He's only been changed for a wee bit over a year."

"Did you change him?" Her tone is accusatory.

"Nae, 'twas nae me. I've nae Converted anyone . . . ever." I pause and then say, "I would nae wish this existence on my worst enemy."

"Meaning *me*."

"Ye are nae my enemy, Winnie! I've only wished to be your friend!"

"Oh, *yes* I am!" she snarls. "And I've *got* you now! I can tell the whole ward, and the bishop wouldn't be able to evade it! He'd *have* to come clean! I can tell the newspapers, the TV stations! I can tell the *world*!" Her voice drops to a whisper. "And there's nothing you can do about it."

I hold my peace.

"Nothing, that is," she says after a tick, "except *kill* me."

"I would nae *do* that!" *But ye almost did, lassie.*

"That's what Sam kept saying," she replies. "All the way to the hospital after that . . . that *creature* attacked us . . . and you stopped him . . . he kept saying how you saved our lives . . . how you could've killed me yourself . . . how you're always fighting your urge to kill."

She's quiet again. Then the tears begin to roll down the sides of her face. "He said you could've hypnotized me at any time and *made* me be nice to you. Is that true?"

"I have that ability, aye."

"Why didn't you just make me be nice to you? Then all your problems would have been solved!"

"Because, Winnie, 'tis nae *right* to force someone to be different than who they are."

"You mean I'm a big, fat, spiteful old hag who nobody is ever going to love or care about."

"*I* care, Winnie! I've *always* cared!"

"*Why?*" she demands. "Why would you give a fig about me? Why wouldn't you just let me *die*? I *wanted* to die! Why wouldn't you just let me die?" Her chest heaves with a huge wracking sob.

"Because ye're my sister . . . ye're a child of God . . . because ye're a human being who's in pain, and I've spent all my life trying to relieve human suffering . . . because I've spent all my life trying to atone for my sins. But I cannae atone! Only the Savior can do that. And if ye lose *hope* . . . if ye give in to the darkness in your soul . . . then ye're lost."

Winnie looks away.

"Today," I say, "some very good and noble people sacrificed their lives. They're people like me . . . and, *like* me, they've killed in the past . . . but they found *hope* . . . hope that Jesus would forgive them . . . hope that He'd *redeem* them. And they decided to *live* for that hope, to *act* on it . . . or to lay down their lives in defense of it. Christ said, 'My grace is sufficient for all men.' Well, they took Him at His word. And ye can do the same. As the saying goes, 'Where there's life, there's hope.' I could nae let ye throw yours away."

"*But he's never coming back!*" she sobs.

She means Heber, her ex-husband.

"Aye, he's moved on," I say. I cross the room to her side and gently take her hand in mine.

And she does nae pull away.

"And so should ye," I continue. "Ye have to believe Christ. He has promised that, if ye live a righteous life, ye'll find happiness again."

"That's the thing, isn't it?" Her voice is wet and burbling as if 'tis bubbling up from underneath an *ocean* of misery. "I haven't been a good person. I drove Heber away with my constant nagging. I drive everybody away. I don't have any friends. My own sister hates me. I don't know how to stop *hating*!" Her voice sinks to a wet whisper. "I don't know how to stop hating myself."

"Lassie, 'tis nae an easy task, to stop hating yourself," I say with a sympathy that goes as deep as the marrow. "I know from personal experience how very hard that is. But the answer's always the same. Ye have to love others and trust in the Lord. When ye give of yourself to others, ye cannae hate them and ye cannae hate yourself. The answer to hate is *always* love."

She looks at me, really looks at me, *seeing* me . . . perhaps for the first time in decades.

"Do ye remember the woman who rescued ye from the barn?"

She nods slowly. "Sarah. She saved me."

"Aye, Sarah. She saved us all. She *died* to save us. She spent almost a thousand years without knowing the love of another human being, but in the end, she understood love better than any of us. 'Greater love hath no man than this . . .'"

I spend the better part of two hours with Winnie, long after visiting hours are over. Sometimes we talk. Sometimes we let the silence fill the spaces. Winnie lies there, and I hold her hand. Eventually she falls asleep.

Chapter 32: Aftermath

LIGHTNING STRUCK the farmhouse, and it was destroyed in the resulting fire. In the end, investigators concluded that lightning started the fire in the barn as well, although it appeared that some "unidentified accelerant" had been a contributing factor.

Nae trace could be found of the registered owner, one Paul Miller.

The abandoned pigs were "rescued" by Animal Control in response to an anonymous phone call. They were found to be well-fed (I saw to that), but anemic.

Rumors of a strange cult that performed bizarre rituals spread like wildfire in the surrounding community. There was even a mention of it on the news.

But *that* story was but a footnote compared to the tale of the "Battling Angels of Temple Square." 'Twas all over the local news for a while. It made the national news once or twice as well. None of the missionaries who were eyewitnesses to the events that morning would give interviews, referring reporters to the Church Public Affairs office instead. Some of the tourists gave interviews, though. What they described was so fantastic, the initial reports were dismissed as some type of illusion created by the lightning and the storm. Some even went so far as to call it a shameless publicity stunt or "fake miracle" perpetrated by the Mormon Church. The official spokesman for the Church stated flatly that the Church had no knowledge of what did or did not transpire. He said 'twas a matter for the civil authorities to deal with.

No pictures or video footage were available from the incident. What tourist would risk their cameras in such a rain? However, the *Tribune* carried an artist's conception of two persons, a man and a woman, flying and fighting in the air with swords. The man was wearing a long white robe and sported great feathered wings. His face looked demonic, complete with huge fangs and eyes of flame. The other figure, the woman, was depicted as wearing black plate-mail to go with her black sword. The woman had nae wings. In the sketch, she had the face and regal bearing of an angel. She looked calm and unruffled by the demon before her. Both of them, the "angel" and the "demon" were described by onlookers as being more than ten feet tall.

The story caused accounts of the "Ogden Temple Incident" to be rehashed. "Eyewitnesses" came forward to describe *that* one, but their stories were so fantastic and contradictory, they were soon given nae credence at all.

After a few days, both stories quietly went away. "Faith-promoting rumors" persisted for some time, though, resurfacing in seminary, institute, and Sunday School classes, as well as in the occasional fast and testimony meeting. With each retelling, the stories got more bizarre and fantastic.

Nary a one of the stories, printed or spoken, mentioned the "angel" as having red hair.

A week after the battle, Carl and I attended a meeting of the "Stake" in Provo. Two more Penitents joined us. They also swore fealty to Carl and joined our little army. I suspected our numbers would continue to increase.

After Carl and I left the meeting, we flew hand-in-hand toward home. The stars which winked at us between the dark clouds were so beautiful. About halfway home, up in the cold night sky above Point of the Mountain, we stopped and hovered.

Carl took me in his arms and kissed me. It was a long, soft, and sweet kiss, and it felt like heaven to be in the arms of the man I loved more dearly than anyone in this world.

I wished we could remain there forever, floating between earth and heaven, locked in a tender embrace. I knew . . . we both knew it could nae last.

We did nae know whether we had weeks or days or hours left. One thing we did know was that we had started down a path that would end in combat to the death with Lilith, the Queen of the vampires, the "Mother of Night."

And if we're faithful and victorious, it'll cost us our lives.

Sarah laid down her life.

Ghalyela . . . Dezba . . . so many others sacrificed their lives. And they did so in the faith that they would find redemption. They gave up this life for the hope of a better one in the world to come.

And I have every reason to believe we will see them again.

SNEAK PREVIEW

The Prophecy
The Children of Lilith, Volume 3

Chapter 1

S *ons of God! Brood of Light-Bearer who fell!' That is how I would render the first half."*

The message is in plain text. The email address looks like a random mix of letters and numbers, and the email provider is one that supports anonymous accounts.

I've been collaborating with colleagues across the country and in the U.K., Israel, and Egypt for more than a week. We've been trying to decipher the twenty-four syllables of Adamic (at least I *assume* it's Adamic) that Lilith uttered at the battle at the farm. My colleagues are experts in Hebrew, Arabic, Egyptian, Greek, and Latin. We've been exchanging emails ever since I asked for their help.

Of course, I've told them I'm not at liberty to reveal the *source* just yet, but I'm certain it's a language that predated all others, a protolanguage. In the beginning, some refused to collaborate on the project because I wouldn't reveal my source, because I was being cryptic. But eventually, most couldn't resist the lure of the *puzzle.* That's something we all share in common, my colleagues and I: we can't resist the potential, the lure of hidden knowledge.

And of course, I can't tell my academic friends that the source is a *native speaker.* I also can't tell them that the text is an outburst from a six-thousand-year-old vampire after she'd been impaled by the very spear that once pierced Christ's side, a spear being wielded by a former Nazi assassin who is now a *repentant* vampire.

In other words, I can't betray my *friends.*

My colleagues and I have been exchanging a veritable whirlwind of email messages for days, with theories, postulations, and outright guesses about roots, word endings, and syntax. It's a fascinating puzzle, but we have so little to go on. So, a *puzzle* is all it is and all it's likely to remain, unless I meet Lilith, the ancient Mother of Night, the mother of all vampires, face-to-face.

And that would be an encounter I'd be unlikely to survive.

I've survived one such encounter with her already ... and *that* only because she had more immediate concerns to occupy her attention than one mortal *stupid* enough to embroil himself in a battle between factions of vampires.

God may watch over imbeciles and fools, but *nobody* has that much luck.

I'm no warrior, like Carl. I'm not a master of the sword, like Moira, Carl's wife. I'm just Tony Lupescu, scholar, professor of ancient scripture at Brigham Young University. I'm just an academic ... and a *mortal* one at that.

I've made up my mind that I'll just have to make do with the sample, *just twenty-four syllables*, that I have. But, hey, it's a heck of a lot more than I knew about the language of Adam *before* I witnessed the Penitent vampires of the "Vampire Stake," led by Carl Morgan, the world's first and only Unwilling vampire, forced into battle with the minions of Lilith.

Twenty-four syllables. It's not a Rosetta Stone with a dead language carved beside a direct translation in a *known* language, but it's all I have, and I'll have to be content with that.

And it's *knowledge!*

And a fascinating *puzzle.*

And I *was* content with the *seeking*, even if I might not find the answer ...

But now ... this almost-anonymous email. And a *piece* of the puzzle that *fits*. I can *feel* it. This is the *correct* translation. I don't know *how* I know it, but I *do* know.

So, with a jumbled mixture of eagerness and trepidation and a dozen other emotions that I barely understand, I reach for my mouse and click the "Reply" button.

"Who are you?" I type. *"How did you get this address? What makes you think this is correct? And why on EARTH would someone say both of these together? It makes no sense: sons of God AND spawn of Satan (that would be 'Light-Bearer who fell') in the same breath. How can someone be both?"*

I sit there for a bit, debating with myself the wisdom of responding. Once I click the "Send" button, there'll be no turning back. I *could* simply ignore the anonymous message, but then I'd never know what the sender knows. And what could be the harm, so long as I don't reveal anything that would betray my friends?

Impulsively, I click "Send" before I can change my mind.

There. It's sent.

I've crossed the Rubicon. *"Alea iacta est,"* as Caesar said: *The die is cast.*

"Tony!" Kathleen calls from the living room. "Lorenzo's here!"

Speaking of points of no return ... The coming meeting is something I'm looking forward to with anticipation and dread. *How will my wife react?*

"Coming," I call back. I glance once more at my email. I click the "Send-Receive" button. No reply. *Of course not. It's too soon.*

I get up and walk into the living room.

Kathleen's sitting on the loveseat, and Lorenzo and Rolf are seated, their backs to me, on the sofa,. Of course, *Rolf's* here: Lorenzo has taken Rolf with him everywhere since Rolf was injured. The kids have been in bed for an hour, so it's just the four of us. Lorenzo and Kathleen are talking in low voices. Rolf, of course, says nothing.

I pause at the entrance to the room and take a deep breath. No sense in putting this off any longer. Kathleen needs to know what we're facing, the danger I've placed our family in.

I glance at the front door. Kathleen usually insists that Lorenzo and Rolf leave their swords at the door. *Surely they didn't come unarmed!* I round the corner of the couch and look at Lorenzo. My concern must be plain on my face because he glances down at his lap and pats the basket-hilted claymore lying across his thighs. Rolf's hand rests on the handle of the broadsword in his lap. His gaze catches mine and he nods in greeting.

Kathleen's allowing them to hold on to their swords? Does she have some sense of what's coming? Did Lorenzo use Persuasion on her? No way! That would be a complete violation of my trust! He wouldn't do that, would he?

One glance at Kathleen lays *that* suspicion to rest. She does *not* look happy. She's sitting, but her back's ramrod straight.

"Tony," she says, her tone reflecting her irritation, "they insisted on keeping those . . . *things* with them."

"My apologies, dear lady," Lorenzo says, his Italian accent more pronounced than usual, "but I fear that we must stand ready at all times, especially after dark." He turns his face toward me and says, "The Morgans intercepted another scouting party last night." He looks at me meaningfully and then adds, "In the *south.*"

By that he means Lilith's scouts were here in the Provo area.

I'm about to ask what happened, but he says, "The engagement was a success."

And by that he means that the scouts are dead . . . and that Moira and Carl are still alive.

"That's the third such intercept since the *incident* at the farm," Lorenzo says. "And this time, there were *six* of them."

My eyes go wide at the number. The previous two scouting parties consisted of only two vampires each.

"She's either getting bolder or more desperate . . . ," I say, but Kathleen interrupts me.

"Will you *please* tell me what in the *heck* all of you are talking about?"

"Kat," I say, trying to calm her. I don't need to see the angry look in her eyes to realize I've just made a *huge* mistake: she hates when I use that pet name in public. *This is* not *going well.* But it doesn't matter. I have to tell her anyway. I cross in front of the couch and sit beside her. I take both her hands in mine and look into her angry and fearful blue eyes.

"You do need to know what's going on," I say. "Do you remember my family legend about my great-great-grandfather Laurentiu?"

"Yes," she says with a quick nod, which is followed immediately by a shake of the head, "the so-called vampire."

"Not 'so-called,'" I reply, my voice gentle. "He really *was* a vampire. Only, he didn't die in the sunlight, like we all believed."

She pulls back from me a bit, but leaves her hands in mine. Her beautiful face is a mask of skepticism. "What? You mean . . . like he's still alive? Sweetie, I *never* believed those stories. I know they're part of your family history, but vampires aren't real. I know that's one of your hobbies, but . . ."

"No, honey," I say, cutting her off, "it's all very real. I know it's hard to swallow, but vampires are very real . . . and so is my great-great-grandfather." I glance over at Lorenzo, and Kathleen follows my eyes. She glances at him and then back at me. Her eyes fix on Lorenzo, and then her jaw drops.

"No!" she cries suddenly and rises to her feet.

Lorenzo rises also, extends his sword behind himself, and bows deeply at the waist. "*Si, signora mia,*" he says, rising, "I was born in 1490 in Roma. I was Converted and became a vampire in 1513. For more than a century I . . ."

"Stop it!" Kathleen cries, and now I can see she's *really* furious. "This is *not* funny!"

Lorenzo nods quickly and says, "Dear lady, please forgive me." He looks at me. "If I may, Tony?"

"Please," I say. It's the only way, and we both knew it would come to this.

Lorenzo locks eyes with Kathleen and then rises into the air about a foot or so. Kathleen gasps and puts both hands to her mouth. I raise a hand and lay it on her arm.

She doesn't flinch away.

"Please do not be frightened, granddaughter," Lorenzo says, his voice calm and apologetic. "Please observe my teeth." He opens his mouth, and I see his upper canine teeth extend until his fangs are quite obvious. He remains that way for several moments, hovering in my living room with his fangs extended. Then his canines retract, and he settles softly to the floor.

Kathleen swallows several times and begins to tremble. "M-m-monster!" she cries at last.

Lorenzo bows his head. "I was *indeed* a monster for more than a century," he said, "but I have been a Penitent, a seeker of forgiveness and redemption, for the better part of four hundred years. I have given my life to God. I serve Him now."

First Rolf's head and then Lorenzo's snap to the left. Lorenzo grimaces. He turns his face back to Kathleen. "Forgive me, dear lady, but we seem to have awakened Abigail."

I can't hear anything.

"Mommy!" It's Abby's voice from her room upstairs. Now I can hear her crying.

Kathleen immediately begins to move. She's off like a shot, out of the room and up the stairs.

I hear the door shut behind her. After a moment, Abby quiets down.

There's nothing we can do now except wait for Kathleen to return.

I sit on the loveseat. Lorenzo sits as well, placing the sword back across his thighs.

"*That* could have gone better," I say with a grimace.

"Abby OK," Rolf says, startling me. I haven't heard him speak since he took some bullets to the brain at Müller's farm nine days ago. Moira told us his speech centers were probably destroyed. The tissue regenerated quickly, but the *knowledge* was lost. He has to learn how to speak and understand speech all over again. Just like a baby.

Only this is a lot faster than I expected.

"He's been doing better," Lorenzo says. "Aren't you, Rolf?"

The German, who now sounds more Italian than German, looks annoyed and a bit irritated. "Not baby," he says. "I . . . I'm learning"—he slaps the side of his head twice and then shakes his fist in frustration as he struggles to find the word—"fast. I'm learning fast."

I notice for the first time that the sword he's gripping so tightly is Sarah's Scottish broadsword. He has abandoned his own Teutonic hand-and-a-half sword and taken Sarah's sword for his own. He knew her for such a short time before she was killed by Müller, but he fell hopelessly in love with her. Lorenzo told me that he often finds Rolf silently weeping, clutching the sword to his chest.

"Yes," Lorenzo says, "you're doing remarkably well . . . better than any of us thought possible."

"I learn fast. I fight. Must understand . . . commands. Must understand Carl's commands. We kill Lilith." He glances back to the left. "Kat comes."

"*Kathleen*," I whisper. "Don't let her hear you say that!"

I can hear Kathleen's footsteps on the stairs. She stops at the bottom, plants her feet, and folds her arms.

"Tell me one thing." Her tone brooks no evasion. "Are my children in danger?"

"Not from *me*, my lady," Lorenzo says. "Nor from any of my friends. I would never hurt my grandchildren. I . . . we are *reformed*. We are Penitents, seeking the grace of God."

"There are *more* of you?" Her expression is stern. Apart from noting her all-business, protect-her-children-at-any-cost bearing, I can't tell *what* she's thinking or feeling.

"Yes, Kathleen," Lorenzo says. "There are forty-seven of us . . . forty-seven Penitents, that is. More are joining us almost every night. There are so many of us now, we must leave the state in order to Feed . . .”

“But,” I say, interrupting him, “we *are* in danger, honey.”

“You played with my children,” Kathleen says, her eyes staring daggers at Lorenzo. “And they were never in any danger?”

“Not from me,” Lorenzo repeats. “I haven’t killed a mortal in nearly three centuries. And I would *never* harm my own flesh and blood.”

“What about *you*?” she says, turning her intense gaze on Rolf. “You, Rolf, the creepy, silent guy! Are *you* going to hurt my kids?”

“I not hurt Abby,” Rolf says. “Not hurt . . . Little Tony. I’m not . . . bad vampire.”

Kathleen looks shocked. She’s never heard Rolf speak before.

“He took a bullet to the head,” I explain quickly. “His brain is completely healed, but he has to learn to talk all over again. He’s made incredible progress. He’s not retarded or slow or a . . . *pedophile* or anything like that. He’s one of the *good* guys.”

She shifts her gaze to me. “I’ll deal with *you* later.”

Yep! I’m in real trouble! But I can’t leave it there. I’m an idiot. I don’t know when to just keep my mouth shut.

“They’ve been *protecting* us,” I say. “There are others . . . many, *many* others who’re *evil*, and they *are* looking for us . . . well, for *me*.”

“Why?” she said. “What did you *do*, Tony?”

Yep! Somehow this was going to be all my *fault! Well, to be honest, it is.*

“He brought us together,” Lorenzo says, “organized us, taught us the gospel of Jesus Christ. He *was* our leader.”

“*You*?” she says, her eyes wide.

“You know me,” I say, shrugging sheepishly, “I just can’t seem to keep my big mouth shut.”

“You *were* the leader?” she asks.

“Yes,” I reply. “Actually, I was more of a teacher. But now they have a *new* leader. He’s a vampire *and* a member of the Church. And he has never killed . . . never killed a *mortal*, that is. There are even a couple of prophecies about him and his wife. You’ve met them. They’re the Morgans . . . Carl and Moira Morgan.”

“Moira is a . . . a . . . ?” she stammers.

“Vampire, yes,” I finish for her.

“But . . . I *like* her!”

“Don’t you like *me*?” Lorenzo says, a fake pout on his face.

“I . . . *used* to,” Kathleen says. She hasn’t moved from her place, her arms folded. She’s still guarding the stairs, still guarding her children.

“I see,” Lorenzo says.

“Oh, my heck!” She unfolds her arms and places her hands over her eyes. Then she drops her hands. “I do, I guess. It’s just a lot to take in!”

Then she steps away from the stairs and gives Lorenzo a quick hug. She pulls back and says, "You're really his great-great-grandfather Laurentiu?"

"That I am, granddaughter," he replies. "But come, we must discuss the very real dangers." He gestures toward the loveseat. "Please sit down."

She walks over to the loveseat and sits. Lorenzo and Rolf both take their seats again, placing their swords in their laps. Cautiously, I join my wife on the sofa.

She reaches over and takes my hand.

I breathe an audible sigh of relief.

Both Lorenzo and Rolf smile at this, although Rolf's smile is tinged with sadness.

"You see, Kathleen," Lorenzo begins, "there is a war of sorts going on ..."

Lorenzo does most of the talking, but Kat asks a lot of questions. *Do they know where we live? Do they know who we are?* The answer to both is, *Apparently not so far, but they are looking.* Lorenzo informs her that there are at least two Penitents guarding our home each night from the air now, and during daylight, there are two stationed outside in Carl's minivan, ready to cloak themselves in darkness and come to our aid in an emergency.

Then her questions shift to inquiries about vampires in general, but she's most captivated by the love story of Lorenzo and Mara, my great-great-grandmother. Lorenzo weeps as he recounts the tale, and Kathleen goes over and hugs him when he's done. Lorenzo talks about how he wanted the two of *us* to have the two of *them* sealed in the temple after he's gone.

"Why can't you just wait until you can do it yourself?" she asks.

"Ah, dear lady," he says, shaking his head sadly, "it may have been centuries, but, long ago, I was a murderer. Even if I *could* get a clearance from your First Presidency, such things take time. And I expect that I . . . all of us . . . the Penitent vampires, I mean . . . all of us will be dead shortly."

"But, you're immortal, aren't you?" She's obviously distressed.

"Yes, I'm immortal, but you see, this war among the Children of Lilith can end in only one of two ways: either in victory or defeat. Either way, we will die."

"You see, Kathleen," I say, "the Prophecy . . . the newer one, at least . . . states that, once Lilith falls, all vampires will die. So, win or lose, Tony, Rolf, Carl, Moira, and all their friends will be dead."

Lorenzo smiles sadly. "But we'll have rid the Earth of the evil of Lilith and her Children."

"But," she says, "can't you . . . I don't know . . . put it off for a while?"

"Every . . . night," Rolf interjects, and all eyes go to him, "people die. Every night Lilith kill people."

Lorenzo nods. "Yes, as much as I cherish life, the longer we delay, the more innocents will die to Feed Lilith and her minions. And," he adds, his eyes moist with new tears, "I have hope that the Lord will have mercy on me and I will see my Mara again."

♦ ♦ ♦

It's nearly midnight before my great-great-grandfather and Rolf leave. Kathleen goes upstairs to check on the kids, while I go to my office to shut down my computer for the evening . . . and check my email.

I sit down at my desk and click the "Send-Receive" button. I wait anxiously, my fingers drumming on the desk beside my mouse.

There's one message.

It's a response from the anonymous sender. I open it hurriedly and read the plain-text message:

How did I get your email address? Let's just say that I have people who have been sniffing around, looking for messages such as yours.

How do I know the translation is correct? Let's just say that I have some knowledge of the First Tongue.

Why would anyone lump the Sons of God and the Brood of Lucifer together? Well, that depends on your perspective. What if the speaker considered both to be insulting, both to be two sides of the same coin, so to speak?

And as for who I am?

I think you know the answer.

So tell me: what do you want to know?

Author's Note

Your book isn't really about vampires, is it?"

I was just leaving priesthood meeting one Sunday when an older gentleman (a former bishop) asked me that question. At first I thought he was being very perceptive (and he is a very intelligent man). I answered, "Not really. Vampirism is just the vehicle I used to tell the story. It's really about . . ." Then I listed off the themes the book explores.

Upon reflection, I realized he was simply taken aback that a good Mormon boy, a member of the Mormon Tabernacle Choir, would write a book about vampires. I asked him and he confirmed that was indeed the case. He said, "I'm OK with it. I just didn't expect it."

So why would a good Mormon boy write a book about vampires? For one thing, the genre has been a favorite of mine since I was nine (when I first read *Dracula* by Bram Stoker). For another, one of the things that has always bothered me about the popular vampire myth is that you have no choice. If you are bitten by a vampire, you become a vampire. While it made for a frightening story, I was bothered by the idea of involuntary eternal damnation.

This aspect of the modern version of the vampire myth inspired me to write *The Unwilling* and *The Penitent*.

God gave us our agency. We are free to choose good or evil. That cannot be taken away. However, we can give it away. We also cannot escape the consequences of our choices for good or ill. If you make a choice to drink alcohol, for example, you will suffer the effects of the alcohol in the short term. If you continue to drink, you may surrender your ability to resist it. If you drink and then get behind the wheel of a car, you may not have chosen to kill an innocent, but you did choose to drink.

On the other side of the latter scenario, you may not have chosen to drink, but may simply be in the wrong place at the wrong time when someone else, who did choose to drink, runs you down and cripples you. Through no fault of your own, you can no longer walk. This is a loss of freedom. However, it is NOT a loss of agency. You are still free to choose. You may choose to become bitter and despondent. You may opt to move your life in a completely different direction by choosing to meet your new and difficult circumstances head on and strive to overcome them.

You can still choose.

Freedom can be taken. Evil can be inflicted on you by others. However, you always have a choice.

I had the same difficulty when trying to explain *The Unwilling* to people. If I said something like, "It's a novel about a Mormon vampire," I could see their eyes glaze over. If I said, "It's hard to explain, but it's a story about agency, the choices we make, and the choices thrust upon us by others; it's about the power of the Atonement of Jesus Christ," some of the members of my faith would listen for a bit, but as soon as they thought to themselves, "There are a ton of books about that," their eyes would glaze over again. If, at that point, however, I would add, "It's the story of the world's first and only unwilling vampire," then that would pique their interest again. What really amazed me was that saying the same thing to people who were not of my faith (even with the addition of, "I warn you: it's heavily steeped in Mormon imagery and theology") got virtually the same reaction.

So, *Mormon vampire story=stupid*, but *agency, hope, and redemption in the context of unwilling vampirism=good or at least "interesting."*

And in the end, this really *isn't* a story about vampires. Vampirism is simply the vehicle I used to tell the tale. It's about hope and redemption in the midst of horrific evil.

I have to add one note about *Twilight* by Stephanie Meyers. I really *loved* those books. I think I've read them three or four times, and I probably will read them at least once more before the final movie is released. I'm a huge fan. So, please don't get me wrong when I say that, as a dad, I *agree completely* with Moira's assessment of them in this book. I love the books, but they also bother me on a fundamental level. Such is the joy of fiction, though. We get to explore worlds we've never visited before. We suspend our disbelief and immerse ourselves in the story.

Having said that, I want you to know that *Twilight* was *never* the inspiration for this work. I've been working on the concept for this story for well over a decade. I don't think Stephanie was even a student in Hal Romrell's seminary class back then.

This is a work of fiction (again). I feel the need to point this out (again) so I don't give anyone the impression that I'm attempting to teach doctrine (or false doctrine). I wanted to tell a good story, and I really enjoyed the opportunity to revisit the world of Moira and Carl.

I sincerely hope you enjoy it as well.

C. David Belt
September, 2011
unwillingchild@comcast.net

Acknowledgements

There are so many people who helped with the writing of this book. I really can't list (and, in some cases, remember) them all, but I would like to mention and thank a few of them here. Cindy Belt, Jeremiah Belt, Bryan Belt, Jacob Belt, Rachel Belt, and Olha Polazhynets provided invaluable help with proofreading and critique. Dr. Brian Hales, Steven Ortgiesen, Bryan Belt, and Dr. Reed Ras-mussen provided medical expertise. Bishop Hal Romrell once again provided counsel on doctrine. Bishop Joe Peterson was extremely helpful with Church procedure. Dr. Eric Huntsman came up with the "Adamic." Rick Steadman helped with the German translation. David Oswald was tremendously helpful in suggesting hang gliders when I kept focusing (and was stuck) on small aircraft. Mable Belt, David Belt (once again, my father, not me), and Ryan Larsen provided encouragement and enthusiasm. Without Elizabeth and George Bentley and their willingness to take a chance on this bizarre project of mine, none of this would have been possible.

My sincerest, heartfelt gratitude to all of you.

About the Author

C David Belt was born in Evanston, Wyoming. As a child, he lived and traveled extensively around the Far East. He served as an LDS missionary in South Korea and southern California (Korean-speaking). He graduated from Brigham Young University with a Bachelor of Science in Computer Science and a minor in Aerospace Studies. He served as a B-52 pilot in the US Air Force and as an Air Weapons Controller in the Washington Air National Guard. When he is not writing, he sings in the Mormon Tabernacle Choir and works as a software engineer. He collects swords (mostly Scottish), axes, spears, and other medieval weapons and armor. He and his wife have six children and live in Utah with an eclectus parrot named Mork (who likes to jump on the keyboard when David is writing).